AVA CROWLEY

VAMPIRE SLAYER

OMNIBUS

BOOKS 1-3

ARIEL DAWN

NAUGHTY NIGHTS PRESS LLC • CANADA

Ava Crowley, Vampire Slayer

Omnibus

Books 1-3

Copyright ©2021-2023 Ariel Dawn

ISBN: 978-1-77357-561-2

978-1-77357-558-2

Naughty Nights Press LLC

Cover Design by Willsin Rowe

AVA CROWLEY, VAMPIRE SLAYER OMNIBUS: BOOKS 1-3

Whiskey, Donuts, and Blood Bonds... Oh My...

Ava Crowley bites off more than she can chew when she finds herself in the middle of a world she never knew existed... one where angelic-faced vampires, sexy-as-sin hunters, and sweet-talking monsters are waiting for her around every corner.

Vampire Cassius Aurelia finds a beautiful college student bleeding out on enemy territory, and he knows time is of the essence. But saving Ava's life means claiming her blood as his, and challenging the monsters he's been trying to escape.

The bond between them is strong, but so is the threat that one day Ava and Cassius will have to make a choice... and only one of them will make out it alive.

The Ava Crowley, Vampire Slayer series is a slow burn, enemies to lovers forbidden romance that may be perfect for fans of Supernatural, Buffy the Vampire Slayer, and The Vampire Diaries.

BLOOD & BONES

AVA CROWLEY

VAMPIRE SLAYER

BOOK ONE

ARIEL DAWN

NAUGHTY NIGHTS PRESS LLC • CANADA

BLOOD & BONES

Some bonds are stronger than blood.

When eighteen-year-old Ava and her boyfriend attend a party on campus, things turn from fun to deadly rather quickly. As Ava bleeds out on the concrete floor, the angel of death comes... only he's not an angel. And he isn't quite dead either.

Cassius Aurelia finds a young college student fighting for her life on the floor of a frat house basement, and he can't turn away. His bite will save her life, but it will also bring forth a litany of consequences for the both of them that neither may be ready for.

Blood & Bones is book one in the Ava *Crowley, Vampire Slayer series, filled with innocent academy students and villainous vampires.*

DEDICATION

I dedicate this book to all the Avas of the world.

Those who see the world beyond the veil.

Those who never back down from a fight.

The ones with a fire in their soul.

And also those who can't live without a strong cup of

coffee.

CHAPTER ONE

AVA'S HEAD WAS *killing* her, and her bones literally ached like they'd been shut inside a coffin for a hundred years. She could hear the sound of the birds chirping outside her window, but they seemed so very loud it was almost comical. A wave of nausea overcame her, and she rushed to the bathroom. Her body heaved with convulsions as she emptied her stomach into the toilet.

Visions of the night slowly came back to her, coursing through her body.

The frat boys she and Ross were playing beer pong with.

Ross obliterated out of his mind, completely missing all his shots.

Ava and him making out in the basement.

Her senses felt heightened, as the loud incessant chirping sounded like nails on a chalkboard. Her stomach dry heaved, as the rest of the memories came forth.

The blood.

There was so...much...blood.

Her muscles ached, the vein deep in her thigh pounding with heaviness against her skin.

The feeling of the knife as it cut into her thigh like a knife cuts soft butter, the creamy texture making way for the impact of the steel.

The boy who'd been making eyes at Ross all night had him up against the wall, his lips on his neck, and Ross moaned with pleasure...before the scream.

The memory of his horrific scream...

Ava threw up again at the memory of his lifeless, drained body in the corner. Covered in blood. Her body shook with the leftover tremors from convulsions as another memory forged its way to the surface.

An angel emerging from the shadows, his glowing green eyes like a cat in the darkness. Like some kind of dream or hallucination...

How she pleaded for him to save Ross.

The sound of his voice, tender and beautiful, offering her a chance to live.

She pushed herself away from the toilet, scrambling back against the sink, the coolness of the pipes chilling the heat she felt within her. Her wrist throbbed with soreness, and she glanced down to see it wrapped in thick, white gauze, only the faintest hint of a lightly pink stain in the center.

The feel of absolute bliss as she watched the angel sink his teeth into her flesh.

The realization struck her, and she unraveled the gauze with a frantic, panicked motion. Her blood chilled as she stared at the bite mark, the raised scarring prominent as if she'd sustained the injury long before last night.

The searing pain as his tongue licked at the wound.

Her stomach twitched at the memory, but it was not

an unpleasant one.

"What the hell?" Her voice wavered aloud in the silence of the bathroom.

When she finally found the strength to move, she noticed the birds had stopped chirping, and her headache was gone.

CHAPTER TWO

"MUST HAVE BEEN one hell of a party last night." Ember pushed the paper cup full of sugary goodness toward Ava.

The campus was crawling with police and had turned into quite the crime scene.

Ava's stomach turned at the memory.

"You have no idea." Ava sipped the warm liquid, hoping it would settle her nerves, if only marginally.

The television reporter showed an image of Ross, with the subtitle *Missing twenty-year-old male, Ross Parish.* Ava's heart stilled at the sight.

They'd only been going out for a month. It just didn't seem real, the idea that their relationship was over before it even had a chance to begin. She was going to ask him to visit for Thanksgiving, for god's sake. If everything went smoothly.

Ross was dead, yet how could she describe what happened when she didn't understand it herself. Speaking up would only make her a suspect as she was the last person to see him alive. Her, and the freakishly beautiful blond man who bit her.

The words were solid in her brain

He fucking bit me. Maybe he was just as tripped out as the rest of the frat boys.

She did remember the one biting Ross on the neck, and quite frankly he seemed pretty into it...until that point anyway. But when had things shifted? Everything was so blurry.

What kind of deranged person goes around biting people, let alone more than one? She thought as she watched Ross's picture on the scene.

Someone on drugs, most likely. She took another sip of her coffee.

"Did you see what happened?" Ember looked concerned.

"Not really, no," she lied. What could she say?

She looked down, catching sight of a familiar pair of eyes across the room

Bright, glowing green eyes stared at her from across the student lounge, and her body went straight as a pole. Her wrist throbbed with a heated sensation, and she nearly dropped the cup of coffee.

"Ava, careful..." Ember leaned toward her, her fingers gently touching her forearm, focusing on the gauze.

"What happened to you anyway?" Her voice broke Ava's concentration.

"I'm not sure. I think I fell on some glass. I was pretty wasted, after all." At least it wasn't a *complete* lie.

"Well, I'm glad Ross had the wherewithal to make sure you were okay." She paused, a look of sorrow on her face.

"I'm sure he's okay. He'll turn up." Ava could see Ember's forced smile. Ember may have been psychic, but Ava knew her talents extended only to reading tarot, and not detective work like her aunt, the famous psychic consultant, Kacie Stone.

"Yeah. Sure," she said as she glanced around the quad, trying to find the green-eyed angel. But he was nowhere to be found.

Perhaps she was truly starting to lose her mind.

CHAPTER THREE

CASSIUS TOOK A deep breath as he made his way out of the student union, passing the young college students as if he were just another face in the crowd.

That was close. Perhaps she hadn't seen him.

She's all right. You can move on now. Forget about her. He walked with swift grace past a group of students coming through the turnstile doors.

The campus was as active as ever, but the news of the party was all throughout the town of Chester. He'd had to act quickly, with the rogue faction so close by, and he was certain they wouldn't be keen to have loose ends.

What was I thinking? He chastised himself. The memory of the night flooded back to him, with clarity.

Cassius followed Taj down to the basement. They weren't supposed to be in this part of the house, but Taj had a score to settle. No one threatened Jasmine and got away with it, especially some young, dumb new recruit. The Boracellis were either getting sloppy or desperate, or perhaps both.

After all Taj and Jasmine had done for him, there

was no way he was letting Taj go off half-cocked without him. It wasn't that his friend couldn't stand off against the new kids; Taj was about as impenetrable as solid marble but the right crack in the right place could make him more than just distracted. Strength was his strong suit; brains.... Not so much.

The stairs creaked underneath him, and the scent of fresh blood assaulted his senses. He stilled momentarily, gaining his bearings. Taj brushed against his back.

"Do you smell that?" Taj whispered.

Cassius nodded.

His heightened sense of smell told him the room hadn't been cared for in some time as the scent of mildew and rotten beer permeated through the concrete like it had been there for years.

Taj sniffed the air behind him.

"I don't smell him. His scent's disappeared," Taj grumbled angrily. Cassius could hear the creak of the stairs behind him, a clear indication his friend was turning around, heading back to the party.

"Please.... Help me..." The sound was small, and almost no more than a whisper. Cassius stepped forward.

"Cassius.... What the fuck? What are you doing?" Taj whispered.

The sight before him angered him in a way he hadn't felt in years.

Since Eden...

The bodies in the corner were piled like discarded packaging, and perhaps to the young vamps they were just that, but not all of them were lifeless shells.

The smell of coagulation was prevalent as he slowly walked toward the sound of the whisper, his gaze settling on its owner.

Her amber eyes were frantic with motion, until they settled on him. He glanced over her quickly, taking in the sight of the young college student who was sitting in a puddle of blood, streams of the crimson liquid seeping out from several gashes on her pale, sweat-slicked inner thighs.

No bite marks, which meant they hadn't fed off of her yet.

"Cassius, come on..." Taj stepped up toward the door, the tone in his voice only slightly worried. Cassius could smell the faint, distinctive smell of the young vamp. Young vamps thought their musk was alluring, and maybe it was to humans. But with his heightened sense of smell, it reminded him of humans who bathed in too much cologne.

"They're going to kill her." He turned toward the shadows where Taj was hidden.

He'd never understood, given the history of their relationships with the mortals, why some vampires preferred to be so cruel.

They'd worshipped their very existence, sacrificed themselves and everything they had once to be chosen, to be gifted with immortality. The humans gave them life, after all. Without their blood, they'd cease to exist.

The girl's chest heaved heavily, and her long, dark brown hair clung to her sweaty, dirty skin. He could feel her pulse like an echo in the air, even at a distance. The rush of blood in her veins. She would certainly bleed out soon if the rogue vamps didn't come back to finish her off.

She struggled to move her legs, frustration on her face. But she kept trying. "We're on their territory," Taj's voice went up an octave, and the reminder was sobering.

"My boyfriend, Ross…he's…he's still alive." Her voice was strong, even though it wavered with exhaustion. She looked into his eyes, and he was in front of her instantly.

He couldn't explain it, but when she looked at him, he felt…seen. Not as a vampire, not as an Aurelia but as a person.

He could not leave her to die alone, and he would not let her die at the hands of monsters, this human who tried with all her fading strength to move.

You're not a monster, he reminded himself.

There wasn't much time to act as the sickeningly sweet scent of the young vampires became more prominent. They were getting closer, but the target was not with them.

He could turn her, it was the easiest option, but it would draw attention he didn't want from the Boracellis. Not as many vampires could turn humans anymore. It would be the most dangerous option, not to mention…

The idea of it didn't sit right with him. He'd never had a choice in the matter, he was born this way. He couldn't take the choice away from her. He knew all too well how it felt.

He could kill her, before the rogue faction showed up. He hadn't had fresh blood in many years, and he couldn't deny the sight of the crimson streaks against her pale thighs, streaming down her legs, was making his throat dry with thirst. It would be a quick, merciful death, thanks to his thrall, but he knew he'd never be able to do it. He'd never liked killing humans, even if he had to do it to survive. He'd managed to stay off of fresh blood this long, he wasn't going to throw all that discipline down the drain, even if it was tempting.

The only other option was, he could mark her. Marking her would buy more time. No vamp would dare try to challenge the claim unless they had a death wish, or unless they were stupid—like the rogue vamp who threatened Jasmine. The Boracellis wouldn't be able to do anything until he either turned her, or fed off her, for at least a few years. By that time, she'd be graduated and likely out of Chester, and the Boracellis... He'd figure something out. He'd have to deal with them one day, after all.

***

The sun was bright and warm, and Cassius started to feel the muggy effects of it against him. His vision blurred slightly, casting a fuzzy haze around the things he looked at, and the feeling of heat in his body flourished like the beginning of a summer bonfire. He wouldn't burn in the sun like the movies portrayed, after all, he needed to blend in with the humans, and his Aurelian blood gave him the ability to do so—but that didn't mean being out in daylight was comfortable by any means. While he'd spent much time outside in the sun in his early newborn days without any incident, the recent years of living in the night had caught up to him.

He walked through the crowds of students, toward the abandoned construction zone where the University suspended work due to lack of funding.

He knew not even students would be hanging out in its dusty, unkempt, forgotten rooms during this time of the day. It would be the perfect place to make an exit.

Cassius sat on the edge of the rafters. He'd had every intention of escaping quietly, but yet...

What if she saw me?

It isn't like she knows who you are, or what you are. If she's lucky she won't remember a thing thanks to the thrall, and she'll just chalk it up to drunken activities.

The vamps should leave her alone, with the mark...

He rolled the thoughts over.

Unless they're stupid. He reminded himself.

What had he done?

It seemed like the best option in the moment, he couldn't just *leave* her there to die at the hands of those horrible monsters. The choice seemed so simple, and yet, in the light of day, Cassius had to acknowledge that perhaps nothing was simple.

The memory of his fangs sinking into her skin... It had been so long since he'd felt the puncture of his teeth in real flesh, the rush of blood into his mouth. It was only a small taste, the blood that touched his fangs, and if he hadn't pulled back so quickly, he knew he would have been no better than the new recruits. But he couldn't deny the feeling of serenity as he drew her wrist to his lips, or the way his thrall instinctively wrapped itself around her, calming her fear and diluting the pain. The sound of her gasp, the feel of her pulse as it ran through him. The feeling of life in his hands, at his mercy.

He'd known marking her was the best option. It saved her life, sealing her wounds with rapid healing, and for that he knew he had made the right choice; but as he sat in the rafters, he could feel the faint thrum of her pulse inside his own veins, steady and strong, and for the first time in what seemed like an actual eternity, Cassius felt alive.

CHAPTER FOUR

EMBER TAPPED HER pencil on the table, and to Ava the sound was like nails on a chalkboard. It was like the sound was deafening.

"I swear to god, if you tap that pencil one more time, my head is going to explode," Ava grumbled.

Ember glanced up from her notebook with a mischievous smile.

Out of all the people in her Medieval History class that she could have been paired with, she ended up with a psychic. An oblivious, anxious psychic. What were the odds?

Ava hugged her knees, her long, dark brown hair falling over her shoulders like a cascading waterfall. Her eyes focused on the group of students that hung around the Chester Cougar statue in the center of the quad. Something about them seemed familiar to her but she couldn't quite place it.

"Sorry." Ember glanced up at Ava quickly.

"No, I'm sorry. I just can't seem to shake this headache..." Ava massaged her temples with her fingers, squinting her eyes in the light.

"It has been three days." Ava watched the small group of students outside passing out flyers. Flyers with Ross's face on them. The group of students at the Cougar statue walked in their direction, and Ava could feel her skin prickle like she'd walked into a freezer. Her wrist heated underneath the gauze and she immediately let her legs down, bracing her hands on the bench.

It was as if time stood still and as the group approached, her eyes settled on one man.

He was average height, wearing an ordinary blue-checkered short sleeve over top of a white tee, and he looked like a California import. Tan skin, dark brown hair with blond highlights, and bright blue eyes.

As he passed her, her wrist felt a searing pain, and instinctively she grabbed the gauze with her free hand as their eyes met.

It was the guy from the party... The one who'd been making passes at Ross all night. The one who had him up against the wall... The one who bit him.

The man smiled seductively at her, and she could have sworn when his lips pulled back...

No, that can't be possible. You're definitely losing your marbles.

When his lips pulled back, she could have sworn she saw an elongated white, razor-sharp tooth.

A fang.

***

"Aren't you scared to go out after what happened?" Stacy looked up from the couch as Ava headed for the door.

"I need to get my mind off things," Ava answered plainly.

Stacy rose from the couch and walked over to Ava with haste. "I know you've had a tough week. With Ross missing, and I know the police interview you gave couldn't have been easy." Stacy ran her hand down Ava's exposed arm, her blue eyes full of concern.

Ava shifted out of her reach. Stacy sighed.

"I'm fine. It's not like we were soul mates or anything. Besides, I was glad to give that interview, if it helps find out who killed him." Her words weren't complete lies.

She'd met Ross at freshman orientation. He was a sophomore brother of Alpha Pi Omega, and he'd volunteered to help the freshman moving into the dorms. It wasn't fate or anything, he just looked really good moving boxes in his polo shirt and khakis, and Ava was excited to finally be able to do whatever she wanted, without judgment.

Like hit on a sophomore fraternity brother who was probably out of her league.

Only when Stacie's eyes widened had she realized her mistake.

"Killed?" Stacy swallowed, and Ava closed her eyes before opening them again. Her pulse quickened with anxiety.

"He's been missing for a week already, Stacy. If he were alive, they would have found him by now." She pursed her lips.

How has no evidence of what happened come to light?

The image of the California import flashed in her mind

His body pressed against Ross, his fingers on his neck.

Ross's moan of pleasure.

Ross's scream of pain.
His body behind her, the sound of gurgling blood.
The angel from the darkness...
She had awakened in her own dorm room...
What had they done with Ross's body?
The memory of the blood covering his shirt, trickling onto the cement floor...

Ava pushed the memory down. She could really use a drink.

Stacy crossed her arms. "You're not going alone." She spoke with confidence.

"I'll be fine," Ava replied quickly.

"I'll go with you," Stacy said as she stepped in between Ava and the door. "Give me five minutes to change." She looked Ava in the eye with a look that said she meant business.

Ava sighed heavily. "Fine." she relented.

Ava leaned herself into the passenger seat of Stacy's bright blue Malibu. Her roommate's car always smelled like laundry detergent, and it was both a welcoming smell and a sickening smell at the same time. Ava stifled a cough.

Stacy turned the car on and backed out seamlessly.

"Where to?" She glanced at Ava.

"The Heights," Ava responded.

The Heights at Chester University wasn't actually affiliated with the school, which made it the prime spot for parties and underage drinking. It was also on the other side of the University, far away from Greek Row.

Stacy pulled up to the parking lot across the street from The Heights, the one everyone parked in to avoid getting a ticket.

It looked as if the party was stretched all throughout the parking lot, and in various apartments. Ava exited the car, the chilly October air biting at her bare legs. She pulled at her red velvet dress for a fraction of warmth as her long hair blew in the wind, tendrils sticking to her lip gloss and blinding her vision.

She swatted at her hair with disdain as she followed Stacy across the street to The Heights.

CHAPTER FIVE

TAJ LICKED HIS lips as a group of college students passed. The scent of chemical vanilla and freesia made Cassius's eyes water.

"We're not here for them," he reminded him.

"You might be a fucking vegetarian, but some of us still require the real thing to live." He leaned against the wall, holding his red solo cup and Cassius had to admit Taj looked like he belonged.

Tajiri's normally long, dark brown hair was pulled back into a tight bun, the style showcasing his high temples, and muscles in his neck. The black Billabong shirt that he deliberately wore was so tight; if he were human, it would have cut off his circulation. The fit made his profound muscles stand out, and that was, of course, on purpose.

A short, petite blonde with cerulean eyes walked up the counter, eyeing up the many bottles, cans, and strewn debris of plastic cups.

Taj's eyes lit up.

"Did it hurt?" He smirked as he pushed off the wall, slowly boxing her in.

Cassius rolled his eyes.

The doe eyed blonde flashed her long eyelashes at him.

"Excuse me?" Her voice was light.

"Did it hurt? When you fell from heaven?"

Cassius turned with every intent to leave, but a solid force stopped him dead in his tracks. Aside from the force of body collision, Cassis felt a strange, heated sensation in his veins. *Warmth...*

His slow heartbeat beat only a fraction quicker, and he could *feel* the thrum of pulse steady like a river inside his entire body.

"I'm sorry," the voice apologized.

Cassius looked down to see the culprit, and if he had human blood, he was sure it would have run cold.

The girl from the basement.

The one he marked.

For the first time in his eternal life, Cassius was speechless.

She looked up at him, and he had to take in the beauty of her amber colored eyes. Flecks of gold in them reminded him of the sun. She brushed past him as if he didn't exist, heading straight toward the blonde who was now running her fingers down Taj's enormous bicep.

He watched as the girl from the basement, the girl he *marked,* walked through the kitchen. She wore a short, red velvet dress, which elongated her pale legs, and the image of her on the floor, with crimson streaks against her flesh, flared his thirst, among other things.

Good thing I stopped at the morgue first. Something about this human... made him long for the taste of fresh blood in a way he hadn't felt in years.

The blonde saw her friend, and gave Taj a playful

shove as the marked girl took her arm and lead her away into the crowd on the other side of the kitchen, in the thick of the living room.

And just like that, she was gone, and the scent of sickening cologne became more prevalent. Taj's stance shifted in response, and Cassius remembered why they came to The Heights in the first place.

Forget about her. You've done your part. She's alive.

But even as he said the words in his head, he could feel her pulse inside of him and he knew forgetting her was out of the question.

CHAPTER SIX

AVA'S SKIN WAS chilled, and her wrist flared with heat as if it were on fire.

She grabbed the silver cuff and turned it against her bite mark, the scar that didn't seem to want to heal despite how much Neosporin she put on it. The cool metal of the silver didn't seem to help as it only heated up in response.

She looked down briefly and ran into a brick wall.

A brick wall wearing black leather pants, and...black and white converse tennis shoes?

What an odd combination.

She looked up the tall expanse of the said brick wall, and her heart stopped.

The angel from the shadows. From the party. The one who bit her.

She cleared her throat.

A thousand words assaulted her senses. A part of her wanted to scream at him, a part of her wanted to thank him, and a part of her wanted to ask him if he knew what happened to Ross's body.

But all she could manage was, "I'm sorry."

She shoved the thoughts down, her fingers pressing against her bite mark on her heated wrist.

She looked up at the angel of darkness for only a moment, taking in the sight of his beauty in the filtered light of the kitchen. His features truly were angelic.

His eyes were the brightest green she'd ever seen, like emeralds, and his golden blond hair was medium length, long enough to sweep back behind his ears and short enough that it barely touched his eyes. He looked like some lost member of the Backstreet Boys mixed with the god Apollo. The sight of him stirred a strange feeling inside of her she couldn't quite place.

She pushed past him and made a beeline for Stacy, who was flirting with some guy who was more muscle than human.

She grabbed Stacy by the arm and pulled her away, and as she walked toward the living room, her heart stopped again.

In the center of the room was the group of students from the cougar statue. The California import stood in the center, with his red solo cup, laughing as though he had not a care in the world.

The images of the party from that night flooded her brain again.

His body on top of Ross's.

The moan of pleasure.

The scream of pain.

Ava's blood boiled.

The smile he cast in her direction, the memory of a long, sharp fang she thought she saw.

Her wrist still flared with heat, and she could see the goosebumps on her arm.

His eyes settled on her, and she investigated them from across the room and all she could see was emptiness.

He nodded in her direction, raising his cup to her.

Ava felt her legs move in his direction as if willed by some unknown force. Her eyes felt heavy, and her body felt strange.

I've only had one drink...

Perhaps someone spiked the punch with some kind of drug...

Her brain felt fuzzy.

Ava watched as someone approached California. His gaze still fixated on her as the other guy whispered something in his ear.

California broke eye contact and turned away, his expression turning to concern.

Ava's skin still prickled like ice, and her wrist still flared with heat, but her eyes felt alert, her brain less fuzzy, and she couldn't quite remember the walk from the kitchen to where she stood. When she looked up, California was gone.

CHAPTER SEVEN

TAJ SLAMMED HIS fist into the punching bag in the gym. "We almost had him!" he growled as his fist thudded against the oversized sandbag.

Cassius sat on the bench like a statue.

"Perhaps we would have had him if you kept your eye on the prize," Cassius retorted.

"Fuck you." Taj pounded into the punching bag again.

"Just saying," Cassis sarcastically responded.

"I was hungry. Some of us *do* actually still need to eat, you know." Taj stilled the punching bag for a moment.

"I get thirsty too. I just have more control than you." Cassius pushed himself off the bench and walked over toward the window. The moon was high in the sky tonight.

"I have control," Taj grumbled. "At least we know their hunting grounds now."

Cassius stared at the silver moon, his mind replaying the night that changed his life.

The way she tried to move her legs.

Her eyes as she begged him for help.

The sound of her voice as his fangs punctured her skin

The feel of her pulse alive within him.

He shook his head and pushed away from the window. "True. But I still feel guilty we couldn't catch him in time." He sighed.

"This isn't about Liam, is it?" Taj walked over to him.

"I saw her. The girl I marked." He turned toward Taj.

"The brunette that stole my dinner? Thought she looked familiar," Taj's words were careful.

"You ever mark anyone Taj?" Cassius asked honestly.

Taj removed the gauze wrappings from his knuckles slowly and methodically.

"A long time ago," he answered quietly.

"What happened?" Cassius swallowed.

"I killed her. Obviously. Man's gotta eat."

Cassius closed his eyes. He knew the answer, but hearing it aloud made it real. Taj couldn't sire newborn vampires. He didn't have the ability to turn humans as Cassius did.

"Why did you mark her?" he asked.

"Her blood...it was like it called to me. I *needed* it...and honestly..." Taj paused before continuing. "To this day it was the sweetest blood I've ever had."

Cassius could see the lust in his eyes at the memory of its taste. "Well, I don't intend on killing her." He turned his gaze back out the window.

"Then *you've* only got one other option." Taj flexed his fingers and Cassius could see it in the reflection of the windowpane.

Marking a human meant Cassius had claimed her

blood for his own use. If he turned her...one bite would spread the venom, and she would be like him. Frozen forever in her youth, with only one true desire. Blood.

Drinking her blood and spreading the venom through the bite...would make her his mate for life. She'd have to bite him after her transformation to solidify the bond but...

No.

Cassius forced the thought down. He'd vowed never to claim a mate, not after everything had crumbled with Eden. He'd come so close to bonding with her...

The memory of Eden Boracelli surfaced, and he had to fight its pull.

The girl struggled in his grasp, and Eden held her still.

"Use your thrall." She instructed him. Her dark blue eyes instilled him with confidence.

Cassius tried to control the thrall, imagine it like some invisible force as Eden had told him. He imagined the invisible force like a shield around the girl. She looked at him with pleading eyes, and her breath hitched.

Eden sunk her teeth into the girl's neck, the sound of crunching muscle and torn tendons sending a shiver through his body. He could hear her heartbeat, feel it like a vibration of bass. The girl rolled her head back, her moan of pleasure a melody of its own.

Cassius was next to her in an instant, his hands braced on top of her heaving chest, her heartbeat thudding against his touch. His lips barely brushed her skin before his fangs punctured the other side of her neck. The feeling of blood as it ran down his throat, hot and wet, was overpowering. Intoxicating.

He glanced at Eden, who licked the blood off her lips, and his heart swelled at such an intimate moment.

He pushed the memory down, as he hurried out of the gym.

"Where are you going?" Taj asked.

Jasmine came into sight, and Cassius felt his speed kick in involuntarily. His mind raced with thoughts and he needed to quiet them.

The streets of Chester were quiet everywhere, but the campus and Cassius found solace on the main street, under the streetlights. He sat on a bench and watched the flickering of neon on the sign of Cory's Diner, focusing on the buzzing sound from the wires inside of it.

The faint thrum of a pulse, steady and warm filled his body and he reveled in its warmth.

CHAPTER EIGHT

THE NEWS HADN'T forgotten about Ross, but he was only a footnote now that two girls had been found dead in one of the apartments in The Heights. The campus was aflutter with gossip and news of the horrific murder was hard to avoid.

Danica and Riley Klume, twin sisters were found in their apartment and had died of blood loss.

The strange thing was…

Except for two puncture marks on their bodies—one on Danica's neck, and one on Riley's inner thigh—there were no wounds or cuts to explain the loss of blood.

Ava felt overwhelmed. Chester U hadn't had a student death in over fifty years. Until her first semester. Not to mention, the constant feeling as if she was being watched…

Ava wasn't a paranoid person, but she still couldn't shake the feeling. Sometimes she'd look up and swear she caught a glimpse of glowing green eyes.

Ember pushed the paper cup of coffee toward her. "Drink up, we've got a lot of ground to cover," she said sweetly.

Ava grabbed the cup, glancing at her wrist. It had been two weeks since the day she received the bite, and it had become a permanent scar. Thankfully, she could cover it up with concealer or jewelry, but it still bothered her.

Her phone rang, interrupting their study session, and Ava was surprised to see the caller. She answered quickly.

"Mal?" Her voice lit up.

"Hey, Simba, how's college life treating you?" The sound of her brother's voice was remarkably refreshing.

"Well, it hasn't been quiet up here, that's for sure." She looked at Ember, and motioned to her she'd return in a moment. Ember nodded and Ava pushed herself away from the table in the quad and walked outside.

The sight of the autumn leaves as they scattered the green grass was comforting as the chill set in. Ava pulled on her grey sweater, the cuff itching her bite scar.

"I heard. That's kind of why I'm calling. I'm stopping home for a bit, and I'd like to see you if that's okay?" Ava could hear the concern in his voice, but he masked it as a question and not a command. She knew him better than that.

"Where are you?" she asked.

"In the parking lot of Grayson Building C," he said plainly.

"Let me wrap up this session with my partner, and I'll be right over," she answered with a smile.

"Sounds great," he said.

She couldn't wait to see her brother.

CHAPTER NINE

AVA WALKED UP to the familiar red Chevelle, and her brother smiled at her from inside the car. "You hungry?" He raised his eyebrow at her.

She came around to the passenger side, pushing her long hair back behind her. "The question is not am I hungry..." she said as he pushed the door open for her from inside. "The question is can I eat food? And to that you know the answer is most certainly always yes." She smiled back at him.

Mal turned the car on, and Ava had to admit, she wondered where Mal would have fit in at Chester U. The eleven years between them should have separated them more than it did, but Ava had always felt closer to her brother than anyone, including her parents.

Especially after they died.

The thought careened through her brain, and she frowned.

It was only three years ago...

She tried to push the memory away. She didn't want to remember the sight of her parents when she came home, their lifeless bodies strewn about on the carpet, saturated in blood in their home. She closed her eyes and tried to imagine anything else.

"Place is a freaking nuthouse with all these reporters and police everywhere," Mal said as he pulled out of the parking lot onto the road.

Ava opened her eyes and let out a deep breath. "Yeah, well, you know how it is. Nothing interesting ever happens around here, so can't say I blame them for all the attention." She leaned back into the squeaky leather seats.

"So, what's good up this way?" He leaned back casually as he palmed the steering wheel, turning onto the main street of the campus.

"Depends, what are you hungry for?" she asked as she peered in the back seat at the amp and guitar that looked as if they had collected dust.

Strange for a musician.

She looked up briefly to see Mal's eyes in the rearview mirror, staring back at her.

"Pizza?" His tone was casual, but his eyes serious. Something about him seemed on edge.

Of course, he's on edge. His baby sister is attending a university where three people were just murdered.

"There's Julian's a couple of blocks from here. Just keep going straight until you hit the traffic light, then turn right on Tucker," she directed Mal.

His gaze turned back to the road.

"Did you know them?" he asked as they pulled up to the traffic light, which changed from yellow to red.

"What?" She turned toward him, with question.

"The...victims. Did you know them?" The way he said the word *victims* didn't sit right with her. She shrugged it off. "I knew the guy. Ross Parish." She spoke honestly.

"I'm sorry." His sympathy sounded genuine, but the look in his eyes was still quite serious. The light blinked green.

Ava pulled at the cuff on her sweater, covering her wrist.

"We only went out a couple times. He was a sophomore. Member of Alpha Pi Omega." It felt good to be honest with someone.

"So... you didn't know the girls then?" He turned right on Tucker Street.

Why was he pressing about this?

"No." Her answer was simple.

"Look, Ava, I know college can be exciting, what with all that goes on up here..." he started as he drove down the street, looking for the sign for Julian's. Ava shifted in her seat uncomfortably.

Please don't try to be the responsible older sibling. It just isn't you, Mal.

"So...you came all this way to lecture me?" She huffed.

Mal, of all people, had no room to lecture her. She wasn't some naive kid. She knew all too well what kind of shenanigans he got up to when he traveled for his gigs.

"I was eighteen once too. I know what happens at college parties. I also know that your friend and those girls were at a party the night they died." His lips straightened.

Ava shrugged as Mal parked the car.

"I'm fine, Mal. Really. You don't need to worry." She opened the door as quickly as she could. Her stomach growled.

"I'm not telling you not to do it. I know you're going to. I'm just telling you to be smart." He shut the car door and leaned against the hood of the Chevelle, as he took out a cigarette from his flannel pocket. He lit it with a stainless-steel lighter and the motion as he did so exposed his pentagram sun tattoo on his forearm, the rays of the sun sticking out like black daggers. Ava pulled her sweater tight around her.

"Finish your cigarette. I'm hungry," she grumbled.

Mal blew a ring of smoke in the air, and just like that the serious tone was gone, and his eyes lit up with a smile. "As you wish, Miss Crowley."

***

Ava closed her eyes and let a small moan of appreciation escape her lips. The cheese was absolutely delectable. "They really do have the best pizza," she mumbled through a mouth full of food.

Mal seemed to be on edge, his gaze darting around the room. It was only a Tuesday night, and still early by campus time, but fall had started to set in, and the outside was bathed in darkness, save for the streetlights and lights from places like Julian's.

Mal picked up another slice of pizza from the platter and scarfed it down equally as quickly as he had the other three slices.

The door jingled and Ava felt the familiar prickling of flesh and heated sensation at her wrist.

She looked up to see a group of students filing into one of the booths. California was with them. He sat with his posse, which consisted of three other men, all of which were impeccably dressed even for brothers of the fraternity.

Mal's gaze darted over to them.

"You know those guys?" he asked between bites.

"Not really, just seen them around campus. I think

they belong to Alpha Pi Omega." She took a sip of her coke and tried to ignore the chills.

Probably some stupid flu.

California locked eyes with her and nodded back at her.

"That the fraternity your friend was from?" Mal asked as he took another bite of cheese pizza.

Ava nodded in response. "Yeah." Her head felt fuzzy again.

"Interesting," Mal said under his breath. Ava broke eye contact with California and shook off the feeling. She pretended not to hear him.

CHAPTER TEN

TWO GIRLS. IN addition to the boy at the frat house, Liam, the Boracelli's newest member, had managed to kill two innocent girls. Cassius was furious at the sight of what the news called The Chester Murders. They'd been killed at the off-campus housing complex, known as The Heights, or rather the apartment complex that they had visited two weeks ago, on the hunt for Liam.

Jasmine had told Taj to let it go. She didn't think Liam would do any harm. "It's just words, Taj. Seriously. He's a kid, let it go," she had said sweetly, but Cassius knew Taj better than Jasmine.

Liam was a baby as far as vampire years were concerned. He'd been turned within the last twenty years, and as Cassius had learned, been sired by a rogue vampire, which in itself was quite a rare occurrence. Rogues didn't usually have the ability to sire as their bloodlines were usually so diluted. Liam had no coven, no real understanding of rules, and yet the Boracelli's took him into their coven, likely because he was racking up quite the body count—which was something the Boracelli's favored above all else. Kills. If the rumors were true, he'd be an apprentice before the fifty-year mark. He'd only surfaced in Virginia a month ago, and already in the course of two weeks, he'd managed to kill three students at the campus. All Greek row, all in their early twenties.

Like him.

It could have been four. He reminded himself as he felt the faint thrum in his veins of a pulse that didn't belong to him.

Still, newborn vamps like Liam were arrogant and didn't understand how to blend in. Their cocky attitudes coupled with the new fondness of eternal life meant sometimes they drew too much attention, where there should have been none.

Taj walked through the parking lot, and his whistle pulled Cassius out of his thoughts.

Taj walked around the red Chevelle and licked his lips. "They just don't make them like this anymore, do they Cassius?" Taj sounded like he'd fallen in love.

The red paint shimmered in the streetlight, casting a glare.

"Not really my type." He shrugged.

Taj flipped him off.

"You wouldn't know taste if it walked up to you and bit you," he retorted.

Cassius noticed something catching a glare from the light, the sparkle glinting against the window.

He peered in the backseat and felt an immediate fear.

The source of the glare belonged to the expanse of a blade, made of what Cassius assumed to be pure silver, its markings all too familiar.

To the naked eye it looked no different than a hunting jackknife, but any vampire worth his blood knew it was anything but ordinary. The symbols etched into the pure silver blade were deadly to his kind.

"Taj, look. Back seat." He shoved his hands into his pockets as he stared at the blade.

"Fucking hunters. Great," Taj cursed.

Cassius could feel the stolen pulse in his veins quicken, and a chill came over him.

What the hell...

He pulled his hand out of his pocket, the feeling of fire dull at his wrist, but noticeable enough to make him jump.

"You alright over there?" Taj walked hastily over toward him.

"Yeah... I..." Cassius flexed his fingers. He could feel the quickening heartbeat, and he knew it wasn't his.

"Lovely." Taj looked in the opposite direction, his sights settling on Julian's.

"What..." Cassius's thoughts felt jumbled.

Taj pulled him closer to the edge of the parking lot.

Cassius felt the pulse become stronger. "What is this? What is happening to me?" he asked.

"It's the mark. It knows she's close." Taj dropped his hand and nodded in the direction of Julian's.

Cassius's own heart stilled, which was a feat considering it was a slow beat to begin with.

She sat there in front of the window, with a dark-haired man, eating cheese pizza.

But it wasn't the sight of her that stilled his heart, not entirely.

It was the sight of Liam and his three henchmen, who walked in the door of Julian's.

CHAPTER ELEVEN

MAL PULLED OUT his wallet and fished around for the proper bills and change. The motion was normal, but his demeanor seemed to have changed. Ava finished the last slice of pizza and took another swig of her coke, and when she looked up California was beside the table.

"I know this may seem a bit forward, but you look awfully familiar to me. Do I know you?" California's voice didn't *sound* like a regional surfer, but more like a Tiffany Jewelry salesclerk. Combined with his preppy style, and expertly styled coif of hair, Ava couldn't help but blush.

Her brain felt fuzzy again, and the chills were still there, and she knew this man...but...

She didn't seem to remember *how*.

That's strange...

"I think so, but forgive me... I can't remember how." She glanced at Mal who's face had gone stone cold as he stood up slowly, against one of the other men who refused to move.

"Back off," he growled.

The man against Mal was wearing a pink polo of all things, and khakis with boat shoes. His backward hat looked slightly out of place with the rest of his ensemble and his dark eyes looked excited as he chewed his lip.

"Looking for a fight, pal?" Pink Polo challenged.

California held his hand out.

"Not tonight, Brody. Take it easy. You need your strength," he continued to speak, never taking his eyes off Ava.

"Well, then I think we should introduce ourselves thoroughly. I'm Liam Bancroft." He smiled, and although her brain felt hazy, she found her eyes had resisted the heavy pull.

"Ava Crowley," she smiled. Something about California...no *Liam's* demeanor felt unbelievably captivating. Memories of lips on her skin, biting at her flesh...

Biting...

Ava blinked and looked down to her wrist for only a second, remembering what lay underneath her sweater. She tugged at the cuff, as something told her she needed to keep it hidden.

The door jingled, and Liam and Brody turned their heads.

"Back up right now, or I will make you," Mal sneered at Brody as he puffed his chest out.

Liam sighed. "Can't a guy just get a decent pizza around here without getting into an argument?" He looked back at Ava, and she cracked a smile.

"See you around, Ava." He smiled in return, his lips pulling back just enough that as he turned, Ava could have sworn that she saw it.

The razor-sharp fang.

Just like in the field.

Liam and Brody backed away slowly as they headed toward the door, and Ava was surprised to see no one was there.

How odd. She thought to herself as she looked out the window.

Where Brody and Liam should have been, there was no one. Not a soul on the street, across the street, or anywhere to be found where a person should be.

Mal's shoulders eased, and he shot Ava a serious glance.

"You're coming home with me tonight." The way he said the words was definitive, and solid.

"What? Why? There's absolutely..." she started to rattle, but Mal held his hand up to stop her.

"I'd just feel better if we were both under the same roof. I'll drop you off at class tomorrow. I'm not going anywhere anytime soon." He stood in front of her, his eyes serious as he waited for her to rise.

"You're being ridiculous, but I can see that you are clearly worried. If it makes you feel better, I'll come home for a few days, but I'm a freshman. I can't have a car on campus, so I'll need you to drive me to and from school for the foreseeable future until you are satisfied. Also, we'll need to stop by my dorm to get a few things." She crossed her arms.

"Always the negotiator," Mal smiled only a fraction as he turned toward the door, and Ava followed.

Stacy's eyes sparkled at the sight of Mal, and Ava's stomach turned with disgust.

"You didn't tell me you had a brother. A very *hot* brother, I might add," Stacy whispered as Ava threw some clothes in her duffel bag.

"My brother is not hot, by any definition of the word,

and most certainly is not suitable dating material. He's a musician, and therefore leaves for long periods of time, and isn't exactly the committed type." Ava wrinkled her nose.

"Like I said. Hot." Stacy shrugged.

"He's at least eight years older than you, Stacy." Ava strung up her laundry bag full of clothes she'd planned on taking to the Laundromat before Mal showed up.

"Age ain't nothing but a number, sweetheart. Besides you have room to talk. Wasn't your boyfriend two years older than you?" Stacy sat on her bed on the opposite side of the room, in crossed leg position as Ava went about packing her things for a few nights. She banked that Mal would get sick and tired of playing responsible sibling after three days. He didn't know how to stay in one place too long, anyway.

"Yeah, but that's different." She dodged Stacy's disapproving glare.

"No, it isn't," Stacy teased.

Ava slung the bag over her shoulder and headed for the door, the laundry bag at her side.

"Okay Mal, I'm ready. Let's head out. I've got class at eight am tomorrow," she said as she threw the laundry bag into Mal's stomach, the motion making him wince.

Mal coughed.

"Jesus Ava, what do you have in there? Bricks?" he retorted as Ava walked quickly out of the dorm room.

"Bye, Stace!" she hollered from the hall, and Mal skipped after her.

CHAPTER TWELVE

MAL PULLED THE car into the driveway of the estate, the headlights casting an eerie white-blue glow on the stone walls. If it was up to Connie, their housekeeper slash pseudo mother, Ava would have remained living at the estate instead of on campus at Chester U for her first semester.

But with Mal gone most of the time, and the rigid structure of their aunt and guardian, Becky Lee Michaels, Ava knew she couldn't stay, even if the estate was a hundred times nicer than her dorm room. Not to mention, cleaner.

"Quiet, or you're going to wake the dead," Ava said as she tiptoed to the porch, waiting for Mal.

Mal fished for the right key on the ring.

"Relax. I called earlier today and told her I'd be stopping home for a bit," Mal replied as he found the key and turned it in the lock.

The click was an ominous sound to Ava, who suddenly worried why she'd agreed to this arrangement in the first place. She *was* perfectly capable of taking care of herself.

"Yes, but I'm sure you didn't mention I'd be coming with you." Ava crept in the open door, glancing around the darkened kitchen, waiting for Becky to show up out of nowhere, like some ghost.

"It's fine, don't worry about it. I'm sure if you tell her you feel safer here, she won't object. It *is* your home, Ava." Mal shut the door and locked it quickly.

Ava glanced at the grandfather clock in the living room, which read ten thirty pm. It wasn't even eleven and the house was already asleep.

When Ava turned the light on in her room, she was surprised to see it was just as she'd left it. The bed was still haphazardly made, the remaining pillows strewn about as if she'd taken a nap, and awakened. Yet, the room was devoid of all its charms as she'd taken the only things she valued with her to college. Her favorite band tees, her records and record player, and of course her tiny collection of paranormal books, and her dream catchers.

Mal dropped her bag on the floor, and it landed with a thud. "It's late, I'm going to turn in," he said quietly.

"I have class at eight, so we'll need to leave around six-thirty." The way she spoke was a command, not a question.

Mal sighed. "Alright. Get some rest." He turned, pausing in the doorway as if he wanted to say something. When the moment passed without a word, Mal shut the door, and Ava suddenly felt exhausted.

Flashes of light flickered in the darkness.

The light from the tiny sliver in the wall.

A door.

Ava wanted to move, but her legs were heavy.

Ross's eyes darted to the light, and all Ava could see was the look of lust.

What had him so worked up?

Why couldn't she move?

The shadows faded into the familiar muted green and beige wallpaper she'd always hated back when living in Loxley, Massachusetts. Ava quietly pushed on the open door.

The sink was running, and the kitchen was empty.

The Record player was still playing Aerosmith, and Ava could tell by the melody it was Sweet Emotion.

"Mom? Dad?" she called out.

But there was no answer.

And there never would be.

It had been weeks since Ava had the nightmare about her parents. She thought perhaps she'd finally outgrown them, or perhaps the dream catchers had worked. But as she tossed and turned, her body heated with anxious sweat, and she reached out into the empty space, searching for something that was not there.

Green eyes gazed down at her, and delicate fingers held her wrist. "I need your permission." His voice was like chocolate ganache on a chocolate donut. Smooth, and decadent.

Ava didn't understand. What was he waiting for? Couldn't they just leave... Surely, he could support her until she found her footing. Her head swelled with a blissful calm and her stomach flipped. She could feel her breathing increase, her heartbeat thudding in her chest, and the feeling of wanting to be consumed, wanting his touch...

The memory of razor-sharp fangs...

Ava awoke in a panic as Mal banged on the door.

CHAPTER THIRTEEN

CASSIUS WALKED AIMLESSLY along Chester's Main Street. The cool air felt refreshing against his skin, contrasting the slight warmth beneath it that didn't belong to him.

Not even corpse blood made him feel this warm.

He ran his hand through his hair, and when he pulled his fingers away, he could feel tiny beads of sweat.

Sweat?

Cassius couldn't remember the last time he felt so warm. The faint thrum in his veins, his pulse—*her pulse*—he reminded himself. It felt...

Heightened.

Cassius stopped for a moment and rescinded his movement. The fainter it became.

He walked quickly, and the thrum became more evident.

The memory of earlier that night resurfaced.

"It knows she's near," Tajiri said.

Cassius followed the feel of her pulse.

Is she in danger?

Is it Liam?

A strange feeling of possession and panic overcame him, and the world around him was nothing but shadow, and the light that drew him was not really a light at all.

Cassius stopped outside a large estate. It wasn't unusual to see a converted plantation home in Virginia, but there weren't many in Chester. The town itself wasn't really large, and was more spaced out, more country than city.

It was why he had stayed. Eden would never think to look for him in a secluded, small country town.

But now...

As long as I don't turn her or consume her blood...they won't be able to do anything. At least...not for a few years.

A few years. That's all he'd have to figure a way out of this. If he could just make sure the girl was alright...

Cassius's legs moved of their own accord as he pushed through the iron gate to the estate.

Her pulse increased.

Cassius followed its call, like a sailor lured by a siren and stopped outside a large window.

He could see rather well in the dark; a trait he'd inherited from his father.

There was no danger.

She lay in bed, tossing and turning as if...

As if she's having a nightmare. He sighed.

It was at that moment he noticed her window was not completely shut.

Cassius stood there for a moment, his brain at some sort of crossroads.

Just shut it, and leave.

She's fine.

You're overreacting.
This mark is messing with you.
He ran his fingers over his forearm, feeling the flush of warmth and slight vibration of pulse beneath them.
Without thinking, he opened the window.
The cool air blew in with him, ruffling cream sheets.
What are you doing?
He had no answer.
It just feels...right.
The girl tossed, her arms reaching out into the empty space next to her, a tiny whimper escaping her lips. When her fingertips brushed the back of his hand, Cassius couldn't deny the shiver it sent through his entire being. Without thinking, he reached out for her hand, his fingers brushing the scar on her wrist.
It was like the entire world had shifted.
No, *his entire world* had shifted.
His thumb brushed the underside of her wrist, where he bit her. Where his teeth had punctured her skin and marked her blood as his.
"I don't even know your name..." he whispered.
Her fingertips grazed his forearm as he held her hand, and Cassius didn't want to let go.
"But...I promise to keep you safe." He let the words fall out in absolution. When the room had brightened with the light of dawn, only then did Cassius realize hours had passed.
The sound of footsteps in the distance alerted him.
In a flash, he leaned his body through the window, stealing one last look at the beautiful mortal who he vowed to protect.

CHAPTER FOURTEEN

AVA STARED AT the scar. It didn't seem to want to fade.

The water ran over her skin, cleansing like rain. Ava squeezed the remnants of her body wash onto a loofah, the smell of bergamot and jasmine filling the air.

The hot water ran in rivulets down her skin, grazing over still tender wounds.

The knife wounds on her thighs were still pink in color, even after two weeks, while the bite mark on her wrist looked as if it'd been part of her skin for years.

How strange, Ava thought as she stared at the raised mark. In the beam of sunlight from the bathroom window, she noticed it shimmered.

The memory of those razor-sharp fangs pushed to the surface, and Ava's breath hitched.

The feel of his warm tongue on her flesh, like it was sealing the wound.

Ava did her best to shake the memory from her mind, and finished her shower, all too eager to leave.

The nightmare had faded into memory as she slept, as fear and pain gave way to bliss and serenity.

The feeling of wanting his touch...the angel from the darkness.

Ava ran her fingers through her wet hair, her reflection staring back at her.

"You're losing your damn marbles, Ava. You're just messed up about Ross. That guy was just as wasted as the rest of them." She pulled on her favorite Blue Oyster Cult shirt.

"Leaving in five," Mal shouted from the hallway. The scent of percolating bold coffee struck her, and her blood chilled. Becky was up.

Fuck.

Ava hurriedly jumped into a pair of jeans, wracked with frays and holes. She grabbed her tote bag and took a deep breath as she opened her door.

When she came into the kitchen, Becky stood there in her fluffy mauve robe, with her unicorn slippers.

Despite being almost sixty-five, her aunt didn't look a day over fifty. Age had been *very* good to her.

"Good morning, Ava." Becky smiled at her with a warm smile.

Ava avoided her gaze. "Good morning," she said as she walked past the countertop where Becky and Mal sat.

"Malcolm tells me you two will be staying here for a while, what with all the hoopla up at the college." Becky sipped her coffee, and Ava pursed her lips.

Hoopla. She called the murders, hoopla.

"Yeah, well it wasn't my idea." Ava glared at Mal.

"Well, I'm glad to have you both." Becky smiled at Mal.

"Yeah, well I'm going to be late, soooo..." She cleared her throat, her gaze fixed on her brother.

Mal pushed off the counter, his dark brown hair

hanging in his eyes as he shook it away.

"On that note, we'll see you later, Becky." Mal saluted her, and Ava all but ran out the door.

Her skin prickled with goosebumps, despite the sun. She ran her hands up her arms as she opened the car.

"You cold?" Mal asked as he got in the driver side.

"Yeah, just a chill." She answered.

Mal reached in the back seat, grasping a blue flannel shirt. He handed it to Ava, who looked at it suspiciously.

"When is the last time you washed that?" She gingerly took the shirt and held it up to her nose. It didn't smell bad. It smelled like tobacco and whiskey, which wasn't an unwelcome smell.

It smelled like Mal.

"Its new. Dallas gave it to me." Mal started the car.

"Aww, how cute. You two are sharing clothes now." Ava fluttered her eyelashes at her brother in a teasing manner.

"It's not like that, and you know it." He shot her a disapproving glare as he pulled the Chevelle out of the driveway.

Ava pulled the flannel on, and she had to admit it was rather cozy.

"Where is your partner in crime, anyway? Aren't you two usually joined at the hip?" she asked as she pulled the warm flannel around her. It was a tad large for her, being that Dallas was much larger than her. Mal wasn't short by any means, but Dallas was a former wide receiver back in his high school days, and Mal...

Although Mal seemed to have put on more muscle in the last few years, she was certain he'd never stand a match with Dallas if it ever came to it.

"He's just hanging out with some friends. Said he'd

meet up with us later." Mal's eyes were serious, but his tone light. "What time are you done with your classes today?" Something about the way he asked, felt...off.

Ever since the pizza shop, he's been weird.

"My last class finishes up at two," she answered.

"Cool. Listen, I've got some errands to run, so if I'm not there immediately at two..."

Ava didn't let him finish. "I'm a big girl, Mal. I can take care of myself. It's fine. Just give me a call or something when you're close." She yawned.

"Should have gotten up earlier, maybe you could have had a cup of coffee." Mal irked her.

"I just had a rough night. I'm fine," she said as she leaned her chin on her flannel covered arm, gazing out the window at the expanse of the trees, the touch of golden autumn among them.

***

Ember pushed the paper cup toward Ava. "You really don't have to do this, you know."

Ava graciously wrapped her hands around the flimsy cup, letting its warmth seep into her skin. "I know. But I like to."

Ember smiled sweetly, her green eyes lighting up with joy.

Ava didn't know what to say. She was never good at this sort of thing.

"Thanks," she said as she took a sip of the mocha flavored coffee.

Ember took her apron off, and hung it on the uniform rack as she punched out from the cafe.

Ava leaned against the cold subway tiles as she waited for Ember to gather her things.

That's when she saw him.

The green-eyed angel from the shadows.

He stood across the room, frozen like an animal who'd been caught in the headlights.

He wore dark black pants, and a grey tee, and even from across the room, Ava could swear his green eyes, *glowed.*

The memory of his lips on her skin...

Of fangs...

Ava clutched her coffee cup.

"Ember I'll be right back," she said as normally as she could.

"Okay..." Ember's voice was faint behind her as Ava walked hastily through the crowd of students.

Why is he following me?

What is his deal?

When a student pushing a cart full of stock cut her off in the middle of her path, Ava cursed.

"Watch where you're going!" the student snapped.

Ava looked up, and the angel had once again disappeared.

About to give up, she saw the flash of golden-blond hair as he walked out the door.

Ava quickened her pace, her legs striding with purpose.

She was only a few feet away.

"Hey!" she hollered. The man ignored her.

She sprinted, the coffee sloshing with animated movement. She reached out for his arm and pulled it. The man spun around in shock. He seemed to be speechless.

"Why are you following me?" She stood on the corner of the sidewalk, casting a glare at him.

"I beg your pardon." He cleared his throat.

"You fucking bit me." She sipped her coffee.

"I...yes. I did." His answer was not cold, or remorseful.

"What the hell?" She pushed him.

He stumbled back.

"Please tell me you don't have anything." She could feel a sense of worry overcome her.

"I...no. I'm...sorry?" he asked as if he wasn't sure what to say.

"Stop following me." She said it with authority. Goosebumps prickled on her arm, inside the flannel.

"I..." He paused, and the look in his eyes was...

Ava wasn't sure how to describe it.

"I wanted to apologize." He cleared his throat, and Ava found herself staring at his mouth.

The memory of his lips on her skin...

Made her stomach flip.

She broke his gaze and took a sip of her coffee.

"Well, consider it done." She refused to look at him, but...

Something about those eyes pulled her in.

"I'm Cassius." His voice truly was like chocolate cake.

Ava glanced up at him for a fraction of a moment.

"Ava." She took a sip of her coffee.

"I'm sorry, *Ava,* if I alarmed you. I didn't mean to." The man named Cassius stood with perfect posture.

"Yeah, well I suppose we're all on edge, after what's been going on around here." She nonchalantly flipped her long dark hair over her shoulder, crossing her left arm in front of her stomach, as she tightened her grip of her right hand on the coffee cup.

"Of course." He blinked, and Ava noticed his eyelashes were dark, and thick.

No wonder she thought he was an angel. His

features were...masculine yet, *beautiful.*
Like a freaking Calvin Klein model.
"See you around, *Cas.*" She took another sip of her coffee and turned back to the union, leaving the man named Cassius in her wake.

CHAPTER FIFTEEN

CASSIUS WATCHED AS *Ava* walked away. He still couldn't' believe she'd caught up to him. When the stalker cut her off...

He thought he'd escaped unseen. But her pulse was louder, and louder with every step until...

She *touched* him. The sensation left the tiniest prickle on his skin.

And she cursed at him. And *pushed* him.

A light smile tugged at the corner of his lips. The memory of a girl who tried with all her might to move, despite a loss of blood.

A fighter.

It wasn't as if she knew *what* he was. If she had, she certainly would not have pushed him. No, if she knew what he was...

She'd run screaming.

As she should, he reminded himself.

She'd rendered him speechless, for the first time in years.

Of course, she didn't understand what had transpired. How could she? She was just an average girl, who had no inkling about the world that lay in the shadows. Of course, to her it must have seemed like he was under the influence of alcohol or drugs. No sane *human* bit another human.

Cassius didn't know what to say, but he knew if he said nothing...she'd leave.

I need to know her name, the pressing thought assaulted him.

"I am Cassius." The words came out differently than he'd meant them.

Ava. Her name was *Ava.*

Simple, beautiful.

Cassius shook his head as he hid in the rafters, trying to ward off his burgeoning curiosity.

When the sound of the doors opening broke the silence, Cassius leaned over the rafters, peering down below.

"I'm thirsty, damn it. How much longer do you expect me to wait?" Cassius didn't recognize the voice.

"We've got to wait, a few more days at most." A familiar head of hair came into his vision, and Cassius recognized its owner immediately.

Liam.

"It's been two weeks." A third voice chimed in. Cassius stayed as still as a statue.

"Yeah, and you can thank Brody for that. I told you to dispose of the bodies. You got sloppy, and now we have to fucking starve," Liam snarled at the one wearing a backward hat.

"I think I saw a hunter today. Red Chevelle. Guy didn't look like one of the locals," the man wearing a green golf shirt and khakis growled back at Brody.

"So now you're going to blame me for the hunters too, is that it, Logan?" Brody cornered the other vamp, his chest puffing out like a peacock puffs its feathers.

Liam snarled, challenging the other vampires. "Silence! You fools." Cassius watched as Liam entered their space, the other two vampires taking a step back.

Brody snapped his fangs at Liam. "I'm not the only one with loose ends." Brody glared at Liam.

"Liam managed to let one get away..." Brody hissed.

"The girl from Alpha Pi?" Logan asked.

"Yes. Someone marked her. I could smell his scent, mixed with her blood." Brody crossed his arms.

"She's nothing to worry about." Liam shrugged.

Cassius gripped the beam next to him tightly.

"What if she remembers... She saw our faces. We were with her and the guy half the night." Logan sounded panicked.

"I don't think she remembers." Liam walked away from them.

"But you're not certain," Brody sneered.

"Are you going to do something about it or am I going to have to clean up your mess again?" Brody stood still, his gaze directed at Liam.

"She's marked, now. That changes things." Liam's voice was solid.

"Well, I've never been afraid of a challenge." Brody smiled.

Liam was in front of Brody within a flash, his fingers poised around Brody's thick neck. Liam bared his fangs. "She's mine to savor, and you best remember your rank." The authority in Liam's voice was direct.

Brody's body shook, his gaze never leaving Liam.

When Liam let him go, Cassius couldn't stand to stay. He crawled through the rooftop latch, and jumped into the shadows of abandoned construction, with one sole purpose.

AVA CROWLEY, VAMPIRE SLAYER

CHAPTER SIXTEEN

AVA SAT CROSS-LEGGED on the bench, peering down at her textbook, a steaming cup of hot chocolate held close to her chest. The sweet wisps of steam filled her senses with warmth and comfort.

When black boots came into her vision, Ava looked up.

The man who stood before her wore dark wash jeans, his black leather belt boasting a rather ostentatious buckle that looked like a pentagram. Ava let her gaze travel up from his waist to see he was wearing a black muscle tank, his black tribal tattoos standing out against his defined muscles.

She'd know those tattoos anywhere.

"You look good in my shirt there, kitten." His voice was deep with bravado, tinged with sarcasm.

Ava's eyes lit up as she stared back into his pale blue eyes. Bright like the crest of a tsunami.

His dark hair was cut short, shorter than the last time she'd seen him, and he looked like he hadn't shaved in a few days. When her brother tried to pull off the grungy look, he failed miserably, but on Jake

Dallas the look added to his charm.

"I believe it's Mal's shirt now." She let her eyes fall back to the book in her lap.

Dallas shifted his weight.

"Mal's running a bit late. So, it looks like I'm your ride." Dallas jiggled a set of keys in front of her.

Ava sat up straighter.

"Where'd you park?" She closed her book and set her hot chocolate down to pack up her tote bag.

Dallas nodded over to the library. "Over by the cafe."

Ava all but leaped off the bench.

She had always been slightly taller than most people, but up against Dallas she felt short.

"Please. tell me you brought the bike." She could feel a smile forming on her lips.

Dallas smiled, the motion reaching his eyes. "Just for you, kitten." He winked at her.

Ava smiled. "Sweet," she said excitedly as she followed him to the library.

Despite the thirteen-year age gap between them, Ava had to admit Dallas looked like he fit in perfectly with the rest of the young students at Chester U, despite being in his thirties.

Probably could wipe out half the football team too.

She noticed quite a few of the students gawking at him as they strode over to his motorcycle.

When Ava climbed on the back of his motorcycle and wrapped her arms around his tree trunk of a waist, she couldn't help but smile.

***

Ava released her hands from Dallas's waist, and took off her helmet, tousling her long, dark hair free. The wind blew long strands in her face, and Dallas let out a small laugh.

"What?" Ava said as she pulled the strands from her face.

"You look like a damn shampoo commercial." Dallas hung his helmet on the handlebar.

"I'll take that as a compliment," she said as she walked past him to the front door. She didn't wait for him to come inside.

"Hello, Ava." Becky sat on the couch with a glass of wine, and the sound made Ava jump only slightly.

"And...Jake? How lovely to see you again." She smiled at him and took a sip of her wine.

Ava felt uncomfortable at the gaze she shot in Dallas's direction.

Dallas nodded to her. "Evening, Miss Michaels," he said politely.

Ava brushed past the kitchen counter, where Connie milled about. It looked as if she was baking something. Ava peered over her shoulder. *Cookies.* Ava reached her hand around Connie, only to be met with Chinese curses and a smack on the hand.

"Don't even think about it," Connie said nonchalantly.

"But I'm hungry," Ava whined.

"You're always hungry, child. It's a wonder you're as skinny as a rail." Connie smiled as she finished icing a cookie. She turned to Ava and held it out to her, her eyebrow raised.

Ava took it gingerly from her hands. "Thank you, Connie." She smiled and graciously took a bite of the cookie.

It tasted like almonds and sweet vanilla. Ava opened the door and walked out on to the patio.

Dallas wasn't far behind her.

"Don't tell me I have to help you with your homework too," he said as he plopped down in one of the Adirondack chairs, letting his legs sprawl out. Leaning up against the chair back, the motion made him look rather enticing.

Ava shot him a glance.

"You wouldn't be much help anyway. I doubt you know anything about the Middle Ages," she said as she took another bite of her cookie and sat down in one of the rockers.

"I know they were big into the occult. Lots of interesting lore and myths."

"Fascinating. Jake Dallas knows something," she teased.

"I know a lot of things, Ava." He raised his eyebrow at her.

"I bet you do." She finished her cookie.

"Ava don't take this the wrong way..." Dallas leaned forward.

"What's up?" She noted the change in his demeanor.

"Mal told me about what happened to your friend. Up on campus—the one from the news." Dallas looked slightly uncomfortable.

"You're not going to lecture me about staying in and being a good girl too, are you?" Ava raised her eyebrow, her frustration evident.

"No. I'm not." He paused, brushing his hands together.

Ava sighed, crossing her arms. "Then, what is it?"

"Have you ever taken...like...a self-defense class?" The way Dallas phrased the question felt odd.

"You mean like, how to fend off a rapist?" Ava shot him a pointed look.

"Umm...yeah," Dallas looked a bit nervous.

"Not really, but..." she started to speak, and Dallas rose from his seat.

"Get up." He motioned for her to get up.

"Wha..." she said as she pushed herself up out of the chair.

Dallas walked over to the grassy expanse of the backyard.

"Come at me." He motioned for her, planting his feet firmly on the ground.

"Dallas, no. Seriously..." She crossed her arms.

"Come on." His eyes challenged her.

"This is stupid," she bit out.

"Humor me, kitten." The look in his eyes was dark, and challenging.

"Fine," she said as she approached him, and without warning, threw the hardest punch she'd ever thrown, directly into his jaw.

Dallas looked slightly shocked, but retaliated, nonetheless.

"Is that all you've got?" He said as he withdrew his fingers from his bloodied lip, a smile forming on his face.

***

She was sweating, and so was he, and it felt *good.* Even though there were no stakes, and she knew Dallas would not harm her, he didn't hold back. Ava had to admit it felt *good* to spar. She'd never considered herself an athlete by any means, not like Dallas was. She'd stuck out cheerleading until she graduated, not because she loved the hustle and bustle of high school football, but because there was something about being thrown into the air, about the training that she really liked. She'd also really enjoyed her kickboxing class over the summer.

Dallas wrapped his arms around her, his hold tight, fingers tightening around her wrist. She backed herself into his hold, angling her elbow, but the touch of his fingers on her wrist *stung* as they grazed her bite. He stilled, and Ava could hear his sharp intake of breath. The fun, laughing tone he'd had disappeared as he pulled her wrist to him.

"How the hell did you get this?" His voice darkened, his thumb brushing the cool mark on her skin.

Ava breathed deep, caught between answering him, and taking advantage of his distraction. She settled on the latter because she wasn't sure *what* to say.

"What the hell is going on out here?" Becky's voice was alarmed and Mal's curses accentuated the air.

Dallas held Ava's arms tightly in front of her, and his body pressed against hers like a brick wall.

Ava wriggled once more, positioning her elbow directly into his groin.

Dallas, distracted once more by the presence of Mal and Becky, was at her mercy. He breathed in a huff of air as she applied the force and stepped on his foot with her free hand, breaking free. He looked at her curiously, but only for a moment, as his natural demeanor returned, leaving that unanswered question in the air.

"Just an old-fashioned sparring session." Dallas chuckled.

"Dallas thought he'd show me some self-defense moves." Ava brushed her hair behind her.

"What a nice idea. Perhaps you could share some of that knowledge with me, Jake?" Becky said.

Ava felt her stomach twitch, and a strange prickling sensation arose on her skin. Her wrist flared beneath

Dallas's flannel, the heat trapped with nowhere to go as she pulled it tight against her wrist, the faint sting from where he'd touched her still present.

The feeling washed over her, and the memories pushed forth to the surface.

Ross carried her, rather unsteadily. She wrapped her legs around his waist, uncontrollable giggles eliciting from her throat.

When Ross fell, she collapsed on top of him, the laughter a full on roar.

"Shh... Ava..." Ross's whisper was less of a whisper and more of a loud beacon.

She rolled off him, trying to catch her breath.

"You are shit faced." She turned her head, her eyes fixated on his bleary, heavy-lidded eyes.

"Oh, like you're not..." He shoved at her, the smile on his face genuine.

Ava leaned up on her elbows, the bottom of her dress riding up her thighs. The floor was cold and wet.

A figure emerged from the darkness behind Ross, but she couldn't make out the face.

He seemed to be wearing a blue checkered shirt.

Ava shook the memory off and noticed Mal was staring at her.

"What's your deal?" she said as she brushed past him toward the living room.

"I don't know what you're talking about." Mal looked at her with question.

Ava watched as Connie made arrangements to the last of the dinner plates on the island in the kitchen.

"You've been weird ever since yesterday." She crossed her arms.

"Maybe I think you're the one being weird." Mal twisted his lips.

"Whatever. You want to be all shadows and secrets, be my guest." She walked into the kitchen and took sight of Connie's dinner. Her heart lifted a fraction at the realization Connie made her favorite cheesy potatoes.

The sound of the door opening broke her concentration.

"Leaving so soon, Jake?" Becky called

"I'm afraid so. I uh…promised to meet up with some friends while I was in town." He smiled lightly.

Mal turned in his direction. "Thanks, Dallas." His voice was serious.

Dallas smirked, and saluted Mal. "Don't mention it."

In the blink of an eye, he was gone.

Becky sat in her usual spot at the dining table, Connie pulling up next to her. Mal stocked his plate full of cheesy potatoes and chicken, leaving out all the other sides, before sitting down.

Ava reluctantly filled her plate and sat next to her brother.

"Isn't this nice, the four of us together again." Becky smiled.

Ava focused on her chicken.

"How long are you in town, Malcolm?" Connie asked.

Ava looked at her brother, waiting for his answer.

"A few weeks." He took a bite of cheesy potatoes.

A few weeks?

Ava couldn't remember the last time Mal had stayed longer than a week.

"I'm so glad you decided to come home for a bit as well, Ava. I can't imagine how terrifying it must be, what with a serial killer preying on the campus grounds."

Ava focused on her food.

"I tell you, I feel so much better knowing you are safe under my roof. And how nice of Dallas to help you feel confident about defending yourself." She took a sip of her wine.

"I don't need Dallas to tell me how to take care of myself." Ava chewed her chicken furiously.

"Of course, you don't. But you can always learn new tricks." Mal spoke seriously.

"I'm the one who gave him a bloody lip." Ava cast a glare at Mal.

She could still feel the flush of heat at her wrist, and a wave of nausea overcame her.

Ava was so tired, and the room was spinning.

Ross was in the corner with one of the fraternity brothers. The one who'd been making eyes at him all evening. Ava was only slightly surprised Ross wasn't offended.

The man had his mouth on Ross's neck.

Ava could feel cold, clammy hands at her shoulder, pulling her away.

"Don't touch me..." She tried to twist out of their grasp, but her legs wouldn't move.

Ross moaned in pleasure, and Ava's eyes felt heavy.

She could feel slick hands sliding up her legs. She tried to shift away, but...

Why couldn't' she move?

"Ross...." She tried to form words, but...

Ross moaned in pleasure, and Ava felt a sharp pain from inside her thigh...

She let out a whimper as she tore her head from Ross's gaze.

She was bleeding...

Another prickle of pain sent a shockwave through her

body, and she could see one of the brothers, the one with the backward hat...

Between her legs.

She forced the numb, deadweight legs with all her might, into his head. The motion knocked him over, and Ava felt exhausted, as her thigh wounds throbbed.

The man pulled his fingers away from his lips, and she noted the blood on his lip. It looked...black.

"Bitch. Just for that I ought to give you another one." He snarled, and Ava could see his teeth looked...odd.

Sharp.

The feel of the knife cutting into her skin was quick, but not without pain.

She attempted to move her leg, but it was like it didn't belong to her. It was heavy, and it hurt.

Ava's stomach felt queasy, and the scent of blood and mildew filled her senses.

Ava pushed herself away from the table abruptly. "Excuse me," she said as politely as possible, trying to hold in her emotion.

"Ava..." Becky started.

"I'm just going to the bathroom. Chill." Ava knew her voice was harsh, much more than she intended. She shut the door quickly, bracing her hands on the cold marble of the sink.

CHAPTER SEVENTEEN

IT WAS A strange feeling for Cassius, the pulsing radar in his veins. Despite growing up in the center of vampiric history, with Leon and Cora, his parents, and even Eden and Octavius, he didn't know much about the claiming of human blood. Leon's studies in the 1980's fared more toward the effect of fresh blood alternatives than they did on the blood of those marked.

Though Cassius knew his father marked his mother first before turning her, he hadn't thought to press his father for information on the matter. He was far too angry at the man for leaving him in the dust because he'd thought Cassius didn't belong to him.

Because he hadn't made his transformation fast enough.

Not to mention, Cassius's blood haze left him longing for one thing, and one thing only.

He'd tried to keep his human friendships at a distance, and romance of any sort was out of the questions. Until Eden, that was, but she was not human. She was a monster. Like him.

He wondered momentarily as he walked past the gates of Ava's residence, how his father could stand such a bright, noticeable feeling in his blood for seven years.

Cassius could barely stand it now, and it had only been mere weeks.

The fading sunset cast a golden glow over the plantation house, and Cassius couldn't help but remember a similar sunset, over the Duquensian Manor only a carriage ride away from Portofino.

Thoughts of *her* crept into his mind, souring the memory.

She'd been a different person then, Eden. She'd been mysterious, alluring, and unlike any other woman he'd met in his short twenty-four years of life. She'd been caring. A friend. She'd taken him under her dark wings.

Before he could move, the front door swung open, and Ava ran down the steps, flinging herself through the gates, and smacked into him.

He held his hands out to steady, her, the feel of his fingers on her skin sending tiny flashes of warmth through him.

"Ava?" he asked as she looked up at him, confusion in her eyes. She pushed away from his light touch, and he noticed the drop in temperature from her departure.

"What the fuck, Cas? Are you fucking *stalking* me...still?" Her eyes flashed with anger.

His gaze dropped to her wrist, and he could *feel* her blood racing as if it were his own.

I am absolutely not stalking you. I just...

His brain wanted to protest. After all, he'd only sought to walk among the main streets, to clear his mind.

He'd given in to the pull of her pulse, followed it to the gates of her estate.

It wasn't *not* stalking.

A sense of shame fell over him.

This isn't me. He thought. But as soon as the thought crossed his mind, so did the memory of Liam, Brody, and Logan discussing their 'loose ends'.

She needs to know the truth. But how do I tell her? Surely, she will cast me off as insane, and why shouldn't she?

"I did not know you resided here," he lied. A small pang of guilt shot through him at the action.

He'd told many lies in his long life, so why was this one different?

Why did he feel the need to tell this mortal everything?

Ava narrowed her eyes at him skeptically. "Why do I not believe you?" She took off down the sidewalk.

"Where are you going?" he asked curiously.

Her long dark hair blew in the rustle of wind, and tiny autumn leaves followed in her dust.

"What kind of idiot do you take me for? Why would I tell you anything? You're the one stalking me, remember?"

Cassius was at her side immediately. "Perhaps, we could talk?" He tried to sound as polite and safe as possible.

Ava glanced at him once more, but she didn't run. She kept up with his pace.

"You have until I reach my destination to plead your case." She smirked, and Cassius noted she seemed to slow down only a fraction.

"About the other night..." He opened his mouth and Ava only rolled her eyes.

"What about it?" They turned the corner block, passing Cory's. The neon flashed, casting an aqua and red glow on her features.

"I bit you." Cassius found strangely enough the words came easily, though he was certain after he told her the truth, she'd probably run.

Far away from him.

A part of him regretted the truth that would undoubtedly separate her from him.

This close to her, he could smell the hint of jasmine, feel her pulse within him like a steady, flowing river.

He followed her stride down the street, passing the tiny accountant office, and homes.

"Yeah, and now I'll have your fucking teeth marks on my wrist forever. That shit left a scar, you know,"

I can work with this.

"I'm not...like you." He struggled to speak the words, knowing the destruction they were about to bring.

Ava stopped, in front of the library and turned to him, causing him to abruptly stop himself.

"Really now? What are you going to tell me you're a vampire or something?" She raised her eyebrows at him, and her tone was sarcastic.

Cassius felt awash with heat that had nothing to do with pulse, nothing to do the weather. It seemed like forever until he found the words.

"Actually, yes. I am. A vampire. It is my venom that healed your wounds." He stood straight, his eyes never breaking her gaze.

Ava rolled her eyes and laughed.

"Fucking delusional too. You're a piece of work, aren't you, Cassius? God damn, it's always the fucking hot ones that are completely bonkers." She turned away from him, as if to move forward and leave him as he deserved, but instead she remained in place. She turned her head once more, in his direction.

Did she just call me...hot? Cassius wasn't sure how to take her words. They were spoken with sarcasm, after all.

"A fucking vampire? Like Dracula-I-want-to-suck-your-blood-vampire?" Her lips twisted in a sarcastic smile, but he could see her eyes betrayed her. And even if they hadn't, the increased pulse inside of him told him she considered the truth in his words.

"Yes. Although, I don't particularly care for that comparison. Most of the stories have it all wrong." He swallowed nervously, his hands finding their way into his pockets.

Ava stood still, facing the dusk.

"Those men...the ones that attacked your friend..."

Ava turned around slowly, her amber eyes tinged with alarm.

"They were vampires too. The girls at The Heights..." The words poured out of him without warning now, faster and faster. The overwhelming feeling of caring, the swell of protectiveness he felt toward this girl, this *Ava*, was startling to him, but he also had to admit that it wasn't entirely the mark's fault. He'd cared for humans before. Friends like Penny, Rocco, Marguerite, Pierre. He'd felt protective of them too, once, without a mark to blame.

You always have to be the hero, don't you? Eden's words swam in his head.

"You're telling me, that the murders plaguing Chester are because of *vampires*?" She chewed at her lip.

"I know it sounds crazy..." The golden sunset lit her up from behind like a halo.

"You're absolutely right. It *is* crazy." Her voice was even as she looked up at him.

"But you know it is true...don't you?" He refused to move from his spot, noting the space between them.

Ava stalked closer to him, her eyes burning with fire.

With her pulse racing beneath his skin, he could tell she was frightened. The last thing he wanted was to frighten her, but—

"Your time is up. If I catch you *stalking* me again, vampire or not, I will make your life a living hell, Cassius. You will regret the day you fucking bit me. Am I clear?" Her eyes burned into his, and he nodded in response.

"Absolutely."

CHAPTER EIGHTEEN

VAMPIRE.

The word reverberated in her cerebellum, and although she knew she should run, far away from this crazy stalker, her wrist burned with heat, her skin prickled with goosebumps, and as she looked into glowing green eyes, she knew it was true.

She knew it in her blood.

She lay in her bed, her gaze settled on the shimmering scar on her wrist. In his presence it burned, while the rest of her skin felt tiny prickles of ice, goosebumps. It was insane to think *he* had something to do with it, but she knew. She'd always been a believer in the paranormal; after all, it was in her blood. She'd known the lengths her family went to, changing their names to Michaels, because they wanted to escape the shadow of their family's lineage. Crowley.

Ava had always felt drawn to her history, being a descendant of one of the most famous occultists in history. She'd amassed a small collection of books on such things—witchcraft, ghosts, divination, cryptozoology. But vampires—

She tossed in her bed, turning over on her stomach, looking out the window at the dark forest beyond.

If what Cassius said was true...that vampires truly were the ones responsible for the murders at Chester...responsible for Ross's death...

How do I fight off something that isn't even human?

Ava could throw a punch, and even evade an attacker, but a vampire? She doubted a solid right hook would deter something with fangs and super strength that wasn't alive or dead.

A knock sounded on her door, and Ava jumped.

Mal stood in the doorway.

"Hey, Simba." His voice was serious, and in the harsh shadows of the hallway, she could see the highlight of the hallway lights on his face. Mal hadn't looked this serious since their parent's funeral.

"Can I come in?" he asked, and she didn't miss the worry in his voice.

"Of course." She nodded and he entered, shutting the door behind him.

"There's something we need to talk about. I know you're going to have a lot of questions...but..." Mal ran his hand through his hair as he took a seat in the butterfly chair in front of her desk. He leaned on his knees, running his hands over his face before continuing.

"Mal is everything ok..."

"Dallas told me you've been bit."

Memories of earlier, of her spar with Dallas flashed in her mind.

His fingers running over her skin, brushing her bite mark on her wrist. The sting.

Cassius's...vampire bite.

Of course, she thought.

He must have seen it and wondered what happened. Any sane person would wonder why one had teeth mark scars on their wrist.

"It's nothing, just... I was at a party and things got...out of hand."

She hid her wrist under her pillow.

"I haven't told you the truth. I thought...I thought I could keep it from you. That'd you'd be safer if you didn't know but...clearly I was wrong."

Mal looked into her eyes, and she could see sadness and fear in them.

"Mal, you're not making sense." She hugged her pillow in front of her.

"All the trips I go on, Ava.... I'm not *just* playing gigs."

Ava's blood chilled. It was as if she knew what was coming, and she didn't want to hear it any more than Mal wanted to speak it.

"I hunt monsters, Ava. The kind that bite you...and leave marks like the one on your wrist. The kind that makes the monster under the bed look tame. The kind..."

"Vampires, you mean." Her fingers tightened around the pillow, squeezing it with anxious energy.

"Yes. Dallas too. He's my partner. We hunt them together."

Ava blinked her eyes, trying to hold back the onslaught of emotion that seemed to be trying to push its way up and out of her through her eyes.

"Vampires aren't real..." she whispered. But even as she said it, she knew it was not true.

"Unfortunately, Ava they are very real. And you've been bitten by one."

100

CHAPTER NINETEEN

AVA TRIED TO focus on the lecture, but she couldn't. Not that she didn't find Medieval history interesting, she'd always loved *history*, but the slides of classical paintings amidst the dark lecture hall made it easy to zone out.

That, and she couldn't stop thinking about Cassius.

Every ounce of her being *knew* he was telling the truth, and if she'd had any qualms about it, Mal's visit squashed any doubt.

That explains the dusty amp.

Ava glanced around the spacious lecture hall, her gaze settling on the various heads in the chairs, and she couldn't help but wonder if one of them was next, or if one of them was not who they seemed.

Ava's skin prickled with goosebumps, and her wrist flared with heat as three men ambled down the steps in the darkness, and she couldn't deny her curiosity as she turned.

Liam and his friends sauntered down the steps, quietly, and as they passed her, Liam shot her a devilish smirk. "Ava." He smiled lightly as he passed her.

His friend, the one who'd irritated Mal at the pizza shop, gave her a sly grin as he passed, and flashes of memories pushed forth.

Brody.

Dark eyes peering up at her from between her legs, black blood on his lips.

That backward hat.

Ava felt her blood chill as she watched them travel the steps to the seats in the front of the room, taking the prickle of ice and heated sensation with them.

Well, that can't be coincidence.

"Do you know those guys?" Ember whispered, poking her arm.

Ava turned to her friend. "I think so," she answered.

Ember's brows furrowed together. "What do you mean you *think* so?" she pushed.

"They were at the party. You know, the one I went to with Ross." Ava slumped in her seat, her head rolling back on the padded backing of the chair. The slide changed, the bright lights in the darkness showing another classical painting.

"Are you going to the service?" Ember asked.

Ava shifted uncomfortably in her seat. Without any leads, and no physical evidence, it wasn't likely Ross's body would be found. They'd declared him deceased, if only for the closure it would provide his family. The funeral service at St. Sebastian's Church was in three days. It was televised everywhere, posters strewn all throughout the bulletin boards and message boards on campus, and she hadn't been able to look at any of them.

The reality of his death was everywhere.

It haunted her every move, and even more so now

that she knew the truth behind his demise.

Fucking vampires. Truth is always stranger than fiction.

"I don't know." It was an honest answer.

Ember pursed her lips, her hand still on Ava's arm. Warm, friendly, soothing.

"Well, if you decide you want to go, you don't have to go alone." She smiled sweetly.

"Thanks."

The lights came on, and Ava glanced at her phone. 2:00.

The sound of bristling students shoving books and binders into bags and backpacks echoed in the hall. Ember slung her backpack over her shoulder as she scooted past Ava to the hallway to join the crowd.

"See you tomorrow." She smiled as she faded out between the stream of students in a hurry for their next class.

When the crowd diminished, Ava exited out of the building as well. When she stepped out of the shade of the building, her lips twisted into a smile. Dallas leaned against his motorcycle, and the bright sunlight shone down on him, casting shadows on his thick arms, his tattoos standing out vividly even at a distance from his sleeveless muscle shirt.

"Would it kill you to wear a shirt that didn't have gaping holes in it?" She stopped in front of him, watching him spin his keys amidst his thick fingers. His blue eyes sparkled with charm.

"You know what they say, flaunt it if you got it." He smirked.

Ava rolled her eyes. "Too bad you're old. I hear things stop working after you turn thirty." She grabbed the helmet he offered her.

"Oh, I can assure you, kitten, my machine is in perfect working order." He winked as he straddled his bike, the motion elongating his thighs, strained against his dark wash jeans.

"Where's Mal?" she asked as she positioned herself behind him.

"He had some business to take care of. He'll meet up with us later."

Ava wrapped her arms around Dallas's waist, her fingers brushing against his abs through his flimsy tank. They felt hard and warm.

"You know, I could get used to this mode of transportation. It's pretty badass." She held on tight to him.

Dallas turned his head slightly, regarding her with a smile.

"I'll show you badass. Hang tight, kitten."

***

"What the hell is this?" Ava dismounted off the bike, staring at the unassuming building buried in the brick wall in front of her. It didn't look like anything....operable.

"Mal told me he had the talk with you." Dallas hung the helmet on the handlebar, kicking down the kickstand to rest on the side of the broken concrete walk.

It was hard to believe anyone even knew about the place, being as it was far out, and not surrounded by much more than an abandoned gas station, and a half-crumbled structure.

"That doesn't explain why you brought me to this hole in the wall." She cast him a rueful glance.

"Is this your idea of badass? Because if it is, I think

we need to have a serious talk. Your dementia may be setting in." She jabbed him.

"Come on." He motioned for her to follow, and she did.

Ava had seen plenty of gyms, both in her cheerleading days in Massachusetts, and in her time in Chester, but she'd never seen a gym like this.

Despite being embedded into a hobbit hole, the place was pristine and well kept. It didn't boast traditional machines, although there were a few she recognized. Leg lifts, barbell benches, push up machines. There was a boxing ring, as well as a track that looked like the paint was fresh.

"What the hell is this place?" She turned to Dallas once more.

"Self-defense is a little different with supernatural forces." His voice was serious.

"Dallas..." she started.

"I know it's a lot to take in, okay? I've been there. Trust me." He licked his lips, and Ava couldn't deny the motion sent a shiver directly to her groin.

Fuck me.

She'd known Dallas as Mal's best friend for the last three years, and though he was *much* older than her, she couldn't deny that she found him insanely attractive.

At least on the outside.

She knew him fairly well, and knew enough that like Mal, Dallas wasn't really the kind of man you brought home to your parents.

Like Mal, he was the kind of guy you *hid* from your parents. Ross may have been out of her league, but at least he was in the ballpark.

Dallas was definitely out of the ballpark. He was out

of the fucking state.

"I suppose next you're going to tell me the tooth fairy is real," she drawled as she dropped her backpack on the floor. She ran her hands along the ropes of the boxing ring.

"Not quite, but the whole teeth thing has some merit. Offering your bones for blessings is pretty much witchy shit 101. Right along with blowing out candles on your birthday."

She turned to see him in the boxing ring, his hand outstretched to hers.

"You up for a round two, kitten?" His eyes settled on hers, and she couldn't help but smirk.

"What, are you going to pretend to be a big bad vampire and come after me?" She set her hand in his and let him pull her up.

"Something like that."

She stepped on the soft floor of the ring and watched Dallas take his stance.

"First thing you need to know about bloodsuckers is their natural defense. Thrall."

Dallas stalked her closely, boxing her into the back of the ring post. She ducked and weaved around him, and he smiled.

"When a vampire corners you, you'll feel this...energy. Like your head gets hazy, foggy." They danced lightly, and he turned, grasping her arm behind her, pressing himself into her back, like they had the day before, when they'd been in the backyard. His other hand held her wrist across her chest, fingers brushing her scar, with that ripe sting. His lips were at her neck, and she could feel his breath heating her skin.

She closed her eyes and tried to focus. Being wrapped up like this, the weight of him against her chilled her bones, and flashes of the party reared their ugly head. That feeling of hopelessness, of terror.

The loss of control.

She struggled against Dallas, but he held her tightly.

"Thrall placates you. It makes you malleable, seeps into your brain. So, when they get close..." His lips were at her ear, and his breath on her earlobe left her stomach in knots.

"You'll likely start to feel aroused. Don't worry, that's a natural reaction. It doesn't mean you *want* them. It just means their thrall is doing what it's supposed to. Sex and blood go hand in hand for vampires."

Ava pushed back against him, trying to angle her elbow just right.

The feeling of the knife cutting into her flesh was vivid in her mind.

Of her legs knocking into Brody's head.

Of green eyes that stared into hers.

Razor sharp fangs piercing her skin.

She'd felt hazy, blissful. Like his lips on her wrist were the most perfect thing in the world. Dallas's words juxtaposed with her memories, and she couldn't deny that as she thought about Cassius's lips on her skin, it awakened deep feelings within her.

That must be the thrall.

"How do I fight it?" she asked, her voice much breathier than she intended.

"Thrall takes hold of your mind, Ava. Not your body. That is yours." His words broke through her thoughts. "Break my hold." He directed her. "Fight me."

His voice was dark, and sultry and Ava had to admit a part of her didn't want to. A part of her wanted to feel his pressure, wanted to relinquish, and give in to the things that filled her head. But if she couldn't fight Dallas, how would she ever fight off someone like Cassius? Death would be inevitable.

And there was no reason she could trust that even though Cassius had saved her, he wouldn't make good on his claim. She didn't know him. Not really.

He was a vampire after all. She might not have known all the finer details of a vampire's biology, but she was pretty sure they didn't save people. They killed them. There were no stories of vampires sweeping in to rescue damsels in distress. *Not that I'm a damsel. Or in distress.*

"Focus your mind. Feel your surroundings, anticipate my moves." He gripped her wrist with his fingers around her chest, while his other hand tightened around her wrist that he held against her back. Her muscles were starting to tense.

Ava closed her eyes, and pushed past the initial shock, and arousal, and focused on the feeling of immobility, the loss of control.

Images of Brody between her legs surfaced, and she remembered the feeling of her leg's deadweight. She was on the brink of death, she knew that. Yet she'd found the will to knock her legs into his head enough to make his lip bleed. Enough to distract him.

When Ava pushed forth against Dallas, there was only one thought in her mind.

The prevailing thought was that she would be better. She would not shrink like a violet in the face of danger.

Especially if danger is tall, blond, and fucking sexy as hell.

It was as if a switch had been flipped, and as she fought her way out of his hold, and he sparred against her, she felt a burgeoning sense of urgency she hadn't had before.

"Not bad for a first shot." Dallas ran his hands through his hair before removing his shirt. He'd worked up quite a sweat. His tan skin glistened in the low light.

Ava let her cardigan fall to the ground, revealing just her Blue Oyster Cult shirt, which was starting to cling to her arms from her own sheen of sweat.

"I can work with that." He smiled as he waved her on, challenging her once more. Ava smiled at the invitation.

CHAPTER TWENTY

"WHAT'S YOUR DEAL? You've been moping around here like a bitch for two days." Taj fell onto the couch next to Cassius. Jasmine sat in the armchair across from them with a beer in hand.

"I do not mope." Cassius scowled.

"What happened, Doc run out of your favorite veggie shake?" Taj teased.

"I told Ava the truth."

"Who's Ava?" Jasmine raised her eyebrow.

Taj grumbled, running his hand over his face.

"Great. The pain in the ass has a name now."

"The girl from the party? "Jasmine smiled, taking a sip of her beer.

"Yeah, that's the one." Cassius leaned back into the cushions.

Her pulse still beat within his veins, but it was faint. As if she was far away.

"What do you mean you told her the truth?" Taj crossed his arms and legs. His ankle rested on his knee, and in the low light of the house, he looked every bit the bodyguard he was once was in the 80's when they'd first met.

Things were so much simpler then.

But Cassius knew he wouldn't trade the present for the past.

He'd come a long way from a scared, newborn vampire in the late 1800's. His life had been racked with blood and death since the day he was born.

He'd vowed to never be like his father; never to force a woman into this bond of blood.

Never to claim a mate.

Never to give his body and his Aurelian curse over to someone he didn't love.

And after Leon had discovered sustainable alternatives to fresh blood, he'd vowed never to drink a human again.

I may have been born a monster, but only I can control whether I am one.

"I told her what I am. What I did to her."

"Why on God's green earth would you do that? I thought we both agreed you needed to—"

"No. I will not harm her." Cassius flashed his eyes at Taj.

"Cassius..."

"I made a vow, Taj. I know you think I'm crazy, but I value human life. I do not wish to be the end of it. I claimed her blood so that she could live another day. I know I will have to make a decision eventually. But until then, she should know the truth. Just in case—"

"Just in case, what Cas? Just in case Liam decides to finish what he started? She's just a girl. She's nothing special, Cas. Just another fucking stray cat you can't keep." Taj's words were bold, and angry but they weren't unjust.

"Taj! That's enough." Jasmine's voice raised an

octave.

Taj balled his fist.

"I'll figure it out, Taj." Cassius pushed off the sofa and walked quietly toward the back porch. It was a quiet night in the woods outside Chester. The sky was starless, and the water in the in-ground pool gleamed like black liquid, the only source of light a tiny reflection on the waves from the moon. He sat on the chaise as he reached into his pocket and pulled out a flyer.

It seemed that a funeral service was being held for the first victim, Ross Parish. Ava's...*friend.*

Boyfriend.

He remembered her words as she looked in his eyes, begging him to save not her, but her boyfriend.

It was such a selfless thing—despite the fact she was bleeding out on the concrete floor, it wasn't *her* life she asked to be spared.

It was his.

Taj was wrong. She was special.

The light in her eyes, the fight that would not leave her as she pushed with all her might to move her legs. To get up, in the face of death and prevail.

A part of him wondered if she'd be there, at the service.

Are you stalking me...still?

It wouldn't hurt to pay his respects. He wasn't like Liam or the rest of the Boracelli's. Human life mattered to him. After all, he was human once too.

The shells his kind bled and discarded had names. Lives.

Cassius folded the flyer neatly back up and set it in his pocket once more, before heading out into the darkness of night to live once more.

AVA CROWLEY, VAMPIRE SLAYER

CHAPTER TWENTY-ONE

AVA HIT THE bottom of the boxing ring with a thump. Her blood raced, her long hair she'd pulled into a ponytail whipping around and hitting her in the face as she scrambled to an upright position.

Dallas bounced back and forth, cracking his neck.

Ava felt the adrenaline surging through her, sweat dripping down her temples, her muscles aching. Though she knew if she sat long enough, the exhaustion would truly hit her. She pushed herself up and challenged Dallas once more.

There was something about the rush of it all, that made her feel...alive.

Powerful.

Ava lunged for Dallas once more, and he captured her in his arms. Breaking his hold was easier, this time. She'd started to anticipate his movement, just as he had told her too.

She pushed against him, her fingers sliding along his sweat slicked bicep, her breathing heavy.

"Getting tired yet, kitten?" he purred in her ear.

"Fuck no," she breathed back, a smile coursing over

her face.

Just as she broke free once more, the door opened, and the scent of Chinese food wafted in. Ava turned her head to see Mal carrying a couple brown paper bags, with two men she didn't recognize behind him.

"Thought I'd find you two here," Mal grumbled as he set the bags down a steel table near the door. His gaze flashed to Ava.

Ava wiped the strands of her messy hair from her face and took in the sight of the strangers. She noted they were both tall, but not quite as tall as Dallas. The man beside Mal had a mop of dark, curly black hair, and even at a distance Ava could see his eyes were silvery grey. Against his tanned skin, the contrast was quite noticeable, especially given the fact he was wearing all black. Black tee shirt, black jeans, black boots.

The other man who walked his way across the track to some cabinet over by the wall, was much less...brooding looking. Against Mal, Dallas and the lost member of a goth metal band, he looked more like a student at Chester than he did a hunter, with his bronze skin, tight-fitting black jeans, and tight-fitting flannel that was rolled up to his elbows. His stature was lean, but Ava could see the muscles in his arm as he opened the cabinet. When he turned to her, she noted his eyes were bright blue, his hair dirty blond. He kind of reminded her of Liam.

"Who's your new friend, Jake?" The dark-haired metal enthusiast asked.

Before Dallas could even answer, Mal spoke up as he opened the bags of take out, pulling out boxes and arranging them on the table.

"Vinny, Tito...meet Ava, my sister."

Tito's head whipped around, and as he did so, Ava could see in the cabinet.

It was stocked with knives and...were those *stakes*?

"You're Mal's sister?" Tito raised an eyebrow.

Ava felt a wash of anger, probably due to the adrenaline, and the surprised tone he took.

"Yeah, what of it?" She stood straight, angling her shoulders, her eyes staring down Tito. After going several rounds with Dallas, she was feeling quite a rush, and as if she could take on the world.

Tito grabbed a long knife and passed the boxing ring.

"Just expected you to be a little less..." Tito's voice trailed off, as if he couldn't find the correct words. Perhaps he just didn't want to offend Mal.

Ava jumped down from the ring and walked up to him, her eyes fixated on his knife.

"A little less what?" She cocked her head to the side, and she could hear Dallas snickering behind her.

"Abrasive, for one." Tito raised his eyebrows.

"That's rich coming from someone who looks like he raided Justin Beiber's closet." Ava turned past him, and she could hear more laughter now.

"Hope you still like pork lo mein, Simba." Mal slid a carton of steaming food in her direction.

"Thanks." She took the carton and a package of chopsticks before sitting on the seat in one of the leg lifts.

"Where's Hunter?" Dallas jumped down from the ring as well and wiped at the sweat on his face and chest with his crumpled-up muscle tank. His thick hands running the fabric over his chest was not a bad view.

Ava stared into her lo mein, avoiding looking twice;

even though she wanted to.

"In Ohio. Working a hunt." Tito answered as he rounded the back of the room. Ava watched him pull down a target.

"So, how'd it go?" Mal came over and sat next to her with his container of sweet and sour chicken.

"I whooped his ass." Ava smiled.

Dallas rolled his eyes. "Easy there, kitten. You did good, but your training has only just begun."

Ava watched him as he grabbed a container and found a spot on the barbell bench.

"So, what is this, like...your lair?" Ava said as she fished around for a noodle.

"Well, when you say it like that, it sounds evil." Mal smirked, his brown eyes lighting up with laughter.

"What defines good and evil, Mal?" She nudged him playfully as sarcasm dripped in her tone.

"Is that what they teach you in college? To sound smart, you just have to rephrase everything as a question?" He jabbed her back.

"The answer to that is simple." Ava watched Tito throw his knife at the target.

"Do tell."

"We're the good guys because we *kill* the bad guys. They're the bad guys because they kill innocent people."

Ava watched the knife as it landed in the middle of the target.

The room fell silent.

"Heard there's going to be a memorial service for your friend, and the other victims," Mal said, breaking the silence.

"Yeah, this weekend." Ava tensed.

"You gonna go?" Mal pushed.

"Why do you care?" She bristled.

Dallas's eyes caught hers, and for a moment it looked as if he understood. Which was really weird. Dallas wasn't the sentimental type.

The sight made her wonder...

"You think those guys from Alpha Pi are going to be there? The ones from the pizza shop?" Mal was serious.

"I don't know...maybe?" She shrugged.

"They're vamps, Ava." Mal looked at her, glancing down at her wrist.

"How do you know?" She cocked an eyebrow.

"Because we've been tracking the one for a few states now," Vinny spoke up.

"But..." Ava set her chopsticks down, remembering Liam and his friends coming into the lecture hall, from *outside*. At two o'clock in the afternoon, with the sun out, when Liam passed her in the quad a few weeks ago. "But they walk around during the day. I thought vampires like...incinerated in the sun." She looked down at Mal.

"Some do. Some don't. I'm not really sure *why* that is, but that's myth buster number one. Some vampires can walk in the daylight, making them much more deadly, and less likely to be detected unless you're a trained professional." Mal smiled at her.

"What else should I know? About them?" Ava hedged, her curiosity piqued.

"They're not all that hard to kill, but they are hard to trap. Pretty much anything that could kill a person, could kill a bloodsucker. The only difference is, you have to burn them immediately, or they'll heal their wounds. Fire is their worst enemy."

"So...do I like, get a stake now? Or a knife? Like the movies?"

Dallas chuckled.

"I don't know if that's a wise idea..." Mal's shoulders tensed.

"Why the hell not? At least she can protect herself with one," Dallas said through a mouthful of fried rice.

"I feel like you're going to need a bit more experience before you go throwing knives like Vinny or staking anyone in the chest. You can seriously hurt yourself if you don't know what you're doing. Especially if you're not capable of fending off their thrall." Mal glanced at Dallas. "I assume you told her about their thrall?" He raised an eyebrow.

Dallas who nodded in response. "Lesson number one—Vampire Jedi Mind Tricks. The college course you'll never find in the books." He smirked.

"What's lesson number two?" Vinny said with a chuckle.

"Lesson number two—Mal finished chewing his food. "Is how to fight the bloody Jedi's mind tricks. How to ground yourself." He looked at Ava. "You have to have a strong mind to fight them too, Ava. It isn't just about strength and adrenaline."

For a moment Ava could see the fear and worry cross Mal's face, as his lips frowned. "And you think I don't have a strong mind?" She couldn't help the disdain that laced her voice.

"Quite the opposite, actually. You're one of the most stubborn people I know, and come hell or high water, when you have your heart set on something..." He smiled, but it wasn't genuine.

"We just need to recalibrate all that power of will."

Ava looked down at her brother, and suddenly she felt like she was ten again. Asking him to help her with her homework. Asking him to teach her how to throw a punch because she wanted to deck Maddox Corsol in the face for pushing around her friend. "You'll teach me how though, right?"

Mal pursed his lips, and the expression on his face was worried. But he replaced it quickly with confidence, even if it was false.

"Of course, Simba." Mal reached out and held her wrist softly. "It's my fault you're in this mess in the first place." he whispered, and Ava tightened her grip on his wrist in return.

When he let go of her wrist, they ate the rest of their dinner in silence.

CHAPTER TWENTY-TWO

AVA SAT ON the ground, her eyes closed, legs crossed. The long blades of grass tickled her knees through the frayed holes in her jeans. It was driving her crazy.

"Focus." Mal's voice was calm.

"I can't focus if you keep nagging at me to focus," she grumbled.

"Tune me out then. You should be good at that." She could hear the laughter in his voice.

"Should I say *ommm* or something?" She could feel her lips cracking a smile of her own.

"Fuck you."

She felt Mal shove her. She opened her eyes and couldn't help but laugh. "Obviously your mind isn't as strong as you think it is if you can't *ignore* me." She shoved him back.

"I'm serious, Ava. You need to be able to block out everything. Focus on *one* thing in your mind. Something to ground you." Mal brought his knees up to his chest, wrapping his arms around them. His dark hair hung in his face and she noted how long it was.

It seemed Mal had forgone the cut and clean look in

the past year and embraced the grunge look. It added to his "rockstar cover" she presumed.

He was silent for a moment, as if he was contemplating something.

"Why so serious, Mal?" She tried to joke with him once more, knowing he'd usually bite on a Batman reference.

"I never told you the truth, Ava." His voice was serious, and all joking, casual tones cast aside brought Ava to alertness.

"What do you mean?" she asked as she scooted closer to her brother, backing herself up against the retaining wall in the backyard of the estate. She sat shoulder to shoulder with him, and he turned to her, and she could see the tears starting to form.

"About mom and dad. What really happened that night?"

Oh. Oh no, Mal...

Ava swallowed nervously. It wasn't as if she couldn't talk about it. She *wished* someone could talk about it. Their aunt never mentioned them. Mal hadn't said a word about them since the funeral. It was like they wanted to pretend it didn't happen. That maybe they were on a long vacation somewhere or something.

Ava knew everyone grieved differently, but she wished just for once, *someone* would talk about how awful her mom's chicken tetrazzini was, or how her dad always lost on board game night. She thought that maybe it would help with the nightmares. Bring her some sort of closure.

"Mal—"

"It was vampires, Ava. They were killed by vamps." His voice shook as he said the words. He couldn't look at her.

The words sunk in. *Vampires.*

"In Massachusetts?" Ava said with surprise.

Mal's lips lifted only a fraction.

"Bloodsuckers are everywhere, Ava. They don't just exist here."

Ava nodded. "Oh."

"I found out...what happened. That's when I decided to become a slayer. I wanted to avenge them." Mal's eyes focused on the dandelions blowing in the breeze in the yard.

"You wanted to find the vamp who did it. That's why you were always leaving, wasn't it? You were looking for them." Ava's gaze settled on the setting sun.

"Yeah. I'm still looking." Mal reached his hand down and picked up hers. His fingers brushed her bite mark gently. "You're lucky, Ava. I don't think you know how lucky you are." His voice was soft.

Ava pulled her wrist from his touch, running her own fingers over the shimmering scar. "He saved my life, Mal. I know that. I was attacked, by *other* vamps. I didn't know that's what they were, but it makes sense now. The one, he—" Her voice caught in her throat. "He cut me, with a knife. Was bleeding me out. They left, and I—"

Mal wrapped his arms around her and pulled her close. "You don't have to tell me if you don't want to, Ava." He ran his hands over her knotted windblown hair.

"No. I need you to understand what happened to me." She said the words out loud, but a part of her was certain it wasn't Mal who needed to understand. *She* needed to understand.

"They left, and I don't know how long they were gone. It could have been hours, minutes. Time stood still. I was dying. I know that." She leaned against her brother, his warmth a comfort. "Then the door opened. I heard voices, and I thought… I only had one thought." She could feel tears forming behind her own eyes.

"He emerged from the shadows like some angel. He wasn't alone, though. The guy he was with wanted to leave, and I saw my chance. I didn't want to waste it."

The moment was so vivid to her, as if she were there. Mal's hold on her the only thing grounding her to this world, as she relived the moment that changed her entire life.

"I asked him to save Ross. I tried to move, but my legs were like dead weight. He told me…" She remembered the glowing green eyes, the way his fingers brushed her skin.

The way her stomach flipped when he looked at her. She ran her fingers over her wrist absentmindedly and felt a strange loyalty within her blood as she remembered him. The man…no, *vampire* that saved her life.

Cassius.

He'd asked her permission first, though she hadn't truly understood what he was asking.

The word echoed in her head; *vampire.* Bloodsucking monsters.

Vampires killed her parents. Her boyfriend.

But one of them also…saved her life.

They couldn't all be ruthless killers…could they?

"He marked you. He may have saved your life at the moment, but…"

Ava looked up at Mal in question.

"But what?" She whispered.

"But it's still a death mark, Ava. One day he's going to have to make good on his claim." His eyes settled on hers and she could see the pain there.

Ava closed her eyes, and suddenly she knew exactly what she needed to ground her. "Is it our parents, that you think about? When you fight them?" she whispered.

"Yes." Mal's voice darkened.

"And that helps you defeat them?" She looked up at him once more.

Mal nodded in response.

"My blood belongs to me. I won't let anyone change that," she said with much more confidence than she felt at the moment.

Mal smiled lightly.

"I might be marked, as you say, but I'm not going down without a fight."

"Then you're going to need to master the art of slaying." He smiled, and this time it was genuine.

"Okay, Mister Miyagi. Teach me the ways of the slayer, and one day I'll help you take down the vamps that killed our parents."

"Okay, grasshopper. But first..." He pulled his arm from her shoulder and rose from his spot on the ground as he looked at his watch. "You need to finish your paper, and I need to meet up with Dallas and the boys, for a jam session." Mal stretched as he spoke.

"I thought the amp was just a prop?" She rose from her seat as well.

"Nope. We *do* actually play instruments. Just not as often as we would like."

"Does your little band have a name?" she prodded.

Mal smirked at her. "Well, it's changed a couple times. Now we're Blood Of My Enemy."

Ava rolled her eyes. "Lame. You can do better than that."

Mal chuckled.

"The ladies don't think its lame." They walked in through the sliding glass door.

"Eew. You're disgusting, you know that." She bristled at the idea of Mal and groupies.

"Why, thank you. I'll take that as a compliment," he said as they parted ways for the evening.

CHAPTER TWENTY-THREE

CASSIUS SLID HIS hands in his pockets as he walked through the doors of St. Stephens Church. The service was for Ross Parish, the first victim in what the news was calling, The Chester University Murders, yet there were flowers and paper signs, and mementos left outside of the church, littering its parking lot, for the twin girls who'd been taken as well. Unsurprisingly the press had shown up, newscasters and reporters milling about the place amidst the large crowd of college students, and likely Ross's family.

The church smelled of an array of flora, as the bouquets lined the central stage around a podium, with a large photograph of Ross. Tawny skin, dark brown eyes, perfectly groomed facial hair, and a coif of dark brown hair that reminded Cassius of the hairstyles he'd seen prevalent on humans in the 1950's.

When I lived with Eden.

Why was it after all these years, the memories came back to him?

He hadn't left Italy on the brightest of terms with her. He'd told no one of his plan, not even his mother.

Or Leon.

The memories tried to weasel their way into his psyche. Memories of crowded rooms, fluffed skirts, and dark eyes as the music buzzed. Things were different then.

I was different then.

Cassius took his seat in the back of the room, sliding into a pew as he gazed around the room, hoping to find a familiar face. After all, he could feel her pulse alive and well.

When his eyes found her, he saw that she was not alone.

She was with the man from the pizza shop, and someone else. A tall, dark-haired man, with blue eyes, who looked like he could give Taj a run for his money in the lifting department.

And then he saw *them.*

Liam, Brody, and Logan, and what he gathered were the other members of the fraternity. They all had that same look that the fraternities often bore. They wore dress khakis, and each one of them boasted green and white shirts, covered with blazers and gold pins that bore the crest of their fraternity.

They've got a lot of nerve, showing up here.

Cassius watched as they all took their seats, and the echoes in the church started to die down.

He focused ahead as the priest started to mill about his podium, waiting for everyone to quiet, and he could feel her gaze from across the room. A part of him did not want to look at her; after all, he could feign that he did not know she'd be there, or quite possibly that he hadn't seen her if she approached him.

Surely, he'd mastered better control than this; after all, he'd stayed off fresh blood likely longer than this woman had been alive. He'd prided himself on his ability to reign in his monstrous instincts. It was safer. But yet despite knowing these things, despite knowing he should refrain from doing so, Cassius met her gaze.

She didn't look as pissed as he thought she would, and that made him feel a sense of relief. She just...stared at him. Amber eyes of fire, deep and inviting. Long, dark hair falling over her shoulder, down her back. Her eyes fixed him to his spot, for a moment longer, before turning back to her companions.

CHAPTER TWENTY-FOUR

AVA SAT THROUGH the service with her brother, and that was enough. It wasn't that she was particularly uncomfortable, after all, she'd only been dating Ross for a month. It wasn't like she was in love with him or anything. But it was the first funeral service she'd attended since her parents.

The memories pushed forth, of the night she'd found them, and she breathed deeply.

The sight of the blood on the carpet.

Her father's eyes—dead, and glassy.

Her mother's lifeless body.

Ava sucked in a breath, as the vivid memory pushed forth.

Mal's eyes were not quite fixed on the podium, with the speeches from all the students, and friends of Ross's. No. Mal scanned the crowd for vampiric threats. Dallas quietly took her hand, not saying a word. The small gesture, kind as it was, was not one she'd expect from him. She let it rest on top of hers, his warmth enveloping her, though her wrist already burned with heat where fangs had marked her. It seemed that her body knew Cassius was near before she could even consider the idea.

The notion both angered her and brought her a strange peace. She'd have to ask Mal if that was normal, for marked individuals who had bites like hers. Ones that didn't turn or kill.

Would her wrist flare with heat like this every time he was near?

You act as if you'll see him again.

She shifted against Dallas in the pew, her long, bare legs bristling against his slacks.

When the service ended, she had every intention of finding Cassius. Giving him a piece of her mind. After all she had told him to...

To what exactly?

Leave me alone?

Take his hot, crazy delusional ass elsewhere?

Ava hated to admit, that while she was certain she couldn't trust the man...*vampire*...there was something about him that intrigued her, and she knew that was a dangerous road to travel.

Flashes of the night of the party filtered in her brain.

Ava was well aware she was being moved. She felt strong arms around her, dark whispers above her.

"You're fucking insane. Just...leave her here. They'll take care of her." The voice was faded, garbled by her own distortion.

"I'm not leaving her." The voice that spoke was close, and she could feel its warmth.

"If you're not going to help me, then you can leave." The voice was steady.

"She's lost a ton of blood."

"My venom will seal the cuts. It'll just take some time."

ARIEL DAWN

The feeling of abrasive fabric on her sensitive skin hurt like a bitch. The darkness pulled her under once more.

"You okay, kitten?" Dallas's voice broke through her thoughts.

"Huh?" She blinked, filtering in the world around her once more.

"You looked a little...spaced out there for a minute." Dallas leaned against the wall, his large stature set against the vases of flowers lining the hallway making him look even bigger than he actually was.

"Yeah, I'm fine." She forced a smile.

"It's okay if you're not, you know. You can tell me. I won't tell anyone." His lips turned up in a slight smile.

"We...weren't that serious or anything." She fell against the wall next to him as they waited for Mal to come back from scouting the area.

"Maybe not, but you were there when it happened, right?" He looked over at her, and she could see his eyes bore a look of sympathy.

A strange realization overcame her.

Who did you lose, Dallas?

Ava watched the crowd disperse, students mingling about. She whispered softly, "Yes."

"You did the right thing, keeping the details to yourself," he whispered back.

"Did I, though?" She looked up at him.

"It's one of the hardest things about this life. It's not something you can just...be upfront about. Most people don't know monsters exist, and it's better that way. Think about it. As far as Ross's parents know, their son died. They might not know the details, but would you want them to? You were there. You know them." Dallas's voice was solid as he spoke.

"No. Not really." Ava frowned, remembering the scream of pain that came after the moan of ecstasy.

"They have their closure. Enough to be able to try and move through the loss. Live life normally again someday."

Ava ran her fingers over her wrist, noting that her skin felt normal. No tingling sensation of ice or heat. Just...*normal.*

Which meant *he* was gone.

"But I know. The truth," she whispered.

"You plan on doing something about it?" Dallas raised an eyebrow at her.

"What can I do, Dallas?" She shrugged, her gaze fixated on his deep blue pools of startling sympathy.

"You can get justice, Ava." His voice was solid and unwavering, and carried a hint of darkness that spoke to Ava's very soul.

"How?" she asked seriously.

"You can take out the vamp that murdered your boyfriend."

He's serious.

"I barely know what I'm doing. Okay, yeah, I was able to knock you around *a little*, maybe I'll figure out this grounding thing too, but—"

"Mal's your brother. It's his natural instinct to protect you. He'll teach you defense, sure. But you need more than defense." Dallas slid his hands into his pockets nonchalantly.

"And let me guess, you're just to person to teach me, aren't you, Dallas?" She licked her lips and a smile started to form.

"I am quite a formidable opponent, kitten. No one slays quite like I do." His eyes twinkled.

"Really laying it on thick there aren't you?" She let

out a chuckle.

"Is it working?" His eyes lit up only a little.

Ava rolled her eyes. "As long as I get a stake, or a knife. I'm in."

"Kitten, by the time I'm done with you, you'll be able to kill a vamp with your bare hands."

"Is there a crash course option? I'd like to be able to kill this bloodsucker before he strikes again." She leaned closer to Dallas, their hushed voices emitting heat in the closed space.

"I'll pick you up tonight, say...nine?"

"You're not going to be with Mal?" Ava's eyes settled on his lips, and her heart started to race.

"I'm a big boy, Ava. I don't need Mal to chaperone me everywhere I go." The sparkle in his eye was mischievous but also alluring.

"It's a date." She smiled sweetly,

"They're gone." Mal's voice broke the silence and Ava moved away from Dallas once more and settled her gaze on her brother.

"Damn assholes are harder to trap than I thought they would be." Mal ran a hand through his hair, his frustration evident.

"Mal! You're in a church!" Ava poked him.

"Seriously, Ava?" Mal regarded her with an annoyed glare.

"Have some respect, Mal." Dallas smirked as he ribbed him.

"Fuck the both of you," Mal grumbled as he sauntered off toward the exit, leaving Ava and Dallas laughing in his dust.

CHAPTER TWENTY-FIVE

"YOUR IDEA OF a training session is Russo's Sports Bar?" Ava raised an eye at Dallas as she dismounted from the back of his bike.

Dallas ran his hand through his short brown hair, after setting his helmet on the handlebar, and kicking down the kickstand on the glistening curb on Chester's main street.

"Well, for starters, I need to gauge your aim, and Russo's has what we need. Darts, axe throwing—"

"You could have just taken me to your top-secret Bat Cave." Ava shrugged as she sauntered toward the door.

Dallas was at her side rather quickly and opened the door for her. "Yes, I could have, but I thought just maybe you'd want some better food than take out Chinese." He smirked at her.

Ava rolled her eyes. "If I didn't know any better, I'd think you were trying to hit on me, Dallas," she joked with him as they walked into the restaurant.

"Kitten, if I wanted to hit on you, trust me, you'd know. There'd be no question." He smiled mischievously as he brushed past her to a high top table.

Ava shook her head and followed.

Russo's wasn't the only sports bar in Chester, but it was the only sports bar that boasted billiards, a dart wall, axe throwing, and an extensive beer menu.

Ave leaned languidly against the high top as she picked up the menu.

The waitress came over rather quickly. "What can I get you...two?" she asked sweetly.

Ava didn't miss the look of judgement on her face.

"I'll take whatever beer you have on special." Dallas smiled, showcasing his perfect teeth, and his eyes lit up brightly.

The waitress seemed to ease up a bit. "That all, darlin'?" she drawled.

Ava rolled her eyes.

"A bucket of buffalo wings, with a side of ranch?" He raised an eyebrow at Ava, who shrugged.

"And what will you have to drink, sweetie?" The waitress did her best to sound nice, but Ava could tell she was judging her.

"I'll have a water, thanks," Ava grumbled. When the waitress finally left, she slammed down her menu. "Can I ask you an honest question, Dallas?" Ava spoke up.

"Kitten, you can ask me anything, you know that." Dallas pulled out a few darts from the abandoned dartboards. The place wouldn't even start coming alive until ten.

"How long have you been...you know. Doing the vamp thing?" She leaned against the tabletop, watching Dallas collect the darts. She didn't miss the opportunity to let her gaze drift upon his ass. In his dark wash jeans, she couldn't help but appreciate it.

It's not like he could see her looking, anyway.

"Since I was about your age." He walked over to her with a handful of yellow and red darts.

"You ever train anyone?" She shifted her weight as he organized the darts by color.

"Yellow or Red?" He glanced up at her.

The waitress dropped off their drinks hurriedly.

"Red." Ava took a sip of her water.

"I *trained* Vinny." He shrugged.

"Vinny's the one who looks like a lost member of The Cure, right?" Ava smirked.

Dallas let out a chuckle as he picked up a dart, and took his stance, his vision fixating on the dartboard.

"I'm surprised you even know who The Cure are." He threw his dart, and it landed with a bulls eye.

"I know a lot of things, *Dallas.*" Her voice dripped with sarcasm.

"Right. Of course, you do, you're a *college girl.*" He said the words with the utmost humor, but there was also an edge to his voice that was most...flirtatious?

"Fuck you." She twisted her lips into an amused grin.

"Quite stalling. It's your turn."

Ava picked up a dart, feeling the weight of it in her hands. She turned it around, inspecting it, before settling it in her fingers properly. She focused on the dartboard, and her wrist flared with heat. The feeling was startling, and whereas it should have been distracting to her, it only fueled her focus more.

She fixated her gaze on the dartboard as her blood boiled beneath the surface. Memories pushed forth of tongues on flesh, of blood rushing to the surface. Of razor-sharp fangs piercing her skin, and they meshed with the sight of her father's lifeless eyes, of Ross's lifeless, blood drained body that seemed to have disappeared into the ether.

She didn't think twice about throwing her dart. She didn't even realize it had left her hand, until she heard Dallas whistle.

"Not a bad shot. I can definitely work with that." He chuckled.

Ava looked to where her dart had landed. It wasn't a bulls eye like Dallas had thrown, but it was much closer than she thought she'd land.

The waitress dropped off the bucket of wings, and sides of ranch as Dallas took a swig of his beer before picking up another dart.

"Do you like it? College, I mean," he said as he threw the dart, before diving into a wing.

"I guess, it's okay. It's an experience, you know." She shrugged as she picked up a dart.

"What's your major?" Dallas popped another wing into his mouth.

"Major in Business Administration, Minor in History." She threw her dart.

"You don't really strike me as the office type."

"Well, you don't really strike me as the musician type," she cracked.

"Your words wound me, Ava. Truly." He chuckled as he took another drink, threw another dart. "I was offered scholarships you know. For Chester, Youngstown."

Ava grabbed a wing herself and had to admit the taste was rather divine. Spicy, tangy, with just the right amount of kick, and accented by the cool taste of ranch. "Why didn't you take it? The scholarship?" She licked her fingers clean before wiping them on a napkin and grabbing another dart, but Dallas's words stopped her from throwing it.

"Because I learned the truth, the hard way. Like you." His voice had lost its air of humor and teasing.

"I'm sorry..." Ava spoke softly.

"Sometimes the world has a crazy way of showing you who you really are." Dallas picked up his glass and took a long pull of his beer.

Ava threw her dart, but this time it didn't land as well as the others.

"Don't be sorry. I know this life isn't ideal, for anyone. But it's who I am. It's what I was meant to do. The rest of it..." Dallas threw his last dart, and it landed smack in the center, a bulls eye once more. His words hung in the air, as his gaze settled on the dartboard, his eyelashes standing out against the lights that illuminated him.

Ava sipped her water as she took in the sight of Dallas. Amidst the red and orange neon lights, she could almost see it.

A young, vibrant Dallas who had the world at his feet.

An attractive, charismatic boy next door who could have anything he wanted with that smile.

A life he never got to live, because somehow, he'd learned monsters were real. He'd left a safe and happy life, normalcy and traded it in for flannel shirts, a microphone, and a stake.

Or maybe he's more of a knife guy like Vinny.

"Your turn, kitten." His bright blue eyes flashed at her.

Ava stilled her breath as she focused on the dartboard. She thought of the ways her life had changed, since that night at the party. Since Ross had been killed. Since Cassius had saved her life. In a way she'd been given a second chance too, much like Dallas. A chance to see into the darkness that most people didn't get to see.

She knew without a doubt, that like Dallas she'd never be able to look away.

The world around her, around *them,* even now left her with the question of who among them was a monster? Her wrist still flared with heat, her skin prickled like goosebumps; but there was no sign of Cassius, or Liam.

She knew within her heart, she'd never be able to look at the world, at people, the same now that she knew what kind of evil lurked in the shadows. In the daylight, even.

Ava focused on her breath, on the heated blood in her veins.

On the feeling of fangs against her soft skin.

On the memories that swam in her head of bloodied bodies, and the feeling of helplessness.

She closed her eyes, and she threw the dart.

When she opened her eyes, she was surprised, and by the tone in Dallas's voice he was surprised too, but there was also another emotion in his voice. *Pride.*

Ava's dart sat snug in the center, knocking Dallas's out of its coveted bulls eye spot.

CHAPTER TWENTY-SIX

CASSIUS RAN HIS hand through his golden hair as he paced back and forth on the patio. He'd heard Liam and his cohorts, even though he hadn't been intent on listening. A part of him was surprised to see them attend the funeral of the man they killed. Although, it was a very Boracelli thing to do, if he had to be honest.

It seemed no matter if one was a born Boracelli or not, the disturbing trait of reveling in your kill seemed to be quite prevalent among the high covens.

That is what happens when you've truly lost your sense of humanity, I suppose.

With Halloween only two weeks away, and a crackdown at the University on Greek events, the rogue Liam and his friends were forced to draw their prey outside of their normal hunting grounds.

The fact that there had been no recent death reports was startling to Cassius. He knew better than anyone how maddening it was to starve yourself for weeks.

In the beginning, in his early days as a vampire, he'd done everything he could to resist the need to feed on human blood.

It wasn't a pleasant experience, and most certainly always ended up putting him in the guiltiest predicament.

As if his body remembered just as much as his mind, his stomach flipped with nausea.

"It's the perfect location, far enough away from the University that no one will think twice about connecting the dots but close enough for all interested parties to get to," Liam had said.

"There's a sense of drama to it, too," Logan said.

"A Halloween Party in an abandoned church on the outskirts of town? Sounds positively perfect to me." Liam smiled.

"And no one will notice a little blood, either. The girls will practically be begging for it. All keyed up on that vampire romance shit," Brody chimed in.

They'd disappeared after that.

Cassius sat in the chaise, his head in his hands. In his heart he knew he should do *something*.

At the very least, I should tell Ava. Make certain she stays clear of that party, he thought as he watched the ripple of the water in the pool.

Taj opened the sliding glass door.

"Where's Jasmine?" Cassius perked his head up.

"Some concert or something over in Willowcrest." Taj took a seat on the rubber chaise, the one that always squeaked from years worth of rust buildup.

"Surprised you didn't go with her, given your protective streak." Cassius twisted his lips.

"I'm trying not to be a dick. Cut me some slack here, Cas." Taj kicked his legs up as he leaned back on the lounge chair. "I'm sorry I went off on you the other day." Taj's voice was low, but genuine. The man was never very good at admitting his faults.

He was a damn loyal, good friend, though. Even if he didn't have a filter.

"Apology accepted." Cas smirked.

"It's just—"

Cassius's smile faltered.

"We've been friends, what thirty some years? I know you better than I knew my own brothers and sisters. I know you have this hero fixation and all, but damn it, Cassius, you can't save them all. Some things are just beyond your control." Taj breathed deeply.

"I know that, Taj. But I can't just sit here in isolation either. I must live my life too. I can't stay scared for the rest of eternity that Eden will find me." His voice hung on her name.

Cassius wished life had been different. He wished so many times that Eden would see the light, but she never did. But he knew the darkness had poisoned her heart long ago.

When she'd lost the only man she ever truly loved, along with a life she never knew she wanted.

Marcellus Medici.

They'd grieved their losses together, gotten close even. Close enough that he'd let her in. That he'd shelved his fear of his Aurelian curse and made love to her anyway.

And then I'd found out the truth.

Cassius ran his hand through his hair. The memory of their last moments, the moment he knew she'd never truly love him, but she wouldn't let anyone else have him either, forced its way through his brain.

"I am not some pawn in your games of dominance, Eden. I am more than some fucking stud for you to parade and commandeer." He turned toward the door, giving his back to her.

"So help the gods, Cassius Aurelia, if you walk out that door..." Her voice was cold, devoid of any emotion she'd once held for him. She no longer cared for anyone, really. She'd lost too much, suffered too much, and the pain, the bloodlust had driven her insane. "I will not give you the choice next time. You will obey me." She growled at him.

He turned to her, taking in the sight of her violet-rimmed eyes that glowed against her pale skin. She stood there in the tower, amidst the stone and tapestries, dressed in the most exquisite plum silk dress, her long, thin legs milky white against the darkness and shadows. With her dark raven hair running over her shoulders like a waterfall, Cassius had to admit that her beauty was only surface value.

Nothing beautiful was left inside of Eden Boracelli's heart.

He'd deluded himself into thinking there was for too long.

She didn't value life anymore. Not his, or anyone else's but her own. She only valued what she could control. Her desire to be Queen was nothing more than a desire to control everything, and everyone around her. Including him.

He'd almost given her an heir, on more than one occasion.

But she did not love *him. There was nothing anymore that she could give him, that he wanted, and even if there was...*

She had blood on her hands.

His father's blood, to be exact.

It would have been so easy to hurt her, so very easy to bring her castle crumbling to the ground. But that was a choice he had made. If he had given in to the need to hurt, the need to make her understand the depth of his disdain for her...he would be no better than her.

"There is always a choice. The fact you fail to understand that is why I will never be yours. You cannot control me, Eden."

"You've got to let it go, Cas. You can't fix everything. You're only one person. Marking Ava..." Taj took a deep breath. "You made yourself *and her* a ticking timebomb. The Boracelli's will certainly be waiting for you to make your move. You *should* just...enjoy her. Savor the blood, and anything else you might want from her." Taj let out a dark laugh, and Cassius's back straightened.

"I don't want any such things from her, I assure you." His voice was short.

"Right. And I'm the queen of fucking England." Taj let out a laugh.

Cassius sighed.

"It's okay you know. You're allowed to *want* her blood. I mean, you did put a claim on it. You're allowed to *want* to fuck her too. It's *normal* to feel and want those things. It's what we're made for. It doesn't make you the bad guy." The way Taj said the words were solid, and Cassius knew they were true.

It was normal. Sex and blood were two sides of the same coin for monsters like himself. He could feel her in his blood, in his veins. A steady pulse of life.

That was all he wanted for her.

For himself, even.

To live.

Liam and his cohorts were planning a Halloween smorgasbord of blood, sex, and death, and in that moment, Cassius knew there was only one thing he truly wanted.

AVA CROWLEY, VAMPIRE SLAYER

He'd tell Ava about the party.
He'd try to save as many as he could.
Even if it meant going against his own kind.

CHAPTER TWENTY-SEVEN

THE MAN IN the shadows stared at her. His eyes followed her no matter where she moved.

"You let me die," the shadow spoke.

"I was dying too!" she yelled at the darkness.

The shadows moved, forming into a shape, and then a body.

Ross.

"You look pretty alive to me." His voice was thick with anger.

"I'm sorry..." Her legs felt like dead weight. She couldn't move them.

Ross stalked closer to her, his blue and white checkered shirt stained with blood.

Why did the shirt look so familiar?

She remembered exactly what he wore. A red shirt and khakis.

"You didn't even try..." He stood above her, and his eyes flickered from brown to green, then brown again.

"I did try!" she hollered back.

"Lies!" His eyes glowed green, and sharp, white fangs glistened as he opened his mouth.

"You knew what happened to me, and you did nothing..."

"There was nothing I could do!" Ava could feel the tears forming in her eyes.

"He's still out there..." Ross looked in the distance, and Ava could see the shining beacon of light coming from the top of the stairs.

"Who?" Her voice cracked.

"The monster who killed me," he answered.

He turned back to her, but this time he had shifted into someone else.

Something else.

Cassius stood before her, his green eyes soft and bright even in the darkness.

Ross's words echoed in the air. The monster who killed me.

Her wrist burned with heat, and her breathing hitched.

Serenity befell her, and all she wanted was to submit to it. Feel its peace.

But the cries of death rang in the air. Ross's broken voice.

There would be no peace.

Not tonight.

Ava awoke in her bed and felt the coldness of the air kiss her skin. She looked at her alarm clock, and could see the red digital letters read three am. She let out a breath as she stared at the ceiling. It had been quite a while since she'd had a nightmare such as this. She took a breath once more.

One. Two. Three...

The images still swirled around in her head. Of an angry, bloodied Ross. Of the beautiful monster who'd saved her life.

Dallas was right. She'd never be able to look at things the way they'd been before Ross was killed.

Before she'd learned the truth that monsters were real.

Perhaps it was guilt, or...perhaps it was just that she was drawn to the shadows, and what lay beyond them. She was a Crowley, after all. Darkness, and the affinity for supernatural things was in her blood.

Whatever it was, Ava knew for certain she wouldn't be able to rest until justice had been served. There would be no peace for Ross's soul, or hers, until she knew his killer had been served. And so, Ava closed her eyes, and focused on the sound of her breath, on the steady beat of her heart, until she found sleep once more.

***

The aroma of coffee in the air was divine to Ava's senses and was almost enough to make her forget her terrible nightmare.

"I don't know how you can drink that sludge," Mal grumbled as he threw his flannel shirt on over top of a plain black shirt.

Ava sipped her coffee slowly as she noticed the stubble making a comeback on his face. Despite his recent shower, he still looked scruffy and unkempt. "I don't know how anyone functions without it," she chided as she followed him out the door, travel mug in hand.

"It's called stamina, Ava." Mal opened the driver side door of his car and wasted no time.

Ava fell into the passenger seat with a scowl. "You are the last person who should be giving a lecture on stamina, Mal. You can barely hang around here for longer than—"

"Dallas tells me you have good aim," he said as he started the car, and pulled out quickly.

"Did he now?" Ava pursed her lips. It shouldn't have bothered her, that Dallas told Mal about their little date.

It wasn't a date.

It absolutely wasn't a date because that would make me the worst person in the world. Going out on a date right after your dead boyfriend's service with another man who's over a decade older than you.

No, it certainly wasn't a date. It was just a meeting of the minds to discuss her inevitable training. Dallas had mentioned he'd trained Vinny to hunt the evil bloodsuckers, and Ava knew without a doubt the chord had been struck within her as well.

"He did. Suggested we test out your ability with actual weapons, see what sticks." Mal stared through the windshield, and Ava got the feeling he was hiding something.

Mal fiddled with the knobs on his radio, and Ava decided not to press him. Not yet anyway. If he was truly hiding something, she'd get to the bottom of it.

When Mal pulled up to the Bat Cave, Ava noticed three motorcycles parked out front.

"I was under the impression it was just going to be a brother sister bonding day." She sighed.

"What's the matter, Ava? Scared you won't be able to hang with the big boys?" Mal shut the door, and a light chuckle escaped his throat.

"Oh, I can hang, Mal. I'm just worried your friends will laugh at you when I beat your ass." She smiled as she made a beeline for the door.

"Keep that enthusiasm. You're going to need it when

you come face to face with those bloodsucking leeches." Mal's tone took on a darker tone as he opened the door for her.

"After you," he said as he motioned for her to enter.

As Ava entered the gym, she could see the ring was occupied with two shirtless, sweaty men who happened to be rolling around legs locked onto one another.

"Go ahead, fucking tap..." the one on top growled, blonde hair falling in his face.

Tito, Ava reminded herself of his name. The one who was throwing knives before.

"Never!" the man underneath roared back as he threw Tito back with force, knocking him to the ground. Vinny stood up, cracking his neck, his steely grey eyes glancing at her as he smiled. Tito took advantage of the distraction and kicked his leg out from under him.

Ava couldn't help but let out a laugh.

Mal opened a cabinet in the corner, and Ava could see quite the collection of blades, stakes and weapons that looked primarily medieval.

The sight alone excited her, but she was soon pulled from her anticipation as a sweat soaked, shirtless Dallas came traipsing around the corner.

Ava couldn't help as her eyes roved over his defined chest, noting the twin star tattoos on each side above his pecs; his hips cutting the most delicious angle, that perfect v shape that was usually only afforded to male models and athletes. Ava felt her mouth run dry at the sight, and so she forced herself to look away.

Hell Ava, get a hold of yourself.

She grabbed the knife out of Mal's hand.

"Hey—"

"Enough deliberating, Mal. Let's do this," she said as

she took a stance she hoped was formidable enough.

CHAPTER TWENTY-EIGHT

AVA PATTED HER hair dry with the towel, her bare feet padding along the cool hardwood floor in the hallway, when the sound of a doorbell alerted her.

It seemed Becky had vacated the premises for the evening, in favor of a wine night with her friends—a weekly event in which they gossiped about their children's love lives.

Though Becky didn't have any children, that didn't deter her from incessantly trying to match Ava with any of her friends' sons, or their friends' sons, and so forth.

You just need to meet a nice boy, and settle down, she had said on numerous occasions. Connie was just as bad.

It was one of the reasons Ava was glad to leave—and why she was so nervous about the idea of bringing Ross home for the holidays if everything went as planned.

But things didn't go as planned, and that was her cross to bear.

She threw the towel in the hamper in the hallway before quickening her pace to the door.

When she opened it, her eyes widened in surprise.

"What the fuck are *you* doing here? I thought I told you—"

"May I come in?" Cassius's lips turned up in a slight smile.

Ava twisted her lips and raised an eyebrow at him.

"If I said no, would that prevent you from coming inside?" She crossed her arms.

Cassius's green eyes sparkled.

"Of course not, but it would be rather rude if I just *walked* in without being invited, now, wouldn't it?"

Ava considered his words and decided instead to meet him on the porch.

She ran a hand through her wet hair, pushing it behind her.

Cassius's eyes dilated only a fraction before returning to normal.

Well, that's kind of strange.

"What are you doing on my front porch?" She didn't mince her words.

"I needed to see you." He cleared his throat.

Ava gazed at him skeptically.

"Does that work on all your victims?" she bit.

Cassius looked offended.

"I can assure you, Ava, I do not go around stalking young women as you may think." He crossed his arms, and the motion brought her attention to his long, slender arms, the slight curve of his bicep. Her wrist flared with heat, her skin with goosebumps, and her heart beat faster.

Fight it, Ava.

She blinked furiously, before meeting his gaze, and remembered the sound of Ross's pained scream.

"Could have fooled me," she drawled.

"The vampires that…harmed you…"

Ava's attention was on high alert at his words.

"You know who they are?" She stood a little straighter, and noticed she came up to Cassius's chest.

Somehow, she'd made it closer to him, and the realization made her take a step back. She fought to look away, but she did not win the fight.

Glowing green eyes gazed upon her, and she could not deny the sight, the way he looked at her—caused her stomach to tie in knots, and her legs to tighten.

It's just his natural defense.

But isn't thrall supposed to make my brain…foggy?

She didn't feel particularly confused.

But she did feel *something.*

A racing heart, an increased pulse.

Wetness blossomed between her legs.

Fucking hell, I need to be stronger than this.

"I do. And I know that they are planning to strike again." Cassius licked his lips, and the sight was like a shockwave directly to her groin.

Ava shifted her weight. "Why should I believe anything you say?" Her eyes flickered to his lips, remembering their soft feel on her skin, his fangs puncturing her wrist.

The memory of it was not…*unpleasant.*

"Because I—"

Cassius could not finish his sentence, for he was punched square in the jaw by a rather pissed off Mal.

CHAPTER TWENTY-NINE

IT HAD BEEN quite a long time since anyone *punched* Cassius in the face. He'd been in his fair share of brawls, what with his frequent stints in and out of bars, taverns, and even hotels throughout his life, but it was usually because he was *breaking up* a fight, not instigating one.

He rubbed his jaw, and the dark-haired man drew his blade.

The very blade he'd seen in the back of the red Chevelle outside the pizza place on campus.

"Mal don't!" Ava put her hands up, and the man looked at her with question.

"Ava he's—"

"I know, Mal. He's...the one. The one who—"

"Bit you?" Mal growled and rushed toward Cassius once more.

"*Saved* me." Ava stood between Cassius and the man she called Mal.

Cassius couldn't help but notice the expanse of her figure, how her curves cut a most luscious silhouette against the fading sun. How his body responded to the sight, how he could feel her pulse quickening within him. His cock twitched, and he swallowed harshly, his mouth suddenly dry with thirst.

No, you can't. You have to fight the thoughts.

Mal's eyes widened, and he pursed his lips, looking from Ava to Cassius.

"Put the blade away," Ava spoke slowly.

Mal gazed at him with anger, fury.

"If you even so much as *try* to touch her—"

Ava scowled at Mal.

"Fuck off, Mal. I don't need you to protect me," she snapped.

I will protect you, my sweet Avarice.

"As I was saying," Cassius spoke up, drawing both of their attention.

"The vampires who hurt you—" Cassius's gaze fell over Ava for a moment, before glancing back at Mal. "—they plan to strike again. At a party off campus. In an abandoned church off route sixty." He stood straight, his voice conveying no anger or offense, despite the fact he'd just been assaulted by a pissed off human.

He has every right to be pissed, you bit someone he cares about.

It was then that the puzzle pieces came together for Cassius. Mal *knew* what he was.

The blade from the Chevelle's backseat.

A hunter's blade.

The similarities in Mal and Ava's features.

Mal was a hunter...and Ava's sibling.

Cassius let out a small breath.

Of course, this would be just my luck. Danger should have been my middle name.

"That's by the—"

"Bat Cave," Ava whispered.

"Bat Cave?" Cassius cocked his head to the side.

"When?" Mal ignored his question.

"Hallows' Eve," Cassius answered to Mal, never taking his eyes off Ava.

"I'll be there," Ava said, breaking his gaze.

This is not how I imagined this going...

"That is a terrible idea." Cassius felt his own blood starting to heat, a feeling he hadn't felt in quite some time.

Since Eden...

"Well, I wasn't really asking your opinion, Cas." Ava shot him a glare which should have been angry, or pissy, but it wasn't either of those things.

In fact, Cassius thought it was rather...alluring.

It's just the mark talking, nothing more, he tried to convince himself.

"You're not ready yet," Mal shot her a worried glance.

"I don't need your permission, either, Mal. I'm an adult."

"You're fucking eighteen, Ava. You're a child!" Mal grumbled.

Cassius felt a shock in his blood.

Eighteen?

The realization made him flush, but due to the lack of human blood in his veins, he was certain no one could distinguish any color to his cheeks.

Corpse blood didn't light up his blush quite the same way human blood did.

"I'm going to that party, and I'm going to put a fucking stake through the vamp that killed my boyfriend, and then I'm going to—" Ava stopped abruptly.

"You're going to what?" Mal's shoulders tensed and

he scowled.

"I don't have to tell you shit." She turned around and faced Cassius.

"This makes us even." She gazed up at him and in her amber eyes, he could see the flecks of gold. In the dying sunlight, with heat in her eyes, Cassius's entire being felt...*alive.*

She was so close. Close enough he could reach out, touch her. Run his hands through her wet, dark hair. Trace his fingertips down her soft skin, feeling her warmth.

Close enough to kiss.

To bite.

He forced himself to look away at the thought.

"I do not think it is a wise idea for you to put yourself in danger," he whispered to her.

"Maybe I like a little danger," she whispered back.

CHAPTER THIRTY

EVERY TIME SHE closed her eyes, she saw bright, glowing green emeralds in her vision. His wet, pink tongue sliding over his perfect pout, and the memory of how it felt against the skin of her wrist pushed forth.

Ava tossed in her bed, trying to think of anything else.

When images of a sweat slicked chest, equipped with dual star tattoos washed away the memory of fangs and bliss, Ava groaned in frustration.

She looked at the alarm clock, which read three am. The witching hour.

This is fucking ridiculous. She stared at the ceiling in the darkness of her room.

Her wrist did not flare with heat, nor did her skin prickle with goosebumps.

Yet her skin was flushed and warm beneath the covers, and the thoughts of Cassius's fangs sinking into her skin, of his tongue on her flesh, made her blood *boil.*

She was safe in her bedroom, beneath her burgundy sheets. Safe, and alone. There was nothing and no one to fight here; except her own thoughts.

The desires that kept her awake.

It was too much to bear, and Ava knew without a doubt she needed release.

To work out the frustrations of the evening, her anger.

To sate the spark of desire that had been ignited within her.

But she knew better. Vampires *killed* people.

They could not be trusted. They were the bad guys.

But yet somehow, in a way Ava could not explain, she knew Cassius was different. She couldn't stop thinking about him. She screamed a muffled sound into her pillow.

He had come to warn her. If he wanted her dead, he would not go to all the trouble of telling her such things. But what reason did he have then, to tell her not to go to the party.

Probably so he can save you for another night, when he decides he's ready to make good on his mark.

Ava had no reason to trust Cassius. But if there was even the sliver of a chance that he was telling the truth, that the vampires who hurt her, who killed Ross—if they were going to strike again, she couldn't waste the chance.

The thought of driving a stake through their chest made her heart skip a beat.

Hallows' Eve was only a week away. She knew she needed to up her training regimen, and as the thought broke through her psyche, her phone lit up with a text.

Who's texting me at three in the morning?

Your brother tells me there's going to be a vamp attack on Hallows' Eve at the church by the gym.

Ava stared at Dallas's text and wondered if she

should respond. Nothing good ever came from texts sent at three in the morning. She could feel her cheeks redden slightly, as the thought of him in the gym earlier resurfaced.

Sweat dripping down his hard abs, down the angled muscles of his hips, which cut into his shorts.

Her insides tightened.

I swear the two of you are worse than a bunch of schoolgirls.

You'd know, wouldn't you ;-)

Ava smirked, the light of her phone a beacon in the dark room.

I may have been a cheerleader, but I'm not a gossiping whore.

Dallas's text bubble faded in and out, as if he was contemplating a response.

With that mouth of yours, I'm not quite sure I believe you.

Believe what you want. I don't kiss and tell ;-) Ava smiled.

You're going to need back up at the party.

You're not going to give me a lecture about not going?

That depends. Do you want me to lecture you?

Fuck no.

What do you want, Ava?

The question caught her off guard, and she was surprised that the answer was not a simple one.

She wanted justice—for Ross, for the other victims who had met their bitter end at the hands of monsters. She wanted to make her almost death, their deaths, count for something.

But she also could not deny she wanted to feel the blissful peace she felt with Cassius's fangs in her skin, to feel the surge of power she felt in the ring, sparring with Dallas.

But she couldn't tell him any of that.

Such deep questions you have at three in the morning. Ava hoped he would not press her.

What time do you get out of class tomorrow?

Two.

I'll pick you up. If you're going to slay your first vamp in a week, we need to make sure there's no room for error.

Oh, so another chance to beat your ass into the ring, then? Can't wait. Her lips turned up into a delicious smile.

Bring me your best, kitten. ;-)

***

Ava swung her arm out, and Dallas dodged her once again. After a solid three days of this, she had to admit her entire body was feeling the strain. Mal, Tito, and Vinny had gone out to assist Hunter, according to Dallas. It was just the two of them again.

Her tank top clung to her body like a second skin, and she could feel the strain in her muscles, in her legs, and all she wanted to do was collapse into a pile in the corner. But there would be no rest. There couldn't be.

"Come on, Ava..." Dallas taunted her as he lunged for her. She angled herself out of his way, and her long ponytail, wet from sweat, whipped around and lashed him in the face.

His hands twisted in the bottom, and he yanked her back by her hair. She fell into his embrace, the heat from his body engulfing her as he locked his arm around her, his free hand sliding over her wrist, brushing Cassius's bite mark with a familiar sting. His lips were at her ear, and she could feel the heat of his breath on her neck. She closed her eyes for only a moment, feeling the ache of her muscles as he tightened his grip, trying to focus.

"I know you're better than this," he whispered.

Ava breathed heavily, her chest rising and falling with rapid rhythm.

"Dallas..." Her voice came out much darker than she anticipated.

"You can't let them get this close..." His lips grazed her ear.

Ava's mind swam with a hundred thoughts, feelings.

She focused on only one, though. The feeling of powerlessness. The vampire who'd bled her with his knife and left her to bleed out on the concrete floor.

The sound of Ross's scream.

Ava backed herself against Dallas, the motion bringing her hands smack against his hard abs, which were slick with cold sweat. She twisted with all her might, snapping out of his hold, and she reached down into her pant leg quickly, pulling out the stake she had hidden. She lunged forth to Dallas, stake in hand as she pushed with her opposite hand and forced him back against the ring.

Her eyes burned into his gaze, and she pressed herself against him, holding him with what force she possessed against the ring.

She noted the sizeable bulge in his pants, but refused to acknowledge it at the moment, despite the fact she couldn't deny it gave her a sense of satisfaction.

"You were saying..."

Dallas let out a dark laugh.

"What's so funny?" She tried to catch her breath,

but she didn't move, and he didn't relent either.

"I think you're enjoying this a little too much." He smiled darkly.

"I'm not the one who's all hot and bothered." She cast him a heated gaze.

Dallas settled his hand around hers, which held the stake against his chest, and he pulled it away slowly.

"Could have fooled me." The low ceiling lights cast shadows on him and his defined muscles, making the sweat on his skin glisten; and all his tattoos stand out.

Her insides twisted.

And suddenly it dawned on Ava, that perhaps getting close to the vampires would be the best way to slaughter them.

It was their nature to use their thrall, to placate humans into becoming wanton little things that would allow them to get close enough to bite, to kill them. But perhaps if one thought they had her, if they could get close enough to bite her...

She'd be close enough to kill them without them realizing their mistake.

But as she looked into Dallas's bright blue eyes, she realized there were some things she just *couldn't* fight.

Because she didn't *want* to.

It all happened so fast, she couldn't be sure who made the first move.

As the stake fell from her hands, it clattered on the boxing ring floor.

Dallas's lips crushed hers with fury, his hands sliding up her back into her sweat soaked hair.

Her breasts pressed against his warm, solid chest, her hands finding their way up his arms, his neck, as her fingers traced his jaw, pulling him closer.

She slid her tongue into his mouth, and he pushed

back against her, his lips traveling from her mouth to her jaw, and her heart thundered in her chest, her nerves at full attention from the adrenaline, the fight. Ava closed her eyes, and the memory of glowing green emeralds, of razor-sharp fangs biting her, pushed forth, and she couldn't help the moan that escaped her lips.

She couldn't deny that it felt good.

The fight.

The feel of Dallas's body against hers.

The building cyclone in the pit of her stomach, in her groin.

"Ava..." His voice vibrated on her skin and made her entire body flush with heat as he pulled away, catching his breath.

"Dallas..." she answered skeptically.

"Fuck..." His breath caught in his throat.

"We shouldn't do this..." He swallowed, and she could hear the concern in his voice.

"Why?" Her eyes focused on his lips, and all she could think about was how good they felt. How badly she needed this. The release. Someone to take away all the thoughts, feelings.

Someone to make her forget.

"Why? There are a lot of reasons..." He leaned his forehead against hers, his hair tickling her face.

"What's the matter Dallas? Afraid I'll bite?" She let out a little laugh.

"Mal—"

"Doesn't need to know," she whispered, her lips brushing his again.

Dallas slid his tongue into her mouth, groaning into her before pulling away once more.

"You're—"

"A consenting adult." She kissed him again.

"Fuck...Ava..."

"If you don't want this Dallas, the door is over there..." Her heart raced; her blood boiled.

It seemed like forever until he spoke.

"I'm not going anywhere, kitten."

"Good. Neither am I."

This time when Dallas kissed her, there was no question or concern. He kissed her with fervor, with desire, and with possession.

And for the moment, Ava forgot about everything else.

About death, and monsters, and revenge.

In the arms of Jake Dallas, it was so easy to forget.

CHAPTER THIRTY-ONE

"You're sure they didn't see you?" Taj took a sip of his beer as he relaxed on the couch.

Cassius stirred the dough absentmindedly as the oven dinged. "I am certain," Cassius stopped his stirring, and he expertly spooned out drops of cookies onto the parchment lined baking sheet.

Jasmine padded down the hall, her hair slightly disheveled from a long sleep. Cassius glanced at the clock. It was still early in the evening, only eight o'clock.

"Oh, you're baking again..." Jasmine's eyes filled with hunger.

Cassius didn't consider himself an expert baker by any means, but after spending so many years in Paris, he'd picked up the skill as a hobby and seemed to have a hard time letting it go. It helped to calm his nerves, whenever he'd feel stressed, anxious. Worried.

And he was most certainly worried about Ava attending a party in which idiotic vampires may try to challenge his claim on her or tie up *loose ends* as Brody had called her.

Taj looked at Cassius, his expression plain and simple. *Don't say anything to Jasmine.*

Cas glanced at Jasmine's cerulean eyes and sighed. "Ava wishes to attend a party in which I know there will be vampires." He scooped out a spoonful of cookie dough, and Jasmine settled on the bar stool at the island.

Taj watched their interaction closely.

Jasmine was as exotic as the flower she was named after, and Taj treated her as such.

He'd only known her for about a decade, after she'd stumbled into the woods of Chester, an escapee of hunters.

Hunters like Mal. Ava's brother.

He hadn't mentioned his little discussion with Ava and her hunter brother to either of them, but somewhere in his depths he knew he needed to tell them. If only for the reason that by association, they would likely be made targets.

But despite knowing the danger it may put him, and even his friends in, he could not deny the truth. He would embrace whatever danger lurked beyond the woman who bore his claim on her blood.

Another cookie dropped to the pan with a soft sound.

"So go the party. Play hero. You know you want to." Jasmine swiped her finger in the bowl, pulling some raw cookie dough onto her finger, her eyes shutting in pleasure as she licked it off.

Cassius could hear a small choking sound from Taj in the living room, and he rolled his eyes. As bristling as Taj could be, there was at least *one* person who could soften his edges.

Cassius wished that he could have someone the way

Taj had Jasmine. The way his father, Lucius, had his human mother, Isabella, before the siring. Before their lives had disintegrated into pain, and betrayal.

"I do not *play* hero, why does everyone keep saying that?" Cassius grumbled as he pulled the bowl away from Jasmine.

She frowned.

"If you continue to eat my cookie dough, there will be no cookies to eat, Jasmine." He raised an eyebrow at her.

Jasmine chuckled lightly.

"Just go to the party. Let loose a little too, while you're at it. Have some fun." She waggled her eyebrows at Cassius who huffed a sigh of exasperation.

"One can hardly have fun when there is danger lurking in the shadows." He shoved the tray of raw cookies into the oven.

Jasmine rolled her eyes.

"Always so dramatic."

Cassius's eyes met Taj's.

"I will go. But I can guarantee I will *not* have *fun*."

***

Cassius held the coffee in one hand and a bag of cookies in the other. Yet, he felt strangely nervous in a way he hadn't felt since he was a young teenager.

Ava sat with her back against a tree in the quad, and she looked rather spent. He could see even at a distance, the bags underneath her eyes, and the deep breaths she was taking. She looked tired, and most certainly in need of caffeine and sugar. Women loved caffeine and sugar, and he prayed she would too. Each step he took toward her felt like a canyon, but he kept going. Her eyes opened, eyelashes fluttering in the shade as he approached her.

"You must have a death wish," she drawled as he came to the edge of the shaded tree, his shoes barely touching the edge of her boots.

"Perhaps it is you who has the death wish." He held out the coffee.

"What is this?" She looked up at him skeptically.

"A peace offering." He nodded at her.

"What's in the bag?" Her eyes glanced down to his fingers that held the bag shut, and he could not deny the way they fixated on his slender wrist.

This close to her he could feel her heightened pulse, and he wondered what she was thinking about.

The sun hit him at his back, and he felt flush and warm, between its heat and the vibrating pulse of his marked human. Never in a million years did Cassius think he would have marked *anyone*. But he had, and he knew because of his actions, it would be rather difficult to stay away. He needed to be near her, if only to keep an eye on her. To make sure she was safe. He had vowed to do so, and he intended to keep his word. Even if being near her put him in danger.

Mal had relented, but he knew it may only be a matter of time before the hunter found a way to discard him. It was what he did.

Kill people like Cassius.

"Chocolate chip cookies." He handed her the bag, and she took it, her fingers brushing his lightly, sending a jolt of electricity through him.

The touch felt so...*good*, but it was rather short lived.

Ava opened the bag and peered in, as if expecting a spider or something to jump out and scare her. "A peace offering, huh? How do I know you didn't poison this shit, and this is how I end up in your fucking lair?"

"I suppose you'll just to have to trust me." He smiled, trying to look as innocent as possible.

"What kind of drink is that?" She looked up at him.

"Coffee."

"Black?" she asked as she wrinkled her nose.

"Heavens, no. No sane human drinks black coffee." The wind rustled his hair, and he could feel her pulse start to race once more. He held the coffee out to her.

She took it from his hands and set it on the ground.

He slid his hands in his pockets, and she pulled a cookie from the bag, looking it over with suspicion before taking the smallest bite.

"Thank you. For the other night," he spoke.

"Like I said, we're even now." She took another bite.

"Please don't go to the party," he pleaded.

"Is this why you brought me sweet treats? Try and butter me up? Did you think if you bought me food I'd just agree to your demands?"

I had hoped so, yes.

As she said the words, Cassius could feel his own dark blood start to heat. It sounded like bribery.

It wasn't *not* bribery.

Suddenly he felt on the spot. "I am not demanding anything of you, I just—"

"Good. Because I don't like to be told what the fuck to do." She rose from her seat, bag and coffee in hand. She took a step closer to him. "Especially by bloodthirsty killing machines who wear leather pants when its eighty-five fucking degrees." She brushed past him.

"What's wrong with my pants?" Cassius felt perplexed as he watched her saunter off.

"See you around, Cas." She waved to him as she

walked off.

"Thanks for the poison," were the last words she spoke before she disappeared around the corner.

CHAPTER THIRTY-TWO

AVA WALKED PAST the array of shops on Main Street, her hands in her jeans pocket. It was still early afternoon, and due to Hunter wrapping up whatever it was Mal and the others had assisted him with, Dallas was occupied. She wasn't angry, jealous, or perturbed by any means. She understood the relationships between Mal and his best friend, and even the other hunters as she'd observed, was something that had been built over several years. They had a bond, the five of them. A bond that was born of blood, and death.

After all, it wasn't as if she and Dallas were...anything really. They'd kissed, sure. But that didn't mean they were together or anything.

She'd just lost her boyfriend. It was a moment of weakness, a moment of just...

Being able to forget. A moment of lust, nothing more.

But she couldn't deny that she enjoyed the moment. She enjoyed it quite a bit more than she probably should have.

Just remembering the feeling of his hands running

up her back, his arousal pressed against her... The way his stubble brushed her skin as he ran his tongue up her jaw... And the fight beforehand hadn't been without its charms either.

Then there was Cassius.

A part of her felt guilty, it had been his image that filled her brain as she kissed Dallas, but she was also thankful that he was able to redirect her desires, if only for a moment.

She didn't want to think about Cassius. About his deep green eyes, his perfect model face, or his sharp fangs.

Or the fact that he had brought her a *peace offering.* Whatever that fucking meant.

He was a vampire. A monster.

The enemy.

Cookies and coffee didn't change that. It never would.

She was grateful he had saved her, but she was also angry.

He certainly didn't have time to explain but...

It still felt unfair. He'd asked her permission, but how was she to know what he was truly asking? He may have saved her life, but she knew as she looked up at him amidst the daylight, that it was much more complicated than that.

Her hair blew in her face, and she remembered the night before, with Dallas. How easy it had been to wade into those waters. How, for only a moment, she had forgotten about all of it. How the fight had transpired into something else when Dallas pulled her by her long, sweat soaked ponytail into his hard embrace.

Even though it had led to a most enjoyable, hot make out session, she had to admit if Dallas could use her long, silken locks against her, perhaps a vampire such as Cas may be able to do the same.

She stopped in front of Lori's Hair Salon, her reflection catching in the window. She'd never *cut* her hair before. She'd had plenty of trims, to keep it long and luscious. It looked so pretty when she'd tie it back, especially with a bow when she donned her cheerleading uniform. But it had started to become a nuisance.

Always flying around in the wind, sticking to her lip gloss. It took nearly an hour to wash and dry every day.

And it could be the difference between life and death, quite literally.

When Lori took the scissors to her hair, Ava closed her eyes. She couldn't bear to watch the years of growth tumble to the floor. When she opened her eyes finally and looked in the mirror, she felt a sting of panic.

Lori brushed and straightened her shoulder length locks, and Ava couldn't deny a sense of excitement swelled in her stomach. It brought forth a feeling of newness, of confidence she hadn't quite expected.

She couldn't stop looking at her reflection in the shop windows she passed, getting used to the new person she looked like. Which was why she was taken by surprise when she ran into a short, familiar red-headed individual.

"I'm so sorry... Ava?" Ember spoke in surprise.

"I uh...didn't see you there, Em, sorry." Ava chuckled.

"You...cut your hair?" Ember raised an eyebrow.

"Yeah, it was getting to be a pain in the ass, so..." Ember smiled.

"Do you like it?" Ava asked, running her fingers

through the shorter locks. It still felt odd, the quick feeling, because of where it stopped, just brushing her shoulder with its edges.

"I do." Ember smiled.

"Where you headed at this hour?" she asked Ava.

"Nowhere, really, I was just...walking. Getting fresh air,"

Getting my mind off the inevitable.

The party was in two days. She was nervous.

She longed to use her stake, to be able to bring justice to Ross, herself, and the victims of the vampires, but...

What if I choke?

What if all this training, all of this...what if I can't do it?

Ava pushed the thoughts from her mind. She couldn't think that way. If she did, she'd be dead. But she was still nervous. She supposed nerves would not relent until she'd followed through.

Until she'd put the monsters six feet under.

Or more accurately, burned them to ash.

You won't be alone, you will have back up.

While Dallas had said he'd back her up, Mal would not hear the word *no* on the matter either.

With the two of them in the same vicinity, she felt better, but she also felt as if it was more important than ever to show them, she was capable of this on her own.

"Are you going to the party up at the old stone church on sixty?" Ember asked.

"Yeah, why?" Her shoulders tensed. "You're not considering going, are you?" Her blood chilled. Ember was not the type to attend parties of any kind, but Ava *had* suggested on more than one occasion that Ember needed to socialize more. Although, she hoped her friend hadn't taken up on her suggestion so soon.

"Ava, you know you can talk to me, right?" Ember reached out and ran her hand on Ava's arm. "You don't have to throw yourself into partying, or drinking or..."

Ava could feel the smile forming on her lips. "I know, Em. But I'm not the kind of person who's going to sit around and mope. You know me. I need to move. I need to be where the action is," she said.

I need to drive a stake through the vampire that killed my boyfriend, and the one who almost killed me.

The two of them walked down the street together, past The Third Eye, the metaphysical shop in which Ava worked and Ember frequented. It was how they met. It had been mere coincidence that Ember and Ava had ended up in the same medieval history class together.

"I know I just..."

"I know. And I appreciate it." Ava nudged her shoulder as they stopped in front of one of the town's most popular clothing boutiques, which was all done up and decorated with Halloween costumes and merchandise for the impending holiday. Tiny red and orange leaves bristled about Ava's ankles, and a shiver ran down her spine. The temperature was starting to drop, and the sun was starting to disappear into the clouds. It would soon be night.

"Are you going to dress up?" Ember twisted her lips as she looked at the display case full of short costumes.

"I haven't given it much thought, actually."

"You could always go as a college kid," Ember said, deadpan. "Wouldn't have to buy a costume." She laughed awkwardly.

Ava rolled her eyes. "What's the point of dressing up

on Halloween if you're just going to go as something you can go as every day of the year?" She looked in the display case of the boutique, which still showcased some regular clothes amidst the pleated skirts and cleavage bearing costumes. Her eyes settled on a thick, black leather jacket with studs on the collar.

Looking at it gave her an instant smile.

I bet that would look badass with all my band tees.

But it was another thought that sparked her interest more.

I bet I could hide a stake in there.

CHAPTER THIRTY-THREE

THE CHURCH ON route sixty had been abandoned for nearly fifty years. The only life it saw was a few drifters, perhaps some thrill-seeking teenagers. It certainly hadn't housed more than a small handful of individuals at once, let alone a smattering of college students all looking to lose themselves in liquor and sex.

Cassius and Tajiri stood on the edge of the rock terrain, the sound of music loud amidst the chatter. Even outside, Cassius could smell the scents of alcohol, sweat, and mildew.

Liam and his cohorts were inside, he knew that.

But so was Ava.

He could feel her pulse beating steadily, and he knew she was near, and that made him feel quite the mixture of emotion.

Taj smiled as he headed toward the main doors, past the scantily dressed angels and demons loitering about the entrance.

How fitting.

Upon opening the door, he was assaulted with a hundred scents: from the crowd of bodies dancing, drinking.

Candles were lit all about; on the dusty altar, in the entryway on cobwebbed tables, in the crevices of windowsills lighting up the expanse of stained-glass windows.

Taj moved quickly, in search of his target, and Cassius tried to keep up, but he couldn't deny that the sight brought back memories he hadn't expected.

Memories of another life.

Eden ran her fingernails down his face, over the throbbing vein in his neck.

Her teeth nipped at his lower lip, and he could still taste blood on the edge of her fangs as his own tongue stroked hers in response.

The candles flickered against the stained-glass windows, all shades of orange against the red painted glass.

The Boracelli's always did have quite the flair for drama.

His tongue licked at her fangs, the taste of blood making him long for more.

Eden giggled, and the sound was both haunting and melodic.

Cassius shook the memories from his mind, as he pushed his way through the crowd, the pulse in his veins getting stronger with each stride.

He watched the crowd, and noted Tajiri was moving faster. He could smell the overbearing musk of Liam, and knew he was close as well.

Then his gaze settled on her.

She stood in the center of the room, her arms around Liam's neck. She looked...different.

Clad in a leather jacket, and a black corseted costume dress, pale legs standing out against the darkness. He could see her black boots came up to her mid-thigh, elongating the slender shape of her legs. Her hair was shorter, angled close to her shoulders, and the ruby red stain on her lips flared his thirst.

It was just makeup, he knew that.

But it drove thoughts of blood and lust through his brain in a way he hadn't felt since he'd fully transitioned.

Liam smiled, the motion showcasing his fangs, and Ava let her head roll back.

Liam leaned his lips against her collarbone, and Cassius moved with heightened purpose. Thunder roared above the music and chatter, shaking the unsteady ground.

Ava ran her hands down Liam's arms, her fingers intertwining with his.

She glanced up in that moment, and their eyes met as the rain fell hard against the roof.

CHAPTER THIRTY-FOUR

IT WAS MUCH easier than she had anticipated, finding Liam. Now that she knew what he was, she trusted her newly found vampiric radar would steer her in the right direction. When she'd told Mal about her suspicions, he'd confirmed the truth. According to lore, and several firsthand accounts of victims, some survivors as well, the marked could sense not only *their* vampire's presence, but that it was nearly impossible to distinguish the vampire who marked them, from any *other* vampire.

"It could be useful for us," Dallas had suggested.

Mal did not want to agree, but Ava felt the same way. While Dallas and Mal, and likely the other hunters as well had trained, and were probably so good at tracking a vamp they could do it their sleep, Ava had to admit it would be rather helpful, and time saving if she could just...follow her vampire radar right into the hands of the monster.

And that is exactly what she did. She hadn't told Mal or Dallas her plan, knowing that both of them would likely try to talk her out of such things, but she knew they were close. If they were concerned something would go south, they'd come to her rescue.

But things would *not* go that way. She would not let them. She'd remain in control. She'd focus her mind. She'd find a way. Failure was just not an option.

And it seemed her plan was working. Liam took her bait like a moth to a flame. His thrall reached out around her, and she could feel the faint cloudiness in her brain, but it wasn't as mind numbing as she'd been told. Either that, or Liam was not running at full power, which she did not intend to push.

She felt *him*, before she saw him.

Not only did her skin prickle with goosebumps, her wrist flare with heat, but her blood *heated* in a way it hadn't when she approached Liam.

Like it knew somehow, someway...it was *his*.

She pushed the thought down vehemently. No one owned her body, her blood. Or any part of her, truly.

She could feel his gaze on her, and the memory of the night he bit her once again forged through the walls of her mind. She closed her eyes for a moment, rolling her head back, and Liam's lips brushed her collarbone. His thrall dissipated, and she knew he thought he had her.

That she was just a victim like the others, so he pulled back.

That will be your first mistake, fucking leech.

When she opened her eyes, she caught Cassius's gaze. He stood only mere feet away, but it might as well have been a vast canyon. His golden blonde hair rustled slightly from the motion of young collegiate drunkenly bumping into him, and he was wearing a simple heathered grey shirt, and those same black leather pants he'd had on the other day.

What, do they assign you a fucking uniform or something when you graduate vampire academy or some shit?

Though she couldn't deny the look wasn't a bad one for him.

He moved closer, and she knew he intended to sweep in and disrupt her plan. Which she could not let him do. Not if she wanted to stake Liam, and the one who'd slit her thighs, leaving a nasty scar.

She pulled Liam, breaking Cassius's gaze as she found her way through the crowd of people, moving quickly so as to lose Cassius in the sea of costumed students.

Liam stopped in his tracks, his eyes alert and she stopped too, looking around to see if perhaps there was something she'd missed. Or someone.

"Logan..." Liam's voice carried the hint of concern.

"There's been a...complication..." This Logan looked at Ava quickly, before continuing.

"It's hunters," she heard him whisper.

Fuck.

A hand touched the small of her back, sliding around her hip, pulling her away from Liam

No...

She turned slightly, to see pale blue eyes staring down at her.

"Hey, baby, I've been looking everywhere for you." His voice was solid, and she knew it was just an act, but she couldn't help the flutter in her heart at his words.

Not now, Ava. Now is not the time...

She scanned the crowd once more, but Cassius was gone.

"Liam..." Logan's eyes cast a glare at Dallas, whose

hand had made its way into his back pocket.

Ava leaned lightly, glancing at his ass. He held against himself something with the slightest silver sheen—a knife.

"Care to introduce me to your friend, Ava?" Liam spoke, and she could feel the beginnings of thrall seeping out, much more powerful now.

Her head started to feel...foggy.

Dallas tightened his grip on her.

"I think we're well past introductions," he answered

Liam glanced at Logan, and back at Ava.

"I will have to catch up with you later, Ava." Liam licked his lips.

When he left, Ava felt as if the world was spinning. Her legs felt slightly like Jell-O.

Dallas braced her against his arm, and for the moment she was glad for the support, but once the fog settled the anger pushed forth.

"What the fuck, Dallas!" She moved out of his touch and shoved him.

"I had him!" she spat.

"Bullshit, Ava, he had *you.*" Dallas slid his knife back into his pocket.

"I was this fucking close to staking him!" She glared at him. "And you let him fucking go!"

"Look around, Ava. We're in a crowded room. Full of witnesses. If you want to fucking end this sucker you need to get him alone where no one can see." He pursed his lips.

"That's what I *was* doing before you so rudely interrupted me." She crossed her arms.

"You cut your hair..." Dallas reached out, running his fingers through the edges and she brushed him off.

"Don't, Dallas," she growled as she shoved past him

with fury.

"Where the fuck you think you're going?" he bit back.

"To kill a fucking vampire. On my own!"

Dallas was at her back, pulling on her wrist. She yanked her arm out of his grip.

"Ava..."

Thunder boomed in the distance, rattling the windows.

She could hear the sound of a struggle beyond the doors of the crowd.

The sound of glass shattering, of a pained scream.

And upon hearing that scream, it all came back.

Ross's moan of pleasure, the scream of pain.

The knife cutting through her flesh.

Cassius's fangs in her skin.

All of it.

Ava didn't think twice about running into the shadows, leaving Dallas behind.

CHAPTER THIRTY-FIVE

TAJ AND LIAM struggled in what Cassius assumed must have once been the office of the church. The two vampires knocked into everything, fangs snapping, fingers grasping at throats. Old, worn and musty smelling papers flew about like confetti in the dank room.

Cassius knew better than to try and break up the fight, knowing Taj finally had his target. Before he'd followed Taj into the office, there was a man who showed up, who broke the thrall of Liam, who pulled Ava's attention from *him.*

But he hadn't intended on having to put up a fight of his own against Logan, the man who'd pulled Liam's attention from Ava.

And by the looks of it, he was a hunter too.

The way in which the tall, muscular man touched Ava ignited a spark of jealousy in Cassius. Which was an odd feeling altogether.

He barely knew Ava, but the sight of this man with his hands on her...

He'd known she had a boyfriend. For God's sakes,

the night he saved her...

She'd asked him to save her *boyfriend.*

He'd just attended the funeral for the man, after all.

Cassius was no stranger to loss, and understood everyone processed their grief differently, but he couldn't help but feel that perhaps this man, this hunter with Ava... Perhaps he was taking advantage of said grief, and that angered Cassius.

But he had no time to *play hero,* as Jasmine would say. Not when the scent of Liam hit his nose, and Tajiri went running after it. Not when Logan swung at him, his fist connecting with Cassius's jaw, fangs bared in a lethal hiss.

That was the second time in a week Cassius had been punched. He hoped this would not become a habit, or a side effect of around Ava. Though, even if it was, he would endure it. It wasn't just the mark on her, though. That was a large part of things, but—

She intrigued him in a way most people didn't.

Just as Cassius bared his fangs against Logan, scrappling against the man's hard chest, the sound of the door crashing open pulled all of their attention.

Mal stood in the doorway, purple and blue lights from the church's main worshipping room lighting him up, his cursed knife glinting off the neon light behind him, and the dark look in his chocolate eyes was a familiar one Cassius had only just discovered in recent days.

The man who'd been behind Ava before was behind Mal now.

Which meant Ava was alone, and Brody was still out there.

Cassius pushed against Logan, delivering a swift punch to his jaw, the sound of cracking prevalent in the air as he channeled his strength and forced Logan up and backward into the wall.

The perks of being a vampire if there were any, included the reserves of strength he hadn't possessed as seeming mortal.

Though a born vampire such as Cassius tended to have more abilities than that of sired vampires, in this moment he was particularly glad for it.

His eyes locked with Mal, who grinned sadistically.

"Well, well, look what we have here, Dallas,"

The man behind Mal had a name.

Dallas.

Tajiri bared his fangs at the hunters, and despite the fact they were fighting their own enemies, suddenly it was as if the lines were crystal clear. Vampires united against the humans that threatened to kill them.

But Cassius did not want to *kill* anyone.

He felt on the precipice of something greater.

He'd had quite the history of caring for mortals, that was his immortal curse. There had been plenty of mortals he'd called friends; those who he'd defended.

Protected.

So, he recognized the look in Mal's face.

Undying loyalty, sworn to protect those close to them.

But he would not let anything, or *anyone* come between him and the woman who bore his claim on her blood. It went against his vampiric instincts, but furthermore, he knew he would not let anyone come between him and the woman he swore to protect, the first person in over a century who'd made him *feel something.*

Alive.

And so, as Tajiri and Liam fought against the

oversized Dallas, Cassius called forth on his reserves and bared his fangs at Mal.

"I am not your enemy, Malcolm. You do not have to do this." His eyes fixed on Mal's sinister stare.

"You are the very definition of my enemy, *Cassius.*" Mal stepped forward.

"I do not wish to hurt you."

"Pity, because I'm going to make you wish for death, you fucking parasite."

Mal swung his arm out, and Cassius instinctively shielded himself from the impact of the blade. The sharp tip cut into his palm, stinging his flesh. Dark, thick black liquid seeped out of his hand.

His blood—black as night.

"You have left her in danger, he is still out there," Cassius growled at Mal, who broke his hold, attempting to get closer.

The sound of agony raged behind him, and the scent of decay and death was prevalent.

Burning.

Cassius did not want to look away from Mal, worried the slight distraction would give Mal an advantage, but he had to know.

His gaze raked over the scene behind him, and Liam's bones disintegrated before his eyes. Tajiri roared against Dallas, and the two fighting together looked rather like two large wrestlers going at it in the ring. They were both men of a certain size, more muscle than was necessary.

Cassius's veins *throbbed,* and his skin felt like ice.

He could feel her. She was close, and the racing of her pulse caused worry to flash in his eyes.

"Ava is in trouble," he said, hoping to reason with Mal.

"Nice try, bloodsucker—"

"I can *feel* her pulse, she is—"

Mal growled and swung again, knocking Cassius against the desk, angling his body on top of him, rearing his arm back to strike.

Cassius pushed back with all his might, his fingers grasping at Mal's, fighting for the knife.

"We can do this another time, Mal. But right now, I am *not* your enemy. Right now, I am your ally." He knocked Mal backward, casting a glare back at Tajiri who had thwarted off Dallas for the time being.

Dallas ran his hand through his hair, and when he pulled it away, Cassius noted the blood.

The scent of it ignited him, stirred his thirst.

But it didn't smell as appetizing as Ava's had.

He'd gone without fresh blood for so long, and though he hungered for it in this moment, there were more pressing matters. Thank goodness he'd consumed his share of corpse blood before attending this raucous, macabre party.

Cassius took off, following the pulse alive in his veins, with only one purpose, one desire.

To protect what belonged to him.

He didn't even notice two hunters, and a pissed off vampire running behind him.

CHAPTER THIRTY-SIX

THE VAMPIRE WHO'D attacked her bared his fangs at her neck. His thrall seeped into her, and it wasn't an unpleasant feeling. In fact, it was quite a desirable feeling if she was being honest.

Brody pushed her up against the wall in the hallway beside the altar, his hands settling over Ava's ass as she wrapped her legs around him.

Ava couldn't deny the thoughts that forged through at his actions, and had she been completely in her right mind, she knew she should be disgusted at the thought.

She closed her eyes, and for the moment it wasn't Brody and his creeping hands over her body, wasn't his fangs poised at her neck.

No, instead her psyche kicked up the image of a rather appealing blond vampire with glowing green eyes, and the thought of *his* fangs in her neck...

She tightened her legs around Brody and let out a deep moan. Her eyes fluttered, and the light from the altar filtered through, and she felt the brush of something sharp against her thigh.

A stake.

Suddenly awash with realization of what was happening, Ava remembered where she was, and what she came to do.

Her brain pushed away all thoughts of Cassius, and the memory of Ross, of the knife in her skin, of her parent's bloodied bodies on the floor reared its ugly head and suddenly nothing was clearer.

Ava continued to play the part as she slid her hand down her thigh, moaning in delight for Brody's ears.

It wasn't *entirely* a lie. What he was doing *did* in fact feel good, but it was his thrall, a natural defense. It wasn't as if she was attracted to the man who sliced her legs open and left her to die.

That would be highly fucked up.

Brody's tongue licked the skin on her neck, right over her throbbing vein.

"I've never stolen someone's mark before. This is going to be—"

Ava slid the stake out of her garter underneath her skirt. Her arms felt like Jell-O, but she forced the movements anyway, and then she felt *him*.

Her wrist flared with heat; her skin chilled like ice.

Her blood heating in response to his presence.

Cassius.

Though she wanted to, she was certain she could *not* look at him right now.

If she did, she'd lose her concentration, her nerve.

Her focus.

Ava's nerves stood on edge, and her breathing caught in her throat.

Images of tongues on skin battled with the sounds of pained screams, and Ava felt the rush of adrenaline surging through her as she brought her stake to

Brody's chest.

At the realization of what she was doing, he growled at her, grabbing her harder, ready to bite.

She fought against him, and she could *feel* Cassius as he approached her.

"Stay the hell away from me!" she roared at him

"Ava—" His voice was soft, and warm, and she refused to let it drive the images she fought so hard against.

"I mean it, Cas!"

Familiar voices echoed in the distance against the muffled music, and she knew them well.

Dallas, and Mal.

Ava and Brody wrestled against one another. Ava struck out once more with her stake, but Brody, wise to her goal, stopped it.

Everything was a blur of rage. Fists flying, backs knocking against the wall. Her arm braced against something sharp, and she could feel the rush of blood to the surface, and it only fueled her more.

Ava breathed heavily as adrenaline coursed through her, and Cassius was at her side almost as soon as her back hit the wall, but his existence next to her was short lived as Mal grabbed him, pulling him away.

"Don't even fucking think about it—" Mal wrapped his arms around Cassius, and Ava noted he only struggled a little bit. As if he was glad Mal held him captive. Which was odd.

It was the distraction she needed. She leapt for Brody and kicked his legs out from under him. He went down with a thud and Ava wasted no time straddling him with her legs. The very one's he'd cut open with knives.

Brody tried to use his thrall, but even his vampire

jedi mind tricks were no match for the feeling of power she felt at the moment.

Holding his cursed life in her hands.

Being able to prevent so much death, with just one plunge of an ash wood stake.

"You fucking bitch," he snarled. "I should have killed you when I had the chance." He fought against her hold, but with all the adrenaline running through her body, her force was stronger than she anticipated.

"Yeah, you should have." She smiled as she pulled her stake back. "But you picked the wrong girl to fuck over, buddy." And without hesitation, she plunged her stake into his chest.

He recoiled around her, letting out a deep growl that sounded all too much like thunder.

The sounds of the party roared in the background, and spurts of dark, black liquid erupted from his chest, splashing her hands and arms, and a stray drop even hit her face.

It felt like blood, but it looked like...

Oil. Sludge.

Vampires have...blood?

The question pushed forth, but she did not have time to be curious. She needed to light the vampire in front of her on fire if she wanted him to truly stay dead.

She slid her hands in her back skirt pocket, reaching for the set of matches Dallas had given her. The world around her fell silent as she focused on the strike of the match, the smell of sulfur. She rose from his body quickly as the match hit him, pulling the stake from his chest with her.

As she stood, she could feel her blood hot like flowing lava in a volcano.

Her eyes found Cassius's as Brody's body gave way

to flames, skin and muscle disappearing, bones crumbling like kindling in a fireplace.

The look in Cassius's eyes was dark, but there was a hint of something else she couldn't place.

Ava nodded at Mal, who looked surprised.

But he let him go all the same.

With the high she was feeling right now, she felt as if she could take on anyone.

Anything.

Cassius glanced at her only for a moment before taking off in the shadows.

CHAPTER THIRTY-SEVEN

CASSIUS WATCHED AS Ava drove the stake into Brody's body with precision and ease. Like it was the most natural thing in the world.

He'd known saving her was the right thing to do. And yet the divide between them was...murky at best when she was *just* a human, and he was just a vampire.

It was more than crystal clear now as he watched Brody's blood spatter onto her hands, and even a bit on her face.

Ava was a hunter.

It was in her blood, that was more than apparent.

Like her brother.

She killed people like him.

Monsters like him.

Yet as he caught her amber gaze, his entire being was flush with heat at the sight.

Her pulse quickened, her chest heaved, her breasts rising and falling with rapid breath. Images of blood-soaked thighs pushed forth, of fangs buried deep in her neck, and his cock twitched at the thought, the sight.

He was both equally terrified and *proud.*

It wouldn't be the first time he felt attracted to someone who could kill him.

He caught the slight nod of her head toward Mal.

"This isn't over, Cassius," Mal hoarsely whispered in his ear, before letting go.

Cassius would not waste the chance to escape the hunters.

He needed to find Tajiri, make sure he was all right.

If anything had happened to him...

Cassius passed Ava and nodded in her direction before disappearing into the shadowed hall in search of his friend.

***

Taj collapsed on the couch in a heap. "Man, I haven't had a fight that heavy in a long time," he grumbled.

Cassius was glad he'd escaped the hunters, although he knew it was likely because the hunters were focused on a different target.

A target with short brown hair, and amber eyes of fire to be exact.

"Yes, well, I fear there may be more brawls in our future," Cassius sighed.

"You can't be serious, Cassius..." Taj ran his hand over his face as Jasmine peeked her head around the corner.

"What's wrong?" she asked inquisitively.

"Ava is—"

"A hunter." Taj finished the words.

Jasmine's eyes widened. "Well, that complicates things a bit, doesn't it?" Jasmine slowly walked up to the couch and took a seat next to Taj.

"A bit, yes," Cassius whispered, his eyes closing in

defeat.

"You need to forget about her, Cassius, for your own good..." Taj's voice held an air of concern and worry.

"I wish it were that simple, Tajiri. I really do," he said as he got up from the couch, suddenly quite exhausted for someone who didn't need to sleep.

Jasmine and Taj did not say anything as he wandered off to his bedroom in search of solace.

CHAPTER THIRTY-EIGHT

THE MEDIA, AND the college lumped Liam, Brody, and Logan's disappearances in conjunction with Ross and the Klume sisters, enflaming the rumors of a serial killer in the town and on campus.

Yet, after a month, the hoopla, as Becky called it, seemed to die down, what with the murders seemingly coming to an end.

Mal had stuck around for the longest time, clear until Thanksgiving, before he'd decided that everything was quiet enough to leave.

Dallas sat in the driver seat of the Chevelle as Mal loaded the last of his suitcases and a clean amp in the back of the car. As Mal headed back indoors to say goodbye, Ava felt it only right to say her own goodbyes.

She leaned her arms on the windowsill.

"Where you two headed?" she asked, trying to focus on anything but the sight of Dallas's lips.

"No destination yet, but I'm sure something will pop up before too long. Lots of monsters out there." He ran his fingers over the side of the steering wheel, his blue eyes catching hers with unspoken words.

"Well, it's been fun." She smirked.

Dallas paused for a moment, his gaze drifting down to her mouth before catching her eyes once more. "That is has, kitten." A faint smile tugged at his lips.

"Try not to get into too much trouble without me." She smiled back.

"You trying to lecture me?" He let out a light chuckle.

"Depends. Do you want me to lecture you?" Her eyes lit up with amusement.

"Fuck no," he said.

Mal walked through the door, making a beeline for the car. He slid into the passenger seat and slapped the dashboard. "I'll try and be back for Christmas." He looked at Ava with slight concern. "But if you need *anything,* and I mean anything..."

"I'll call you, I promise." Ava rolled her eyes.

"Okay." His shoulders eased just a fraction, and Dallas started the car.

"See ya when I see ya," Mal shouted as Dallas backed the car out of the driveway.

Ava watched them drive off, as she had many other times. This time she felt a pang of sadness, but she did not dwell on it. She walked down main street with her hands in her pockets, toward Cory's Diner.

The air was chilly, but she preferred it much more to the blistering heat that was often prevalent even in the autumn in Virginia. It wouldn't be long before snow finally made its appearance, which she also detested. But for the moment, it was a perfect fall afternoon.

She sat on the bench across from Cory's, taking in the sight of the world around her. The few people walking by the light of the neon sign.

A light fluttering sounded beside her, and her wrist

flared with heat.

Goosebumps erupted on her skin.

"You must have a death wish. Clearly that, or you are certifiably insane." She turned her glance to Cassius.

"I can assure you I have exquisite mental awareness, my sweet Avarice." His lips bore the ghost of a smile.

"That's not my name." She shifted her body, the motion causing her legs to bristle against his.

"I know." He leaned back against the bench, crossing his ankles.

Silence fell between them.

"I could kill you, you know," she whispered.

"I know," was all he said.

But today would not be that day, she knew that.

Though death was inevitable.

It would either be hers...or his.

And Ava Crowley had no intention of dying.

Thank you for reading!

***

Turn the page for Blood & Lust: Ava Crowley, Vampire Slayer, #2...

BLOOD & LUST

AVA CROWLEY
VAMPIRE SLAYER

BOOK TWO

ARIEL DAWN

NAUGHTY NIGHTS PRESS LLC • CANADA

BLOOD & LUST

Some people run from danger...
Ava Crowley flirts with it.

When Ava and her brother embark on a trip to TerrorCon, a horror movie convention in Oklahoma, chaos follows. The kind that involves blood, sexy vampires, brooding hunters, and even a renowned demonologist. But Ava and the hunters aren't the only ones searching for answers.

Cassius is pulled back into a world of blood, lust, and death, a life long forgotten. In order to help clear a dear friend's name, he must travel to Oklahoma, all while fighting a magnetic blood bond between him and the snarky vampire slayer he can't live without.

Will Ava and Cassius be able to fight temptation surrounded by blood and lust?

Blood & Lust is book two in the Ava Crowley, Vampire Slayer series, filled with snarky heroines, sexy-as-sin monster hunters, and other seductive supernatural beasts.

Blood & Lust

Ava Crowley, Vampire Slayer

Book Two

Copyright ©2022 Ariel Dawn

ISBN: 978-1-77357-423-3

978-1-77357-424-0

Naughty Nights Press LLC

Cover Design by Willsin Rowe

Love is a smoke made with the fume of sighs;

Being purg'd, a fire sparkling in lovers' eyes.

— William Shakespeare

Love isn't soft, like the poets say.

Love has teeth which bite and the

wounds never close.

—Stephen King

CHAPTER ONE

AVA WATCHED THE doorstep from the comfort of her Chevy Impala.

She leaned one arm on the window, her cheek resting on her fist, while her other hand stretched out, fingers tapping against the steering wheel.

She'd expected more... something.

Everything seemed quiet in the sleepy town of Chester.

The town was no longer the center of media frenzy.

Sure, there were still *murders*, but nothing quite as scandalous as attractive college kids with strange marks on their thighs and necks, like the Chester Murders two years ago.

She could have sworn the man she'd followed had *all* the signs of a vampire, and even if she didn't believe it to be so, her vampire radar never lied.

The bite mark she'd sustained only two years prior—the bite that saved her life—flared with heat while her skin prickled with goosebumps every time a vampire was near.

As if she could have willed it with thought alone, her

wrist heated, and a soft knocking on her passenger window alerted her.

Her lips twisted in annoyance as a rather attractive blond with a penchant for leather pants smirked at her.

Cassius.

"What do you want?" she bit as she tried to look around him.

"May I come in?" He held a coffee in his hand.

Though she knew she should say no, she could not bring herself to do so, and that aggravated her.

"If it means you are no longer going to obstruct my vision, then, yes, by all means, enter my humble abode," she drawled sarcastically as she heard the click of a door.

Cassius opened the door and slid into the passenger seat, the motion accentuating his long legs—and the curve of his ass—in his black leather pants.

Ava pretended not to notice.

Especially when her blood *heated* at the sight.

"I was once told never to attend a stakeout without coffee." Cassius offered her the coffee cup.

Ava raised an eyebrow as she took the coffee from his hands, quickly opening the lid. The scent of vanilla and cream was divine.

"I was told never to invite a vampire into your house or car, yet here we are." She took a sip of coffee and had to admit it was divine.

"Thanks for the poison, but you didn't have to—"

"I was in the neighborhood." Cassius's eyes sparkled with amusement.

"Uh huh. Sure..." Ava rolled her eyes, focusing on the doorstop.

Nothing.

No movement.

Cassius casually leaned back in the seat.

"What if he does not show?" His voice was smooth, like caramel.

"He'll show," she answered as she took another drink of the sweet liquid.

"But if he does not..."

"Then I go home," she grumbled.

"But you will not rest, will you, Ava?"

She closed her eyes, letting the coffee warm her insides. She refused the idea that anything but the coffee could warm her like *this*.

"Until I put a stake through his chest, you mean? No, I won't."

Cassius sighed, turning his head to look out the window.

"Well, I suppose we wait then."

"There is no *we*, Cassius. This is my life, and—"

The door budged and Ava sat straighter.

"Bingo," she said as she set down her coffee, turning her car off.

CHAPTER TWO

THERE WAS NOTHING Cassius could do about Ava's extracurricular activities. He understood her reasons for slaying those like him; after all, it was his kind who killed her boyfriend, Ross. It was his kind that left her for dead; would have bitten, fed on, and killed many others without her intervention.

But he was not like those other vampires. He did not wish to kill, or maim, or indulge in the many pleasures vampires could indulge in without fear of retribution.

He had saved her life with his bite, with his venom, and though he knew she could dust him at any moment *if* she wanted...

She hadn't. She had threatened to do so on more than one occasion, but she had not moved to do it, and he had not made any move to finish his claim, to turn her. He hadn't made any indication toward her that he was interested in consuming her, either.

It seemed they were at a standstill. But as he sat in Ava's car alone, he could feel her pulse alive within him, and he had to admit his weakness.

He'd watched her drive a stake into a rogue vampire

only two years ago. The black blood of his kind sprayed on her pale cheeks, across the creamy expanse of her cleavage, her eyes alight with adrenaline and power. A power that reminded him of someone else.

They are not the same.

Cassius shifted in his seat, yet his gaze did not leave the entrance of the door Ava had walked through. Though he hated that she put herself in danger on an almost constant schedule, he also knew he had no way of truly stopping her.

The bite that he had given her had undoubtedly changed both of their lives, and the repercussions of that bond affected them both quite differently.

For starters, Cassius could feel her pulse within his own veins; a feeling he had grown rather fond of in the last two years. Yet, in her presence, his blood heated as if he were a boiling pot, and she the fire. In the beginning, it was startling, but now... Every fiber of his undead body being lit up like a star in her presence, pulled him to her like an unyielding force of gravity. The fight was becoming much more difficult.

"What are you doing?" he mused aloud to himself as his gaze stayed fixed on the entrance. He wasn't sure if he was talking about himself or Ava.

It seemed to be getting harder to separate his desires from those of the bond they shared.

As he sat in her car, surrounded by her intoxicating scent of jasmine and bergamot, Cassius worried his control was slipping.

His phone vibrated in his pocket. When he did not answer, it vibrated again. Incensed, he relented and pulled it out of his pocket.

"Yes," he snapped.

"Where the hell are you?" The voice on the other end of the phone was one he knew well, but not one he'd shared his phone number with.

"I believe I do not have to disclose my whereabouts to you, Malcolm." Cassius breathed deeply.

"I swear to God, if you're with her…"

"I can assure you, your sister is safe." He noted a flicker of light in the window.

"I know what you are, Cas," Mal's tone was cut and dry.

"A vampire? A little late for that discovery, isn't it?" Cassius kept his voice controlled.

"An Aurelia."

Cassius stiffened at his surname.

"And what do you plan to do with this information?" Cassius could not help the desperation in his voice. The last thing he needed was Malcolm to tell Ava he was the last of a fabled bloodline among the covens. He'd spent so many years trying to escape his name, and all that came with it.

Death, heartbreak, and immortal misery.

When Ava looked at him, she didn't see an Aurelia. He wasn't sure what she saw truly, as she was quite cantankerous most of the time, but she certainly didn't see him as the bounty he knew he was. Had she known, she would have certainly staked him without a second thought.

For the Aurelian line was cursed with the gift of life.

The rate of born vampires had dwindled ostensibly since the rate of vampires with the ability to sire seemed to be lessening. Above all, there was only one line which could bear descendants by birth, or by blood.

His.

The last of his bloodline would die with him. That much he'd promised himself. He would not burden anyone with a claiming bond, with the curse of immortality. And he certainly wouldn't burden anyone with a child.

A child who would be cursed to end up just as he had.

No, it was quite safer to stay hidden, blend in.

To leave his past in the past.

"If I told you, I'd have to kill you," Malcolm snickered.

"Yes, well, forgive me if I have to decline your offer."

"I'm going to find a way to break your bond," Mal said with conviction.

"There is no way—"

"There is *always* a way," Mal's voice echoed through the cell phone, and then the sudden click was deafening.

Cassius nearly jumped as Ava climbed into the car once more, black blood spattered on her jeans, some on her shirt.

Her skin was free of blemishes, though.

"Don't you have anything better to do than sit in my car like a fucking stalker?" she bit as she started the engine.

"Perhaps, I prefer your company," he answered honestly.

Ava rolled her eyes. "And I prefer a well aged Bordeaux and a man with a pulse, but when life gives you lemons..." She looked in the rearview mirror and backed up rather quickly for Cas's liking.

I have a pulse...

He wanted to defend her allegation, but what could he say?

He had a slow, dying pulse that belonged to him, but he had hers, too. Even at this moment, he could feel its elevation, the adrenaline still running through her.

He could feel her fear, her excitement.

Her lust for such things.

It stirred dark things in his own being, and he had to force the thoughts far away. For when they started their onslaught, there was only one way to truly quiet them.

Cassius shifted in his seat, stifling his rigid erection. This close to her, the scent of jasmine and bergamot was overpowering, and the feel of her pulse in his veins—alive with excitement—was like a thrall of its own.

He knew how Ava liked to make her kill.

How she liked to get close enough to her prey they could sink their fangs in her neck.

She was more than a slayer.

She was the spider, and he was nothing more than dead in her web.

So he said nothing. Instead, he leaned his arm out the window, and turned his face to the moon, praying the crisp air would cool the fire that surrounded him on all accounts.

CHAPTER THREE

AVA STOLE A glance at the stunning vampire in her presence. Against the black interior of the Impala, his flawless skin illuminated by the moonlight, he looked positively angelic.

Golden blond hair blowing ever so faintly from the gentle breeze that crept in through the window. The planes of his face were soft as if he was no younger than she was; barely twenty.

But she knew he was much older than he let on.

Though, she'd never asked. Such things didn't really matter and would only make things more difficult when the time came to put a stake through his heart.

And undoubtedly, she would put a stake through his heart.

Because he was a monster.

Like Brody, the vampire who'd slit her legs and left her to bleed out on the floor.

Like Liam, the vampire who killed her boyfriend, Ross.

Like the vampires who killed her parents.

Yet, Cassius had made no move to feed off her, or

turn her. Instead, he brought her coffee and donuts. Instead, he showed up out of nowhere, swooping in to dismantle her plans. He always dismantled her plans, whether he meant to or not. Because no matter what, when he walked in the room, her skin chilled with goosebumps while her blood boiled beneath the surface, and her pulse quickened.

And when she looked at him—

Bad idea, Ava.

You know better.

Ava forced her gaze back on the desolate road. The radio flickered between stations, and she reached for the dials just as Cassius did.

His fingers brushed hers with the lightest of touch, and she noted they didn't feel cold and dead.

They felt soft and warm.

She pulled her hand back as if he was a flame and she'd been burned.

Cassius cleared his throat as he turned the dial. Songs faded in and out until he'd settled on a station. The dark beats filled the car as the singer crooned on about holding someone's hands in the holes of his sweater.

Ava scowled, but she didn't change the station. The bass thumped, while the deep, breathy sounds of the singer filled the space.

She stared at the road and refused to acknowledge the thickening fog surrounding her while the singer droned on as she shifted in her seat, feeling strangely flush.

Which had nothing to do with Cassius.

No, she was just keyed up from a fresh staking.

When she pulled up the driveway, the headlights shone on the empty garage.

Cassius was out of the car within seconds, opening

her door.

She flashed him a gaze of annoyance, but he only had the audacity to look just as charming as always. Like some picture-perfect leading man in a romantic comedy, or something out of a cheese-induced dream.

She wanted to say a hundred things to him, but all she could do was truly get as far away from him as possible. His visits were becoming much more frequent, and she worried that perhaps he'd started to get the wrong idea. Their *bond* did not make them friends. In fact, it was quite the opposite. There wasn't enough coffee or Danishes in the world to make her forget the reality of *what* Cassius was.

What he'd done to her.

What he'd probably done to several other people throughout his long life.

She stopped at the door, sliding her key into the lock. She could feel him behind her, but he kept his distance. He always kept his distance.

As he should.

"You can go, Cas." She huffed as she stepped across the threshold of the door and turned on the light. She nearly stumbled over her duffel bag and suitcase by the door.

Fuck, Connie must have moved them.

Cassius's gaze flicked down to the luggage.

"Are you leaving?" She didn't miss the sadness in his voice.

"Not that it's any of your business—" She leaned against the doorframe, crossing her arms.

"But, yes. I'm leaving town for a few days." Her eyes searched his, gauging his reaction. His glowing green eyes looked hurt. As if her words alone could cut him like a knife.

He just wants your blood, Ava.

Nothing more.

"I see," was all he said as he stood on the other side of the threshold, in the cold autumn air on her front porch.

He wouldn't dare cross it without her permission.

Not because he couldn't, but because, as he once pointed out, it would be rather rude to insist on coming inside when he was not wanted.

"Where are you going?" Ava watched as he slid his hands into his pockets, the motion jostling his leather pants just enough to be noticeable in the lamplight, casting shadows on his pale skin.

"Again, not that it's any of your business, but..." She twisted her lips. A part of her screamed to shut the door on him. She didn't owe him anything. He had saved her life, with his bite mark, but she had not known the cost of such things. The bond between them was nothing more than circumstance.

Cassius was not her friend.

He was the *enemy.*

Who happens to look quite appealing in leather pants.

But Ava found herself divulging her plans far too easily to Cassius, despite wanting to keep them to herself.

"Oklahoma." She pursed her lips and imagined locking them up and throwing away the key.

"What's in Oklahoma?" Cassius smirked at her.

Ava felt her shoulders relax only slightly.

"TerrorCon." She smiled.

"What is... TerrorCon?" He raised an eyebrow, looking perplexed.

"Only the biggest horror convention in the United States." Her eyes glittered with excitement.

"Horror movies, you mean?" Cassius tilted his head to the side.

"Yup. It's five days of pure horror."

Cassius twisted his lips.

"That sounds awful," he chided.

"It sounds like heaven," she said as her lips tugged into a smile.

Cassius hesitated, and she turned, seeking her moment. But for some reason she couldn't shut the door.

"When do you leave?" His voice stopped her.

"Tomorrow." She turned once more and took in his lovely features. Ava had the startling concern that Cassius would not let her go. Such a thought was unnerving to her, and instantly flared her defenses, her panic.

"Don't follow me," she ordered.

"I would not—"

"I mean it, Cas." She stood her ground. She'd told him so many times to leave her be, but he always came back. Before she could hear any more of his sweet, decadent voice, she shut the door.

CHAPTER FOUR

CASSIUS WALKED THE empty streets alone, with only his thoughts for company. Thoughts of amber eyes and luscious pink lips as they gazed back at him only moments before her cutting blow.

Ava was leaving.

It is not as if she is leaving you.

Of course, that was not the case at all—but Cassius could not deny the sharp sting in his heart at her words. Since the night he bit her, he'd barely been away from her for longer than twenty-four hours.

Not that she knew that, of course. He'd gone to great lengths to appear in her proximity sporadically. But every night it was the same routine. He'd venture close to the estate and check to make sure she was safe and sound.

On the nights she'd have nightmares, he'd creep in through her open window, and he would be there, offering the gentlest of touches along the back of her hand until she relented back into a quiet slumber.

He would find his way to the piano bar on the nights it became too unbearable to be near her. Anything to pull his attention away, make him forget even for the slightest moment that his life was no longer his.

That he was as much as marked as she was.

Those nights were becoming much more frequent, much to his dismay.

He longed to touch her, more than a gentle caress of his fingers on her skin. To feel her blood as it pulsed beneath her skin, to feel the soft flesh against his palms. Against his lips.

How could my father stand this?

Cassius knew his father had claimed his mother's blood before turning her, but seven years?

How did the thirst, the *need* for her not drive him completely insane?

Because they were together.

In love.

His thirst for her blood may not have been fed, but they'd had you...

It was obvious the other main need of a vampire was being met.

The thought made Cassius somewhat jealous. It had been a good twenty-five years since he'd been intimate with anyone, and his diet of corpse blood wasn't exactly the most fulfilling. Perhaps, that was why the desire was so strong, but alas, he refused to partake in feeding on a live human, or in casual sex, blood induced or not. He would not give himself and his Aurelian curse to someone he didn't love.

Not after Eden...

He wished the cold autumn air would cleanse him, but he knew better.

Nothing would cleanse him of Ava Crowley.

No, nothing could chase such a siren song away, and yet she thought he was a *threat* to her.

It had been two years.

Two years of fighting a blood bond that was maddening, yet somehow, he had remained controlled. He had not stepped out of line once, and he never would. Not unless she asked him to, in which case he would most certainly oblige.

But the way she had regarded him, when she told him he was leaving...

How she commanded him to stay away.

As if he would go against her very demands, but only moments before...

She seemed at *ease* with him. Those moments, as infrequent as they were, were exactly the thing that kept Cassius from going mad. Deep down, below the bitterness, and the sarcasm, the threats to end his existence...

She felt it, too.

The magnetic pull that had *nothing* to do with the bond.

But Ava Crowley's life was etched in blood and bones. Her world shifted on its axis the night Liam and his cohorts killed her boyfriend and left her to die.

In the wake of it all, she was reborn.

A hunter.

Like her brother.

Like her parents.

He knew it was asinine–it went against all the codes and made absolute perfect sense–she would despise him and what he was. That one day, she would truly end him.

Yet, all of his life Cassius strived to be more than what he was admittedly born to be.

As he walked through the dark doorway of his residence, he knew Ava's wishes were founded in truth. Despite the fact she'd started to move closer to him, that he caught her stolen glances at him... the truth was still bright and clear. There was quite an obvious divide, and Cassius knew he must stay on one side of it. The thought of her being so far away—far enough away he couldn't feel her pulse, couldn't smell her intoxicating scent— Made his slow beating heart tighten in his chest.

Perhaps she is right to put some distance between us.

Perhaps this is for the best.

Cassius quietly slipped out of his heather-gray shirt and leather pants and folded them neatly before setting them on the armchair in the corner of his bedroom.

The cool air kissed his fair chest, the shadows playing over the expanse of his toned abdomen. He ran a hand through his hair and took a deep breath.

Images of Ava filled his brain, of the car ride home.

Her fingers as they brushed his skin, sending bolts of electricity through his entire being.

Thankfully, she had pulled away, but the action left him feeling a sense of sadness.

As if she was repulsed by his touch.

Cassius did not need sleep, but he crawled into bed, anyway.

The quiet of the night was most comforting, and he knew he was alone.

Tajiri and Jasmine would not be home until dawn.

So he let the thoughts come unabashedly in the welcome solitude.

Her deep eyes of fire as they fixed on him, speckles of black blood across her cheek, in the corner of her ruby red lips.

Legs straddling Liam, stake in his chest.

Her cleavage spilling out of her tight corset top.

His eyes closed, he did not fight the memory.

Crimson streaks spilling out of her creamy, pale

thighs, the look of abject terror on her face, streaks of mascara and tears staining her perfect cheeks.

The feel of his fangs piercing her soft skin, and the way she gasped.

His thrall begged to wrap itself around her, his thirst clamoring to be met.

It was only a drop. A small, minuscule drop of blood that ran down his fangs, simmered on his tongue.

Hot, sweet.

Cassius slid his hand beneath the waistband of his boxers, and the memories replayed like a song on repeat.

The sound she'd made when he bit her, that stirred a deep instinctual desire within him.

Every stolen touch: a brush of a finger here, a side-by-side touch of her arm or leg, or bump of her shoulder, sent little shockwaves throughout his being, heated his blood.

Ignited a thirst within him that even blood couldn't quench.

His breath hitched, and the feel of her pulse—its steady rhythm within him—made him feel warm all over.

Images in his mind flashed of perfect, pink lips; lips that housed a sharp tongue no less, traversing over his, biting, sucking at his before making their way down his neck. He quickened his movements on himself, feeling the familiar tightening in his muscles, his desire culminating like a whirlpool. Building and building with each thought, each fantasy, each memory spiraling into thoughts of what he longed for.

The thought of that sharp tongue he'd grown so fond of sliding across his, licking his fangs. Leaving trails of warm saliva down his neck. Tracing the shallow, toned lines of his hips...

Cassius stifled his groan of release into his pillow as a mixture of relief and guilt overcame him.

He closed his eyes as he tried to catch his breath, his heart beating a fraction faster than it normally did. Coupled with Ava's pulse, the feeling made Cassius feel almost human again.

Five days.

That was less than a week.

Surely you can manage that...

Though, as Cassius left his bed to wash up, pushing through the familiar feelings of guilt, he knew it was a lie. But for Ava's sake, he would find a way to manage. After all, he'd managed hundreds of years without a mate, and thus far, two years without giving in to the pull of the bond.

Yes, five days would not make a difference.

At least, that was what he told himself before he allowed slumber to overtake him.

CHAPTER FIVE

AVA SMILED BRIGHTLY as Mal threw her duffel bag in the backseat. His hair had gotten longer, covering his ears; a true sign that it had been far too long since she'd seen her brother.

"Ready to get this fucking road trip started?" He looked positively as giddy as she felt.

"Abso-friggin-lutely!" she said as she settled into the passenger seat of his red Chevelle.

The car actually smelled clean, like fresh laundry detergent.

"You cleaned the car? For me?" she teased.

"A man has to keep his house in order every once in a while, right?" he jabbed back at her.

It wasn't entirely a lie.

Mal lived his life split between hotels, motels, and his car. Such was the nature of a musician and a hunter.

Mal was both.

He'd started to leave for much longer periods of time, ever since discovering Ava had been bitten.

She understood his reasons.

After all, finding a way to break her bond with Cassius was his priority next to finding the vampire who had killed their parents.

He chased dead end leads all while working tirelessly with his partner, Jake Dallas, and his hunter friends—Vinny, Tito, and Hunter—to eradicate the world of the evil bloodsuckers.

And the quest for answers, the promise that came from wielding a stake into the chest of those monsters... well, Ava understood its pull completely.

Still, she couldn't deny she missed her brother and had been looking forward to this one on one time with him since he'd brought it up only a few months prior.

There were eleven years between them, but despite the age gap, they had always been close. Growing up in their home in Massachusetts, with their parents, had been a happy, fulfilling life.

Eating junk food on the oversized couch with her brother, curled up in blankets, watching movies like *Halloween* and *A Nightmare on Elm Street*—in the dark—were some of her most favorite memories of her childhood.

While most children favored the likes of princesses and cartoon animals that talked, Ava preferred the thrill of a good horror movie. The way the anticipation built, drawing her to the edge of her seat until the scary part came and made her jump.

And strangely enough, it had been those films that helped her through the darkest moments of her life. Her parents' deaths. Moving to Chester to live with her aunt.

Becky Lee Michaels did not care for such things as scary movies. She only cared about the finer things in life.

Mal started the car up, and the radio blared loudly,

and Ava couldn't help but smile.

"I hear Skeet Ulrich is going to be there," Mal said flashing a smile.

Ava squealed with delight.

"I'm definitely meeting him, if that's the case." She could hardly contain her excitement.

"I heard they have a zombie run!" she said as she settled into her seat, ready for the long drive.

"They have a Carrie-style prom, too," Mal's voice hitched an octave as well.

"This is going to be so much fun," Ava said as she leaned against the window and watched all of Chester pass by in a blur.

***

The Silver Starling Hotel was quite ominous looking, set against the gold and orange hues of the setting sun. It looked less like a hotel and more like a haunted mansion.

It had been a long eighteen hours cooped up in Mal's car. They'd taken turns driving, naturally, but sleeping in Mal's car was not all that comfortable.

Her muscles ached as she stood on the pavement, her red skull suitcase and black duffel slung over her shoulder.

Mal arrived next to her, sans suitcase. He lived out of a backpack, anyway.

Ava had to appreciate the beauty of the fabled hotel. Tales of ghost sightings and stories of the many things it was used for throughout the ages had always intrigued her.

It looked as if it housed a plethora of secrets within its walls.

The inside, however, was not as beautiful as the outside. On the outside, it looked positively elegant, but inside it had been renovated to reflect a modern age. Stale blue carpet, a lounge with tiers of continental breakfast offerings, and slightly worn rubbery chairs.

The lobby was busy for eight p.m. Visitors bustled about as she watched the room.

Mal handed her a room key. "There's been a bit of a mix up and they actually booked us for two rooms, but I figured you wouldn't mind," he said as he started off in the direction of a hallway.

Ava followed quickly, dragging her skull suitcase behind her.

"There really is a God," she teased.

Mal scowled. "Really, Ava?"

"Would you have preferred a sock on the door instead?" She smirked.

"Oh my God, Ava!" Mal's voice hitched an octave and she laughed.

"I'm kidding, Mal, take it easy."

"I'm going to need to scrub my brain now, thank you."

Ava chuckled. Their rooms were right next to each other, as luck would have it, but Ava was still thankful for her own privacy.

"I'm fucking beat. Think I'm going to turn in early so we can get a head start tomorrow on the opening festivities," Mal said as he leaned against his door, twirling the key in his fingers.

"Okay." She shrugged.

"You should do the same." He raised an eyebrow.

Ava smiled. "Of course."

***

Hamlet's Bar was decently packed for a Wednesday night. Ava had heard that many of TerrorCon guests liked to partake in liquid refreshments the day before the convention, mingling with the guests. She wondered who she would see there, perhaps she'd run into Skeet Ulrich and get her picture. Maybe share a drink.

Who cares if he's old enough to be my dad, he's still fucking hot.

She'd forgone her leather jacket and band tee for the night, and instead, had opted for a black *Creature from the Black Lagoon* top with the sides cut out, a pair of tight black jeans, and her studded boots.

It didn't take long before some man—dressed in all black with more chains than an oil rig—offered to buy her a drink.

Which she gladly accepted. It wasn't as if she was incapable of purchasing her own. After all, she did have a fake ID. But at least she wouldn't have to pay, and if a man got too handsy expecting payment other ways, she kept her stake on her at all times. As well as pepper spray and a switchblade.

Ava downed her whiskey rather quickly, and her skin prickled with goosebumps.

Her wrist flared with heat, and she felt a startling feeling.

Like she was being watched.

She looked around the room inconspicuously, but she could not fathom where the vampire was in such a dense crowd. Or if there was more than one.

Her gaze caught on a man across the bar, surrounded by a throng of women. Dark eyes set amidst his olive skin, a hint of stubble peppered along his jaw. His black hair was short enough it curled around his ears, but long enough for him to have swept it into a messy coif. He held a beer in his hand, his red button-up sleeves rolled up to his elbows, a few select buttons unhooked. In the red light of Hamlet's, he looked absolutely devilish. She recognized him almost immediately.

Sam Kingsley.

The controversial demonologist from the show *Hell on Earth.*

Ava contemplated walking over and saying hello, but her thoughts were interrupted by a sheer wind that left her skin with goosebumps.

She turned without thinking and followed her vampire radar like a bloodhound.

And perhaps in a way, that's what she was.

For it was the black, slick blood running down her stake that she chased.

The fire as it consumed bones and supernatural muscle, disintegrating it into nothing more than ash to be swept away in the wind.

Her senses heightened, but her vision blurred only slightly, and Ava found herself out in the cold midnight air of Ansley, Oklahoma, in a patch of dark forest.

Lured like the unfortunate mortal such creatures thought she was.

"Hello," she called out, her heart pounding in her chest. She knew he was out there, and she knew without a doubt he'd make himself known if he thought she was but a frightened, innocent little thing.

Ava waited impatiently for him to make his appearance.

But all hopes of staking a bloodsucker went out the window when she heard a shrill scream, coming from the direction of the bar. Instinct overran her, as she turned and ran out of the woods and into the arms of danger once more.

CHAPTER SIX

CASSIUS DID NOT need an alarm or device to wake him up, as his internal clock always seemed to know when the sun had risen. Like the waves of the ocean moved in tandem by the draw of the moon.

He opened his eyes to the sunlight that poured in his room, and he knew it was still quite early. But the morning felt quieter than usual. Where the chattering of birds was usually heard this deep in the woods, there was nothing. Nothing but the near whisper of tree branches scratching against his window.

He sat up, stretching his arms, and the soft blankets fell from him, highlighting his fair torso. It was then he noticed that he felt... *empty.* His slow heartbeat still ticked away in his chest, yet...

He felt different.

Because the pulse he'd gotten used to feeling in his veins over the last two years was suddenly gone.

Because she is gone.

He pushed himself out of bed and forced himself to move. Lying in bed and moping about things he had no control over, or rather a slayer he had no control over, was not good for anything.

He quietly padded his way into the kitchen, nearly tripping over something on the floor. When he looked down, he sighed in exasperation.

In the midst of their return home, it seemed Jasmine and Tajiri had lost their clothing piece by piece in a rather unkempt trail of breadcrumbs. Cassius picked up the lump that was Taj's jeans and chucked them at the couch.

The kitchen, it seemed, had stayed clear of any of the remnants of Taj's and Jasmine's dawn arrival.

Thank heavens for that.

Cassius focused on the motions of his morning routine, taking note of the details if only to distract himself.

The sound of coffee percolating, the sizzling of bacon grease in the skillet. The flaky texture of his chocolate croissant.

He sat on the barstool, his bare feet touching the rims as he swiveled back and forth. A loud, mechanical chime sounded, the sound of his phone going off once again.

He debated leaving it, just in case it was Malcolm calling to harass him once more, but when he saw the number was one he recognized, he picked it up immediately.

Especially because he hadn't heard from the owner in quite a long time.

"Leon... how..."

"It's not Leon," a soft, sweet voice spoke on the other line, and Cassius froze.

"Cora?" He hadn't heard Cora's voice in ages. Since he'd left Oklahoma...

"I...I didn't know who else to call..." He could hear what sounded like a faint sob.

"Cora, what's wrong?" He tensed immediately.

"It's Leon... I...I think he's in trouble."

"What kind of trouble?" Cassius pressed.

"There was a murder, but I *know* he had nothing to do with it!" She let out a wail.

"You and I both know Leon is not capable of such things," he tried to reassure her.

"I think someone is trying to frame him..."

"Whatever for?"

"The club..." She sniffled.

"What club?"

"The Dark Hearts Club, of course." Cora said the name as if Cassius should have known.

But he didn't. He'd left in haste all those years ago.

Twenty-five years ago, to be exact.

In the middle of the day, without a word to anyone... Except for Leon.

He'd preferred it that way, for he wasn't certain who he could trust. He needed to be as far away from the Boracelli Coven as possible.

Far, far away from the vampire who had betrayed him.

Eden Boracelli.

"What makes you think I can help?" Cassius spoke as he readied about the kitchen, cleaning up his dishes rather quickly.

"Because you're the only person I can trust. I know you care for him as I do..."

Cassius made his way to his bedroom once more, opening drawers, pulling out clothes.

"Where are you?" he asked as he pulled a suitcase out from his closet. He hadn't used it in over twenty years, and it was covered in dust.

"Ansley." Cora's voice seemed to have calmed itself.

"Ansley..." he pressed. "Oklahoma?" Cassius's heart

stilled, which was no small feat considering it was a slow beat to begin with.

"Yes," she answered softly.

Oklahoma is a large state, I doubt it is in the same place Ava is visiting.

Do not get your hopes up.

"I will inform you when I arrive. Do not tell *anyone* I am coming. Even Leon. Do you understand?" He brushed off the dust from his suitcase before opening it.

"I understand," she said.

The phone went dead, and Cassius was left alone once more.

He knew, better than anyone, that Cora would not have called if the situation wasn't serious.

She knew just as well as Leon did that Cassius valued his privacy, that he wished to stay under the radar. Yet, he'd all but shone a damn spotlight the moment he marked a dying college girl in Boracelli territory, so perhaps fleeing Chester would be the smart thing to do to get his head right. If Ava could leave, so could he. At least, that was what he rationed.

His friend was in trouble and needed his help.

Eden had said once that he always had to play a hero, and perhaps she was right.

For Cassius did not have to think twice before he zipped up his suitcase and headed for the train station on the first train to Ansley.

CHAPTER SEVEN

"AVA LOOK OUT!"

Ava heard a voice holler from her left. Before she could even get a good look, she collided into a solid mass.

"The hell..." She recognized the solid mass too little, too late.

"What the fuck are you doing here?" She stumbled backward only slightly as large, muscled arms held her at bay.

"I could ask you the same thing." Dallas looked at her with curiosity.

Ava looked around his lumbering frame, toward Hamlet's.

Toward the sound of the scream.

"I don't have time for this... There's—"

"Ava, what the hell—" Vinny said as he came upon Dallas's behind.

Dallas's fingers gripped her arm, his grasp firm and warm against her chilled skin.

"You're supposed to be in bed!" Mal's voice cut in.

Ava looked at Dallas, and Vinny, and then to Mal.

"So are you!" She broke Dallas's hold and readied

her stake.

"You still didn't answer the question." Dallas crossed his arms, his bright blue eyes looking her up toe to head, his gaze strangely... possessive.

"Well, I was hunting a vampire, then I heard a scream and—"

"For the love of all that is holy—" Mal ran his hand over his face.

"And I was on my way to—"

"Ava, no one's there." Vinny took a step toward her.

"You don't know that, I just heard—"

"We just came from the same direction. Tracking a vamp. Probably the same one you were. There was no scream." His gray eyes were soft, his lips pursed.

"Oh hell no, I know what I heard!" Ava crossed her arms.

"Have you been drinking?" Dallas raised an eyebrow at her, his lips turning up in the corner only slightly.

"I'm not drunk, if that's what you're implying. Takes a hell of a lot more than one glass of whiskey to get me tipsy, thank you very much." She scowled at him, and for the moment imagined setting his annoyingly sexy smirk on fire.

The memory of just how enticing those lips could be came flooding back to her, and she pushed them down.

Now is really not the time.

"He's gone, probably scared him off." Mal spun his blade around like it was nothing more than a toy, his brown eyes carrying a hint of disappointment.

"That's because the lot of you are louder than a fucking freight train." Ava pushed past Vinny, knocking him in the shoulder.

Dallas sighed behind her as she approached Mal.

"This is supposed to be a trip for *us*. Not us plus the fucking Goon Squad."

"It wasn't supposed to happen like this—" Mal huffed as he headed toward the strip where Hamlet's stood out like a sore thumb.

"Forgive me if I don't believe you," she grumbled.

"It wasn't! Dallas and Vinny were tracking a vamp from upstate. They followed the trail here, that's all."

"Oh, so it's just a coincidence that the vamp led them straight to the freaking town where TerrorCon is? Maybe he's dying to check out the guest list?" The sounds of the bar carried, getting louder with each step.

"Yes, Ava. Not everything is a damn conspiracy theory." Mal slid his hands in his jean pockets.

"Although, if you think about it, it's the perfect place to find victims who are into that sort of thing." Mal cocked an eyebrow at her, and Ava didn't have to ask what he meant.

Though they didn't speak of it often, he'd been more than crystal clear in his concerns Ava would give in to the blood bond and fall for a tall, lean vampire with a penchant for leather and eyes like the brightest emeralds. She scoffed in response, rolling her eyes.

Never going to happen, Mal.

Trust me.

"Well, he's not likely to come back out now that we've spooked him, so it's as good a time as any to call it a night," Vinny interrupted them.

"Where are you guys staying?" Mal asked as he lit a cigarette.

Ava watched as he blew smoke into the cool air.

"The Silver Starling," Dallas answered. In the light of the neon signs, his muscles rippled in orange and red glow. The shadows fell on his expanse of skin from the open sides of his muscle tank, and as he shifted just a fraction. Ava could have sworn she saw the points of a star tattoo on his right pectoral.

A sight that immediately brought back images of just how taut those muscles were, the black lines standing out against his skin. The memory caused her to flush, even if it was only momentary.

"Funny, that's where we're staying." Ava shot Mal a suspicious glare.

"What are the fucking odds?" Mal grumbled between puffs.

***

Ava tossed and turned in the hotel bed. It wasn't terribly uncomfortable. In fact, it was a king size bed with rather soft bedding. But even if it had been made of clouds, Ava would not have been able to rest.

For her mind swam with thoughts of screams, chilled skin, and a solid slab of abs.

"Tomorrow, Ava. You need to sleep. Can't very well be looking like death if you want to rub elbows with all the guests at the con tomorrow," she spoke the words aloud to herself.

Still, she couldn't fathom the serendipitous occurrence that put Jake Dallas in her path once more.

It had been two years since she'd last seen him. While Mal had ventured home in recent months, Dallas's presence was not to be found. He'd always traveled with Mal, and his sudden absence was startling to Ava.

Why did she care if he came home with her brother, at all?

Because you like playing with fire, that's why.

Truth be told, just because they'd shared a kiss—a very hot kiss to be exact—did not mean they were bound to one another in the slightest.

Yet, Ava could not help but wonder if their secret

kiss had anything to do with Dallas's sudden lack of availability.

The way he'd gripped her arms in the forest, smirked at her with those deceptive blue eyes, as if he was challenging her to make a move.

Challenging her as he had in the boxing ring of the Bat Cave. To anticipate his movement.

Well, two can play at that game, Jake.

CHAPTER EIGHT

AVA SCANNED OVER her appearance in the hotel mirror, a long oval-shaped thing that appeared older than it probably was. Still, she was thankful for a full-length mirror so she could take in her look from top to bottom.

It was only the first day of the convention, and thus, she had decided to try and keep her outfit simple, and comfortable. Her costumes wouldn't make their debut until the sun was down... as long as the vampires kept themselves at bay long enough for her and her brother to enjoy themselves.

She smoothed her hands over her overalls, one strap left unbuttoned in the haphazardly dressed look which seemed to pull her casual *Chucky* outfit together.

A knock on her door pulled her from her thoughts as she finished putting on her lip gloss.

When she opened the door, it was not who she expected to see.

Instead of Mal dressed up as Michael Myers, Dallas stood there. He leaned in the doorway, his blue eyed gaze traveling over her body, leaving her with a sudden warmth that both annoyed her and intrigued her.

"Morning, Kitten." He smiled.

"What the fuck do you want?" She twisted her lips as she braced her arms against the doorway, blocking him from any further entrance. He looked just the same, standing in dark wash jeans, and a Jack Daniels muscle tank. His tan arms exposed, as always, showing off his pentagram tattoo and a new addition which looked like a black cat with a crescent moon in between its eyes underneath it.

Interesting.

"I was heading down to the lobby to grab some breakfast. Thought you might want to join me."

"And why would I want to do that?" She narrowed her eyes at him.

He had the audacity to laugh. A low, dark chuckle that made Ava nearly stop breathing for a moment.

It had been two years.

Two years since she'd discovered the monsters in the shadows. Since she'd trained with Dallas.

Since they'd kissed.

She could still remember the taste of his tongue in her mouth, his hands as they coursed over her, touching her everywhere.

Though Ava was not looking to jump from fire to fire, she could not deny such a kiss had diluted all the chaos, even if it was only short-lived.

For when she kissed Dallas, she felt *nothing.*

No thoughts of Cassius, no memories of bloodied bodies in the corner of a frat house basement, no knowledge of vampires and other creatures of the night.

All she could feel was *him* against her thighs, his searing lips against hers.

She let herself wander into the darkness, lost in all the unsaid words and unspoken desires that clearly existed in the space between them no matter how hard Dallas insisted against it.

Dallas's words broke her memories once more.

"Because I know how you get if you don't have your daily dose of sugar and caffeine."

The way in which he smiled was rather flirtatious. Ava could not hide the smirk on her lips as she turned away from him. She would not let him see.

As if perfectly on cue, her stomach growled. Rather loudly for her liking.

"Fine. But this is purely out of survival alone," she said as she left him standing in the doorway. She dug around in her suitcase to retrieve her crossbody bat purse.

While she knew he should stay in the doorway, a part of her wanted him to follow her inside. Wanted him to come in, lock the door, and kiss her again. Run his hands over every inch of her. Fill her head with *nothing*, to take out all the chaos and replace it with fire...

Focus!

She threw on her purse quickly and hurriedly escaped through the doorway, past the attractive lumbering hunter in her way.

She did not wait for him to catch up. Instead, she kept her pace quick.

"If I didn't know any better, I'd say you're *not* happy to see me," he said teasingly as he caught up to her stride. They walked down the neutral-toned hallway, a silent race to the elevator.

"And what makes you think you know better?" she said as she grabbed hold of her purse strap. Gripping it tightly as she refused to look at him and his sexy, smug face.

As she came to the elevator, she pounded the down

button impatiently.

Dallas's body slowly enclosed her proximity, and before she could even have time to process it, the doors dinged and opened.

She hurried inside and mashed the buttons just as he entered the space. Once the doors swished closed, it was just the two of them.

Dallas hit the hold button and the elevator stopped in place, before taking his spot next to her.

Although he only stood next to her, with an ample amount of space no doubt, she couldn't deny that her heart was pounding.

It's from the run to the elevator...

Not.

But Dallas's voice broke her thoughts as he put himself in front of her.

"Because of this..." He slowly encroached on her space, and Ava's body heated in response. He was only inches away from her, his arms leaning out, hands gripping onto the elevator bar on both sides of her, and she was trapped.

But being a prisoner of Dallas's gaze, the way he was looking at her...

It was so radically different than he had been two years ago when she'd last seen him. Hesitant to even kiss her, at first.

He leaned closer, his lips only a fraction away from hers, and every bone in her body told her to fight back, to yell and scream at him, yet she couldn't find the words.

She also felt the instinct, the desire to close the space between them and kiss him until she couldn't breathe.

"If *I* meant nothing to you, Ava, you wouldn't have blinked an eye when you saw me."

"It's been two years, Dallas. You had your chance." Ava looked up at him, taking in the sight of him, all the finer details. His bright blue eyes, chiseled jawline. Dark hair that looked shorter than she remembered. His full lips. Despite the thirteen-year age difference between them, he still didn't look a day over twenty-five.

All the familiar warnings came flashing back.

He's too old for you.

He's your brother's best friend.

Ava tried to push the thoughts away.

She felt her heartbeat quicken as she moved to release the hold button, but he stopped her by stepping in her way.

"Two years I've been fighting to try and forget you... forget what happened between us... because I thought..." He licked his lips and reached out his hand, pushing a strand of her dark hair behind her ear.

"What did you think, Jake?" she breathed as her heart pounded away in her chest. She could not break his gaze, and she could not deny that his touch felt more than welcomed.

"I thought... I thought maybe *you'd* gotten over it. Regretted it, maybe?" Dallas's gaze dipped to her lips, and Ava couldn't help herself.

She'd never been good with self-control, or regrets. And in the presence of Jake Dallas, both seemed to evaporate completely. Even after a two-year absence. It was as if they were right back where they had started, the elevator becoming a boxing ring.

Ava fell into his kiss, savoring the taste of him on her tongue once more. Her entire body melted, and the embers of yesterday sparked once more.

Dallas's hands found her hair, his fingers twisting her locks, pulling her closer.

She parted her lips, settling her hands on his hips, her fingers grazing over the open expanse of his skin, visible from the loose open sleeves of his muscle tank. Close enough, she could feel him harden against the flesh of her exposed thighs, and the realization only made her wish for more.

To see how far he'd let her go.

Yet, the image that filled her head as his lips caressed hers was a shocking splash of cold water to her system. One that she'd become all too familiar with in Dallas's absence. It seemed any time Ava decided on partaking in any kind of romantic pleasure, the thoughts were always there to douse her with their chilly remembrance.

Memories of glowing green emeralds, of soft lips on her wrist, surged forth. Of her blood rushing to the surface, of a hot tongue searing her wound.

Of Cassius.

No, this isn't supposed to happen...

Last time...

The images she'd tried to keep locked away rushed to the forefront with new intensity.

The very *thought* of Cassius's angelic Calvin Klein-model features elicited a soft moan from her lips, and she hated that it did so. Hated that he'd taken this from her, too. There was nowhere she could escape the looming presence of Cassius.

He was everywhere.

She hated that his thoughts pervaded her consciousness night after night, day after day.

Dallas did not know that, and instead he responded to the sound of her desire by trailing his lips over her jaw.

The memories of the night Cassius bit her melded with ones that never happened, and ones she knew *could never* happen. Ones Ava couldn't help but think of in the dead of night, alone. In the crevices and cracks of her dreams and nightmares. Ones that she could only quiet with a touch of her hand and regretful release.

Cassius's lips biting at hers, his soft tongue and lips leaving trails of ice and fire along her neck, her breasts, biting at her nipples, his fangs pulling back to show the hint of a smile she found sexy as hell.

She fought the thoughts the only way she knew how. The only way she'd been fighting them for two years.

"Dallas..." she groaned into his mouth as she wrapped her arms around him, deepening their kiss, her tongue eagerly seeking out his, letting her hands travel down his chest, settling at the waistband of his jeans.

She needed this.

Touch.

Release.

To chase the ghosts away that haunted her thoughts.

To chase *him* away, the vampire who marked her.

And then, as if her thoughts could speak of their own accord, Dallas stopped his motions.

He stopped, looking her over once and he just... walked away and pressed the hold button.

Ava was left dizzy from the onslaught of feelings, thoughts, her head spinning from Dallas's sudden departure from what would have been a rather lovely way to start the day.

He stepped aside and cast her a smug smirk.

"I'm happy to see you too, Kitten."

"Fuck you," she bit, her fingers wiping her mouth of the remnants of Dallas on her lips.

The elevator doors dinged, and Dallas exited the space.

***

"What's your deal, you've been in a mood all day? I thought this trip would, you know, make you *happy, not* pissy," Mal said as he sat down in one of the many chairs in the empty panel room.

"I am happy, she bit.

"Are you still pissed about last night?" he asked curiously.

Ava crossed her legs and sipped on her iced coffee. "You could have told me you took on a job," she said as she flashed a disapproving glare at her brother. Attendees filtered into the empty room, lining up in the seats.

"I wasn't *supposed* to be working a job, so there was nothing to tell." Mal crossed his arms and kicked his legs out, crossing them at the ankles as the rest of the attendees filled in the spaces of empty chairs.

"I won't be mad if you let me in on it."

"Ava..." Mal sighed.

"Practice makes perfect."

"I can handle it," he rebutted.

"I know you can. But I want in." She held her ground.

In the light of day in the hotel, she could see Sam Kingsley's face much better.

He looked less like a devilish creature and more like a sexy lumberjack in the flannel shirt he was wearing over his Van Halen shirt.

Mal did not respond to her inquiry, and she knew he wouldn't. He still wasn't entirely on board with her interest in staking vamps. He'd trained her, along with Dallas—with the intent that she could *defend* herself should the situation arise, especially given the circumstances surrounding her claiming. But he had not anticipated that she would be *good* at slaying vampires all on her own. That she would search out the bloodsuckers of her own accord and disintegrate them into ash.

The doors shut on the panel room with a loud thud that echoed in the expansive space, and the chatter in the room quieted.

Ava focused her attention on Sam Kingsley and the moderators of his panel, abandoning the conversation at hand with her brother.

It seemed like an eternity of rehashed information as the moderators reiterated Sam and his story. How he'd gotten into the study of demonology, the success of his show, *Hell on Earth.* He'd answered the questions with finesse and even a smile. But something about the way in which he did so, Ava thought there was an air of annoyance in his voice. As if he detested such events as this.

"We will now open the floor to questions, but please keep them short, and to the topic of this panel. No personal questions about Mr. Kingsley's life, please."

Mal huffed. "Only people with shit to hide say that," he grumbled next to her.

"Maybe he just likes to keep his *work life* and his *personal life* separate, unlike some people I know," Ava bit back.

The string of attendants started to line up in front of the microphone, but no questions would be asked.

As the doors slammed open and in walked three police officers, and TerrorCon security, all while making quite the entrance.

"This panel is over, and all of you are to return to your rooms at once," the officer spoke loud and clear, and chatter erupted once more.

He bellowed louder, and the chatter turned to silent hushes.

"There has been a murder at this convention. Please, remain calm and return to your lodging."

Ava's eyes widened and Mal pursed his lips.

"Ava..."

"It can't be a coincidence..." she whispered to her brother as the room erupted into chaos once more.

"Mr. Kingsley, please come with us," another officer spoke plainly at the table.

"Of course, officers. Anything I can do to be of assistance."

As Sam quietly stepped down from the stage, Ava could not help but steal a glance at him, and she could swear for only a moment his eyes glowed red.

CHAPTER NINE

CASSIUS STEPPED OFF the train into the murky, dull station. He looked around the concrete building, which was not as busy as he imagined it would be. Then again, it had been a long time since he'd last visited Ansley...

The memories pushed forth and he could not squash them, for there was no pulse to distract him and he was alone.

Eden scowled in disgust at the small station.

"If this station is any inkling of the town we are looking at, I don't like it already."

"What is wrong with middle America? Is that not the ideal location for happy families?" he asked curiously.

"I prefer something with a little more taste."

"I know what you prefer." Cassius's lips turned up in a smile.

"The covens will expect more," she sighed as Cassius reached for her hand with his free one.

"The covens expect us to look the part, Eden. If we at least look like we are trying to make a family—"

His voice trailed off and he could not finish the

sentence.

Eden stopped and turned to face him.

"I know you have as much at stake as I do, I am sorry, I—"

Cassius dropped the bags at her uncharacteristic show of vulnerability. He settled a hand at her hip gently. Careful not to push, to ease her strain only slightly. Neither of them had asked for this arrangement.

An engagement.

It wasn't a proposal of love in the least.

With his father dead, his mother was left alone and in danger from many enemies. She'd done the only thing she thought she could to keep herself safe. She'd approached the very coven, the very woman who'd forced her and his father out to begin with.

Isabella begged for forgiveness and protection in exchange for what Francesca had long desired. An Aurelian stud to unite the Boracelli bloodline and create the perfect vampire.

Eden had fared no better; forced into the arrangement because of her ties to the late Marcellus Medici. Though the extent of their ties had not been disclosed to him at the time, even Cassius knew he would have said yes regardless. To keep them safe, both his mother and Eden.

He'd considered her a friend, at least. Arranged marriages happened all the time, after all, and some were not as lucky to even know the person beforehand. It was not an ideal situation in the least, but the arrangement was for more than just a wedding.

They needed to produce an heir; a legitimate one. Or, at the very least, as Eden had claimed, look like they were doing everything they could do as such.

Something that should have come rather easy to the both of them, given their long-standing friendship with one another.

But neither seemed to be able to treat the engagement as anything more than a death sentence.

But perhaps it did not have to be that way, Cassius thought.

Friends become lovers all the time. At least, that was what he believed from all the years he'd studied mortals, befriended them. Read their literature.

Friendship could very well be the foundation a good marriage was built upon.

And with nothing but time on their hands, perhaps...

Perhaps, one day it would be love.

The clock sounded with a large chime, pulling Cassius from his thoughts.

"Cassius!" the lilt of a young, feminine voice called to him, and he could not help but smile. She looked different than he'd seen her last.

While Cora had always bore eternal youth, being forever sixteen, he had to admit she looked much older in the modern day.

Her once bountiful red curls were now poker straight, mixed in with thick golden blonde streaks. Her bright blue eyes still sparkled like the sky on a sunny day, and her complexion was as pink as ever.

She's fed recently...

Cora all but ran toward him, her pointy black heels clattering against the dull, unswept floor. She threw her arms around him, her round breasts squishing up against him in a tight hug.

Cassius lightly hugged her before removing her ever so gently.

"Cora."

"You look just as I remember!" She squealed in delight. "How long has it been?"

"Too long, I am afraid. Although, I cannot say the

same for you, my dear." Cassius shifted his stance as Cora collected herself.

"Yeah, well, when in Rome... you know," she said as she flashed her baby blues at him, running her fingers through her waist-long locks.

"Do you like it?" She smirked.

Cassius was not sure how to proceed with compliments when it came to Cora.

While he cared for the girl, being his best friend slash pseudo father figure's adoptive daughter and all, he did not wish to stoke Cora's insatiable crush.

He'd always known she fancied him.

But Cassius did not see her as anything but a fond family friend.

A child, even, given Leon had taken her in and considered her such.

Leon never married or claimed a mate. He'd lived alone, an eternal bachelor, until he had stumbled upon a dying young prostitute in the middle of England. She'd been bitten, but it seemed her sire had been disposed of by hunters, and as his body lay dying, decaying—Cora was in dire straits.

Leon sealed her wounds himself and took her in. He'd always wanted a child, but as his inclinations were toward men and he was not an Aurelia, producing an heir was not in the cards for him. Taking Cora in had changed many things for him; suddenly the rumors of his predilections ceased.

"If you like it, that is what matters most," he answered.

Cora frowned only slightly. "I thought you liked long hair."

"What I like, my dear Cora, should be of no interest to you," he said politely.

Cora rolled her eyes and motioned for him to follow

her.

"Why must you always be so bloody noble?" She sighed.

Cassius followed her outside the train station to a limousine that lay in wait.

"You did not have to bring the cavalry, Cora. I said to remain low key."

"Cassius, Cassius, when will you accept that you deserve the finest things in life?" The driver opened the door for her and she slid in, her eyes never leaving his as she pat the seat next to her.

He languidly slid in as the driver took his luggage.

When the door closed, he felt strangely overwhelmed by the scent of chemical freesia.

"My dear, when will you discover that the finest things in life are not things you can buy."

Cora smiled, her ruby red lips stretching sweetly.

"Everything and everyone have a price, Cassius. Even you."

CHAPTER TEN

AVA LAY BACK on Mal's bed, staring at the ceiling.

"The one time we actually get a chance to do something fun and it's over before it even began."

"I would have thought you of all people would be most excited about a murder at a horror convention," Mal sighed.

"I would be more excited if I could leave my hotel room and hunt some fucking vampires. Or murderers," Ava huffed.

"And here I thought you wanted to spend time with your dear old brother." A knock in the door interrupted them both.

Mal slowly ambled to the door and Ava leaned up on her elbows.

"Dallas..." Mal didn't seem particularly excited at the arrival of his partner.

"Where's the rest of the Ghostbusters?" Ava said, not taking her gaze from the ceiling.

"Tito and Hunter were headed down to Hamlet's for a drink. Vinny is out on patrol," Dallas said gruffly, and Ava could feel his presence like a poltergeist, even though she was certain he was far enough away he could not see the rise and fall of her breath as it quickened from his voice alone.

There'd been plenty of times the memory of Jake Dallas had crept into her dreams, popped up unannounced in her wandering mind. But Ava was no fool, and she did not expect Dallas to show up on her doorstep, begging to sweep her off her feet.

A kiss was only a kiss, no matter how delicious it was.

It wasn't a relationship, and she would not delude herself into thinking Dallas wanted more. But then he showed up at her door and boxed her in in the elevator, kissed her with desire, a hunger that she couldn't deny, and for once she was glad Mal stood between them.

For Ava was not certain what would happen if it was just the two of them behind closed doors.

"I thought the place was on lockdown?" Mal said, perking up.

"That's what I came to tell you. Seems word around the hotel is they've got nothing. Just stirring up shit to try and see what comes up. They had nothing on that Kingsley guy, he was out in minutes 'Cause he lawyered up."

"Figures," Mal grumbled.

"What about the convention?" Ava said as she sat up, looking at the two hunters.

"What about it?" Dallas settled his eyes on hers, and Ava couldn't help the flutter in her stomach at the sight.

The way he looked at her was as if...

As if he, too, were glad to have a buffer.

"Please, tell me they're not going to cancel..."

"Nope. No canceling. But there will be a curfew. I guess they're changing the hours or something. Con hours will end at like six, or something, through Monday."

"Oh thank God!" Ava said with relief.

"Well, that's good news for us. Means we can hunt this thing in peace," Mal said as he got up and headed toward the cooler, grabbing a cold bottle of water.

"You want one, Dallas?" he asked nonchalantly.

"Sure," Dallas responded, just as the bottle nearly missed his head. He caught it so quickly, Ava could actually see the breeze rustle his hair.

"Well, shouldn't be a problem as long as *some people...*" He shot Ava a smirk before continuing. "As long as some people can keep quiet."

"Fuck you, Dallas," Ava shot back as she rolled her eyes.

Dallas let out a dark laugh.

"I bet you couldn't stay quiet to save your fucking life," he taunted her.

"Unlike you, I know when to keep my mouth shut." She huffed as she got up and headed for the door.

"Where are you going?" Mal asked.

"To Hamlet's. I need a drink."

***

Ava tossed back another shot of whiskey.

Hamlet's was packed with bustling congoers all worked up about the "bust" that never was. It was all anyone wanted to talk about in the damn place. She'd already started to tire of the "where were you, what were you doing when..." discussions no sooner than she arrived. She hadn't even seen Tito or Hunter, despite Dallas's claims they'd gone to have a drink. Perhaps she was too late.

Why she let Dallas get under her skin was a mystery to her.

She was usually so much better at dealing with cocky assholes like Dallas. They were a dime a dozen on campus, not to mention she'd been a cheerleader in high school; a label that brought with it plenty of assholes in the wake of her pom-poms.

But there was something about Dallas, about the way he spoke, the way he looked at her, that made her want to put him in his place, but also...

There was something about Jake Dallas that called to some deep, dark corner of Ava that she didn't quite want to acknowledge.

So, instead, she drowned the thoughts with shots of whiskey.

What would Cas think?

The thought was intrusive and came out of nowhere, startling Ava. She opened her eyes, slamming the shot glass down on the bar so hard from the shock she thought it may break.

What the hell?

Why would I even care what Cas thinks about... anything?

Even the thought of the vampire seemed to make her blood rush. Though, the scar on her wrist did not flare with heat as it usually did. Instead, she found herself slightly chilled as images of his hurt expression on her porch filled her brain. The sight of such things left her feeling guilty, as if causing the vampire pain of any sort was... wrong.

Ava cleared her throat, her gaze catching the bartenders once more.

"Can I get another one, please?" she said boldly. She did not want to think about Dallas or Cassius. Not now. Not here. Though, it seemed the further she tried to run from them, they always followed, showing up in the darkness as she lay in bed, in her wandering daydreams.

The bartender nodded in response, and Ava let out a deep breath.

"Where's your boyfriend?" A cool voice pulled Ava from her wayward thoughts. She turned to see a familiar face, and as her gaze settled on the man, the scent of fire and teakwood filled her pathways. It was a most masculine smell, and it was rather divine to Ava's senses. Paired with the dark, inviting eyes and boyish grin on Sam Kingsley's face, Ava couldn't help but gasp in awe.

"Ummm... I don't have a boyfriend," she said sweetly as she swiveled on her barstool toward the delectable demonologist.

"You were in the front row at my panel with that guy, I thought..."

"You thought what?" Ava said with a smile, feeling the effects of her whiskey and her natural confidence mingling together to heighten her boldness.

Sam Kingsley may have been a celebrity, but he was still at the base of all things, a regular man. A man with an extensive knowledge of the supernatural who was also quite attractive, smelled heavenly, and was hitting on her.

"I thought a woman as beautiful as you would *have* to have a boyfriend."

"Does that line work on all the girls, Mr. Kingsley?" Ava said with a sexy smirk.

Sam leaned on his defined arms against the bar. Ava could see the shape of his muscles all along the curve of his shoulder, the slight outline of his chest through the flimsy black t-shirt he wore.

"Call me Sam," he said, flashing her a smile. "And no. I know what you must think, a guy like me travels all over the place and picks up girls in every city, but I can assure you that is the furthest thing from what my life is like."

"Oh really, Sammy, do tell me how utterly boring and unaffected your super-cool life really is," Ava said with a chuckle as the bartender dropped off her shot.

"Is that what you want to hear about? My boring life? No theories on cryptids or creatures of the night? Or about the murder looming over this convention?" he said with a raise of his eyebrow.

Ava felt a strange feeling in her stomach at Sam's words. Her head felt slightly hazy, likely from the alcohol, and she half-considered telling him everything.

The truth about who she was.

What she was.

A slayer.

It was a truth she hadn't admitted to anyone, not even her closest friend, Ember.

Sam waved at the bartender authoritatively.

"The last thing I want to talk about is fucking bloodsuckers," she drawled, noting the sparkle in Sam's eyes.

"Thank heavens. Most of the time that's *all* people want to talk about with me. Exorcizing demons is my *job*, but it's not who I am, you know?" he said with a deep sigh, his shoulders relaxing. Ava had to tear her sights away from the man; the look of vulnerability on his face was too much for her.

His dark hair fell in his eyes, the mixture of blue and red lighting from the bar casting shadows on his boyish features.

Her skin prickled with goosebumps and a shiver ran down her spine, like a splash of ice water.

"Unfortunately, I know *exactly* what you mean," she grumbled. The bartender made his way over to them, catching Sam's attention.

"I'll have one too, thanks," Sam demanded; the bartender nodded back in response.

"I didn't catch your name, *bellus*," he said as he angled himself closer to her.

The motion caused Ava's blood to heat even if only a fraction, and her insides felt tingly. Ava rolled her eyes, not at all impressed by Sam's compliments. But for the moment, she did not care about the demonologists' social skills, and she engaged him, anyway.

After all, was this not what she wanted?

To go on an adventure far away, to forget the sinfully delicious vampire who had gotten too close?

To meet new people, discover new experiences?

"Call me Ava," she responded with a wink as she raised the glass the bartender finally dropped off alongside Sam's.

"Beautiful name for a beautiful woman," Sam said, flashing her a smile. "Very well, *Ava*. What should we toast to?" The lighting of the bar and throughout Hamlet's had shifted into a smattering of red and orange hues as a band took the stage, readying to play.

When the beginning notes of "Bark at the Moon" filled the air, Ava couldn't help herself.

"How about... cheating death," she said with a laugh. "To living to hunt the monsters another day."

"I can definitely toast to that," Sam said with a grin.

CHAPTER ELEVEN

AVA'S BACK CRASHED against the wall as the door slammed shut. Sam's hands roved down her side, settling on her ass as he squeezed. Her head felt slightly foggy and warmth blossomed between her thighs as Sam pressed his hardness against her.

A giggle escaped her throat as she grabbed him through his jeans, eliciting a deep growl from his throat.

"Ava..." he groaned, his hands finding their way up her back, into her hair. His lips crushed against hers and he tasted bitter, like whiskey and day-old coffee. But for the moment Ava didn't care.

There was only this moment.

There was only *him*.

The feel of his hands, of his dick rubbing against her through his constrictive jeans.

There was only the feeling in her stomach of growing arousal, and a deep *need* to sate the madness building within her.

To *forget*.

To lose herself in someone, so she could not feel the

heat of her scar, could not think of glowing-green emerald eyes, or the memory of fangs piercing her skin.

Sex always did the trick to make her forget, even if the forgetting was short-lived.

"Let me guess, you don't do this sort of thing, normally, right Sammy?" she said darkly and bit her lip, looking up at him through hazy eyes.

Sam's hotel room was dark, and they hadn't moved to turn on the lights. Though in the darkness, she could still make out his fine features, and it only added to the spinning sensation in her head and body.

"I don't..." he whispered as he kissed her right below her ear. He moved his lips farther down her neck, stopping over the throbbing vein in her neck, a deep groan leaving him as he did so. "You smell so good..."

"I, um... need to use the bathroom," Ava said as she took a deep breath. Something about the proximity of his body to hers, the way his hands gripped her, his voice...

Her entire body felt alive, but she was cold. Freezing, actually... and every ounce of her body begged to feel his touch, to feel the warmth of his body against hers, all over. Her head was spinning, and nothing was making sense...

"Of course," he breathed deeply, the sensation of his breath on her skin causing her blood to heat.

Ava swallowed nervously as she backed away slowly, feeling her way to the bathroom in the darkness. When she found her way to the door, she entered, shutting the door quietly after turning on the light.

The room had been renovated, but it still retained some of its original charms in the crown molding, in the ornate pedestal sink's design.

Ava gripped both sides of the sink, forcing herself to look up at her reflection in the mirror.

Her short hair was slightly disheveled, her dark eyeliner smudged out slightly farther than the corners, and her lipstick had worn off. Likely, from the extensive kissing marathon they'd engaged in on the way back to his hotel room.

"What are you doing?" she whispered to herself in the mirror. The bright lights were jarring, and she had to blink a few times to adjust.

Ava turned the faucet on, splashing cold water on her face, if only to cool down. Her entire body felt flushed and warm away from him, as if she was boiling from the inside out.

Though she did not expect an answer—from her reflection or herself—Ava could not deny in the solitude of Sam's bathroom, she was certain of two things. The first was that this moment was a once in a lifetime moment.

The host of *Hell on Earth* was on the other side of the door, waiting for *her*.

The second was that something about the whole situation: the bar, the toast, the walk back to the hotel room—

I don't even remember the walk back to the hotel room, Ava realized as a knock sounded on the door.

I know I only had three shots...

"Are you okay in there? You're not sick, are you?" Sam's voice sounded from the other side.

Ava noted the slight concern in his tone, and her shoulders eased as she pulled her gaze from the mirror.

"No, I'm okay... uh... be out in a minute..." she said as innocently as possible.

Ava shook her head, the thoughts gone like dandelions on the wind. Her stomach flipped with anxiety, her nerves standing at attention.

That's probably just the alcohol.

She squared her shoulders, glancing at her reflection once more, and pushed it down. Forgetting all about her nerves, about her instincts. It wasn't like her to get cold feet, especially when it came to sex. Then again, Sam Kingsley wasn't some college frat brother or biology tutor with no shame. He was an established, thirty-something-year-old man who looked like trouble, and Ava *loved* trouble.

She sucked in a deep breath and turned on all her charms as she shut the faucets off and exited the bathroom into the darkness of Sam Kingsley's hotel room... like a lamb to the slaughter.

CHAPTER TWELVE

THE DRIVE TO Leon and Cora's home was longer than Cassius had anticipated. He sat stone still next to Cora, like a statue. She tapped away on her phone mindlessly, and for the moment he was glad. He rolled the window down only a hair, taking in the sights of the world as they passed him by.

Nothing looked familiar, but then again, he knew it wouldn't. It had been years since he'd been in the town, and historical landmarks, businesses, and establishments were falling through the cracks all across the United States, across the world, really.

A part of him was saddened by this, that the world he'd once known was buried underneath a layer of skyscraper and steel, that the ornate, romantic buildings and idyllic towns had all shifted into cookie cutter replicas of one another; indistinguishable.

I wonder if that donut place is still here...

Cassius's thoughts were interrupted as the car pulled up to Leon's house, and Cassius couldn't help but smile.

It seems as if some things will never change.

Leon's house looked just as he'd remembered. It was as preserved as the day he'd last seen it, as if time itself had evaded Leon and his microcosm.

Though Cassius was not prepared for the onslaught of memory that pushed forth through his thoughts.

Cassius sat on the veranda with a tall glass garnished with a small lime wedge. He wasn't entirely certain what alcohol it was, the liquid was as clear as water.

Leon smiled as he took a seat next to him, but Cassius could barely look up from his glass.

"I'm sorry about your father," Leon said softly.

"I know I should feel upset, or angry... or something..." Cassius sighed deeply, closing his eyes. "But I don't."

"What do you feel, Cassius?" Leon leaned back in his wicker chair, resting his ankle on his knee, balancing his long, sinuous elbow on the arm of the seat, his kind eyes staring at Cassius as if he could see right through him, down to his very soul.

"Nothing," Cassius said as he ran his fingers up and down the side of the glass, feeling the cool condensation against his fingertips. "I feel nothing, Leon. I feel numb." Cassius took a sip of the drink, noting the prominent taste of lemon on his tongue and it reminded him of home.

"I know the two of you had a... complicated relationship, but I know without a doubt your father loved you."

"He left me, Leon. He left my mother and me because he thought I was not his, and when he found out I was... I thought for a moment things would change, that we could repair what he'd broken, but..."

Cassius took a long drink, nearly emptying his glass as a mixture of emotion overcame him.

"I thought, perhaps, we could make amends, and maybe things could be like they were before. The three of us, a happy family... Well, five of us, really, if you counted Theodora and Sylvie."

Leon did not press him, only waited for him to continue.

"But he had to go back to the covens. Because somehow, some way, he'd been found out. His actions put us all back in the spotlight, and it was his actions that led him to his death. Led my mother to fend for herself with the only bargaining chip she had."

"You," Leon said softly.

The words fell over him like a heavy blanket.

"I had no choice in the matter," Cassius said as he finished his drink. The remains of dusk fading into night.

"You always have a choice, Cassius. Even when it feels like the cards are not in your favor, you have the choice. It is just not always an easy one."

"I did not want to watch my mother struggle again without him. You know the man had his enemies, and now that he's gone... I couldn't risk it. I—"

"A noble notion from a noble son." Leon leaned forward, pulling the glass from Cassius's hands.

"But nobility is not always heroic. It masquerades as selflessness, as martyrdom.

When there is no one left for you to fight for, Cassius, who will fight for you?"

Cassius blinked the thoughts away as the car pulled up around a cobblestone driveway, in front of a large Grecian fountain.

"It looks just as beautiful as I remember," he said in awe as the driver opened his door.

Cora looked up from her phone with a smile.

"Well, you know how much of a stickler Leon is about *preservation*," Cora said with a roll of her eyes.

Cassius took a moment to take in the spectacular features of the Victorian-era home, from its wraparound porch to the high windows and textured roofing.

A warmth blossomed in Cassius's chest, and relief overcame him as he walked up the steps, following the driver who was carrying his luggage. As soon as the doors opened, Cassius could not help the smile that crossed his face.

He felt *happy*.

The winding staircase and its ebony railing, the parquet flooring that looked freshly waxed, the ornately-carved entry table which boasted a vase full of peonies and lilies freshly cut from the garden. The air smelled of flora and fresh wax, and the scent relaxed him in a way he hadn't expected, his shoulders easing up for the moment as joy settled in his stomach.

Though Cassius had called many places home over the course of his long life, none had felt like such. He looked around the preserved foyer, taking in the beauty of it all.

He felt as if he was finally *home*.

"Cora, sweetheart, where did you put my—" Leon's crisp, clear voice echoed in the entryway as he rounded the corner and stopped dead in his tracks as he looked at Cassius.

In many ways, it was as if he had not changed at all, but in so many ways, he was different.

His eyes were still the same, bright and sparkling in the artificial lamplight against his olive complexion, his dark hair swept back behind his ears. His glasses had changed, from the round academic ones to sleek, rectangular frames that made him look older, more refined. Though, he'd forgone his stuffy academic-style suits and traded them in for a simple pair of khakis and a blue button-down silk shirt. He looked more like a young golfer than an ancient vampire.

"My word, has Hell frozen over?" Leon said with a genuine smile.

Cassius could not help but return it with one of his own.

"Last I checked, no."

Leon walked with a steady pace toward Cassius, reaching out and pulling him into a tight embrace.

"It's been far too long, Cassius," Leon said as he hugged him.

Cassius's arms found their way around the man who did not look a day over thirty.

"I missed you, too," he said as he hugged him back. Once the shock of his arrival had worn off, he held Cassius by the arms a short distance.

"Do not get me wrong, I am overjoyed at your company, but I must ask... what exactly are you doing here?" Leon asked curiously, his gaze traveling from Cassius to Cora then back again. "I thought you were laying low, trying to—"

"Cora called me..." Cassius answered before Leon could finish.

"Whatever for?" Leon said, his dark eyes shooting up in alarm.

"She said you were in trouble, that there's been some deaths..."

Leon's face went pale, a feat for a vampire such as he.

"I... I have things under control," Leon said, his entire demeanor changing completely.

"No, you don't. You're too focused on your breakup, too wrapped up in your damn project to see that the club is in danger!" Cora huffed angrily.

"Leave Grayson out of this, Cora! Those deaths have

nothing to do with the club!" Leon bit at her.

"Those deaths have *everything* to do with the club, Leon! You cannot trust your investors, I have told you, I—"

"Cora, leave us." Leon's voice had taken on a much more demanding, authoritative tone that left Cassius rather surprised. In all the years he'd known Leon, he had never truly known the man to yell or command anyone.

Not even Eden...

"But Leon—"

"I said, leave us." Leon turned, flashing a dark look at Cora. Cassius noted her eyes looked as if she were on the verge of tears, and she actually had the audacity to stomp her foot like a petulant child in frustration before storming out of the entryway to God knows where.

Leon picked up Cassius's suitcase and motioned for him to follow.

"Come, we have much to catch up on," Leon said as he headed to the opposite side of the house with Cassius's luggage held hostage.

CHAPTER THIRTEEN

AVA STIRRED IN the dead of night, her eyes fluttering as they tried to adjust to the darkness. The heavy hotel blanket fell from her instantly, the chilly air hitting her skin, causing a shiver to race down her spine. She wiped her eyes and let out a groan as her head throbbed.

A quick glance to her left and the events of the night came crawling back as her gaze fixated on a shirtless Sam Kingsley who clung to his pillow, dead to the world.

Ava's gaze trailed over his exposed torso, and she swiftly lifted the covers only a fraction, just enough to see if she was really dreaming or if she'd lost her marbles completely.

Her cheeks heated at the sight, as reality set in, as the memory came flooding back to her.

The memory of Sam's heated kiss, of the dizzying feeling she'd felt in his presence, likely from her alcohol consumption. Although, she was still quite puzzled about that. Ava was no stranger to drinking, and it usually took far more than three shots of whiskey to do her in.

Perhaps, it was the heat of the moment, perhaps, it was the shots, perhaps, it was the fact that he was Sam-freaking-Kingsley, and he was attractive, famous, and her number one celebrity crush.

He was also extremely knowledgeable and well versed in all the things Ava knew now to be true. Though he was a demonologist first, in the last year or so he'd been building up interest in his to be released *Unbound: Vampires in History & Among Us* documentary, something she had wanted to ask him about but refrained from after his admission that was more than the things he hunted, the things he spoke about on television.

Ava dropped the sheet once more, her senses coming back to her slowly. Aside from her splitting headache, she felt a stinging pain along her inner thighs, where her scars lay.

The memory of how she'd gotten such scars always made her feel uneasy, but she was not embarrassed by them by any means. They were a reminder of her survival, the moment her entire life changed.

The vampire who'd carved through her flesh like butter, leaving her to bleed out had since met his demise, by her hand no less, but it seemed more often than not, the few men who'd actually seen the scars since she obtained them were more than put off by them. They found such scars unsightly, unflattering, and as one brutish asshole had stated, *a turn off.*

But Sam did not seem to mind one bit, as the memory of his teeth nipping at the flesh they covered caused Ava to flush once more. It hadn't hurt at the time, but now in the dead of night after the fact, they did.

Ava closed her eyes, recalling how Sam had run his

tongue over them, causing goosebumps to form on her flesh before diving in to taste her.

Remembered how he'd devoured her like she was his last meal.

And as if such a thing were a curse in itself, the memory of her pleasure melted into memory of the *most* blissful feeling she'd ever felt. Ava's mind wandered to the very thing she'd undoubtedly been trying to forget, the thing she could not seem to escape.

Bliss...

Cassius.

Her mind instead wandered to a wet, warm tongue on her wrist, sealing her wounds with venom, to the blissful feeling of fangs piercing her skin, the rush of blood to the surface.

Even the memory made her heart race, her blood heat, and her thighs clench, As if Cassius were not merely a figment of memory in her brain, but as if he were lying next to her instead of the delicious demonologist who was rather skilled with his tongue.

And in the dark, with her eyes closed... she could pretend he was.

Such a desire caused shame, guilt, and anger to overcome her, as it always did, but Ava did not have time to wallow in her qualms about the sexy vampire who she'd left in Chester, far away from Oklahoma—far away from Sam Kingsley's hotel room.

A scream startled her out of her fantasies, bringing her back to the here and now. Ava sat up straighter, flinging the covers away as she all but leapt out of the bed.

She hurriedly felt around on the floor for her clothing, dressing as quickly as she could, nearly tripping over her stake, which had fallen out of her boot from the haphazard, clothes-tearing session.

Fuck, I hope Sam didn't notice that...

Another scream, and Ava was out the door in a flash, never looking back as she followed the sound of terror like a moth to a flame.

CHAPTER FOURTEEN

THE MOONLIGHT CAST an ethereal glow on Leon's expansive backyard, turning the grass a shade of deep blue. The trees on the edge of his property loomed over with their full, leafy bounty bristling in the wind. Cassius thought it was a rather beautiful sight, even if it reminded him of *her*.

Eden.

"Why do you insist on running?" Cassius asked as he hunched over, his hands braced upon his knees, catching his breath.

"Ah, yes, well, this is what happens when one no longer needs to hunt for their food. You become fat and lazy," Eden taunted him.

"I will have you know I am in top shape, my dear."

"Your undead lungs say otherwise," she said with a laugh.

Cassius looked up at her, his gaze much more haunting than it should have been, given the light of the full moon on this night.

The sounds of smooth jazz filled the air, faint like a ghost. They were far from the party at hand, and a part of Cassius longed to go back.

To where it was safe, to where it was warm.

"Perhaps, if you stay in one place, Edie, for more than five seconds you will see just how lively I can be."

Eden turned to him, her ruby red lips curving into a sinful smile he knew all too well.

"Perhaps, I like to be chased, darling. Perhaps, I like the thrill of the hunt."

The moonlight shone on her fair skin, making her bright sapphire blue eyes glow in its wake.

Cassius stood tall, finally catching his breath as she stalked over to him slowly. When she stood only inches away from him, her jeweled eyes caught his with interest. She reached out slowly, pushing a lock of golden hair behind his ear.

"Forgive me, Eden, but I always thought you more of a hunter than prey," he said darkly, feeling the effects of his champagne, the chill of the wind, and the stirrings of desire in the pit of his stomach.

"Perhaps, for once, Cassius, I want to be captured," she whispered against his lips, and Cassius did not wait as he obeyed her and captured her lips with his.

Leon motioned for Cassius to take a seat, and he did so. It seemed that despite his looks, not much about Leon had changed. Including his hospitable demeanor, as he tried to make Cassius as comfortable as possible. He'd been living with Tajiri and Jasmine for nearly thirty some years and among the three of them, Cassius was the one who took care of most things regarding their abode, and it felt good to be waited on, for once.

"I was not certain I'd ever see you again, Cassius, after our last meeting," Leon said softly.

The memory of their last meeting would never truly fade away, no matter how many years went by.

The rush, the urgency.

Cassius could still feel it as if it were no time at all, even though it had been thirty-five years.

"Cassius, sit down. Please. We can talk about this—"

"There is nothing to talk about, Leon. I am leaving this god-forsaken hellhole and I am never coming back..." Cassius bit as he brushed past Leon with his suitcase.

"You are being irrational right now because you are angry, and rightfully so. Eden has that effect on many people."

"She killed him, Leon! She killed my father—"

"Cassius..."

Cassius could feel the tears forming in his eyes, and his heart felt as if it were in his throat at the words, the reality of them hitting him like a bag of heavy bricks.

"Because he found out the truth. The child—" Cassius's throat tightened, a mixture of grief, anger, and frustration coursed through him.

He should have known better. It wasn't the first time Eden had kept the truth hidden from him, and he felt a fool for abandoning such notions that she could change, that she was different.

That she loved him.

She'd never loved him. She'd only loved Marcellus Medici. He'd kept her secret, stood by her in her darkest hour. Yet, she'd fought to preserve her own name, preserve her ranking. Had the covens discovered the truth, that Eden and Marcellus had been carrying on an affair, that their affair had resulted in an illegitimate heir—despite the fact that that she'd lost both her lover and her child—

The covens would surely bring her to justice for her actions. After all, she was bonded to the vampire, and that evidence was as solid as the earth beneath his feet.

The treaty between the covens would fall into ruin, and it would be war. There would be no trial.

His father, Lucius, posed a threat to her existence, and she killed him so she could live another day. So she could kill, lie, and chase the ghosts that haunted her until there was no magic left to dull the pain.

The worst part was Cassius understood her reasons, but it didn't make any of it right, and it left a sour taste in his mouth.

He could not trust her.

Not now.

Not ever.

And she'd had the audacity to threaten him. As if she could command him like some obedient dog, as if she could make him see he was the irrational one. Her words filtered through his brain, the memory of her expression as her eyes filled with tears.

"So help the gods, Cassius, if you walk out the door..." Her voice shook with fury, with anger. "I will not give you the choice next time. You will obey me," she growled.

"There is always a choice. The fact you fail to understand that, is why I will never be yours to command. You cannot control me, Eden."

Darkness swelled in Cassius's vision as he closed his eyes, trying to fight the hunger inside of him that begged for blood, for release.

A body to sate his turmoil; to quiet the monster inside. What had Eden turned him into?

"I need to leave," he said, his voice echoing in the cavernous room.

***

Cassius brushed his fingers along the glass, feeling the cool water against his skin, pulling him from his painful thoughts.

"What about your mother?" Leon pressed, following Cassius as he hurriedly ran down the steps. The way Leon spoke made Cassius stop dead in his tracks, his shoes squeaking on the freshly waxed floor. He turned on his heel, taking a look at Leon before he answered, stilling his breath.

"That is why I came here, to see you. To tell you what I must do. I need you to make sure she is safe, that neither my mother nor Eden will come looking for me."

"You can't be serious," Leon sighed.

"I am. I do not belong here, Leon. I never have. I was not made to be a pawn in some grand scheme erected by the Boracellis, or to be some stud for breeding. I was not meant to love... I—"

"Cassius, you are hurting. It is natural to feel this way, it does not mean—"

"How can you defend her? After all the pain she's caused you?" Cassius felt enraged as Leon's words settled on his ears.

"I am not defending her. I am merely concerned that you are too emotional, right now, and you are not thinking straight."

"I need to be as far away from Eden Boracelli and the god-forsaken High Covens as I can get. I'm done playing their games, Leon. This ends with me."

"And where will you go?" Leon's eyes took on a glassy shimmer of their own as he stood in the foyer, his hands at his side.

Cassius could see the pain in his eyes, and his heart sank.

He'd miss him the most.

"Yes, well, I was rather... what did you say? Emotional?"

Leon smirked. "Yes, I think that was the word."

"Not one of my finer moments," Cassius said with a raise of his eyebrow.

"You were in pain, Cassius."

"I was. I was damn heartbroken. Everything I thought was real... it wasn't. And Eden...

"I just couldn't stand to look at her anymore. She'd fallen further into darkness and knowing the truth, about what she did to my father and *why* she did it, knowing that Marcellus was the reason for her madness..." Cassius sighed deeply as he sat back in his chair.

"But I am not here to talk about Eden. That is ancient history."

"She is still alive, you know."

"I know."

"Really?" Leon said with a raised eyebrow of his own.

"The cabin I reside in, in Virginia, is on the border of Boracelli territory."

"Is that so?"

"A wise man once told me to keep my friends close and my enemies closer. And that is what I do. I keep a low profile, I get by. I stay under the radar. Octavius and his lackeys are too focused on expanding their territory. I don't anticipate them coming back until—"

Cassius shifted in his seat, feeling his throat tighten once more. He wanted to say the words, wanted to tell Leon about Ava. About claiming her. If anyone knew about blood bonds, it would be Leon. The man was a wealth of knowledge and had never steered Cassius wrong before, but Cassius could also feel a strange protectiveness at even the thought. Though he trusted Leon more than anyone, he felt a strange possessiveness to keep her all to himself. The world had taken much from him, but in its wake, he had found her.

He looked down to his wrist, and for a moment he could have sworn he felt the faint thrum of a pulse in his veins; like a ghost, it slipped away just as soon as it had made its presence known.

"It doesn't matter. All that matters is that you apparently need some guidance of your own," Cassius said with a smirk.

Leon rolled his eyes.

"Cora has always had a flair for the dramatic. I assure you I am fine. She is just blowing things out of proportion."

"Tell me about the deaths."

"The local law enforcement has been trying to pinch me for years because of the club, but I can assure you I run a legitimate establishment."

"Club?" Cassius asked curiously.

"The Dark Hearts Club. To the humans, it is just an average club, nothing more to see than strippers and adult entertainers, but it is built for our kind, it is—"

"A blood den."

"Yes. I've been conducting my research there for the last thirty years. Studying the link, the attraction and sustainable relationship between mortals and vampires."

Cassius felt his blood run cold, and the faint buzzing danced in his veins again. He shook his head, trying to dispel the tricks of his mind. After all, Oklahoma was a large state. But something about Leon's words hit him hard in the chest.

Sustainable relationship.

Cassius had known about Leon's academic undertakings. He'd been studying their biology for centuries at this point. The thought that perhaps he'd uncovered something about the *link* between his kind and the mortals, perhaps could be of use to him somehow, someway... Thoughts of Ava flooded his brain as the flutter of a pulse caused his heart to race.

You're just working yourself up.

You need to relax...

"Cora believes someone is trying to frame you. An investor or someone interested in the club."

"I think she watches too much television."

"Is it possible, though?" Cassius asked.

"The recent string of murders indicates something that is not of our kind. Though the killer has gone through a great deal of trouble to try and present the bodies as vampire victims, which means they are familiar with our kind."

"What do you mean not of our kind?"

"I cannot be certain as I don't have enough evidence, yet. If I could get my hands on the toxicology reports, I would be able to corroborate my theory—"

"English, Leon."

"I believe the one responsible for the murders is not a mortal, or a vampire. I believe, and it is just a hunch at this point..."

"What? What is it?" Cassius felt on the edge of his seat.

Leon looked back at him with a cold expression.

"I believe it is an Incubus. It's been nearly a hundred years since one was seen in these parts, but the details are similar..."

"An Incubus? A sex demon?" Cassius raised his eyebrow. He'd been fortunate enough to evade demons, save for a brief time in the '20s... but even then, the demons he'd known then were run of the mill crossroad demons, save for a few Succubi. He'd never come into contact with an Incubus before.

"As I said, I cannot confirm or deny my theory

without substantial evidentiary findings."

"Perhaps I can help with that," Cassius said, feeling bold. "I am quite the professional when it comes to morgues," he said seriously.

Leon only smiled. "Perhaps you can."

CHAPTER FIFTEEN

THE BRIGHT FLUORESCENT lights buzzed loudly in the hallway, their vivid light only adding to the pounding in Ava's head. She brought her arm up to shield herself from the light for a moment, adjusting to her surroundings. The deafening sound of a thud sounded to her right, and without thinking Ava turned to follow.

The hallway loomed in front of her like some carpeted labyrinth, twisting and turning until the sounds of struggle, of wet sucking became louder. With her stake poised in her hands, Ava leaned against the wall, keeping as quiet as possible. The scar on her wrist heated, and she could feel an energy in the air that was most profound.

Thrall.

Ava knew without a doubt the vampire was near, and she took a moment to catch her breath.

As she turned the corner, stake at the ready, her eyes widened in surprise. The vampire turned, eyes glowing with anger. The short red-haired woman had her claws wrapped up in Vinny's jacket, and Ava could see he was struggling to fight off the young woman who looked like she couldn't be a day over sixteen.

"Let him go," Ava said as she rushed toward the vampire.

The woman reared her teeth in defense, a deep hiss escaping her throat.

Ava moved to push the vampire off but was not so lucky.

The vampire let Vinny go, but within moments her long nails were wrapped around Ava's neck, and her blue eyes were filled with rage.

Vinny slid down to the ground, coughing, trying to regain his breath.

"Ava... what the..."

Ava wrapped her hand around the vampire's wrist with all her might.

The red headed vampire focused her angry gaze on Ava like a hypnotizing snake.

Lust started to form in Ava's belly, her head started to feel foggy.

The telltale effect of thrall hard at work, vying to make her pliable to be vampire chow.

The very same images that always accosted her, especially when feeling a vampire's thrall, filtered in through her thoughts without warning. Thoughts of glowing green emeralds, of the warmth of Cassius's mouth on her skin, how it would feel against her throat.

How his fangs would feel deep inside her flesh.

Ava could not help the moan of ecstasy that escaped her throat as the vampire *giggled*.

She'd been in this exact position quite a few times, and thanks to Mal and Dallas's training, she was more than well versed in how to combat the vampire's Jedi mind tricks.

Ava fought against the thoughts, battling them with memories of her own; vicious ones that would forever be rooted within her, would haunt her nightmares forever.

The memory of her parents' bodies, cold in a puddle of blood on the living room floor.

Of Ross, her college boyfriend, his life drained from him, discarded like a shell in the corner.

Of the vampire's sneer as he plunged the knife in her skin; of the pain.

Ava leaned forward, bringing her heavy hand up, fingers grasped around the stake.

A groaning Vinny moved to stand, but a loud banging sound distracted them all, and before Ava knew it, the vampire headbutted her.

"The fuck!" Ava said as she dropped her stake, her hands moving to her head, which was throbbing now more than ever.

Ava stumbled, falling to the floor, her vision blurred.

Out of her peripheral vision, she watched the vampire disappear into the shadows of the stairwell.

"Fuck, Ava... Are you okay?" Vinny said as he moved in front of her.

"Did she bite you?" Ava asked as she squinted her eyes shut, the light more intrusive now than when she'd awakened.

"No, I'm not bit... but... there was a girl... in the stairwell... I—"

"Fucking hell..." Ava groaned.

Vinny's hands softly wrapped around Ava's wrists, and the touch made her jump. His hands on her skin were rough to the touch, but he pulled at her hands gently.

"Let me take a look" His breath was hot on her skin, and he smelled vaguely of cigarettes and whiskey.

"I'm fine, I—" But Ava did not have the will to fight him, and she was suddenly very tired.

"Stay with me, Ava," Vinny said, his voice slightly panicked.

"I'm tired..." Ava said as his hands settled her own in her lap. He brushed his thumb against her eyebrow, the motion bringing him closer to her.

"Shit Ava, you're bleeding pretty bad. Probably going to need some stitches." His voice vibrated on her skin, and she could feel slumber beckoning her.

"Nothing a good sleep can't fix," she whispered.

Vinny wrapped his arms around her, and she felt him pull her up. He placed her arm around his back, his arms holding her at his waist.

"In a little bit. First things first, we gotta get you cleaned up, okay?" His voice was soft, even.

It reminded her of Cassius.

Ava could hear the clicking of the lock, the electronic whirr that told her the door was ready to open. Vinny held her closer as he entered the doorway, his arms tight around her. Ava brushed against his chest, breathing in his smokey scent.

It smelled like Mal.

Like home.

"What the hell, Vinny? What happened?" A dark voice broke the silence.

"Where's Mal?" Vinny asked as he maneuvered them over to a bed.

Ava fell onto it instantly, wanting to curl up on the pillows.

"No, no, no sleep yet," Vinny soothed her.

Ava groaned.

"Fuck if I know. Do I look like his mother to you?" the voice bit.

Ava knew that sarcasm, that bite anywhere.

Dallas.

"Well, considering we were just attacked by a fucking vamp, I'd be a little more concerned."

"He said he was meeting up with someone," Dallas said as he lifted Ava up, pulling her into his lap. A part of her felt angered by the motion, but another part felt a satisfying warmth as he held her up while Vinny moved about gathering supplies. She could not help as she sunk back against him, closing her eyes. She took a deep breath, focusing on the sounds of the hunters' voices.

"Well, for the moment that's probably a good thing," Vinny said.

"Did you get a good luck at the bloodsucker?" Dallas asked, his hands tight on Ava's arms, and she could almost feel a tremble in them.

Then again, it was probably the mixture of a hangover and a rattle to the brain.

Because nothing made Jake Dallas tremble.

The man was built from steel.

"Yeah, you could say that. Got pretty up close and personal," Vinny answered definitively.

"I saved his ass," Ava said, flashing a smile.

"Damn right you did," Vinny's warm voice sounded close to her face, and she could feel his rough fingers on her temple, touching a spot on her head that stung. A cold liquid mixed in with the blood, with her flesh, the sting somehow worse than only moments ago.

"Fuck... that stings."

Dallas's hand slid down her arm, resting just above hers, his thumb brushing her knuckle.

"I know, I'm sorry. I'll try to be quick, here," Vinny said as she felt a pinch through her skin, and the pain heightened.

"Christ!" Ava lurched forward. "Aren't you supposed

to like, warn me? Give me an anesthetic or some shit?" Ava grumbled.

Vinny ignored her, focusing on his tight stitching.

Dallas grabbed her hand and squeezed.

"Squeeze if it hurts, okay? That way Vinny gets to live another day," Dallas whispered in her ear just as another stitch went through.

Ava squeezed his hand tightly, so tightly she thought her own fingers may break.

"Good girl," Dallas whispered, his breath hot against her neck, his voice dark and somehow relaxing.

The tone, how faint it sounded, Ava knew only she could hear him. She was not sure how to feel about that, not sure how to comprehend anything except the innate desire to fall into Dallas or Vinny or whoever's bed it was she was camped out on.

"Okay, that just about does it," Vinny said as he cut the last piece of thread and Ava felt all the tension, all the exhaustion as the evening's events caught up to her.

"Can I go to sleep now?" she murmured.

"Yeah, you can go to sleep. We'll take turns taking watch," Dallas said matter-of-factly.

"Watch?" Ava said as she pushed out of Dallas's hold, curling up on the unmade bed, pulling herself against a pillow that smelled vaguely spicy, like smoke and cinnamon.

It wasn't a terrible scent, and she breathed it in, letting it fill her lungs.

"Well, I mean you were hit in the head. Probably should just keep an eye on you to make sure you don't have a concussion," Vinny said as he put away the needle, thread, and alcohol.

"Don't tell my brother," Ava grumbled.

"Wouldn't dream of it, Kitten," Dallas said as he ran

his hand up and down her back, the motion lulling her into a well-deserved sleep.

CHAPTER SIXTEEN

CASSIUS WALKED ALONG Ansley's Main Street, taking in the sight of the bars and shops, the businesses that littered the sides of the street. Like Chester, it was positively perfect in design, right down to the shiny mailboxes that were without graffiti or marking.

The last time he'd been on Main Street, it had looked quite different. In fact, it was a different time altogether. Where the White Barn Candle shop lay, Cassius could still see fresh in his mind the café that existed there once upon a time in the days after Prohibition. The ornate bronze trim molding still existed around the exterior, reminding him of the shimmer it had in the moonlight of long ago.

When he'd been a different man.

A man who thought he'd found love but was sorely deceived. What existed between Eden and him was not love. It was lust, half-truths, and lies. It was fabricated, arranged by those who knew nothing of love.

Not really.

Though it was late, the streets were fairly empty. The neon lights of the bars cast hazy pink, purple, and blue shadows on the cobblestone street, reflecting in the puddles in the cracks in the sidewalk, a most relaxing sight. When he finally found himself in front of The Dark Hearts Club, he stopped to take in the sight.

Cassius had been to a few blood dens back in his early years as a newborn, that first time being the night he'd agreed to venture out with Marcellus Medici and his friends, with Octavius, Eden's brother. His friend.

At least, at the time Octavius was not a foe. In fact, he was the closest thing Cassius had to a best friend. Someone in his corner, no matter what.

He'd never cared much for the blood dens, feeling a strange sense of protectiveness over the men and women who chose a life of servitude to their *immortal gods.*

Many entered the ring of servitude willingly, but there were those who simply had no other option.

It's no different than a whorehouse, Cassius.

Octavius's words still made his stomach twist several centuries later, what with the way he'd carelessly spoke them, Cassius should have known his value for life was more in line with his sister's than either of them would have liked to acknowledge.

The outside of The Dark Hearts Club was lit by the same pink, blue, and purple neon glow that seemed prevalent on all the bars on this street, but the shimmering black obsidian pillars, the sleek glass...

It was all very modern, sensual even. Cassius's stomach growled once more, his mouth watering at the prospect that lay behind the walls of the club.

Leon's club.

Cora had claimed Leon was being blackmailed, that someone was out to frame Leon to try and gain the upper hand, gain access to the club.

To cut him out of the equation completely.

But why?

Cassius knew his answers lay on the other side of the door. Though the nerves flooded his body, his wrist flaring with heat as his blood warmed, and thoughts of fresh, warm blood pushed forth.

It wasn't just the thought of blood that persisted in his memory like a record on repeat.

Oh no.

It was the thought of his fangs piercing soft, pale flesh, of his fingers brushing away silken chocolate locks, trailing his fingertips along her skin.

Ava's skin, in particular.

The woman he'd *claimed.*

It was the fantasy of tasting her blood, letting it run down his throat, letting it fill him to the brim until he was so sated on it there'd only be one way to calm the fever that fresh blood brings.

Cassius swallowed nervously, sliding his hands in his pockets.

I can do this.

It's just a little recognizance.

I'm just getting a lay of the land, just checking things out.

I am stronger than my instincts.

Though as he thought the words, he knew it was more than that. He chose to believe the lie instead, as he pulled open the heavy glass doors and headed into The Dark Hearts Club.

The inside was just as cool in color and temperature as the outside and didn't look all that different from the average strip club.

Cassius had done his fair share of gallivanting with Tajiri in the years since he'd shown up in Chester, if only because he enjoyed the company of the man rather than the thrill of hunting. After all, he didn't hunt anymore, but he'd always enjoyed being a part of the world, even as a wallflower keenly observing life as it went on in his midst.

Though the world may have changed around him, some things remained constant forever. Parties, sex, alcohol; the high of youthfully being free... of living in the moment... Those things never grew old for humanity.

Cassius casually stalked over toward the bar, taking in the sight of the club and its inhabitants before him like a cheetah observing its prey. He'd forgone such vicious things as hunting, as feasting on the living— there were always blood dens like The Dark Hearts Club throughout the years, which made feeding much more streamlined, but Cassius never felt right about it, not after what had happened to Marguerite... The only woman he'd ever fed off of, even if it was only a brief time.

Instead, he traded such things in for a steady supply of corpse blood from the local morgue. Before long, he'd have to make the trip, if the dryness in his throat and mouth was any indication.

His gaze scoured over a dancer on the main stage, teetering on her Lucite heels, wearing some sort of black vinyl contraption that strategically covered just enough of her pale flesh to be considered a bikini. He watched, frozen in his tracks as her crystalline-blue eyes caught him, watched as she ran her hands up from her navel, squeezing her breasts softly before sliding them around her throat. She rolled her head back, long, dark hair cascading over her shoulders, lit up in the blue neon. The sight stirred a mixture of emotion in him, of desire and memories long forgotten.

Memories of *her.*

The wicked queen.

Eden.

His fangs *ached* for the blood coursing beneath the dancer's neck, which her fingers traced over suggestively. Her tongue graced her pouty lips just before she took the flesh in between her teeth, and Cassius forced himself to break her gaze.

I do not have time for this.

This is not what I came here for.

He moved to the back of the room quietly, observing the foxes and the vixens of the den. And as he hid in the corners, watching life as it lived right before his eyes, he noticed a familiar head of red hair turning the corner, looking around panic-stricken before a man stepped up and blocked his view.

Cora looked around the man once more, her eyebrows knitting together in slight worry before they too disappeared into the shadows, into the crowd.

Cassius sidled up to the bar, which wasn't looking overly populated, at the moment. In fact, there were only a few club goers spread out between the barstools. The same pink, blue, and purple neon lit up the back of the bar and all the frosted liquor glasses, and Cassius noted the large smoked glass mirror that stretched the length of the bar. He could see his reflection, illuminated by the neon glow.

He'd been in several blood dens over the years, but this one was the first since he'd gone off fresh blood completely.

Though the times had changed, he knew the structure would not, and without a doubt the real attraction was below deck, and likely, one needed special access to attend the actual dens in which feedings took place. Which is why the upper level was so important. Something needed to distract the humans so they would not be the wiser to what was really going on. The smoke and mirrors were a part of life for a vampire. One needed to blend in seamlessly into the background, into the fabric of life in order to live another day, undetected.

"Slow night?" Cassius asked nonchalantly as the bartender came to his end of the bar. The man was quite stocky, the sides of his head shaved, while a sleek, generous coif of hair was gelled into a perfect shape on top of his head. His strategically cut and lined facial hair only added to the brooding look this man had about him, and he leaned against the bar, swishing around a toothpick in his mouth.

Behind him, Cassius could hear the music changing, signaling the next stripper to take the stage. The melody of some man crooning about "preying on you tonight" and hunting one down to eat them alive filled the air.

"No, actually, I'm kind of glad there's a break. Must be a big event or something over at the Starling. This place has been packed nonstop since that fucking convention rolled in. Not that I'm complaining, though," the bartender said as he dragged a clean rag up and down the sleek black marble bar.

The neon, the marble... even the mirror.

Everything about the place felt familiar to Cassius, and when the first notes of "Cherry Pie" by Warrant started to play, Cassius couldn't help the smile that formed across his face.

Memories of the first time he'd met Taj, in a club in the mid-eighties, pushed forth and Cassius had to appreciate the finer details. But, unfortunately, he was not here to appreciate the ambiance.

No.

He'd spent nearly all his life in and out of bars, clubs, and cafés, so he knew better than anyone the best source for information on the town happenings was the man who poured the drinks. The anonymous ear of a bartender was worth its weight in gold.

"What can I get you?" the bartender asked as he swished his toothpick around in his mouth again.

Cassius eyed the lit expanse of bottles, noting the labels were top shelf. Leon always did prefer the finer things in life.

"What is the oldest wine you have?"

"Oldest? Like shelf life or..."

"Aged," Cassius said.

"Up here, the oldest I got is this Cab." The bartender brought the bottle over to Cassius, who inspected it. The label was not particularly helpful, but it did say the wine was a vintage, bottled during the early nineties. He preferred a well aged Bordeaux, but it would have to do.

"I'll take a glass, please."

"Shit, I never thought I'd see *anyone* else drink this sour cherry shit. Only the owner requests it, which is why we keep it on hand."

"Surely, he won't mind," Cassius said with a smirk.

"I won't tell, if you don't," the bartender said with a smile as he poured the wine.

"Thank you," Cassius said as he swirled it around, letting the aromatic notes fill his airways. He took a deep breath before taking a sip.

Sour my ass.

"Ah. Delicious. Your owner has good taste."

"He thinks he does, anyway." The bartender chuckled. "I'd rather get shitfaced on a good scotch than over some stuffy old wine, but what do I know. I just work here."

Cassius figured it was now or never and decided to go for the kill.

"Have you heard anything about that case... the... murder at the Silver Starling? They ever find the guy who did it?" Cassius said as he leaned casually on the bumper rail of the bar, looking nonplussed. He took extra attention to speak casually, eradicating the refined touch of enunciation he'd garnered throughout the years. Though it wasn't something he utilized frequently, he could make himself sound modern, natural. Like any other twenty-four-year-old.

"Actually, they tried arresting my boss for it, which is crazy. He might be an eccentric dude, but he ain't a killer."

"Eccentric?" Cassius couldn't help the smile that formed on his lips.

Well, that's one way to describe Leon.

"Yeah. Lives in this old creepy house, keeps to himself, mostly. Aside from his weekly visits here, that is. I swear he's either perpetually single or gay, even though he hangs out with this smoking redhead." The bartender whistled.

Cassius took another sip of his wine.

"How does one get access to the dens downstairs?" Cassius said as if he was asking for the weather.

The bartender's smile faded, replaced by an unreadable, impenetrable one.

"How do you know—"

"Your owner is a friend," Cassius answered softly, and the bartender pursed his lips. When Cassius had thought his venture had failed, the man spoke.

"What kind of friend?"

Cassius felt a relief come over him and he sipped his wine once more, draining the last bit. The liquid came too quickly, and some of it dribbled down his chin. He casually wiped it away with his thumb before speaking.

"Why, only the best kind," he said with a smile,

exposing just the tip of his fang.

"Unfortunately, we close in an hour, so... the den is booked for the remainder of the evening."

"I can make a reservation?"

"You can come when the club opens and speak with Louie. He's in charge of the basement, and... payment, of course."

Cassius slid his hand into his pockets pulling out his wallet.

"Thank you," he said as he counted out a small stack of bills that were probably too much for the sole drink, but he did not think twice about leaving a large tip.

The man had been more than agreeable to answering his questions. As Cassius turned on his heel, readying for his exit, his gaze settled on the stage once more. The woman on the stage looked familiar with her lithe, pale frame dangling from the pole, only held up by the crook of her knee latching on for dear life. She pulled herself around the pole slowly, angling to get a look at the crowd before flexing her leg straight up the side of the pole as if she had no bones in her legs at all.

Cassius watched as she pushed away once more, feigning disinterest as she tried to escape the confines of the neon light of the stage.

When she turned to face the audience on her left, toward him, his heart stopped.

Crystalline-blue eyes stared back at him once more, long, straight red hair falling over her pale shoulders down to her waist, the swell of her pert, round breasts straining against her tight blue, triangle bikini top that looked like it was barely held together by string.

"Like what you see?" The bartender jabbed him with a chuckle.

"I, uh... need to go," Cassius said as he turned away, sliding into the shadows and away from Cora's line of sight.

CHAPTER SEVENTEEN

THE BLOOD WAS everywhere. Saturated in the threads of the carpet, streaked against the floral wallpaper. The bodies, lifeless in the corner, discarded like trash. The eyes of her parents, once so full of life were now nothing but soulless voids.

Ava reached out across the space between, but it was too distant. There was nothing she could do. Nothing could bring them back. Nothing could turn back time.

Her vision was blurry, mascara streaking down her cheeks like black oiled tears. She wiped them away, smearing the makeup all along her cheeks. She saw what she'd missed all those years ago.

The puncture marks in her father's neck, all along her mother's wrists and forearm.

And the world turned to dust and debris once more, the wallpaper dissolving into the dark, dank walls of a frat house basement, and Ava was no longer reaching for her parents.

She held her hand out in the darkness, and something reached back.

Warm, soft fingers stroked her wrist, grasping around her, pulling her closer.

How desperately she wanted to follow, wanted to rise from the depths of the puddle of blood, and fall into the arms of her savior.

But when she looked into the eyes of her hero, she knew he was no savior.

For the fangs he bore and the blood that stained his porcelain skin would never go away. No, this gallant angel of death who had saved her life was not a hero.

He was a monster.

He killed people, people like her parents. Like the monsters who had killed Ross, who had left her alone to die. But he'd spared her, for some reason...

Ava rose from the puddle of blood, which had turned from blood to ash. The embers surrounded her like the dust and leaves around her ankles on a mid-evening walk in Chester in the fall.

Ava let Cassius pull her close. Close enough he could wrap his arms around her waist, close enough she could run her hands up his heathered-gray shirt and feel the solid expanse of his chest beneath her fingertips. Close enough that his breath on her skin could elicit goosebumps and make her blood boil like a witch's cauldron on Halloween.

"What are you waiting for?" he whispered, his voice sultry and smooth in the dead of night like some beautiful lullaby.

Ava blinked, looking around, trying to fight the fog that had settled in her brain, and all around them.

They stood in the open, underneath the moon, where she was acutely aware they were indeed alone. No one would find them here.

Not Mal, or the hunters.

Not Dallas.

Certainly not Dallas.

No, in the corners of her subconscious, they were truly alone. She leaned into him, gazing up at him through her long lashes into his emerald-green irises. The shadows fell across his angelic face, the blood from his fangs dripping down his chin almost black in the light.

It would be so easy to just... give in. To let herself submit to the salvation, the promise she knew her stake would bring.

She could stake him easily, like this. He wouldn't even blink, this close, entranced by her blood.

By her mark.

His mark.

It would be so easy to just... end it all. Kill him, as she knew she should. There was no proof it would take away the mark, but... perhaps, it was the only way. Every other option Mal had come across hadn't worked, and it was a long shot...

Cassius's fingers trailed over the scar on her wrist softly as he brought his lips to her ear, his hair brushing against her temple.

"I don't..." Ava swallowed harshly, trying to find the words, trying to fight the maddening feeling radiating all throughout her body, the haziness of her thoughts, her racing heartbeat.

The building warmth and moisture between her legs.

It didn't feel like thrall, but what else could it be?

"I don't know," she whispered back as her fingers ran up his neck, finding their way into his hair, tugging on the locks tightly.

Cassius embraced her, his hold tightening like a vice.

"Oh, my sweet Avarice. I think you do. Perhaps, you need to stop fighting, stop running... for there are monsters out there..."

Cassius's lips brushed the skin of her neck softly, suckling at her flesh, his warm tongue causing butterflies in her stomach and a most pleasant wetness that spread like wildfire in between her thighs.

"Monsters I can't save you from," Cassius whispered, his voice vibrating on her skin, dark like the shadows that pulled him from her grasp into the darkness once more...

Ava shifted into a hard, warm mass as the edges of her dream started to fall away. The warm mass smelled good, felt rather cozy and comfortable, and she burrowed her face into it once more.

"Well, good morning to you, too," a gruff, gravelly, sleep-tinged voice settled on her ears and, for a moment, it sounded just as comfortable as she felt snuggled against...

Dallas.

Ava's immediately opened her eyes and shot up to confirm she wasn't still dreaming.

No.

Her gaze settled on Dallas, on his deep blue eyes, his five o'clock shadow. On that chiseled jaw, thick arms, and...

She pushed herself away from Dallas and nearly jumped off the bed, but the motion was too much and she felt dizzy.

Dallas wrapped his hand around her wrist and tugged, causing her to fall back into the messy covers.

"Rule number one when dealing with Hunter Triage..." he grumbled as she groaned.

"There are rules, now?"

Dallas let out a chuckle.

"There have always been rules, Kitten. You and your brother just don't seem to think they apply to you."

"Well, that's because they don't," she said with a

huff as she moved to get up.

Dallas's grip tightened.

"Rule number one," Dallas continued as if she hadn't even spoken.

"No man gets left behind. We take care of our fellow hunters. Always."

Something in the way he said the words made Ava feel panicked. Why, she could not be certain. It wasn't as if it was a terrible rule. To watch out for one another, make sure your other hunters were taken care of if injured. But something about his words, the tone of his voice... it was as if he was saying something else.

Something she did not want to hear.

Not now.

"Let me go, Dallas," she said, turning her head and casting him a warning glance.

"What were you doing there last night? Vinny was all the way on the other side of the hotel, and you two weren't patrolling together. I would know."

Ava pursed her lips, and her blood started to heat at his insinuation.

"What's it to you? You don't fucking own me." She pulled against his grip, but instead of breaking it, she only ended up pulling him closer.

Dallas looked past her, and she turned to follow his glance. Vinny lay sound asleep on top of the covers, soft snores coming from his half open mouth. Dallas's voice was a dark whisper; full of things Ava didn't want to acknowledge at the moment.

I don't have time for this...

"You're right, I don't..." Ava's gaze caught Dallas's, and in them she could see fire.

Anger, jealousy.

But what did Dallas have to be angry about?

It wasn't like they were... anything. She didn't owe

him shit.

"But if you did, you certainly wouldn't have ended up with fucking stitches. I would have made sure you were safe."

Ava pulled with all her might against his grip and broke away. His hand fell to the mattress, and though every bone in her body told her to leave, every siren blaring that this... whatever *this* was between them, was not something she should pursue, she could not help rising to the occasion.

She could never resist having the last word. She couldn't resist a fight, and Jake Dallas made her feel as if every moment was fight or flight.

"Maybe I don't need anyone to keep me safe. Maybe..." She leaned closer, close enough she could stake him.

If he were a vampire, which he was not.

But from the way Dallas was looking at her, and the slight sting she could still feel from his touch, she was not certain he wasn't some creature sent from the depths of Hell to destroy her and her quest for... vengeance?

Sanity?

Ava wasn't sure.

"Maybe I'm capable of rescuing my own damn self," she said as she got up from Dallas's bed and made her way to the door.

"I believe the words you're looking for are *thank you*," Dallas growled.

Ava stopped in front of the door, turning only to give Dallas a one-finger salute before leaving and slamming the door shut so loud she was certain it would have woken the dead.

***

Ava cursed as she realized upon her arrival to her hotel room, that she'd left her clutch in Sam Kingsley's hotel room. She leaned her head against the door in defeat, the motion stretching her skin only enough to send a twinge of fresh pain through her head.

"Get your shit together, Ava," she mumbled to herself as she pushed off the door, heading for the front desk. A quick glance at the giant grandfather clock in the hall told her the convention's panels and programs likely would have already started, which meant Sam was likely nowhere near his hotel room.

Ava slid her hands in her overall pockets as she sauntered down the corridor, her disheveled hair, smeared makeup, and fresh stitches only adding a more gruesome element to her original Chucky cosplay. In fact, the number of nods, thumbs up, and people who'd stopped her along the way for a picture made her wonder as if she should truly consider splitting skin every time she dressed up in the future, for authenticity's sake.

Upon reaching the lobby, the sunlight streamed through the revolving doors, and it was terribly bright. Bright enough when she tore her vision from it, she could still see spots. She leaned on the cold acrylic countertop, peering down at the concierge.

"May I help you?" he asked drudgingly.

"I lost my keycard. Can I get another one, please?" she said as politely as possible.

"You were given two."

"Yes, but I lost the one, and the other is locked in my room," she huffed.

When the concierge rolled his eyes, Ava had to bite her tongue. She knew the best way to get what she was asking was to be polite and understanding; every bone in her body wanted to holler and shout a few choice words at the man behind the desk who was testing her sanity.

She was tired, aggravated, and very much in need of a hot shower. Her fate lay in the hands of a concierge who looked like he'd rather be anywhere than the Silver Starling.

So she changed her tactic. She loosened her shoulders, sighing in desperation, feeling her eyes already starting to water.

"I'm sorry to bother you, really, but I just... I don't know what else to do. I..." She even added a fake sniffle for effect as she wiped her eyes.

The concierge's shoulders softened, and his face looked panicked.

"Miss, please, don't cry..."

Bingo.

Perfectly on cue, she let out a rather loud sob, loud enough the people behind her could hear, and the people in the line beside her looked over in worry and disgust at the concierge.

"I'm sorry, I just..."

"What was your room number?" he asked in a low whisper.

Ava had to fight a smile.

"Room 213," she said with another sniffle.

"Okay, I'm not usually supposed to do this but... please... just... don't cry, okay? We can fix this just... hold on, okay?" he said dejectedly.

"O...okay," she responded.

Within minutes she had a brand new, shiny key card to room 213.

***

Ava had showered long enough the water had gone cold.

But she had a plan. The ghost hunt being led by select members of the cast of *Hell on Earth* she'd hoped to get in on did not start until nine, which meant she had more than enough time to get herself together and enjoy the convention as she'd planned to. That included attending Sam's panel on vampires at noon, where she hoped she could nonchalantly ask about retrieving her clutch.

She towel-dried her hair, glancing at herself in the mirror. The stitches above her eyebrow did make her look slightly menacing, and a part of her wondered if covering them up or camouflaging them with makeup would only irritate her wound. Perhaps, she could just tell her brother it was makeup, anyway. If she even saw him today. They'd planned on going to the vampire panel together, but Dallas had mentioned Mal had gone out and off the radar. Likely, he had a better night than she did, wherever he was waking up, stitches-free.

She slid into a pair of dark wash jeans with more frays and holes than should be classified as pants, and a plain black tank top, tousling her hair for added volume. Sliding the keycard into her back pocket, she opted for just a simple swipe of dark plum lipstick and some black eyeliner.

Her body still ached from exertion, from her rigorous activity of sex and fighting off a bloodsucker—the combination leaving her feeling in desperate need of an Advil and a venti caramel macchiato with at least two shots of espresso.

She kneeled on the ground, fingering through her envelope of cash she'd stashed in a small zip pouch. Everyone on the forums mentioned bringing a Ziplock of cash and only allotting a small amount every day to try and save money. At this moment, she was thankful she'd taken the advice, if only because her clutch with the remaining forty dollars she'd had for yesterday was currently sitting in the room of the man she'd...

Fucked.

The reality hit her in the light of day.

She'd gotten into bed with the host of *Hell on Earth,* and though part of her experience was foggy at best, she remembered it had been rather enjoyable.

The way he'd used his mouth to bring her to the edge.

Or the way he'd kissed her neck, while thrusting deep inside her, his teeth grazing her skin like...

Ava forced the thought down.

No, best not go down that road.

Not like it's going to happen again, anyway...

The moment of forgetting was gone once more, and she closed her eyes, trying to force the thoughts of lips on skin, of fangs in her neck away.

That will never happen, either.

Over my dead body.

***

"What the hell are you doing here?" Ava said in surprise as she came up to the line for Sam's vampire panel.

Dallas slid his hands in his jean pockets, looking bored, while Vinny, Tito, and Hunter seemed to be enjoying their own coffees with smiles on their faces.

"Babysitting," Dallas grumbled.

"Fuck you, you didn't have to come, you know." Hunter jabbed Dallas in the arm.

"And miss this asshole trying to spout off a bunch of lies? Why would I want to miss that?" Dallas drawled sarcastically.

Ava pursed her lips. "What makes you think they're lies?" she asked as she forced her way in line with the hunters, garnering her a few choice looks from others in line.

"Please. Guys like Sam Kingsley are a dime a dozen. They think they know shit because they read some books, watched a few Stephen King movies, but they don't know shit. They're just there to look pretty and boost ratings."

"Have you ever watched *Hell on Earth*?" Ava said, feeling strangely defensive.

"I don't need to watch it. I live it, Kitten."

"Dallas hates TV," Vinny chimed in.

"What are you, an alien?" Ava jabbed as she took a sip of her coffee.

"Ha, ha. Very funny. No, I just don't see the point in wasting my time on shit that isn't real. I have bigger things to worry about than whether or not the stupid ghosts showed up and answered some guy who shouldn't be in their space to begin with."

"Then leave. Why force yourself to do something you don't want to do?"

Before Dallas could answer her, the onslaught of the line lurched forward, and he broke her gaze. Ava followed the crowd into the expansive ballroom, realizing there was one person missing from the equation.

"Where's Mal?" she asked as she squeezed past Dallas to get ahead.

"Probably somewhere better than here." Dallas winked.

"Gross," Ava said as she wrinkled her nose.

"What?" Vinny asked innocently. "It's not a secret or anything Mal is a bit of a..."

"I do not need to know the sexual practices of my brother, thank you very much, Vinny," Ava said as she grabbed a seat near the front. Dallas sat next to her, while Vinny took the other side, Hunter and Tito finishing up beside him.

The stream of people kept pouring in.

"Whatever, I'm just saying I wouldn't worry about him right now. I'm sure he'll turn up this afternoon somewhere. If he doesn't, then I'd worry."

Just as everyone had gotten settled in their seats, the man in the row in front of them turned and looked at Ava. "Did you hear they found another body?" His eyes sparkled with excitement as he spoke, all too eager to discuss the information.

"No, I didn't. Where..." Ava glanced at Vinny.

"I guess they're trying to keep it hush, since the big fiasco the last time. Startled everyone too much when they came barreling into Sam's last panel."

"Oh really?" Dallas crossed his arms, raising an eyebrow.

"Maybe they just don't have any evidence he did anything. Maybe they're actually looking for the person who—"

Ava's words were cut off when the lights dimmed, the spotlight shining on the stage where the table of speakers lay empty.

Within seconds, the applause was roaring as the cast of *Hell on Earth* took the stage. Sam and his team of investigators walked out in the spotlight, taking their seats.

Ava couldn't help the way her eyes roved over Sam, over his defined arms, remembering the feeling of his fingers, or the force from his hips. She pressed her legs together, trying to still the sensation building within her, her fingernails digging into her jeans as she held her breath.

Sam's fingers slid over her stomach, down to her aching center and pushed her thighs apart, fitting himself flush against her. Fingers traveling all over, her nerves lit up like a powder keg. His dark voice in her ear, his lips hovering over her throbbing vein in her neck as he urged her to come.

Ava felt the blush sting her cheeks as she tried to force the thoughts down, but looking at Sam in the spotlight, his features more prominent against the contrast of shadows and light, it was all too difficult to fight.

And when he took his seat up front and center on the stage, when he looked out into the crowd and saw her...

He smiled, and suddenly Ava felt flush with heat, her brain slightly foggy again as the desire came back full force, but she pushed against it, knowing she needed to focus. It wasn't like her to come undone over a man so quickly, but then again, Sam Kingsley wasn't just a man. He was a demonologist, a celebrity, and he had been more than a good time. Perhaps, as luck would have it, she was not so unlucky after all. Perhaps, fate had intervened and left her clutch in his hotel room for a reason. Leaving a belonging in someone's house or car was a surefire way to get an invite back. It was one of the oldest tricks in the book, and Ava couldn't help but smile at Sam in return, a most wicked grin of her own, and when he smirked at her, licking his lips slowly, she thought perhaps Sam Kingsley was not meant to be a one night stand after all.

CHAPTER EIGHTEEN

CASSIUS DID NOT *need* to sleep, but sleeping was a difficult habit to break. Especially when given the fact that, from time to time, he did feel tired.

Perhaps the ever-present memories that would not go away in this wretched town were to blame. For every corner he seemed to turn, he was assaulted with bits and pieces of a life he'd lived long ago.

Especially here, in Leon's mansion.

Cassius twisted and turned in his bed, which was much larger and much more comfortable than the one he'd grown accustomed to in the woods of Chester. His bed at home was a solid queen size bed, though big enough for two people, of which Cassius knew no one but him would ever sleep in. Therefore, there was no need for anything larger or fuller.

Taj had been much more favorable to sating the lust that was always present with the hunger for blood and until he'd met Jasmine, their bachelor pad was mostly Taj's bachelor pad.

He'd never judged the man for feeding his desires. Unlike most vampires, Tajiri kept his hunting, feeding, and his desires on a strict schedule. Selecting victims, he'd always chosen individuals he knew would not be missed, or who had no one to question if they'd gone missing. A skill he'd no doubt picked up through the years by patrolling the nearby university and dive bars when the drifters tended to fall.

But in Leon's mansion, in his large guestroom, Cassius found himself surrounded by memory.

Cassius stared into Eden's deep sapphire eyes, and he knew there was no going back from this. On some instinctive level, he knew.

They'd both lost people in this invisible war; the one fought between covens.

She'd lost a man she loved.

She'd lost a child.

There were many who thought Eden was damaged, incapable of such things.

But Cassius knew differently.

Eden Boracelli was not a monster.

She was broken, but wasn't he as well?

Cassius reached out across the space between them, pushing a stray raven hair behind her ear.

He'd always found her to be attractive, from the moment they'd met. But now...

Covered in blood—blood from the hunters who had almost killed him—he was certain he'd never seen anything quite as beautiful.

"Leon will have a fit if he stains the carpet," Cassius whispered.

Eden smiled. "Then perhaps, we should take care of him, now."

But Cassius could not find it within him to move from this space. Not here, not now.

His heart beat steadily, a side effect from the blood they'd consumed.

"There are more pressing matters," he uttered.

Eden slid her arms around his neck and pulled him closer, until her lips brushed his softly. Cassius felt on the edge of a precipice. He wanted to kiss her back. He wanted so much more than to kiss her back.

"Why do you fight this, Cassius?" she whispered as her lips traced his jaw.

"I don't know..." he answered as he shut his eyes, as he let himself feel her lips on his skin. Lust pooled in his stomach, both in part to the fresh feeding and because...

Eden was most desirable.

"But I think you do. I think you know the reason. But you do not have to be afraid." She set her hands on the side of his face, looking into his eyes once more with something he'd never seen before. Understanding.

"It does not have to mean anything. It is a natural part of who we are." Her words were thickening the silence in the air between them.

Cassius ran his fingers through her hair, his gaze dipping to her crimson, blood-stained lips.

"But that is the thing, Edie. I want it to mean something. I want it to mean something to you, because it means something to me."

His words left a heavy silence between them, and for a moment Cassius thought he'd said the wrong thing. He'd opened up and told her the truth, and she...

Eden pulled him close once more and kissed him with the fire of a thousand suns.

Her tongue stroked his fangs as her fingernails traced down his arms, digging into his skin. The taste of blood on her tongue, her scent of roses and vanilla, intoxicating.

She turned him against the poster of the king size bed, his back smacking hard against it.

And where he expected to feel thrall, there was none.

Every time they'd gotten close, this close... the walls went up. The thrall stopped him. He was powerless against it, and though he knew the act of her doing so was more than illegal, he'd understood. He'd come too close, and she could not let him in.

But in this moment, there was no thrall.

Just the feel of Eden's soft, pillowy lips on his; her nails digging into his skin hard enough he knew she'd draw blood.

But he didn't care. Because her words stopped all time and space.

"How do you do that?" she whispered against his lips.

"Do what?" His voice was dark, even to his own ears.

"How do you ignite this desire within me? These things that have been long dead that I never thought I could feel again. This need, this insatiable hunger to be more?"

Cassius looked at the vampiress before him, and he did not see a vampire.

He saw a fighter.

A woman who'd been knocked down countless times, who held secrets and was ambitious.

A force to be reckoned with.

He saw a burning fire, and the beauty of its flames entranced him.

For he burned, too.

He burned with the fire of pain, of loss, guilt, and hope that one day he would find someone who could take it all away.

And in that moment, he was certain Eden Boracelli was that person.

So he kissed her with all the fire he could conjure, letting desire and bloodlust overtake him, for though he was a creature of the night, he was still at the core of all things, a man.

A man with hopes, desires, and needs.

"Edie, my dear. You are more. You are more than anyone, especially someone like me, deserves."

"I think that is the bloodlust talking," she teased.

"Maybe it is. Maybe it isn't, but a vampire once told me to fight our instincts is insanity. To give in... to give in is salvation."

Eden's lips curved into a wicked smile as she ran her fingernails over his chest, looking up at him with dark eyes.

"If it is salvation you seek, darling, then your submission means more to me than you will ever know."

Cassius sat up in bed, raking his hand through his hair. The memories were too strong here, and he did not want to relive them.

For they were all lies.

Lies Eden had fed him for so many years. He'd thought perhaps despite all of the turmoil, the rumors, the deaths they'd both endured... even the infidelity...

He'd thought she loved him.

Because he so desperately wanted to believe it.

Because he loved her.

You loved the mask she wore.

The lies.

Everything was a lie!

Cassius threw the covers off of him, and wandered over to his suitcase, agitated. There would be no sleep tonight. Not here, not now, not in this prison of memories.

I need to get out of this house...

A knock on the door pulled him from his thoughts.

"Cassius..." the sweet voice was most recognizable, and Cassius let out a sigh of annoyance. Of course, Cora would have impeccable timing.

"Yes, Cora?" he drawled.

Cora entered the room wearing a form-fitting black dress and stilettos, her bright red hair tumbling over her shoulders in candy apple waves. With her bright blue eyes, she looked quite stunning, but her features were soft. They would always be so, thanks to the vampirism in her blood and the fact she would be frozen forever in the youth of a sixteen-year-old.

"If you want access to the den, all you have to do is ask me, you know."

Cassius turned to face her, his blood cold.

"I beg your pardon?"

"RJ told me you were asking about the den."

"RJ?"

"The bartender from the club. Don't even try to deny it. I saw you there, talking to him."

Cassius crossed his arms, never moving from his spot.

Cora slowly padded closer, her heels click-clacking on the parquet.

"Ah. The bartender. Chatty guy, isn't he?" Cassius raised an eyebrow.

Cora was now only inches away, and he stood perfectly still.

She looked at him with a doe-eyed expression he was certain worked on many men but would not work on him in the least. Because Cassius would never see Cora the way she wanted him to, even in the light of a blood den.

"Seven-thirty," she whispered.

Cassius glanced down at her. "Come again?"

"I will grant you access to the blood den. Under one condition."

"And what is the price for this... access?"

"A date."

Cassius laughed, rolling his eyes. "Cora..."

Cora held up her hand to stop him.

"You will be ready at seven-thirty. We will go to dinner, you will pay, and then we shall attend the club, and I will grant you whatever access it is you seek to help build a case to prove Leon's got nothing to do with those murders."

Cassius blinked at her words. He'd never known Cora to be so forward, but it had been many years since he'd seen her, spoken with her.

People really do change.

Once her words finally hit him, his eyes widened in surprise. "Murders? I thought it was only one..."

"Another girl showed up dead last night."

Cassius sighed, weighing his options. He could just ask Leon for access to the den himself, if he could get a hold of him.

Since his arrival and their initial chat on the veranda, Leon seemed to be making himself scarce. He'd always been a bit of an introvert, favoring his books and academic research more than socializing with the vampires in the covens, but even this seemed slightly out of character for him.

No, Cora was likely right. His best chance to get into the den was her. After all, next to Leon, she was the rightful heir to the properties he held. It only made sense that she would have access most others wouldn't on Leon's payroll and making a reservation with Louie was a fifty-fifty shot, especially if they did not believe Cassius's claim of friendship was sound.

Regrettably, Cassius had to agree.

"I will take you to dinner, but it is not a date," he said sternly. The wicked smile that graced Cora's lips reminded him of a devilish queen, who smiled every time she won the argument.

"Whatever you say, Cassius," Cora said as she spun around on her heels, exiting the guest room.

When she was gone, he grabbed his suitcase, and headed out of the luxurious, haunted mansion in search of a vacancy anywhere but where the ghosts of his pasts would find him.

CHAPTER NINETEEN

THE PANEL HADN'T proved as interesting as Ava would have hoped. Rather than answer questions about vampires or his research, Sam and the panel discussed the upcoming documentary and pored over legends and myths Ava already knew like the back of her hand.

But it didn't matter what he said. Not really. Ava knew it was a stretch to think he'd mention anything about the way vampires lived, let alone know anything about their marks, and though she was well versed in lore and legend, she could have listened to the man read the phone book and been invested.

There was something about his voice, its tone, volume. It was silky, hypnotizing almost. Even in a crowded room, somehow, Sam commanded the floor as if he was the only one there, but alone...

Ava could not deny she wanted more of the pleasure she'd felt with Sam, which was why, as soon as the panel had ended and everyone had gotten up from their seats, she pushed past Dallas toward the aisle.

"Excuse you," he said gruffly, but she did not care.

She only had one goal.

To make it to Sam before he left the room.

She pushed against the crowd like a salmon swimming upstream.

"Sam!" she yelled over the chatter, just as he was taking a drink from his water bottle. Security, who she hadn't noticed prior, took a step forward, but instead of completing their step, Sam halted them with his hand.

"It's okay, I got this, fellas," he said as he smirked at Ava, nodding for her to approach.

The other cast members rolled their eyes, but did not say anything, which annoyed Ava. She was not some rabid fan looking for an impromptu meet and greet. The man *did* have her belongings, after all.

"Ava, to what do I owe the pleasure?" he said as he stroked his lips with his thumb, dark eyes alighting with interest.

"I believe you have something that belongs to me," she said as she crossed her arms and raised an eyebrow at him. Just as she spoke the words, she could feel eyes on her, watching her.

Familiar eyes.

Jealous eyes.

She refused to turn around and meet the gaze of the perturbed owner. He would have to wait.

"Oh, do I now? And what might I have that belongs to you?"

"My skull clutch. It has my hotel card in it, and obviously my ID, cash..."

"Had you not left in such a hurry, perhaps, you would not have forgotten it."

"I did not leave in a hurry..."

"I must say, I am rather used to waking up alone, but I had hoped we could have had a repeat this morning..." he said with a wink.

Ava smiled as she leaned closer, breathing in his

sweet, masculine cedar scent.

God does he smell good...

"You know the definition of insanity is repeating the same thing over and over and expecting different results," she said sweetly.

Sam leaned closer to her, close enough he brought his lips to her ear, his voice dark and deep.

Like forbidden fruit.

She bit her lip to refrain from letting out any sort of sound that would alert him to the effect he seemed to have on her. Her insides twisting with the familiar warmth all over again.

"I guarantee, Ava, that some things are best enjoyed over and over again." His voice was thick with lust.

Ava looked up at him, and the world seemed to get foggy again. It was as if a haze of lust had replaced all sense and she did not care they were in public. If Sam Kingsley did not take her right here against the stage, she felt as if she would die on the spot. Such things should have alarmed her, but they did not, for Ava was not in her right mind.

"Ahem," Dallas's voice boomed not far from her, cutting through the fog.

Ava blinked furiously, her lips straining into a thin line.

Dallas...

Realization overcame her and, suddenly, she remembered where they were, and who she was with.

What the fuck, Dallas...

Not now...

"I believe your harem is calling you," Sam teased as he kissed the underside of her ear.

"When can I see you again?" she whispered huskily, her eyes never leaving his.

Sam smiled a most sensual smile that turned the

butterflies in her stomach once more.

"Meet me at my hotel room in an hour. I believe you know the way."

Ava smiled, her insides doing flips at the thought of seeing this man again, all clutches be damned.

"Yes, sir," she said sweetly as she broke away from his proximity, and headed toward a group of shocked hunters who looked like they'd just seen a ghost.

CHAPTER TWENTY

"SO, THAT'S WHAT you were doing on the other side of the hotel," Dallas snapped.

Ava sighed indignantly as she kept walking.

"You could do better, you know," Tito said nonchalantly, Hunter jabbing him in the arm.

"What? It is true..."

Ava stopped abruptly, turning to face the group of hunters, who she suddenly wished she could erase from existence at this moment.

"I didn't ask for opinions from the fucking peanut gallery, thank you very much."

"Isn't Sam a little... old for you?" Vinny said cautiously.

Ava glared at him.

At all of them, really.

"I don't need to explain my life, especially my sex life, to any of you. This conversation is over."

"Good. No offense, but we've got bigger problems than who's tapping your ass," Tito said, rolling his eyes.

"What's that?" Hunter asked curiously as Tito

tapped away at his phone.

"I just got a tip from a friend, something I think might explain the vampire reports, the murders around here..."

"Well, don't just stand there like a stone, spill," Ava said, crossing her arms. A part of her was glad in that moment the conversation had shifted to something much more comfortable.

It wasn't as if Ava was ashamed of her attractions, or her choices. Something about the idea of having to explain herself to a group of men just made her feel angry and agitated. No one would bat an eye if the situation was reversed and any one of them were in her place and Sam was some model or stripper.

Besides, it didn't matter how *old* Sam was. Age was just a number. She was over the age of eighteen, after all, and it wasn't as if she was being taken advantage of or naive or anything.

She knew exactly what she was doing.

"There's a hot spot nearby," Tito started to speak.

"A nest?" Vinny cut in again, taking his spot next to Ava, sliding his hands into the pockets of his black jeans.

"Worse." Tito shook his head.

"What's worse than a nest?" Ava asked, looking back and forth from Tito to Hunter to Vinny—ignoring Dallas altogether.

"A blood den."

Gasps erupted around Ava, and also a string of curses.

"What the hell is a blood den?" she asked, both intrigued and annoyed. If their reaction was any indication, it obviously wasn't good, but she needed to know, especially, if it was something she needed to be on the defense about.

"Bloodsucking whorehouses," Dallas growled, and Ava realized he was beside her, flanking her opposite of Vinny, who had gone pale.

"Where there are dens, death usually follows. Vampires are known not to be able to keep their fangs or their dicks to themselves," Hunter drawled.

"It's not something we have seen a lot of, most of them were wiped out back in the early 1900s, but some are still rumored to exist across the country in pockets. Guess we found one of the remaining ones," Tito said, twisting his lips. "The sole purpose of a blood den is to provide slaves for the vamps to feast on as well as..."

"I think I get the picture," Ava said with a huff, holding up her hand.

"And you're sure there's one here?" Hunter asked.

"Well, my friend isn't usually wrong and he says there is. A place called The Dark Hearts Club. It's a couple blocks away from the hotel," Tito stated.

"Should we check it out? See if we can make a bust? Maybe find the vamp responsible for the murders? Or at the very least, I mean, we could probably put a stake through one or two and do the world a favor. Maybe if we're lucky we'll find an actual nest." Hunter's eyes crinkled in the corners as his smile spread over his face, and Ava noticed the smile on Tito's in return.

"We should definitely check it out. Do some poking around. Might find something useful, might pick off a few ticks in the process." Vinny nodded in agreement.

"Sounds good to me. When should we head over there?" Dallas said, shifting his weight.

"According to Google, the place opens at seven," Tito said.

"Um, there is no *we*," Ava said, glancing at Dallas for only a moment when she was certain he wasn't looking. This close to her, she could smell his natural scent, and it wasn't terrible. In fact, his spicy scent made her feel relaxed, and she could remember the last time she'd been this close, the last time she'd smelled him like this... She'd wanted nothing more than to fall in his arms and sleep like the dead.

And the haze that had started to form over her once again made her feel as if she could do the same again.

"Don't tell me you have plans with Doc Hollywood?" Dallas bit at her.

"Actually, I was hoping to check out this ghost tour tonight..."

"If it's ghosts you want, Kitten, I can save you the five hundred dollar ticket and show you some real haunts."

Ava pursed her lips. The premise *did* sound rather intriguing. A blood den... a place vampires could go to fulfill their hunger, their desires? Hunting vampires in their own territory? Where they'd least expect it? It would be like taking candy from a baby, and Ava had to admit her fingers twitched at the very mention of going and casing a place likely riddled with vampires.

"I mean, you don't *have* to come, but we could always use some extra back up," Vinny said with a friendly smile.

"I'll think about it," Ava said with a smile of her own as she turned and headed for the escalator.

Just when she thought she'd escaped entirely without argument, Dallas pulled her by the shoulder, turning her around forcibly on the escalator stairs.

"What is your fucking problem? You've had an attitude ever since I woke up today," Ava said angrily to Dallas.

"Me? I'm the one with the attitude? Oh, please. You've been in a bitchy mood since I fucking arrived."

"Gee, that sounds like maybe you're part of the

problem, don't you think?" She turned away from him once more.

"You are infuriating, you know that!" Dallas snapped again.

"I'm infuriating?" Ava gasped in shock as she raced off the escalator as it came to the end, letting them both off on the floor.

She turned around and pointed her finger directly at him, poking him in the chest.

"You are the one who fucking kissed *me*, then left without a god damn word for two fucking years, and then you show up here and—"

"And what, Ava? It's not like I was planning on running into you or your brother when I took this gig with the guys."

"You had your chance, Dallas."

"I didn't know you were giving me a chance, Ava. So that hardly feels fair."

"My bad, I assumed grabbing you by your fucking balls was a pretty clear invitation."

A few congoers passing them by shot wide-eyed looks their way. Dallas ran a hand through his hair, his lips tightening into a straight line.

"I—"

"What? What's your excuse now, huh? Going to tell me you wanted to protect my god damn virtue or some shit? Because if that's the case, you're really late to the party on that one."

"I was trying to be respectful of your feelings and boundaries. You just lost your boyfriend..."

Dallas's words hit Ava, and the memories came flooding back.

The memory of Ross's body on the floor, bled dry, his eyes vacant.

The sound of his moan of pleasure as the vampire

bit him, sucked his blood down like a bottle of beer.

She pushed them back, not wanting to fall into the hole of that darkness again. The nightmares still plagued her quite frequently.

She didn't want to remember that night.

The night she almost died.

The night Cassius saved my life.

Ava looked up into Dallas's eyes and in them she could see many things, but the most prominent was pain and regret.

Did he regret what had happened between them?

Did she?

"You don't get to do this."

"Do what, Kitten?" Dallas's voice had taken on a calmer tone as they stood head-to-head, or more accurately, as Ava stood head to Dallas's chest.

"You don't get to start this fire then douse it with water, only to spark up the embers whenever you feel like it. You can't just waltz in and out of people's lives and expect there to be no consequences."

"And you can't just hop from dick to dick in hopes you'll forget the shit you're running from. It doesn't work. Trust me, I know."

Ava scoffed and let out a small laugh. "Awww, have you and Mal finally taken your bromance to the next level? I'm so happy for you."

"Shut the fuck up, Ava."

"Make me, Dallas." She glared at him with a challenge.

"Do not push me," he growled.

"You're all bark and no bite, anyway," she said as she moved to turn around, but Dallas caught her by the wrist.

His grip around her was tight, and he pulled her back, the motion landing her right against his chest.

His right hand slid around her waist, holding her flush to his body, while his left traveled up her back, sending a shiver down her spine. His fingers found the edges of her hair and he wrapped the ends around his fist, yanking on her hair and forcing her to look up at him.

Lust started to pool in Ava's stomach once more, her heartbeat pounding in her chest. And when she looked into Dallas's deep blue eyes, she couldn't deny the fire in them. For not only were Dallas's eyes full of flame and fury, but she could see her own flames staring back at her in the reflection of his irises.

Jake Dallas seemed to have a way of getting under her skin like no one else was capable of doing. So when Dallas brought his lips to his hers, instead of drowning out the fire, a new spark formed. It caught on brittle branches, on the last bits of dead leaves that lay in the memory of two years ago. And though Ava knew she should push him away, slap him, tell him to fuck off, and leave her be... She could not fight the magnetic pull of this man who both infuriated her and awakened her all at the same time.

Ava kissed Dallas back, her tongue caressing his as a soft sound of contentment escaped her lips.

His fingers tightened their grip in her hair, and it stung. His body pressed against hers was warm and solid as Ava slid her hands down his side, fingers resting on the waistband of his jeans, traipsing down his thighs.

It was the most effective way of shutting her up, and, for the moment, Ava didn't fight it. Instead, she let Dallas lead her into the darkness, into the space between what was and what could be. But the moment was too short-lived as a vibration against her thigh broke the spell over her.

"Fuck," Dallas growled as he pulled away from her.

He looked back into her eyes, and the unspoken words hung between them.

This isn't over.

Far from it.

"Hello?" he said gruffly into the phone. It took all of one second for his tone, his demeanor to completely shift, and one word; one name for Ava to understand why.

"Mal? Where the fuck you been?"

***

Ava knocked on Sam's door not once, but twice. The silent pause as she waited made her feel some sting of anxiety.

What if he wasn't here?

What if he was playing some kind of cruel joke?

What if he didn't really intend on giving her stuff back?

But before Ava could fabricate another unlikely scenario, the door opened to reveal a rather delicious sight.

Sam stood in the doorway, his dark hair slightly disheveled, his warm eyes sparkling with mischief. He smirked at her devilishly, and for a moment Ava felt as if she couldn't breathe. The sight of him leaning in the doorway and his long, defined arms the only barrier between them.

"Hello, Ava," Sam said smoothly, and the sound of his voice was like melted butter. It reminded her of someone else's voice, someone she could not quite remember at the moment...

The twist in her stomach, the heat between her legs was almost instant.

How the fuck does he do that?

I'm not usually this easy around men... but it's like

ever since I arrived at this damn convention...

"Hey..." she said with a smile, feeling almost giddy. She could not take her eyes off this man, and it was as if she was waiting for something, but she couldn't be sure what it was.

"Come on in," Sam said with a raise of his eyebrow, motioning her to come into the room.

Ava had the strangest feeling she was crossing some sort of line, some invisible threshold she didn't remember existed. So, she stepped into the room one foot at a time, and within seconds the door closed, sealing them both in. The curtains were closed, only a sliver of light exposed around the window's edges, which lit up the room in a velvet-red glow. The lamplights were on, on the lowest setting, also adding to the dark, somewhat hellish landscape.

Ava's gaze settled on the bureau, where her skull clutch lay perfectly untouched, perfectly kept. She walked over and grabbed it, opening it quickly to check and make sure everything was there, just as Sam came up behind her.

"It's all there, I promise," he said smoothly, his fingers tracing over the soft skin of her neck. Ava closed her eyes, breathing in the warm, cozy fireside scent of him as he surrounded her, and the reaction was instinctual. She rolled her head back against his chest, her hands settling the clutch on the bureau once more.

Sam's fingers traced down her chilled arms, his fingers brushing over her knuckles, entwining with hers, gently pushing the clutch away. His hands against hers were warm. In fact, it seemed as if heat radiated from his palms outward, heating her entire body.

"O... okay..." she said, trying to find the words. Her

head was spinning once more.

"Mmmm, your lust smells delicious." Sam breathed huskily, his tongue lapping against the taut skin of her neck.

Ava's heart pounded, her legs tightened, and resistance was futile.

"Yeah? You don't smell too bad yourself." She could hear the lust in her own voice as she spoke the words.

Sam pressed his body harder against hers, sandwiching her between the bureau and his warm, solid body. He wrapped one hand around her throat, while the other trailed over the exposed cleavage of her tank top, over her breasts and down her abdomen. His fingers slowly caressed her thighs before sliding between them, pushing apart her legs with urgency. His fingers brushed over her apex, and she could feel the heat coming from his touch, the heat he seemed to be able to pull from her body.

"You are so responsive to me... I have to say, I enjoy that very much."

The words disappeared in the air as Ava settled her hand over top of his, pushing him further below, to stroke her.

"And so impatient." Sam's voice took on a hypnotic tone again, and she almost could have sworn he *hissed*.

Like a snake.

But her brain was foggy, and nothing made sense. Nothing but the insatiable need to feel Sam every way she could, until he was buried so deep within her he'd be a part of her, and even then, it wouldn't be enough.

She'd still want *more*.

He held her wrist in his hand delicately, his thumb brushing over the scar that would always be there now.

"Sam..." she groaned. The feeling as he brushed over

her scar sent a shiver up her spine. "Don't be such a damn twat tease."

Sam let out a dark chuckle as he removed his hand from her throat and slid it down her back, before circling around and deftly working at the button of her jeans.

"And that mouth. Gods, I haven't had anyone tell me what to do in ages. I kind of like it."

Ava felt her internal temperature start to heat once more, and she removed her shirt instantly, a heavy sheen of sweat burgeoning on her skin. Aside from the mark on her wrist, every other bit of her felt practically combustible.

"Is it hot in here or is it just me?" she teased.

"I believe it is *us, meum delicium.*"

"What did you say?" Ava blinked as Sam slid her jeans down to the floor.

"*Meum delicium...*" he purred against her ear, his voice vibrating all throughout her body. His fingers slid between the straps of her underwear, sliding them down to the floor with ease until she was naked from the waist down, pressed against the bureau with the heat of Sam Kingsley behind her.

"What... what does that mean?" Ava breathed huskily, trying to find her breath and stability. She felt lightheaded.

The sound of a belt buckle and shifting clothing sounded behind her loud like a church bell.

There was a moment of silence before Ava felt warm fingers pushing their way into her slick opening, felt a hardness pressing against the seam of her ass. She could not contain the moan that escaped her mouth, or the shockwave of pleasure that rippled through her as she brushed against his fingers, which stroked her with a slow rhythm, with instinct. Her fingers grasped the edge of the bureau; only to keep herself from falling.

"It means... my pleasure." Sam's tongue stroked her ear, and Ava noted it felt... different.

Different than the last time.

His voice was still hypnotic, but the *hiss* of the way he said his s's... the word pleasure... was like a snake.

Something was off.

With his free hand, he grasped her wrist once more, bringing it up to his lips. His tongue licked at the scar, and the chill returned.

But Ava could not care about such things, right now. Right now, there was only one need, one desire that filled her brain.

"I need more..." Ava said without thinking.

"You *need* more?" Sam pulled his occupied fingers back, the emptiness striking Ava like a barren desert.

"Yes, I... I need you inside me..." She struggled to speak, her brain a foggy mess, her body nothing but sensation.

Sam let out a dark sound, a sound Ava could not distinguish. His teeth nipped at the taut skin of her wrist, and the feel struck a chord deep within her.

Why did that feel so familiar?

"You are bound..." his voice wavered only slightly, and Ava felt flush with warmth at the words.

"Yes," she breathed without thinking.

"How very interesting." Sam's lips curved into a smile as he brought them against her neck, letting his tongue lave over her skin.

"Tell me, Ava... tell me what you desire most..." he purred.

Ava moaned in response, trying to find stability to answer him.

"I..." Ava found it difficult to form words.

"Tell me... let me in and I will give you *everything*

you ask for, *meum delicium.*"

His lips settled on her neck, his tongue stroking her skin once more, and Ava let out a strangled moan. Something about his words seemed alarming, but she couldn't quite place what it was.

Let me in...

It was as if his voice was a thickening fog of its own, surrounding her, invading her thoughts and every beat of her heart—making it hard to breathe, hard to concentrate.

"I want to be bitten," she whispered the words like a prayer.

"Hmmm... I sense the weight of this desire... this lust for blood... it drags you down, doesn't it?"

Sam's hands left her body only for a moment, and she missed the feeling. He unclasped her bra and let it fall to the ground before his fingers softly pulled at her nipples, eliciting another moan of pleasure from her.

"You chase after anything to dull the ache, the pain... because you want it..."

"Yes..." Ava responded without thinking.

"You want it so bad, but you know it is wrong, don't you?"

"Yes."

"And what would you do if I told you I could make it all go away?"

Ava sighed as her head rolled back against Sam's chest as the world spun around her. Yet, his smooth, decadent voice kept talking, and it sounded so serene. Like someone else... someone she couldn't quite place, but whose voice could also melt the ice within her veins.

"You think about it all the time, don't you? In the darkness, it's him you want. Filling your brain, your every desire. You want the bite." Sam's voice was dark and hypnotic, and Ava was certain she would have given this man the winning lottery numbers if she had them. She was putty in his hands, a puddle of desire and lust, and yet...

Release was still so far away on the horizon.

Would she reach it?

Or would she only chase the dream of it, at the mercy of this man who fueled a hurricane of lust within her?

How is it he seemed to elicit this willingness from her?

It was almost as if she was under a spell, a spell that smelled strangely of fire and caramel and everything, every man she'd ever wanted in her life... Yet, their names were on the tip of her tongue, but she could not remember them, because there was only...

Sam.

"Yes..." she moaned. Images of glowing green eyes pushed forth in her brain, and they felt familiar, almost like she knew the owner, but like her pleasure, the name was only on the horizon, and she could not reach it. But the thought of those eyes staring into her soul from above, watching her face twist into an expression of utter ecstasy, caused her insides to twist with pleasure once more.

"Oh, Ava... you are perfect. It is as if you were made for me..." Sam whispered before pulling his hands away from her.

In the wake of their exit, she felt chilled, exposed. Every nerve was on fire, begging to be touched once again, to be brought to release. And as the emptiness overcame her, it was soon forgotten, for when Sam Kingsley pushed himself inside of her, sliding in with much ease, Ava could not think about anything but the maddening sensation of him within her.

"I want to taste you, *meum delicium.*"

"Sam..." she groaned.

"Mea..." he growled darkly in response.

Ava was certain he was speaking Latin, but she was not fluent in such languages, therefore she dismissed his plea, his declaration. She could not discern what it was he was truly asking.

For she was not in her right mind, under the spell of Sam Kingsley.

Her pleasure was his, and she would have done anything to stay in that moment, to feel what he made her feel. She could not find the words to speak, and instead, a satisfied grunt left her throat.

The bureau clicked and clacked, screeching with every thrust from Sam, and Ava gripped on for dear life as he quickened his pace. The sounds of wet skin slapping, of the creak of wood against the floor, of deep, throaty moans filled the hot room.

"*Mea voluptus unica,* Ava," he hissed in her ear, and the sound was pure heaven, dragging Ava down into Hell as her body pulsed around his, pleasure so intense she was certain she would die in its wake, and become nothing but...

Meum delicium.

My pleasure.

And when the moment had passed, Sam Kingsley slid out of her, and Ava dropped to the floor in a heap of exhaustion, sleep overcoming her once more.

***

Ava awoke in a hotel bed, naked. She sat upright, the memory hitting her like a flashback on a television show. She looked around, expecting to find Sam Kingsley, but was alone.

Alone in his hotel room.

She ran a hand through her hair, as reality set in.

She and Sam had...

Again.

Her head was pounding, as was the rest of her body. Her knees and legs felt sore as well, and she closed her eyes, taking a deep breath.

What did this mean?

Were they just... fuck buddies?

Could this... whatever crazy connection *this* was between them—could it be something more?

Sam's words echoed in her brain, *mea voluptus unica.*

Ava wasn't very keen on Latin, but something about the words made her feel somewhat suspicious.

What did they mean?

Was it some kind of blessing or curse?

Sam had uttered the words in the midst of his release, maybe it was some term of endearment like, "I love you."

Which in itself would be a good thing, right?

Celebrities *could* fall in love with fans, right?

But even as Ava thought the words, they made her tense.

She liked Sam, she'd always liked him on television, and in person he seemed like a nice guy, but then again, they hadn't done much talking since the night at Hamlet's only two days ago.

A blush creeped onto her cheeks at the realization. Perhaps, they didn't need to talk. The connection they shared was much deeper than words, anyway, and Ava couldn't deny it spawned a hunger within her.

She had been bitten by Sam Kingsley and she did not want to give up this feeling, this excitement so soon.

She turned to swing her legs out of bed, only to see

a note written on the hotel notepad, taped to the lamp.

I had a panel to attend, and I did not want to wake you. You looked too cute asleep, and I wish I could have stayed, but duty calls. This might sound forward, and I'm not really good at this stuff but... I want to see you again. Maybe we could get dinner tonight? Seven p.m.? If you agree, meet me in the lobby at six thirty.

I hope to see you, meum delicium.

— Sam

Ava's lips formed a wide, giddy grin as she stroked her fingers over the dried ink.

Maybe she was right.

Maybe this could be *more.*

The ghost hunt could wait.

There would be others.

The Dark Hearts Club could wait.

There would always be vampires, that she was most sure of, but there would never be another Sam Kingsley. There would never be another moment like this, and if life had taught Ava anything, it was to seize the moment.

So, as Ava dressed herself in Sam Kingsley's hotel room, she decided she would do just that.

CHAPTER TWENTY-ONE

CASSIUS WALKED WITH his suitcase in hand, and it reminded him of his first train ride from the sandy beaches of Portofino to Paris.

He'd only brought one suitcase then, packed with not much more than one suit and a few personal belongings. A pair of pants, a change of shirt. He had not intended on being gone much longer than a few days in Paris with Eden and Octavius, no inkling in the world all that would transpire from the moment he walked off the train.

He'd had every intention of returning to his meager apartment in Portofino, but after the coronation of Amora Medici, he'd found himself unable to leave the great city of Paris.

Not much had changed in over a hundred years for Cassius. He still stood with one suitcase, a fancy suit and a change of pants and shirts with scarce personal belongings.

But he was wiser now, older.

He'd accumulated more than wealth, he'd accumulated memories.

Memories that would not leave him be.

Still, Cassius moved with purpose, only stopping dead in his tracks when he saw a familiar face in line for the coffee cart in the small park.

"I do not recall you being a fan of coffee," he said with a friendly smile. Leon turned, startled for a moment until he set his eyes on Cassius and relaxed once he'd realize who he was.

"Cassius, how nice to see you out and about on such a lovely day," Leon said with a smirk. It was a chilly, gloomy day in Ansley, most perfect for the ambiance of a haunted town such as itself.

"Yes, well, could not sleep, I suppose."

Leon's gaze shot down to Cassius's suitcase. "Leaving so soon, are you?"

"I appreciate your letting me stay on the premises but—"

"Well, this should be good." Leon grabbed his coffee from the call out window, taking a long sip as Cassius took a deep breath.

"But I cannot stay in your home. There are far too many memories, too many ghosts within your walls."

"How long has it been since you've seen her?"

"Leon..."

"How long, Cassius?" Leon did not raise his voice, only kept it plain and solid.

"Long enough."

Thirty-seven years.

"And yet, you still can't face your demons."

"I have no demons to face, Leon. Eden is the one with blood on her hands, not I."

"Our demons are not always recognizable to us, you know. Sometimes, they come in the form of what we know best. They do not come from the world around us, but from within us."

"Yes, well they don't speak quite as loud when I am far away from all of this."

"I understand. I do wish you'd change your mind, but I digress. As long as you are comfortable and happy, Cassius."

"I would be much happier if I could get a decent meal," Cassius grumbled.

"Ah, yes. Cora told me the two of you are going out for a night of Ansley's tip-top culinary delights."

"Yes, well, she insisted."

"Nevertheless, I am sure you will find something that fits your... preferences at the den, thereafter."

"I am not partaking in the den's refreshment. I only want to observe. Perhaps, there is something that can help us find the evidence you need."

"I seem to remember you felt differently in Paris." Leon's eyes furrowed in confusion.

"I was a different man then, Leon. That was over a hundred years ago."

"And what of the man you are now?" Leon said as they strolled through the park to a bench, where Leon sat down.

"Is this... new man... content with his solace?"

"Enough. I only require that you point me to the nearest morgue, so that I may be fed and content."

"The morgue?" Leon wrinkled his nose in disgust.

"I have not had fresh blood since I left... her. In Massachusetts."

"Dear God, you don't mean to tell me you've been drinking..." Leon tilted his head to the side, curiously.

"Corpse blood, yes, Leon."

"Corpse blood?" Leon said, raising his eyebrow.

Cassius shrugged.

"That's nearly fifty years you haven't had a drop of fresh human blood." Leon's eyes lit with excitement, and Cassius wondered if disclosing such information was a good idea. He'd known Leon long enough to know the look on his face meant the gears were turning and soon he'd be subjected to a hundred questions for "research."

"Fascinating. How do you do it? Is it an acquired taste? Do you still long for the real thing or do you not remember how it tastes, memory fuddled by cold blood?"

Cassius pursed his lips, but he figured it was no use, and so he gave up standing and sat next to Leon.

"I have a man who works in the coroner's office. His name is Bryan. I saved him, but the circumstances of how I did so..."

"Exposed what you were, ah, yes. Isn't that always the case."

Cassius sighed, nodding in agreement. "Far too much in my long life, yes, it is."

"And this Bryan? He trusts you?"

"Yes. Enough. He knows I would never harm him, and I think that is enough. He leaves the discarded blood packaged and ready for me. Usually, I can get by with the minimum, make a jug or two last for weeks. It isn't the most fulfilling diet, but it has kept me alive."

Cassius looked out against the grayed, gloomy landscape as the storm clouds rolled in above them.

"Alive. That word means something different to all of us, doesn't it?" Leon glanced down at the coffee cup in his hands.

"For the humans, it is a word they cannot describe fully what it means. They do not know what it is to truly live, their lives so short in comparison to ours. They merely exist. They do not *live*." Leon spoke with grace.

"I would argue that we do the same. Empires rise

and fall, and yet, we do nothing. We do not fight or intervene. We hide in the shadows, feasting on blood like animals, driven by that one instinct in which nothing else will ever compare. How can one call that living? When death becomes no more commonplace than the Sunday paper."

"We are not all Eden, Cassius."

"I know that. But what exists in Eden... it exists in all of us, does it not?"

Leon sighed, reaching his hand out fondly, setting it on Cassius's thigh as he squeezed, forcing Cassius to look into the eyes of the man he'd come to know as more than a friend.

In the absence of his father, Leon had become that man.

"Eden Boracelli is a cautionary tale of what happens when one forgets their humanity. You, dear Cassius, are an exemplary example of who we can be if we remember it. And those that fall in between are no less good or bad. They just are who they are. Is that not enough?"

"I am not qualified to answer such a question."

Leon squeezed his leg once more before letting go.

"The morgue is about two blocks in the opposite direction. Past the Silver Starling Hotel, on the other side of Ansley, bordering Cardello."

"Thank you," Cassius said with a nod.

***

It had been too long since Cassius had infiltrated a morgue in the daytime.

He'd gone to three hotels along the way to the Silver Starling, and none had vacancy due to the TerrorCon convention.

The same TerrorCon convention Ava had mentioned.

When the pulse in his veins came back with a vengeance, the hunger was so intense, Cassius thought he may expire on the streets of Ansley.

His chest ached, his muscles tight as they all twisted around his slow beating heart, his stomach and insides. His fangs longed to push into flesh, to feel warm blood, or *any blood* at that point, and suddenly, the harmless mortals surrounding him looked more than appetizing.

But it wasn't their blood he truly desired.

No.

And when he had managed to secure a room at the Silver Starling, he'd wondered if he should stay sequestered. If she truly was nearby, as the quickening pulse in his veins indicated...

No.

You need blood.

You need to eat.

Though the wave of nausea that overcame him at the thought of feeding was nearly too much, he knew without a doubt the only way he'd fight such sickness would be to find the morgue. How he'd get in wasn't even a thought in his mind. His only goal was to find something to sate the need, something to quench his thirst and quiet the demons inside that begged for blood.

Yet, it had almost been much too easy. He'd simply smiled at the front desk attendant, turning on his charm as he had in his younger years with Eden and Octavius, or Tajiri. He'd resorted to one of his old stories, about coming to identify a body of a loved one.

Humans rarely questioned a grief-stricken, attractive man, after all.

Though Cassius once felt disdain and shame for using his charms in such a way, life with Eden had taken that from him, too. While he valued human life and the sanctity of it, years alongside the Boracelli siblings had strengthened his ability to blend in, to pull the wool over wandering, desperate eyes.

And the satisfaction of the blood, no matter if it was cold—made all the guilt and lies worth it in the end, because it quieted the pain.

It gave him the chance to live another day.

The radiating pulse in his veins was maddening, and his stomach turned, twisting in agony as he shut the door. His mouth was so dry, he thought he'd surely crumble to ash on the sterilized morgue floor. The stench of embalming liquid and bleach was so overwhelming to him, his eyes watered.

He leaned against the counter as another wave of hunger rang through him, noting the papers laid out evenly.

Papers with pictures of victims.

The murders, he realized as he took in the sight of the photographs.

All looked to have suffered the same puncture wounds that were prevalent with vampire bites, but something else stood out to him. The markings around the neck looked like *claw* marks, not strangulations as the papers implied. But Cassius did not have time to read the reports, not when his stomach twisted, the hunger growing more insatiable by the minute.

Cassius scanned the room, until his gaze settled on the slab in the center of the room. The air was frigid and the light fell on the corpse of a man, lighting him up like a halo, only his face visible. The white sheet covering him stared at Cassius like the fabled light, and next to him, he saw it.

A container of fresh corpse blood.

The hose was no longer attached, and it sat there,

still.

Crimson and thick.

Cassius's pupils dilated at the sight, his tongue flicking out to lick his dry lips.

It had been nearly a week since he'd last fed, and he was very hungry.

He zeroed in on his target, not even registering the toxicology report that flittered to the ground in his wake.

He wasted no time, knowing the door was locked.

He'd be quick.

His hands wrapped around the glass container, bringing it to his lips as if it was nothing more than a cherry slushie.

Cherry...

His mind hung on the word, and all the connotations that came with it.

Ava loved cherries.

Cherry pastries, cherry slushies, cherry pie with enough whip cream to be considered its own level on the food pyramid.

The thought of her pervaded his brain as he let the cold blood run down his throat, a deep groan of satisfaction escaping his lips. His head started to feel fuzzy, and he turned around, glass in hand as he leaned against the countertop, causing a cup of pens to fall over from his motion.

It wasn't the best tasting corpse blood he'd had, but it was enough. Enough to make his body heat with warmth, his cock twitch with life once more from the taste, the thoughts that bloodlust always brought him.

He closed his eyes, gulping down the thick liquid as if it were nothing more than a milkshake, careful to not let it run over his lips, down his neck; careful to avoid any evidence or staining of his clothes.

The image of her the first time he'd laid eyes on her pushed forth. The crimson streaks running down her creamy, pale thighs from the wounds in her legs. The fight in her eyes as she struggled against her own imminent death to stand, to reach out.

He'd never seen anything quite as beautiful as the sheer will, the defiant ambition that was Ava Crowley. He'd felt drawn to her in that moment, in so many unexplainable ways, like a moth to a flame.

Like Icarus, drawn to the sun.

He'd done the right thing, hadn't he?

He'd saved her life, but in return he ached with pain and desire, the intensity of the claiming bond ever present in his brain, his being.

Even now as he let the chilled, semi-congealed blood slide down his throat, he could feel her pulse within him like a beacon, and the thought of seeing her somehow, someway, was difficult to fight.

The sound of her gasp as his fangs pierced her skin only for a moment.

How her bountiful cleavage heaved with heavy breath after she'd staked Brody only two years ago.

The light catching in her eyes as she looked at him in those moments.

Black vampire blood splattered across her beautiful face and skin.

Cassius's cock hardened at the thought, the memory, and it was no use fighting. There was only one way to truly quiet the unrelenting desire that blood and thoughts of Ava brought him. Though, a strange sense of heightened urgency seemed to hit him, like the first hit of caffeine from a cup of coffee. Only this feeling was much, much more intense, and it only fueled his arousal.

His *need.*

Cassius shakily slid his hand down his leather pants, the haze around him thickening. He gripped himself tightly and let the thoughts drag him under once more, the desire in him building like a crescendo. A part of him knew every bit of what he was doing was wrong; the sane part of him.

The human part of him.

But it was as if some unknown force compelled him, some spell and control was out of his reach. The vampiric part of him did not care about right and wrong. It only cared about blood and lust. Drinking corpse blood would not erase the lust that came with drinking blood.

No.

Though, the thought of *fresh* warm blood—Ava's blood to be exact—even as he consumed his sustenance, was enough to stir the instinct, let alone the fact they were *bonded*. He'd claimed her blood as his own when he'd saved her life and knowing her blood was *his* to take... was enough to drive him mad.

He needed *release*.

He needed a quiet, serene peace. So he let go of the glass, letting it clatter against the countertop, and the euphoria of bloodlust settled over him like a velveteen blanket.

But something was off.

He'd never felt quite *this* aroused by the thoughts alone, or the corpse blood.

He opened his eyes, and the room seemed to blur, a jarring discovery. Instinctually, he closed them once more, trying to fight the effect, and when he did so, he only saw *her*.

Ava sat on her knees before him, looking up at him through her long dark lashes. Pale and naked on the concrete floor she sat like a statue, the only light visible was the fire in her amber eyes that called to him. She looked delicate, like the goddess Venus perched on the dais, waiting for him. But he knew she was anything but delicate. She reached out for him, crooking her finger as she cast him a most wicked glare and he came to her beckon call.

In life, it seemed as if the existence of him was nothing but an annoyance to Ava. Come. Leave. Come. Leave. He was at the mercy of her command, and always would be. As long as she wore his mark, as long as her blood was *his*... He'd be a slave to Ava Crowley and all that she was. All she had to do was say the word.

"Yes," she purred in his ear as her lips hovered over his neck, as her hand traveled between them, wrapping her fingers around his thickness, squeezing tightly.

"Yes, Cassius. You can come for me, now."

CHAPTER TWENTY-TWO

CASSIUS TURNED THE corner, the overly bright fluorescent lights of the Silver Starling casting a glare directly in his eyes. His thoughts seemed to be going a mile a minute, ever since he'd broken into the morgue. He'd managed to leave without drawing too much attention, but somewhere between his exit and the few blocks it took to reach the Silver Starling, Cassius realized two things.

The first was that he'd been careless. He'd been so used to receiving purified, clean blood from Bryan that he hadn't even thought twice about checking the reports of the corpse on the slab.

Though his vampiric genes prevented him from falling ill with blood borne disease, they did not prevent him from feeling the effects of certain toxins within the blood, which led him to the second realization—the blood he'd feasted on had been laced with some kind of euphoric toxin.

Though Cassius was no stranger to alcohol or drug infused blood, something about this felt... different. He'd lived through the eighties and nineties with Tajiri, when such drugs were frequently the cause of many deaths, cocaine and ecstasy being quite popular at the time, and he thought that must be it.

For what else *could* it be if not a drug?

He blinked furiously, as his eyesight settled, the light dissipating, shifting into sharper vision as a body came through from the ice room, nearly smacking into him. As his vision adjusted, he felt his skin crawl, his blood boiling beneath the surface as a pulse *throbbed* in his veins, louder than anything he'd ever felt before, and his eyes took in the sight before him.

Perhaps, I am hallucinating...

It was Ava, with a bucket of ice in her hands. Her short, chocolate hair was wet, and the scent of bergamot and jasmine filled his senses like the room had been sprayed, bathed in her scent. She wore nothing but a Van Halen t-shirt, large and boxy and long enough to barely be considered decent as it stopped just a hair above her mid-thighs.

He fixated on the sight, noting the flesh of her long, beautiful legs was still a tinge pink, as if she'd left the shower only moments ago. Cassius rubbed his eyes.

"What the fuck are you doing here?" Her voice was sour, like a tart cherry, but sweet to his ears.

I'm not hallucinating...

The realization hit him and he blinked, tiny spots splintering in his vision as his heart beat louder, as her pulse rocked his body. She smelled quite intoxicating, and Cassius noted another scent, not as prevalent but still quite intoxicating.

His eyes roved over Ava, settling on the hem of her t-shirt as understanding dawned on him. The scent of...

Dear lord, have I died and gone to Hell?

Think unsexy thoughts...

He felt the familiar stiffening in his groin. He

groaned in defeat.

He'd already sated his hunger, his desire, hadn't he?

Cassius knew the answer, but it did not matter. For whatever toxin was laden in the corpse's blood, it seemed was only getting started and he needed to regain control.

"What's the matter? Cat got your tongue?" Ava said as she shifted her weight, raising an eyebrow at him, tapping her foot.

This is really happening...

She is here...

I am...

Cassius let out a deep sigh as he ran his hand through his hair, feeling the beginnings of sweat forming on his brow.

Out of all the hotels in Oklahoma...

"Paying a visit to an old friend." Despite feeling as if he was out of his wits, his voice did not betray him. Cassius shifted his stance behind the vending machine, the feeling of rigidity building against his leather pants again, the thrum of her pulse and the bloodlust making his throat dry with thirst, as if he hadn't fed nearly an hour ago. As if, somehow, his afternoon lunch had already metabolized through his system, leaving him vacant and ready to be filled once more.

She smirked as she held the bucket of ice in front her.

"I thought I told you to stay away," she said the words, but for once they carried no bite.

"I do have other friends, you know," he said with a smirk.

"Mhmm..." She squinted her eyes narrowly at him as if she was weighing the sincerity of his words.

"I was born at night, you know, but not last night." She twisted her lips, the motion lighting up her eyes in the fluorescent halo from above.

His vision sharpened as he found himself falling into the depths of them, fixating on the gold flecks that reminded him of a morning sunrise.

I must be dreaming if she is being this friendly.

She's never this... relaxed...

A startling thought popped into his chaotic brain as her smile elicited one from his own mouth.

Is she flirting with me?

Somewhere in his brain, he hoped she was. The thought alone that she would even entertain such a thing, *flirting* with him, would indicate that she...

Cassius could not complete the thought for all attention went to his cock, straining against his leather pants. He shifted his weight once more, propping his left leg out nonchalantly, hoping to heaven she didn't notice. If she did... Well, he would rather not die against a vending machine in Ansley, Oklahoma.

"I didn't follow you here, Ava." Cassius shifted uncomfortably in her gaze. He felt an overwhelming desire to make her understand this. To make sure she understood he was not some stalker, not some person who disregarded her wishes at the behest of his own.

"No, it's just all some big, serendipitous miracle that we'd wind up miles away in the same fucking city." She twisted her lips, the ghost of a smirk on the edge of the corners.

"Choose to believe me or not, but this is not a pleasure call," he responded defensively. He didn't mean for his voice to sound so harsh, but the aching in his cock was beginning to border on unmanageable.

His body temperature rose, and he swallowed nervously. A part of him longed to touch her, to know he wasn't imagining this. But the desire to brush his thumb over her bite mark, *his* bite mark, was not the only one fighting for dominance in his brain.

He longed to run his hands along the expanse of her exposed long, smooth legs and feel her pulse beneath his fingertips. He longed to run those same fingers through her soft hair, to hold her close against him and feel her life, her lips against his own... but another, the sane part of him; whatever shred was left at the moment, knew he should keep his distance.

For both of them.

Not only because he feared he may get carried away with his whims, but because he had managed to restrain himself thus far, and he did not want to falter now. The thin line he walked with Ava Crowley was a tightrope, at best, and he knew if he wanted to see her again, share coffee in the Impala, or find himself crawling in through her window at night without being staked, he would have to keep his feelings, his desires, in check. He would do whatever it took to keep his presence in her life, one that did not end up in death.

For a life without his sweet Avarice was no life at all.

Perhaps, it was the toxins making their way through his system, or wishful thinking, or perhaps, it was just a matter of serendipity, like a comet traipsing across the sky—but something about Ava felt... different.

Something had infiltrated the walls of her fortress, and in its wake was this alluring creature who was *flirting* with him. As if she herself had been affected by some sort of spell or toxin. One that disintegrated her walls, her own misgivings and preconceived notions.

Realization dawned on him, as he hung on that word.

Toxins.
The photographs, the murders.
The bite marks, claw marks...
Leon's hunch.

Of course, it all made sense.

There was only one creature who could secrete euphoric toxins that would rival any drug, even ecstasy, and leave marks like that.

Incubi and Succubi.

Though they were hard to come by normally, unless it was mating season, which only happened every hundred years or so. Cassius closed his eyes as reality set in, as Leon's words reverberated in his brain.

There hasn't been a sighting in this area for nearly a hundred years.

His thoughts raced at the horror of what that truly meant. Leon had suggested an Incubus was responsible for the murders, yet, he had no substantial proof, needing toxicology reports.

Toxicology reports that Cassius took for granted during his luncheon.

Where there was an Incubus, there was likely a den of Succubi not far away, and if he was truly working through the effects of Succubi toxin, he knew he was in for a long ride. Such toxins usually had catastrophic effects on the mortals, who could not handle the physicality of such a creature, especially when they transitioned to their full form, and those who could handle the sexual congress become prime targets for mates to host the Succubi's essence until they overtook their male targets in every way until they became them.

Like a parasite with only one purpose—to spawn more Succubi.

Though relations between the demonic creatures and vampires wasn't likely, it was possible, and their toxins would still work their lust-fueled magic. He'd seen it before. The only difference was it would wear off quicker on him than it would on a mortal, and he would just have to ride it out until it was completely out of his system.

Before Ava could respond, the sound of her stomach growling pulled him from his thoughts. He could have said anything, but all he settled on was, "You are hungry?"

Ava let out a soft sound of contentment.

A *laugh.*

A genuine, sweet *laugh.*

The sound was music to his ears.

"The question is not am I hungry, Cas. The question is, can I eat? And the answer to that is always *yes.*" She smiled.

She is flirting with me.

I don't believe it.

Of all the luck, the one time she lets her guard down and I'm high as a bloody kite.

Perhaps, it was the moment, the toxins. Perhaps, it was because they were in the middle of nowhere, surrounded by temptation on all sides. Cassius couldn't be sure what it was that spurred him to seize the moment.

But seize it he did.

"Donuts." His voice was starting to waver.

"What?"

"There's a place not far from here that makes the most delectable donuts. Let me take you." The words were out of his mouth before he could really hold on to them.

Her facial expression shifted to one of distrust, and her stance tensed as she grabbed the bucket tightly like a shield.

Anxiety spread through him as his heartbeat quickened, and he felt quite on the spot waiting for her answer.

Perhaps, the toxins had gone to his brain.

Perhaps, he'd overstepped.

Before he could open his mouth to speak, to apologize, Ava spoke.

"Fine. But you try anything, and I mean *anything*—" She pointed at him with one finger. "I will fucking dust you." Her voice was solid, and the threat was real as she glared at him with warning.

Doesn't she know I would never hurt her?

The realization of her words hit him, and immediately the panic set in.

She'd said *yes*.

And that changed everything.

"You okay, Cas? You look a little... jumpy." She regarded him with a suspicious gaze.

"Scout's honor, my sweet Avarice." He smiled nervously, feeling as if his slow beating heart would jump clear out of his chest at her words.

She said yes.

"I'm going to drop this off and grab some pants. I'll meet you out here in, like, ten minutes." She was definitive in her commands.

"And your weapons," he muttered quietly. Cassius knew she did not usually leave her house, or anywhere, without at least one or two weapons of choice. Most favorably, it was two stakes and a backup pocketknife.

Ava's eyes perked up.

"Who says I'm not packing right now?" She taunted him.

"Where on earth would you be hiding a stake right now?" he said as he cocked his head curiously, his gaze once again wandering over her freshly showered form, traveling down her long, slim legs to her boots.

Ava batted her eyelashes at him as a chuckle escaped her lips.

"Wouldn't you like to know?"

Cassius watched her turn the corner, and when he was certain she was gone, only then did he remember to breathe. The dizziness overtook him as he closed his eyes, leaning against the cold ice machine.

"What the hell have I gotten myself into?"

CHAPTER TWENTY-THREE

AVA DROPPED OFF the bucket of ice abruptly, like it was a hot potato and burned her fingers.

What the hell is wrong with me?

I should be pissed.

I should stake him right here...

I should...

Ava's thoughts spiraled in all directions, fraying at the edges. She could not pretend that Cassius's appearance meant nothing to her. She'd told him not to follow her, and whether he was telling her the truth or not about "visiting an old friend," it didn't change the fact that he was *here*. In Ansley, Oklahoma, in her hotel, offering her sugar confections.

Which he always does.

Only, this somehow felt different than all the other times he'd shown up to her Impala parked outside vacant lots at two in the morning with a bag of cookies and coffee. Something about the way his eyes looked, slightly glassy, and the way her scar *tingled* in his presence... Even the way he spoke—though his smooth, velveteen voice was still dreamy, it carried the hint of something she'd never heard in it before.

Fear.

But what on God's green earth did Cassius have to fear?

Ava removed Sam's Van Halen shirt, discarding it on the bed haphazardly; wondering for a moment if she should confiscate the thing as a souvenir. With all the other clothes strewn about his hotel room, she thought he'd likely not even notice it had gone missing but settled against the theft.

She jumped into her jeans, fastening the belt with haste as her stomach growled again.

"Shut the fuck up, you'll get yours soon enough," she grumbled in retort.

She dressed in her black tank top once again, smoothing the fabric over her abdomen. Looking herself over in the mirror, she ran her fingers through her hair, smoothing the stray locks into place before sliding her feet into her boots. Once again, she scoured the floor for her stake, and upon finding it, slid it into the side of her boot.

Whether or not Cassius was telling the truth, she could not deny the inkling in her gut that perhaps, it had *something* to do with the murders. Ava did not believe in coincidences.

The murders, the blood den, the congregation of all those vampires in one place...

I wonder what Cas knows about the blood den...

Is that why he's here?

The thought of Cassius in such a place caused a flurry of emotion in her. Anger pushed to the forefront, right behind it was envy. Her body flushed with heat, and her insides twisted at the thought. The desire to set something or *someone* aflame at the thought of Cassius's fangs in *anyone*... Ava did not want to think about it. So she pushed it away.

I'm just hangry, that's all.

Nothing more.

She grabbed the note from the lamp, shoving it in her clutch before finally leaving the aftermath of Sam Kingsley's love nest.

When she arrived back at the spot she'd left him, she was only somewhat surprised to see he was still there. A part of her thought perhaps, she'd imagined the whole thing, that perhaps, she was still asleep in Sam Kingsley's warm bed, but there was another part of her that would have *jumped* at the chance that maybe, just maybe...

Maybe he *did* follow her all the way to Ansley, Oklahoma because...

"How close is this place?" she asked before she could let her thoughts run away from her again. When Cassius was around, she found it rather easy to let them wander.

"A couple blocks," he said, sliding his hands in his pockets as he turned his back to her.

It wasn't the first time he'd done so, but something in the way he did in that moment gave Ava a startling thought.

He trusts me.

He trusts that I will not stab him in the back and turn him to dust.

But why?

Ava shook her head, dispelling the thoughts. She was out of sorts, it seemed, ever since she'd awakened in Dallas's bed this morning. Perhaps, it was the aftereffects of her attack from that redheaded vamp. Perhaps, she *was* suffering a concussion. It would explain her sudden shift in behavior, her mood swings, and her thoughts...

"Okay. But fair warning, if I don't make it, I'm not against eating you to survive, you know," she said with a smirk. She watched Cassius's shoulders tense at her words. As he looked over his shoulder at her, his glowing green eyes sparkled with something she couldn't quite place.

"Fine by me, as long as your hunger has been abated."

Ava felt a strange pooling in her gut, a strange flush of heat radiating from her scar at his words, his gaze, and therefore, she forced herself to look away.

I think I have completely lost my fucking marbles.

They walked past the lobby, past all the signs and congoers, and Cassius seemed to be picking up pace, almost running at this point.

"Where's the fucking fire? Can you slow down?" she grumbled as she tried to keep up.

Cassius abruptly stopped, and she almost collided with him, just before the revolving doors.

"I'm sorry, I thought you could keep up," he said, flashing her a charming smile.

Ava crossed her arms.

"I can. I just didn't plan on running a 5k to the donut shop."

"Very well. I shall adapt to your leisurely pace, if it pleases you."

Ava raised her eyebrow, fighting the smile that wanted to spread over her lips. She'd never seen Cassius this at ease. Usually, he was more reserved, a bit stand-offish, even. But here, now...

He was different, and though that should have alarmed her, should have been some sort of red flag, it wasn't. In fact, she found that she enjoyed this side of Cassius, and a part of her wanted to see more of it.

No.

That's a terrible idea.
That is how he'll get you.
Pull you in and end your fucking life.
Don't fall for his charms.
He's a monster and always will be.

But yet, after two years, he hadn't made a move to bite, attack, or... anything. He'd only stood off to the side, showing up with snacks and coffee, or in the middle of the night when she'd had a nightmare.

Ava was not certain what it all meant, and so she decided to focus on the task at hand instead of the labyrinth of thoughts this strange being seemed to build in her mind.

"I... thanks. I guess," she grunted as she pushed through the revolving doors, finding their way out on the street.

It was raining, and Ava let out a curse as she realized.

"Damn it, I should have brought a hoodie."

"No need for that," Cassius said smoothly, popping an umbrella over her head.

"Where the hell did you get that, Mary Poppins?" she asked as she looked up at the golden-haired vampire who held a black umbrella over her head, shielding her from the rain. Yet, it fell on him, and the sight of water droplets running down his smooth, pale skin stirred the heat inside her once more and she had to remind herself to breathe.

Even now, wet and pale, he looked like some angel fallen from the heavens, too beautiful for a place like Ansley, sticking out like a sore thumb, like a man from another time.

Because he is a man from another time, Ava.
He's an immortal, bloodsucking monster.

"Hotels such as the Starling usually keep a canister

of available umbrellas just for this occasion."

"Oh. Guess I haven't stayed in a lot of hotels this nice."

"Neither have I."

Ava wrapped her hand around the base of the umbrella, just below his hand. She pushed only slightly toward him.

"There's enough room for the both of us," she said solidly.

Cassius's lips turned up in a smirk.

"Is that an invitation?" His gorgeous green eyes searched hers, looking for something she couldn't quite grasp.

"It's common courtesy," she retorted as he stepped closer, underneath the umbrella, a sliver of space between them.

"Such excellent manners." The sly smile that spread on his lips exposed just a hint of his fangs, and Ava had to admit the sight was most appealing.

"Uh huh. You start running again and I might have to stake you," was all Ava could manage as they took off for the donut shop, and true to his word, he kept with her pace.

"Your wish is my command," he murmured as she dropped her hand, leading them through the rain into salvation.

"Are you enjoying your... convention?" he said the words as if he was unsure of himself, unsure whether or not she would bite him or snap at him.

A maddening flush crept up on her cheeks at his words, as images of Sam filled her brain, as her muscles strained with ache with every step, a reminder of just how much she'd enjoyed *him* and how he made her feel.

"I, uhm... guess you could say it's going pretty well.

Except for the murders." She looked at Cassius, who was looking straight ahead and likely would not notice, watching his facial expression at the words.

His lips formed a thin line, but other than that, he was expressionless, unreadable.

"I must confess that is why I am here. A very good friend of mine was accused of those murders."

"Does this very good friend happen to be a vampire?"

"Yes," he answered plainly as they stopped on the corner of the street, waiting for the walk sign to light up.

"And what can you do about any of it?" She realized the words sounded much harsher than she'd intended, but Cassius did not flinch.

"You have your skills, Ava, I have mine." The way in which he answered her forged a new path of questions, and Ava wondered momentarily what sort of *skills* someone like Cassius would have.

She followed the alluring vampire across the street, and when they came to the building, Ava felt a wave of disappointment. It was a small building, barely distinguishable as a restaurant at all, except for the window set in the dark brick that showed a lit-up dining room with hardly any individuals in it, and a neon sign that read *open*.

"This is it?" Ava asked, raising an eyebrow as Cassius closed the umbrella beside her.

"Indeed, it is." He smiled at her.

"It doesn't look like much." She shrugged as she headed for the door, but Cassius cut her off, opening it for her instead.

She rolled her eyes.

Who does he think he is, Prince Charming?

"In my experience, the best things in life are always

the things we take for granted."

"Whatever, I'm starving," she said.

"That makes two of us," he said as he followed her into the light of the dining room.

CHAPTER TWENTY-FOUR

AVA SIPPED HER coffee, and Cassius leaned back in the booth languidly, thankful for the table obstructing her view.

The crash of the Succubi toxin was at its peak and would likely taper off soon. Though, at the moment, it surged through him like a buzzing vibration, alighting his nerves, making every sensation magnified—including the uncomfortable tightness in his leather pants—and the dry, scratchy feel of his throat.

Ava relaxed as she pursed her lips, reading the menu of outlandishly named confections, none the wiser.

"So, how do you know about this place?" she asked as she turned the page.

She seemed quite conversational this afternoon. Most of the time she just rolled her eyes and shirked past him as if he were nothing more than a nuisance.

"I spent some time traveling when I first came to this country from Italy," he answered. It wasn't a lie. Though, he'd left out the part about *why* he'd traveled so much after setting foot on American soil for good in the 1940s.

When he'd found Eden up against the brick by a dastardly warlock in 1923, he'd only meant to find her and bring her back to Rome, but the lure of all America had to offer, and the woman who had managed to snake her way into his bed and arms were, too difficult to leave behind.

And after the Boracellis and the High Covens had arranged their engagement, the hunt for where to lay roots was quite strenuous and long because Eden was never satisfied with any of it. The towns. Him. Nothing was good enough for Eden, and never would be... The hole in her heart could never be filled. The darkness would only consume her until nothing was left but vengeance and greed.

Cassius pushed the memories—the thoughts of the wicked queen—out of his mind, glancing around the restaurant at the decor. It still looked just as it had in the fifties when he'd last visited it. The checkered floor was still just as shiny, the silver-edged bar bright against the faded yellow acrylic. Even the lamplights looked original, still casting their dewy glow over the pale-yellow booths and empty tables.

There were only a few people at this hour, being a few blocks from the convention and looking as quaint and unassuming as it did. Only the locals truly knew what delicacies lay behind its doors.

Eden never cared for sweets, not like he did. To her, they were merely human fodder, something that gave no value to their kind, and provided no real sustenance, and Cassius could not forgo such indulgences. Not when vampirism made everything taste better, even the most mundane of foods.

Ava settled her gaze just as the waitress came over.

"What'll it be, y'all?" she asked as she popped her

bubblegum. Cassius looked at Ava, awaiting her answer.

"I'm going for a dozen. I'd like two strawberry-frosted, two chocolate, two raspberry jelly-filled, two cookies and cream and..." She looked at Cassius with a devilish smirk.

"What would you like?" she asked sweetly, but Cassius knew it was an act. Sweet and Ava Crowley were not two things that normally went together. Her tone may have been sweet, but she did not hide her sarcasm well.

He smiled just enough that the edge of his canine fangs showed only to her, and almost instantly felt the faint increase in her pulse through his veins. The notion made him feel like king of the world, knowing that even if she would not admit such things, that he did have *some* effect on her. An effect that had nothing to do with thrall.

"I'll have two of the Red Velvet Supreme," he said as calmly as he could muster.

Ava squinted at him, weighing his response once more. She said nothing as she handed the menu to the waitress. She waited until the woman left, before speaking.

"You're not going to actually eat that, are you?" She crossed her legs underneath the table, a motion which bristled her boot against his long legs, and he found himself shifting again as his desire throbbed with need at her touch.

This is madness.

You are better than this...

"Although it does not sustain me, I can eat it. I can still taste sugar, among other things," he answered.

"What were you doing before I ran into you?" The words fell out without warning.

"None of your business," she bit. Cassius watched the heat crawl into her cheeks, watched her eyes rise with surprise as if he could see into her very soul, and the walls were up once more. He could feel Ava closing up like a clam and instantly regretted his words.

"What were *you* doing before I ran into you?" she retorted.

"Investigating." He shifted his arm so it strayed across his lap.

"Investigating? Since when do you do the Nancy Drew thing?"

"I have done the *Nancy Drew* thing for quite some time, though it has been a while. I enjoy solving puzzles, actually. Keeps my mind stimulated."

Ava scoffed and rolled her eyes. "I take it your *investigation* has to do with your 'friend'?"

Cassius nodded. As long as the conversation kept on this topic, fighting the effects of the toxin would be much easier. Procedural conversation was a mood killer, after all, no matter what century he was in.

"Yes. In fact, there is something I need to tell you about my... investigation."

Ava raised an eyebrow, and he could tell she was weighing whether or not to take the bait. She leaned back in her booth, bouncing her leg nervously against his, and his cock twitched again.

Devil take me now.

"And what do you *need* to tell me, Cas?"

He fought the smile as she looked at him with curiosity. If there was one thing Cassius had learned about Ava in the last two years, it was that the woman had a hunger and ambition for knowledge. She soaked up the books she read like a sponge, retained even the most off-kilter facts in her head like they were required reading.

She hated to be the last to know anything, especially when it came to the supernatural. She was a Crowley, after all. Such lust for things was in her blood.

"The murders are being made to look like a vampire killing, but in fact they are not."

"And how do you know that?" she said as she took a sip of her coffee. Her tongue darted out, licking her lips of the remnants of whip cream, and Cassius had to concentrate on his words. It should not have been as difficult as it was.

"Because it is mating season for the Succubi and Incubi."

"Come again?" Ava said, nearly spitting out her coffee.

"Every hundred years, the Succubi awaken, and they seek out human males to mate with. When they find humans who are capable, they..." Cassius could feel his throat going dry, not from thirst, from slight panic.

Even his unruly member tensed, waiting for the description, the rest of the explanation, which left him feeling slightly uncomfortable.

Ava blinked, waiting for him to continue. "They what? Come on, Cas, don't stop there," she taunted him, a smirk playing on her lips.

Cassius shifted his stance, crossing his legs, and sitting up straighter, away from her incessant bouncing leg.

"When the Succubi find humans who are capable of... copulating... they... absorb the male's essence, which gives them the ability to attach themselves to the male like a... like a parasite. Eventually, they take over completely, fusing themselves with the male to become an Incubus, and when that happens, the Incubus seeks out a female mate to breed with, to spawn more

Succubi for the next season, and the cycle repeats endlessly."

The air was silent between them as Ava wrinkled her nose in disgust.

"Ugh. Demon spawn. Great."

"The mating season occurs every hundred years, and Leon..." Cassius stopped as he realized he was saying too much.

"Leon's your friend, I take it."

"Yes."

"So you think the murders are what? Angry Succubi and Incubi who got carried away or something?" she asked.

"Or something. I think... I think for whatever reason, they are targeting the vampires. Though, I'm not sure why. Our kind tend to... stay away from demons."

Ava looked surprised at this revelation, and then she dropped a question Cassius did not see coming.

"What do you know about the blood den? The Dark Hearts Club?"

Cassius could feel his blood run cold.

How did Ava know about the blood den...?

"I beg your pardon..." His voice lost all its vibrancy and went flat.

"The Dark Hearts Club. Rumor has it, it is one of the only remaining dens in the country."

"It is," he answered cautiously.

"So you do know about it." She grinned.

"Leon owns it," he blurted out.

Ava nodded, just as the waitress came and dropped off a platter of confectionary delights. Her eyes looked like they were going to pop out of her head.

Cassius felt a warm smile spread across his lips at the sight, grateful for a slight reprieve from the dangerous conversation.

"Do you think the two are connected, somehow?" she asked as she took a jelly filled donut off the top of the platter.

"What do you mean?" He reached for one of the red velvet ones, his fingers brushing hers as he did so, and the touch sent a jolt of electricity directly to his groin.

"I mean, the Succubi are like, sex demons, right? And vampires go to a den for more than just blood," she said as she bit into her donut.

Cassius watched her bite into it, the red jelly clinging to her lips, and the image of her covered in blood—*vampire blood*—resurfaced. She was right, but he did not want to travel down that road of thinking. Not when the sight of red jelly all over her lips forced the memories on him with unrelenting fervor.

Her heaving chest, blood-soaked skin, eyes wild with the rush of her kill.

His cock twitched and he pursed his lips.

"Some do, yes."

Ava moaned in delight as her tongue darted out and licked the remains of jelly from her lips. Cassius stifled the reciprocal groan in his throat as he focused on his own uneaten donut, stilling his breath.

The thirst was lessening. The thirst for *blood*, that was. The thirst for Ava Crowley was only getting worse.

Maybe this was a bad idea...

"Well, I mean, it makes sense *maybe* the demon fuckers might want to use the den as hunting grounds to find their mates, and vampires can be territorial as hell."

Cassius scoffed in response. "Not all vampires are *territorial.*"

"Yes, they are." She waved him off as if his pleas were nothing, taking another bite of her donut, stuffing it in her mouth like a chipmunk. Red jelly spread on her lips once more.

"I suppose you could be on to something. I hadn't considered that the Succubi or the Incubus could be using the den to seek out their mates."

"Do they have any tells? Like, demons have red eyes, vamps have thrall..." Ava stopped, as if she was remembering where she was and who she was talking to. She took a long drink of her coffee before setting it down.

Cassius sighed.

"Well, those who do not... take the toxin *well*, the lust drives them mad, and usually a Succubi will feast on their blood."

"So they have fangs like vampires?"

"Yes. Succubi in their true form have fangs and a forked tongue and red eyes. Like traditional demons."

"What do you mean, in their true form?" Ava asked cautiously.

"They can only turn to their true form during mating. Otherwise, they look just like you or me."

"So, there's no way to tell in a crowded room who's human and who is a demon fucker?"

Cassius rolled his eyes at her coarse description. He nearly let out a laugh and would have if the conversation was not so serious. Thankfully, the toxins were thinning out and he was starting to feel slightly normal. His thirst for blood had quieted, yet, there was still the matter of his lust he'd need to take care of sooner or later.

"If there is, I'm not sure I know the answer. I haven't cavorted very much with the likes of demons. I try to stay away from such things."

"Are you going to eat that or what? You've been staring at that damn donut for at least five minutes."

"Don't even think about it. You've got at least seven

other choices on that platter to choose from." He nodded at the spectacular array of donuts in between them.

Ava narrowed her eyes at him, challenging him.

"Besides, you aren't fast enough." He smirked at her.

"Is that a challenge, Cas?" She smirked back, biting her lip. The sight was downright sinful.

They stared at each other like it was a standoff, one waiting for the other to flinch, and then make their move. And suddenly, it was as if the weight of the world had lifted and they were not in the middle of Jim Bob's Diner, as if they were not on opposite ends of the mortal slash immortal chain. It was almost as if they were just, Cassius Aurelia and Ava Crowley, nothing more.

Their hands collided, a mass of fingers and icing, as Cassius snatched up the dessert, pulling it out of her reach. He bit into the donut, fangs and teeth piercing the soft cake, sating the desire to bite, if only for the moment. The icing on his tongue was so sweet, the taste of vanilla and cream dialed up to eleven. He swallowed the bite, casting Ava a sly smile, wearing his victory proudly.

"Your enthusiasm is endearing, my sweet Avarice." He licked his lips.

Ava's eyes sparkled with mischief.

"Who says I lost? The icing's the best part, anyway." She retorted.

Cassius shook his head as he swallowed down the sweet pastry. Ava glanced down at her icing covered fingers, before placing one directly in her mouth, and Cassius bit down harder on his donut.

He was certain if he'd had a mortal heart, it would have stopped beating on the spot at the sight of Ava's fingers in her mouth. He fixated on the way she slid them in and out over her jelly-stained lips, how her tongue wrapped around her long fingers, and Cassius could hold off no more.

"Ahem... if you'll excuse me..." He nodded over to the restrooms. He needed some distance, and it seemed like the best excuse. If he didn't leave her right now, he would be far too tempted to taste her raspberry flavored lips for himself until he'd cleaned every last drop from her luscious, divine mouth.

Ava licked the icing off her thumb, her gaze fixed on him through long, dark, thick eyelashes.

She nodded in silent response, as Cassius all but sprinted to the restrooms.

CHAPTER TWENTY-FIVE

AVA PICKED APART a frosted donut, savoring the sweet taste; hungry for more. It was almost as if she was starving for something she couldn't quite put her finger on.

Well, I guess I haven't really eaten much in the last couple days...

The realization struck her like a bucket of ice water. Normally, when she'd travel to a new place, the first thing she did was scope out the local cuisine, but she hadn't thought much of food, or anything really, since she'd met Sam Kingsley at Hamlet's merely forty-eight hours ago.

Well, the man is quite the distraction, that's for sure.

Her vision blurred only slightly as the feeling of exaltation and happiness she'd felt since waking up in Sam's hotel room started to dissipate, replaced by a wave of tiredness and a headache.

Perhaps, I just need another cup of coffee...

Or perhaps, it has to do with the vampire who showed up once again out of nowhere to drive you fucking crazy.

Ava let out a sigh as she bit off another piece of dessert.

Of all the things to happen in the middle of Oklahoma, *he* had the audacity to show up and *claim* he hadn't followed her. As if she would believe his pleas.

Vampires lie.

It's what they do.

It's how they're programmed.

Say whatever they need to, to get you alone, to get their fangs in you, and call it a day.

Yet, she'd gone willingly with a *known* vampire—the very one who'd marked her blood as his—regardless of knowing this.

Why?

What the hell is wrong with me?

God, it's like I'm not even myself anymore...

She closed her eyes and took a deep breath as a wave of heat overcame her. She felt as if she was clearly losing her mind. In the two years she'd known Cas, he'd always been reserved. Yet, something about the glassy look in his eye, the way he seemed *loose*, less inhibited...

She could not deny that it was most intriguing. If she'd had any sense, she'd follow along until his guard was down completely, until he wouldn't suspect a thing, and then she'd put a stake through his chest, just like all the other vampires she'd come to slay since that fateful day in the frat house basement, where they'd first met.

Yet, she could not rationalize such actions when he smiled as he did, exposing a hint of fangs. When he smirked at her, eating his prize donut like a king on a throne. When he held the umbrella over her head, not even blinking as he stood drenched in the rain.

He's been gone awhile...

Ava's phone vibrated in her pocket, pulling her from her thoughts. Sliding it out, the lit-up screen displayed a text message. It was her brother.

Team meeting in my hotel room in ten minutes.

Be there.

"Cryptic and dramatic, as always," she grumbled as she set the phone down on the table, just as Cassius returned, looking as stoic and gorgeous as ever.

Why does he always have to look so fucking pretty?

Just once I'd love to see him have a bad hair day or something...

"I was starting to think you'd bailed on me." Ava sat back against the booth, gazing up at him, taking in all the fine details of the immortal creature in front of her.

His bright green eyes sparkled in the light, soft shadows falling across his pale skin from his golden hair, which was still slightly damp and pushed back to show his angelic features. His perfect jaw, smooth cheekbones.

"A gentleman never leaves his date unattended for long," he said with a smile that exposed just a hint of fang.

Ava's skin prickled with goosebumps, her wrist flaring with heat the way it always did when he was around. When she was around *vampires* in general.

"Well, good thing you're not a gentleman and this isn't a date," she said the words plainly, and did not miss the slight furrow of his eyebrows. It wasn't a date. After all, a date was something you did with someone you liked.

Ava didn't *like* Cas. Not like *that*. He was sexy and mysterious, yes, but he wasn't *alive*, and she certainly didn't trust him as far as she could throw him, and yet...

Before she could speak, or completely process such a thought, the waitress dropped off a box, and Ava started filling it with the leftover donuts as Cassius reached for his wallet.

"I got it, Cas." Her voice was solid.

"My idea, my treat." He smiled at her, as if nothing had happened. As if the man who'd left for the bathroom and the one who returned were two entirely different people. She twisted her lips into a wry expression.

Did I miss something?

"Really..." she started, but he waved her off and handed a wad of bills to the waitress.

"Keep the change," he spoke clearly, politely.

Ava glanced at him with suspicion once more but closed the box as the waitress nodded and sauntered off, leaving the two of them once again at odds.

"You didn't have to do that," she said, sliding out of the booth with the box in her hands.

"I know. But I wanted to..." The words made Ava uncomfortable and she averted her gaze.

"Well, thanks. I guess."

"You are quite welcome," he said as he rose from the booth and came to stand in front of her.

"I, uh... wish I could stay, but... Mal texted me, wants to meet up."

Cassius looked as if he was struggling with something, his eyes dancing back and forth nervously.

Ava moved to turn, his voice stopping her.

"Would you like some company along the way?" He looked into her eyes, and in them she saw something she hadn't expected to see.

Hope.

Don't be ridiculous Ava, he just wants your blood.

Nothing more.

He's not capable of wanting anything else.

Her brain battled with the twisting butterflies in her stomach and the feeling of guilt. Though, why leaving a vampire alone in a donut shop would make her feel guilty, she was uncertain. It didn't make sense. Then again, lately nothing was making sense, and it was as if the world was upside down. So, instead of spouting an angry remark or sarcastic comment, instead of turning heel and leaving him in the dust, she found herself going against the grain, against what she knew she *should* do.

"Okay." Her answer was short, but it was enough to make Cassius's lips turn up ever so slightly in the corner.

***

Ava set the box of donuts down lightly on the bureau, sat on the edge of her bed, and only then did she finally let out a deep sigh. Her head was pounding, and she felt slightly queasy, like she felt when hungover. Except, Ava knew the alcohol she'd consumed at Hamlet's was out of her system by now.

Perhaps, I shouldn't have eaten four donuts in one sitting.

That was probably not a good decision.

She fell back on her hotel bed, looking at the ceiling as the events of the past forty-eight hours hit her. She let her hand fall to her chest, feeling the beat of her heart as she closed her eyes.

Meeting Sam in Hamlet's.

The first night they'd spent together; exploring one another.

Tasting each other.

The vampire who attacked Vinny and then her.

Dallas's arms holding her tight.

Waking up snuggled against his solid, warm chest.

Sam's sexy smile at the panel.

Cassius shielding her from the rain.

His fangs tearing into a donut, all but ripping it to shreds with that sexy, victorious smile.

Her impending date with the sexy celebrity demonologist.

She'd come to TerrorCon to relax, to enjoy a celebration of movies and fandom, but yet she had barely made it to any panels, or met anyone aside from Sam.

"That's it! After your date tonight, it's panels and movies! No more of this fucking around!" she chastised herself.

"You need to focus on the important things," she whispered aloud, her fingers running over her raised scar on her wrist.

The important things.

Finding a way to remove Cas's mark.

Finding the vampires responsible for killing her parents.

Her phone vibrated against her hip, and she sighed, knowing exactly who it was.

"I'm coming," she said as she forced herself up off the bed, grabbing her skull clutch and heading next door to Mal's room for the impromptu meeting with renewed focus.

CHAPTER TWENTY-SIX

AVA KNOCKED ON the door, tapping out the beat of "The Final Countdown" like she used to do when she was little, wanting to get into her brother's room to play with his Legos. Though they hadn't said anything about it in ages, it had become a sort of language for them both. Even after moving in with their Aunt Becky, the elaborate knock was something that brought both of them comfort.

The door opened to reveal Vinny on the other side, and Ava could see Mal sat on the edge of his bed, next to Dallas, looking a little worse for wear. Dark circles under his eyes indicated he hadn't slept well, and his pallor was slightly paler than usual.

"The prodigal son returns," she drawled as she entered the room, brushing past Vinny's flannel sleeve.

"Glad to know you were so worried about me," he grumbled, raking his hand through his hair.

"Dallas said it wasn't all that abnormal for you to be gone awhile."

Malcolm shot Dallas an annoyed glare, but Dallas didn't react. Just stood against the wall by the bed, his large arms crossed over his chest, leaning like he was over everything.

The vampires, the convention.

Mal's sudden emergence.

"Did he, now?"

"I mean, it wouldn't be the first time you stayed out past your bedtime." Dallas shrugged, avoiding Ava's gaze.

She pulled out the chair in front of the desk across from Mal, flipping it around so her legs straddled the back, her arms resting across the back languidly.

"Normally, I'd agree with you, but I wasn't gone because I wanted to be."

Tito and Hunter were camped out against the air conditioner, both looking to be eating from a large bag of barbecue chips.

"What do you mean?" Hunter asked through a mouthful of chips.

"I was abducted by a fucking Succubus."

Ava felt her blood run cold.

Cas mentioned something about Succubi and Incubi...

Maybe he was telling the truth...

"How do you know it was a Succubus?" Vinny asked.

"Well, honestly, she *seemed* normal enough, and I thought everything was kosher until we started getting our clothes off and—"

"Spare me the dirty details, please..." Ava shuddered.

"I thought I saw her eyes flash red. I just figured it was a trick of the light, but then... when she was... um... going down, her tongue felt... different. I tried to open my eyes, but everything was blurry, and I felt like a... *need* to..."

Ava twisted in her seat, uncomfortably.

"She called me *meum delicium*."

Ava felt her heart stop, felt her blood chill.

No, that has to be a coincidence...

"My pleasure," she whispered.

"Yeah, how do you know that?" Dallas asked, his eyes settling on her.

Ava met his gaze. Though a part of her knew she should come forward, another told her not to divulge her secrets just yet. She needed to be sure first, before throwing around an accusation like that.

Just the thought, *Sam Kingsley is an Incubus* sounded too outlandish, too far-fetched.

But those words...

What were the odds the Succubus would use the same phrase the demonologist had when he was deep within her walls, pushing her over the edge?

"I mean, you can learn a lot of things if you go to college, you know," she bit back at Dallas. He regarded her a moment longer, as if contemplating the truth in her words, but when he looked away, she knew he had bought it.

"You didn't..." Tito asked cautiously.

Mal shook his head.

"No, I didn't. When she said those words, something just... something clicked. I remembered that job we worked a couple years ago, the one in Vermont. Where we went to investigate that lead... which turned out to be nothing?"

Mal's gaze danced around the room, and Ava got the feeling there was something he was implying, some code of secrecy among them that she was not sworn in on, and that made her angry.

Why would Mal keep something from her?

Especially if it was so important, he couldn't say it out loud in a private hotel room?

The hunters exchanged glances, silent nods in agreement.

"Yeah, we stumbled upon that Succubi den by accident, when we saved that guy we thought was vamp chow."

Mal nodded in agreement.

"I remembered hearing those words. Remember their significance."

"What significance?" Ava asked, and they all turned to her, as if remembering she was there.

"The words are like... like hypnotizing. You know how magicians will hypnotize you to do something when they say a certain word, then snap their fingers and you're awake? But the minute they say that word—"

"Boom. You don't know what hit you and you do whatever they ask." Hunter clapped his hands together.

Ava swallowed nervously.

"It's like a spell they put you under to make you more pliable so they can get what they need to become an Incubus."

"How did you get out?" Tito asked as he popped a potato chip in his mouth.

"I fought my way out, of course, and when I managed to get a knife in that bitch's chest, I took whatever blood I could for anti-venom, just in case we need it, and I fucking ran out of there as fast as I could to warn you all, but I was still intoxicated. I mean, we fooled around quite a bit before she—"

"Seriously, stop. I think I'm going to throw up," Ava grumbled. It wasn't a complete lie. Her stomach seemed to be in knots.

"So we've got a vampire blood den and a Succubi den, and probably an Incubus floating around somewhere where there's a massive concentration of humans?" Vinny sighed.

"Yeah, and I think those fucking demons are the ones responsible for the murders."

"And how do you figure that?" Ava asked skeptically.

"I heard them talking, when I was trying to escape. They're planning some kind of attack at The Dark Hearts Club in the dungeon, where all the bloodsuckers are going to be."

"So, they're after the vampires?" Tito asked curiously.

"No." Ava shook her head, Cas's words finally making sense.

"No, I think they want the den. For breeding grounds. A vampire owns it, so it only makes sense they'd try to squeeze them out."

Dallas twisted his lips, his gaze heated as it fell on her.

"And how do you know that?"

"Call it a really good hunch," she said as she stared back at him.

"Ava's right. It's the perfect motive. How many people visit a strip club on a daily basis? There's enough lust in one of those places to keep an Incubus or Succubus *rolling* in human ass for eternity."

"We have to stop them," Mal said definitively.

Dallas looked at Mal, nodding in response. The other hunters did the same. Then, they all turned to her.

"What are you looking at me for?"

"Are you in or are you out, Ava?" Mal asked.

Ava felt on the edge of a cliff, as if she was being pressed to jump. To jump into uncertainty and potentially wind up vampire chow or worse, an incubator for a demon spawn. Yet, the predator advancing on her would surely take her under if she did not jump.

She wanted to say no. To walk away and let the Succubi take out the vampires, to let it all dissolve into dark matter, far, far away from her. But she knew deep down in the depths of her soul that she would not be able to turn away.

The lives they could save if they worked together...

They could take out a den and a nest, and it would be a hell of a win, and Ava was always good at calling the winning horse.

"I'm in," she said.

"But you should know I have a date tonight."

Mal rolled his eyes. "Of course you do."

"With Sam?" Vinny raised his eyebrow, a soft smile playing at his lips.

"As a matter of fact, yes. We're going to dinner around seven." Ava smiled, her nerves alighting at the mention of his name. If he truly was what she did not want to say, she'd find out tonight. She had to know, and there was only one way to truly find out. She'd gotten up close and personal with vampires quite often, right before she delivered the blowing kill.

"Maybe it's better that she doesn't come. I mean, it'd be one less person to worry about," Dallas grumbled. The tone, the way he averted his gaze, and his words ignited a fire within Ava that stoked her dormant rage.

Who the hell do you think you are, Jake?

"Dallas has a point..." Tito added.

"Who says I can't find time to dine and slay?" she bit.

Mal chuckled, rolling his eyes.

"I mean, he's not wrong, but we can always use backup if you think you can handle it." Mal smiled at her, and in his eyes, she could see he had faith, trusted her to watch his back and everyone else's. She also knew her brother well enough that he would prefer to keep her in his line of sight for peace of mind, rather than out of it.

"Please. You had me at the den of vamps."

"Think you can get your demonologist date to bring you to The DHC?" Mal raised an eyebrow.

"I think I can manage that," Ava responded solidly.

"Good. Get some rest, guys, because tonight we're going hunting."

CHAPTER TWENTY-SEVEN

LEBLANC'S WAS LIKE stepping back in time. From the ornate woodwork and marbled tile to the art deco-frosted glass and framed prints on the wall. In the historic town of Ansley, it screamed opulence.

Cassius sipped his Bordeaux anxiously. Of course, Cora would pick this place.

She'd lived under Leon's roof long enough to form an attachment to all things decadent and luxurious, not to mention she didn't know Cassius's history. She only knew what had been visible to her over the decades, and his relationship with Eden was off the table of knowledge.

"It does not have to be this way, Eden. You do not have to shut me out."

"How noble of you to come to my rescue," she drawled.

"You and I both know this arrangement is what is best, given our circumstances." Cassius reached across the table, his fingers brushing the top of Eden's hand. She pulled away, setting it in her lap.

"Is that all I am to you? A circumstance?" Her dark

eyes were vacant, no glimmer of life in them. No hope, no sadness, just empty pools.

"Of course not. How can you say that after I—"

"After you what? Rode in on your white horse to sweep poor damsel Edie off her feet? Oh, what would I have done without you, my dear Cassius?" she mocked, her eyes grazing over the form of a young busboy who had his arms stacked with dishes.

"I am a victim, too, you know!" Cassius grumbled, leaving his hand on the open table.

Eden licked her lips as the young man hefted his dishes through the kitchen doors, her gaze settling at his backside.

"A victim of what? You are not the one riddled with the pressure of delivering an heir. A perfect heir, might I add."

"I am your victim, Edie. Every day I fight for your attention, fight to try and make this arrangement more than something we have to do. I threw myself on the fire for you, and you won't even fucking look at me."

Eden's eyes shifted to Cassius, taking in the sight of him.

"If you just give this a chance, a real chance..."

"We both agreed to uphold this engagement. You said so yourself, feelings would be left off the table." She grabbed her glass of wine, fingernails scratching the glass.

"Because I did not want to rush you. You had just lost Marcellus..."

Shattered glass rained over the table, across her lap, red wine bleeding onto the fresh white linens, spreading quickly.

"Don't say his name."

"I cannot keep on like this. Competing with a ghost."

"Then don't. I am not forcing you to stay."

Her words were true, but yet, they were not. She was not forcing him to stay, but his duty to uphold the agreement, the agreement that kept his mother protected and safe, was of the utmost importance. If he left, surely the agreement would end. He'd do whatever it took to make sure those he loved were taken care of. Though, at the time, it hadn't seemed like such a miserable sentence. He'd been hopeful that perhaps in the ashes of Marcellus's death, in the space between their friendship, perhaps, they could be more.

Despite being an engagement of convenience and breeding, Cassius hoped they could build some semblance of a life together. Yet, that life was an uphill battle wrought with thorns and storms that would not relent, would not cease to give Cassius one breath of serenity.

"Can you look at me and honestly say you wish me to go?" His voice was strained, full of remorse, pain.

Eden rose from her seat, gazing down at Cassius like a vengeful goddess ready to strike her killing blow.

"I will make this simple for you, then." She sauntered closer, trailing her long fingers along his jaw, lifting his chin with her pointer finger.

Cassius looked up at her, taking in the sight of her beauty. The scent of vanilla and roses filled the air once more.

Thrall.

Eden's thrall seeped around him like a blanketing fog, and his cock hardened at her touch, his pupils dilating. He found himself unable to move and that both alarmed him and excited him all the same.

"I belong to no one. Not you, not Francesca, not the damn High Covens."

Her fingers traced his neck, nails dragging over the veins softly, before they gripped his neck tighter. Not tight enough he couldn't breathe, but tight enough to imply the seriousness of her words.

"You cannot have my heart, Cassius," she whispered as her thrall sank deep into his bones, into his brain, taking over.

It was an almost heavenly feeling, except for the fact he could not move of his own accord, something that left him feeling alarmed. Her words left a sadness, an ache in his chest, and she looked at him with a spark of interest, and in her eyes, he could see his own fear.

She'd never exuded her thrall on him before.

"But my body is yours to take, should you decide to put your emotional agony aside. Now, I am done with this dinner and this conversation."

Cora prattled on about the menu, her bright pink lips moving a mile a minute.

"I know circumstances could be better, but I am truly glad you came," she said sweetly, folding her hands in her lap.

She looked stunning against the luxurious setting, her bright red hair falling over her shoulders in long curls, parts of it in the front had been pulled back to frame her heart-shaped face. She'd always been a beautiful girl, no matter the fashions of the decade.

"Yes, well, Leon's done much for me over the years, it was only right I return the favor."

"Why did you leave the house?" she asked and then took a sip of her water.

"Too many memories. Not all of them are good ones."

Cora nodded in agreement. "I get it. Still wish you could have stayed. I liked having someone else in the house for once. Someone I know."

Cassius ran his fingers around the base of his wine glass, debating his words. With the toxin out of his system, he was finally able to think clearly, process everything he'd learned.

The more he thought about Ava's words, the more it made sense. If they truly didn't look any different than the average human mortal, plenty of them could have already infiltrated the club. He decided to take a chance.

"I believe I may have a lead on the situation with Leon."

"Oh really?" She tore into a piece of bread, dredging it around on the plate of olive oil between them.

"It is Succubi and Incubi mating season, you know."

Cora did not flinch at his words. "Yeah, I know."

How interesting...

"How do you know about that?"

"Well, there's this guy who's been filming a documentary in the area. Sam Kingsley, I think is his name. Anyway, he's making some kind of 'vampire tell all' and has been filming at the club for a while, and I overheard him talking to someone on his crew about working a case that turned out to be a Succubus, where they only come out every so many years when it's 'mating season.' Guess he's like, some big demon exorciser or something." She shrugged. A couple passed them, and Cassius did not break his gaze from Cora.

"How does Leon feel about this documentary?"

"He's been a bit of a stickler about it. You know Leon. Loves information but doesn't always want people to have it. Likes being the smartest guy in the room."

"You didn't think *any* of this was pertinent information?" Cassius pursed his lips, feeling agitated.

"Not really. I mean, the documentary has nothing to do with the murder accusations, and Succubi are harmless to us. It's not like they pose a threat or anything."

"How long have you been locked up in that mansion?" Cassius huffed. "Of course they pose a threat. They are demons, Cora."

"Yeah, and who's to say we aren't the very same thing?"

"We are *not* creatures from Hell." His voice only rose an octave.

"We feed on blood and sex just the same."

"They feed on *lust*. Their only function is to overtake a host and spread their seed. That's it. One goal. We are more than what we feast on. We are more than our hunger for blood and our libidos."

"They are just doing what is natural for them! None of them asked to awaken during the mating season! They're just trying to make sense of what they are, the same way we are."

"I cannot believe you are defending them. They are likely responsible for *murders*. The very ones that Leon has been accused of!"

Cora huffed indignantly.

"And you are not? I remember you have killed your fair share of mortals in your day."

"That was different, Cora, and you know that. And furthermore, I have never taken pleasure in what I have had to do to survive."

"I do not wish to argue with you, Cassius," Cora said, crossing her arms.

"We are not arguing. We are having a discussion."

"Well, I do not like this discussion or your insinuations. We can agree to disagree, can we not?"

Cassius weighed her words. She'd been careless in her regard to tell him everything, and such a thing did leave him feeling perturbed. But she did have a very good point. While he was adamant they were different from the demon spawn, he could not help but see the similarities, and seeing Cora passionately defend them, even if she shouldn't... made him slightly proud. It would appear Leon's teachings had taken, after all. He did not like her insinuations, either, but he knew he needed to keep a clear head.

He also knew he needed access to the blood den. If Ava was right and the Succubi were there... he needed to find out. He needed to gather his evidence and be a hundred percent certain before going to Leon with his findings.

"I do not wish to argue with you, either. We will table this discussion. For now, but it is far from over."

He brought the glass of wine to his lips and took a long drink as another couple passed by, heading to their table, and a familiar scent filled his nostrils.

Jasmine and bergamot.

Cassius set his glass down, snapping his head in the direction they'd walked.

No, it can't be...

His gaze settled on long, pale legs that left his throat dry, and made the throbbing pulse in his veins ebb like a sonar. His gaze traveled upward, settling on the sway of the hips said legs belonged to, onto the curves he knew all too well. And when she turned around, looking over her shoulder—amber eyes ablaze—Cassius did not look away.

CHAPTER TWENTY-EIGHT

THE LAST PERSON Ava expected to see at Le Blanc's on her date with Sam was the redheaded vampire who'd attacked Vinny. Sitting with Cassius, of all people.

Who is she?

Ava felt awash with hunger, jealousy.

What the hell is she doing with Cas?

A part of her wanted to stake the beautiful creature, right here in the middle of the room, but she knew better than to draw attention to herself in a public setting. Having to explain to a room full of people that you'd just killed a vampire didn't always go over well, as most people didn't know vampires even existed. Not unless you were thrust into the world of blood and ash the way she or Mal, Dallas, or even Sam had been. No, if she staked this woman making eyes at Cassius, she'd only look like a psychopath.

Sam slid into the open booth, and Ava followed suit. The man really did clean up nicely. Even on the show, he was quite casual, wearing nothing but band tees and horror-centric shirts and jeans, despite being in his thirties. Yet, when she'd met him in the lobby at six-thirty as directed, she'd hardly recognized him, dressed in a well-tailored gray suit with a stark-red tie.

Ava hadn't planned on fancy dinners with her brother and, therefore, was pressed for something to wear that could pass as appropriate for a date. She'd settled on the long, form fitting black dress she'd brought for her *Elvira: Mistress of the Dark* cosplay. By the look on Sam's face upon her entrance, he did not mind one bit.

Sam leaned in close to her, setting his hand on her exposed thigh.

"I'm really glad you showed up. I was worried I was going to have to dine alone again."

"Well, one thing you should know about me is that the way to my heart is through my stomach."

"I will remember that," he said with a light squeeze as he picked up his menu.

So far so good, he doesn't suspect I know anything, which is good.

"How was your panel?" she asked, attempting to make small talk. The realization they hadn't spoken much made her anxious, and it was as if she was clear of mind for the first time in days. With her wits about her, she was acutely aware of all the visible flaws between her and the attractive man next to her.

"It was all right. It was just a basic Demonology 101 panel with Kristen."

"Your co-host. Yeah, I haven't really seen much of her during the con."

"She hates these things, so she's usually holed up in her hotel room any time she's not on the clock." Sam air-quoted his last words, and Ava couldn't help her smile.

She started to feel slightly at ease, but nevertheless,

the edge was still there. She could feel a fiery gaze from across the room and she didn't have to look to know where it was coming from. Her wrist flared with heat and her skin prickled with goosebumps under her long black sleeves.

"I know you don't like to talk about work, but I did have some questions I was hoping I could pick your brain about?" She crossed her legs, angling herself toward him, the motion pushing her breasts together, all but popping out in the space between her plunging neckline.

Sam's gaze dipped to her cleavage, his tongue flicking out over his lips. The lights dimmed, and for a moment Ava could have sworn she saw a flash of red in his eyes, but when he looked back up at her there was no evidence. No red eyes, no shimmer or glow, but once she got him alone in the den... she'd know for sure. Still, she needed to act as if nothing had changed, for if he was truly an Incubus as she suspected, he would be dying to close the deal, the ritual tonight.

I really do need to get a grip on myself.

"Sure, shoot."

"I um... kind of have a secret. I don't normally tell people this but—" She leaned closer, settling her hand on his thigh, rubbing slightly. The need to touch him, to feel him was becoming difficult to fight the closer she was, and when his sweet, fiery scent surrounded her she couldn't help but give in.

She traipsed her fingers up his thigh, resting them just alongside his groin.

"And you want to share it with me? I'm flattered," he said with a smile, placing his hand on top of hers.

The touch, even as faint as it was, stirred butterflies in her stomach, her skin crawling with the need to feel his touch everywhere. Somewhere in her rational brain, she understood the reason, but a part of her wished it was something else. That the connection she felt with Sam was because she liked him, and not the ever-flowing toxins he secreted. She wished her attraction was beyond chemical, but when she looked into his dark, alluring eyes she knew at that moment it was both. Which made everything she was about to do, so much more difficult.

He needed to trust her.

Needed to think he had her, for her to get close to him; close enough she could exorcize the demon within him.

But it was a risky process.

Dallas would assist her; he was the hunter with the most experience exorcizing and cleansing in their little band of misfits. As long as Ava could get Sam downstairs, in the private dens, Dallas and Mal would take care of the rest, and the vampires...

The thought of sinking her stake into a fresh vamp caused her heart to skip a beat. So much had happened, and she wasn't entirely sure how to feel about any of it, but the promise that came with her stake was enough to make her forget, enough to abate the turmoil even if it didn't last.

"I know the truth. About vampires, I mean. Well, actually, I know the truth about a lot of things, but if I had to pick one line of study, it'd be vamps."

"Oh really?" Sam's eyes focused on her intently, but before Ava could speak, the waitress was at their table.

"We'll have a bottle of champagne, please, to start," he said, barely even looking at the waitress, and within minutes she had disappeared.

"Please, continue," he said as his fingers grazed her skin, his thumb brushing over her raised scar.

The touch felt... *cold.*

Like ice.

In the presence of vampires, her skin always prickled with goosebumps, but her wrist... her wrist where Cassius's fangs had marked her skin, was always *warm*. So warm, in fact, she felt as if her blood was boiling. But despite being in the same room with a vampire, she did not feel what she always did.

Instead she felt the opposite.

Chilled, cold.

Perhaps they do have a tell after all.

"Two years ago, my boyfriend... he was killed. By vamps. I saw the whole thing." It wasn't hard to feign sadness, for Ross's death would always haunt her. His moan of pleasure, right before his scream of pain as the vampire fed on him.

"Oh my God, Ava..." Sam's eyebrows furrowed, and he scooted closer, taking her hand in his free one, moving the other to around her back, pulling her close. Up close, she could smell his aftershave. She closed her eyes and breathed him in deeply. It was the most pleasant smell.

"It's... it's okay. I mean, it's not *okay*, but... anyway—I learned all about the monsters hiding in the dark that day."

Sam's fingers brushed over her scar slowly. "I wanted to ask you about this, but I didn't think it was any of my business."

His dark eyes dipped to where his fingers caressed her, and she couldn't deny the touch stirred the butterflies in her stomach once more.

"Ask away," she whispered, feeling overrun by emotion.

"Claimed by a vampire?" It was a statement more than a question, definitive. His words were heavy, and the way they made Ava feel...

Guilt, shame, anger, and sadness all pushed forth. She hadn't understood in that very moment what Cassius was asking. All she knew was she would have done anything to live.

"Yes," she whispered. "I've been searching for a way to break the bond for two years."

Sam licked his lips, his fingers splayed at her back, brushing along the edge of her hair.

"Are you scared he'll come back to finish what he started?" Sam's words were heavy in the air between them.

Ava's eyes lifted only a fraction, and she gazed at Cassius through her long lashes, watching as he gracefully sipped his drink.

Red wine.

A well aged Bordeaux, probably.

She knew how much he favored red wine, always raiding her fridge in the middle of the night when she'd awakened from a terrible nightmare. She'd always threatened to end him if he kept showing up without warning, yet, she could not close her window at night.

Her housekeeper, Connie, had even started stocking wine in the fridge more often, if only to appease Cas. She was always prattling on about him; about how perfect he was.

As if I don't already know that.

He's designed to be perfect, but I will not fall into that web of deception.

"Every day," she answered, looking away once more.

"But I'll be ready when he does. I've trained. I've learned everything I can. I don't leave home without my stakes."

"Stakes? So you are..."

"A slayer," she whispered the words and the silence between them was most palpable.

Sam pressed his lips into a thin line, a look of contemplation on his face.

"I get why you don't tell people that."

"Yeah, well, I just... I'm not saying this is going to go anywhere, but if it does... I just... I need you to know the truth."

"I remember the first time I exorcized a demon. I was fourteen. I'd been studying exorcisms and demonology for a while at that point, but I hadn't really told anyone about it. I suspected there was a crossroads demon praying on people in my town. I couldn't prove it, until my friend made a deal and wasn't able to hold up their end of the bargain."

"I'm sorry, that must have been difficult for you, being so young and all."

"Sometimes, you don't know what you're made of until you're made." A soft smile tugged at his lips as he drew her closer.

Ava looked into his deep brown eyes, and started to feel lightheaded, the desire in her stomach only spreading under his serious gaze.

"What are you made of, Sam?" she whispered, her gaze dipping to his lips, remembering how they tasted, how they felt against her own. Somewhere in her mind, she sensed danger. But that was the difference between Ava and everyone else. Most people sensed danger and they fled. Ava flirted with it, instead, dancing the tightrope just to see how far she could fall before she lost herself completely. In the presence of this man, she could not think clearly.

"I think you know by now, *meum iuvat*."

His words were like smooth caramel over chilled vanilla ice cream, and when Ava brought her lips to his, she fell from the cliff into the abyss below. And as his lips moved hungrily against hers, a soft moan escaped her throat. He tasted like the icing of a red velvet supreme donut, and for a moment, as she closed her eyes, she let herself enjoy the taste and all the desire it stirred within her soul.

CHAPTER TWENTY-NINE

THE DARK HEARTS Club was in full force.

Cora clutched his arm tightly as they moved through the thick crowd of mortals on the top floor, the pink, purple, and blue lights roving over the crowd. There were two dancers on stage, one at each end of the catwalk. While one was crawling around on her hands and knees seductively, the other he recognized from the previous night. The blonde, who'd looked at him with her hands around her throat. She danced gracefully around the pole, the motions reminding him of a ballerina he'd once known.

Marguerite.

The one and only woman he'd ever had as a sustainable food source, in his early years with Marcellus and Octavius. Though, like most of the women Cassius had cared for in his long life, her fate did not end well.

Because of Eden and her jealousy.

Even in the days Eden fought him, she could not keep her hands clean. Spurred by the madness of her addiction to supernatural blood—witch blood, demon blood, it was all the same to her—she did not want him, but she could not stand anyone else coming close to having him, either.

I did it to protect you.

Her words were always the same, every time, but they did not change the reality of the deaths that were on his conscience, merely because of one's relationship with him, even if said relationships were platonic at best.

"Maybe we could hang out for a bit before heading downstairs? I always like to have a little fun first before I retire to my den."

"*Your* den?" Cassius raised an eyebrow in question.

"Well, of course *my* den. What do you think I do? Hunt like an animal?" She rolled her eyes.

Cassius pressed his lips in a thin line. "I am just surprised."

"You aren't the only one who dislikes spontaneous feeding or killing, Cassius. It's messy. I don't like messy."

"Do you have a... what is the word? Fox?" he asked nervously.

"I do. But I also entertain others from time to time." She stopped in the middle of the crowd, turning her body close to his, snaking her arms up around his neck.

"When was the last time you danced, Cassius?" She gazed up into his emerald eyes, searching for something from him.

Acceptance, permission.

What, he was not sure of.

He wrapped his arms around her waist, yet left space between them. A dance was just a dance, after all. It did not mean anything.

"I spent much of the late eighties and nineties

working and traversing clubs."

"And since then?"

"Since then, I have kept to myself. I do not indulge. Not anymore." He scanned the room, at the bodies beside them, in front of them, of the dancers on the stage, and the waitresses and waiters dropping off drink orders. In many ways the world had changed in appearance, but at its core it was still the same, and always would be.

Cora pulled herself closer, closing the gap between them, and Cassius pushed her away only a fraction.

"This is a good distance."

"What are you afraid of? I don't bite. Much." She giggled.

"Cora..."

"Don't think, Cassius. Just... enjoy this for what it is. Stop fighting what is in your nature."

Cassius breathed deeply, and she pulled herself closer once more, letting her small fingers trail over the fabric of his black dress shirt, over the tiny plastic buttons.

"It's okay to have fun," she said as she slid her hand over his heart. "It's okay to live in the moment, without expectations or guilt. You carry too much."

Cassius moved back and forth to the rhythm, and Cora followed without question.

After a couple songs, Cora ventured to the bar for refreshment, returning with two drinks.

"What is this?" Cassius asked skeptically.

"A cocktail," she teased as she offered him the drink.

"I know that, but what is it?" he asked as he took the glass from her hand.

"I recall your favor for sweeter things in life, so I offer you a little concoction known as a Dracula's Kiss." She twisted her lips in amusement.

Cassius sipped the dark liquid, and the tastes exploded on his tongue.

Cherry, of course.

"It is delicious." He smiled as he took another sip. Though vampirism made it difficult for him to get drunk, it was not uncommon for him to feel slightly inebriated. Though, keeping the alcoholic buzz going was not an easy feat and usually required a litany of cocktails and hours of drinking. But after nearly a bottle of red wine, and nearly half a Dracula's Kiss, Cassius was starting to feel a little more relaxed.

Cora smiled at him through her lashes, spinning the liquid around with her cocktail straw before putting it to her lips and sucking. She watched him carefully as the lights and music shifted, signaling the change in dancers.

He drained the rest of his drink almost instantly, savoring the sweet taste on his tongue before biting into the candied cherries at the bottom just as the speakers came on to announce the next set of dancers.

Cora grabbed his drink from his hands before leaving him to dispose of their glasses, and he had to admit it did feel good to just... dance. To just be in the moment, for the moment, carefree. He'd venture down to the den soon enough, and it would all disappear.

"Please welcome to the stage, Avarice!"

Well, that certainly isn't a name you hear every day...

The dark guitar riffs of "Sweet Dreams" filled the air, but it wasn't the version he was familiar with from living during the era of the Eurythmics. No, this one had a deep, male voice crooning about "some of them want to use you..."

And when Cassius turned to get a look at the new dancer, he gasped in surprise.

Perhaps, Cora has spiked my drink and I am

hallucinating.

For the second time in twenty-four hours, Cassius was battling with whether or not he was surely going insane.

My sweet Avarice...

Ava sauntered down the catwalk, all long legs and curves, just the way Cassius had always dreamed about. He was only half certain he was dreaming, as if somehow the Succubi toxin had leeched its way into his brain and brought forth an image directly from his fantasies.

Though, she was still much more clothed than the previous dancers, wearing her long, skintight black dress she'd worn to dinner with the man she was with.

Is he here as well?

Surely...

The high slit in her dress accentuated her slender legs and when she moved, the movements were deliberate and confident. When she made her way to the pole at the end of the catwalk, he waited with bated breath to see what she'd do. For once, he was glad to be anonymous, lost in the sea of people.

She did not waste a moment as she circled it, arching her arms behind her, grasping onto the steel. She pointed her toes and arched her back, the motion rather graceful, but somehow more appealing than anything he'd witnessed in The Dark Hearts Club, yet.

His gaze trailed over the curve of her spine, dipping farther down, following her movement as she slid down the pole. Her eyes fluttered, she bit her lip, and his throat went dry. The overwhelming *need* for release hit him like a ton of bricks, and he found it hard to breathe.

"Someone looks hungry." Cora's tiny fingers slid across his chest as she came up behind him, her voice hazy with lust.

Lust...

Didn't I come here for...

A wave of euphoria washed over Cassius, and he moved to shift his erection.

"I see the toxins taking effect." Cora giggled as her hands slid over top of the waistband of his pants. She turned him toward her, breaking his gaze for only a moment as her words registered.

"What did you say?" he breathed darkly. His vision blurred, and he could see her pupils had dilated."

"I think it's time we head downstairs, Cassius," she whispered as she snaked her arms up his chest, her fingers pulling him by the neck down toward her.

Alarm bells sounded all throughout his brain as Cora's thrall wrapped around him like a snake.

The euphoria.

The drink.

Her thrall.

It all felt too similar, like history was repeating itself.

"No one fights like you do, Cassius," Eden purred in his ear as her fingernails dragged across his bare chest, eliciting tiny slivers of black blood from his pale skin.

"Not everything has to be a fight, Edie," he said as he claimed her lips with his own.

The toxins from the Succubus they'd consumed were in full effect. Where there should have been pain, there was only pleasure, and the maddening desire to bury himself inside of Eden until there was nothing left.

"Cora, I—"

His words were soon cut off by a searing kiss, a wet, warm tongue forcing its way in his mouth.

But it didn't feel right.

Didn't taste right.

The music thumped loudly, vibrating his being.

This was wrong.

All sorts of wrong.

He brought his hands up, placing them on Cora's chest and he *shoved* her away.

"No."

"Cassius..." she groaned, reaching out for his hands.

His head was splitting, and the world was foggy. His cock ached for release and his throat was drier than the desert, and he was angry.

So very angry.

Cora had drugged him.

Intentionally.

He'd trusted her, and she had betrayed that trust.

Didn't she understand?

"No means no, Cora," he growled as he turned away from the crowd, anger running through him like electricity.

"Wh... Where are you going?" she mewled.

"Do not follow me," he snapped.

"Cassius, wait! I can explain!"

Cassius slid up to the bar, catching sight of RJ.

"What it'll be?" he asked, chewing his toothpick.

"I'd like to go down to the lower level."

"I told you, you're going to have to talk with Louie."

"Then get me Louie." Cassius could feel his anger spreading, no doubt elevated by the toxin in his blood.

"Well, well, if it isn't a giant pain in my ass," a familiar voice sounded next to him.

"Hello, Malcolm." Cassius tried his best to still his building fury as he turned to see familiar brown eyes and shaggy dark hair.

"Cassius. Should have known you'd follow my sister across state lines."

"I am not here for your sister."

"Good. Then I don't have to tell you if you touch her,

I will kill you."

"Your threats are wasted. I would never hurt Ava."

"You already did, the day you bit her."

Cassius's blood boiled like an overflowing pot on the stove, and he ran his shaking hand through his hair.

"I saved her life." His words rattled in the space between them, and in a flash he was closer to Mal than he'd ever been, and though he should have remained cool, he was at his wit's end. With Mal's callous demeanor, Ava and her hot and cold attitude, with Cora and her disrespect for boundaries, with the Succubi who were throwing a monkey wrench in the whole ordeal.

So he did not remain cool.

No.

He bared his fangs to Malcolm Reynolds, in the shadows of The Dark Hearts Club.

"And I would do it again."

"If you know what's good for you, *Cas—*"

Hearing Malcolm use the nickname Ava had given him made him feel all sorts of emotions.

"You'll do as I say and leave. Stay the fuck away from this place tonight."

"Why is that?"

"Because this place is going to go down in flames," Mal said as he drained the last of his drink, turning away from the bar, the lights catching on the gleam of his blessed silver blade.

His words were serious.

Was he *warning* him?

Was he insinuating he was going to...

Cassius did not want to finish the thought, as a mass killing of vampires made him sick to the stomach. Of course, the toxins would also be partially to blame.

"You would not burn down a building with your

sister in it."

"Cas, my sister's gonna light the match."

CHAPTER THIRTY

AVA WAS CERTAIN of two things as she walked into The Dark Hearts Club.

The first, as her wrist flared with heat and her skin chilled upon entrance—somehow it was magnified—was that the place was crawling with vampires. Her entire being felt like a divining rod, her nerves standing at full attention. The second, was that Sam Kingsley was truly what she feared him to be.

An Incubus.

A creature of lust whose only design was to spread his poison to an unsuspecting victim. The way she felt in his presence, the maddening *need* for him to touch her, to get him alone, to let him possess her from the inside out...

She knew better, now. Those feelings didn't belong to her, they were a reaction to his power, his toxin. Toxin she'd allowed into her body more than once.

In the few hours before her date, after Vinny and Hunter had left, Ava spent what little time she had learning about the demon spawn from Tito and Mal. When Tito had left, she'd come clean: the knowledge and similarities to Mal's story too much to pass off as coincidence. To her surprise, neither of them jumped down her throat or were condescending, though, the dark look in Dallas's eyes was not one she'd soon forget. Instead, they'd only nodded in understanding, forming a plan to put an end to the demons, while trying to keep casualties to a minimum.

The mating rituals of both the Succubi and the Incubi were very different. For the ritual to culminate and impregnation to occur, the Incubus's victim needed two things. Their blood and their semen, at which point at that stage in the mating ritual, the female would have likely built a tolerance to the toxin and the chant, and submission would be a slice of cake, their willingness to feed the Incubus something more than desire. It would be *needed*.

Just the thought made Ava shiver.

Gross.

If things were going to go as planned, all she had to do was get close enough to attempt an exorcism, and avoid drinking Sam's blood, avoid his *toxin*. Yet, she looked at Sam in the light of the club, bathed in the glow of the neon, she was also certain that she'd let herself fall too far into the fantasy, and reality was a bitch.

Believing someone like him could really be interested in someone like her, how had she ever entertained such an idea?

It was outlandish, at best, and she knew, now, that he'd managed to tap into her darkest desires.

To be *wanted*.

To be worshipped and adored.

A part of her hated that she wanted such things to begin with. Life was more than finding some guy to shack up with and have a couple kids. For a brief moment, she'd thought that what she and Sam had could have been something.

Something real.

But it was all toxic lies.

It had been a sheer stroke of genius that as Ava made her way back from the bathrooms, the stage manager mistook her for someone else. Never one to back down from a challenge, a part of her understood the need for an Incubus to feed on lust; she would play the part. She would dangle herself like a carrot and be exactly what he wanted.

Meum delicium; my pleasure.

What was more lustful than watching your mate avail themselves to a roomful of spectators?

It'll definitely make a good story to tell later when all this is said and done.

As she sauntered to the edge of the catwalk, sliding down the pole like her life depended on it, she looked out into the crowd in search of Sam, but it was not his eyes she found.

Instead, she locked eyes with glowing green emeralds.

Cassius stood in the middle of the crowd, his golden hair falling, casting shadows over his perfect, angelic face. He was still dressed in his signature gray shirt and leather pants and the redheaded vamp pressed herself tightly against him, his hands around her waist. Her pulse throbbed, her heartbeat quickening.

The sight stirred a mixture of feelings within her, dancing with the Incubi toxin, a dangerous waltz.

The way he held her, his fingers against the small of her back.

The way he looked at her, and then...

Ava's heart twisted as she watched the redheaded vamp pull Cassius to her, locking lips with him like he was some leading man in a romantic movie and they were not in a crowded room. It was like time stood still, and there were only the two of them, the neon lights dancing over them like laser beams.

She was not prepared for the flurry of anger, the pang of jealousy that pushed forth, the way it heated her blood. Her fingers twitched, and she silently prayed the vampire would meet her end at her stake.

But why do I care what he does?

He isn't anything to me.

But even as she thought the thought, she knew it was a lie.

He'd claimed her blood as his, that counted for something right?

She shut down the dangerous thoughts, forcing herself to look away. Whatever fantasy she had indulged in earlier was just that.

A fantasy.

It could never be anything more.

Because one day it would come down to him or her.

And she would do whatever it took to survive, including putting a stake through his heart.

When she'd made her exit, it was not Sam who waited in the wings. Dallas stood with his arms crossed.

"Are you done playing around?" he grumbled.

"Ah, so I assume you watched the show."

"Only because I had to," he said gruffly as they walked back out toward the crowd, stopping in a shadowed alcove.

"Regardless, I think your little display worked. I saw Sam talking to the guy over by the stairs, slipping him a nice wad of cash."

"Well, then, guess my stripper skills paid off," she chortled.

"Please, Kitten. That was hardly stripping. You didn't even take your clothes off."

"Is that why you're so grouchy? Didn't get the show you wanted?" she bit as Dallas loomed over her.

"I'm *grouchy* because you're wasting my time by playing showgirl instead of taking this seriously."

"Don't tell me I'm not taking this seriously. You're not the one who got fucked by an Incubus."

Dallas's lips thinned, and a look of fury flashed in his eyes.

"Now, if you're done playing asshole, I've got a demon to entertain."

She pushed past him, searching for Sam once more. He stood by the stairs, just as Dallas had claimed, looking positively devilish. The closer she got to the stairs, the colder she felt; until she stood in front of him, a sweet smile on her face.

"You are just full of surprises aren't you, *meum delicium*?" he said darkly.

"Surprise is my middle name," she responded flirtatiously.

"I've managed to get us a private table downstairs. It's much more... intimate than those up here," Sam said as he ran his finger up and down her arm seductively.

"Isn't that where the vampires are?" She raised an eyebrow innocently.

"It is."

"Quite an invitation for a slayer. Should I be on my best behavior?" She flashed her eyelashes at him.

"In public, of course. But behind the doors of the den..." He leaned in closer, his lips brushing her ear.

"Give me your worst," he said, his eyes flickering red once more.

Cassius's words echoed in her brain.

They can only return to their true form during the mating process.

She was counting on it.

For the minute Sam gave way to the demon that possessed him, Ava would be waiting with her crystal and holy water ready to trap the monster that claimed Sam Kingsley.

"With pleasure." Ava smiled slyly.

CHAPTER THIRTY-ONE

OUT OF THE corner of his eye, Cassius spotted Ava and her date moving down the stairs as Malcolm's words hit his ears.

Just as he noted the flash of red ghosting over her date's eyes.

His own widened in panic.

"What have you done, Malcolm?"

"I haven't done anything. Yet."

"How can you put your sister in danger consistently and not think twice about it?"

"Because if I tell her no, she'll just go in hot, and that's when you make mistakes." He shrugged, heading for the stairs.

"How do you expect to get down there?" Cassius sneered.

"Dallas already took care of that. Last chance, Cas, to get the hell outta dodge. Otherwise, I can't promise you won't end up at the end of my fucking stake."

Cassius's pulse quickened, his temper burning hotter.

"Do you know what he *is?*" he growled.

"Yeah. And so does she."

The words agitated him. Ava *knew* the man was a demon of lust, what he was capable of, and yet there she stood on the edge of the stairs, with a wicked grin on her face. Baiting an Incubus was nothing like baiting a vampire. The two were not the same, and the way he'd looked at her...

There was no way in hell Cassius was going to leave. He'd made a vow to protect Ava the night he saved her life, and he intended to keep it.

"I am not leaving."

"It's your funeral," Malcolm said as they walked over the staircase, his pulse throbbing with every step.

True to his word, the man, Louie, took Mal's reservation and opened the velvet rope. Cassius was slightly impressed the mortal had managed an in, but he would not let him know that.

Instead, he focused on trying to fight the toxin, which was now hitting its peak. When they came to the bottom of the stairs, Cassius wondered just what he'd signed up for.

While the room upstairs was basic in its layouts and design, echoing the clubs he'd seen in the eighties, the basement level of The Dark Hearts Club looked like something straight from the pits of Hell.

Deep, crimson walls with black molding that stretched up the crevices of the walls and across the ceiling like black thorny vines, a glittering black and red crystal chandelier sparkling ruby prisms all across the black marble floor. The red velvet chaises and lounges were spread out in a circle around the stage, where the blonde-haired dancer who reminded him of Marguerite, gracefully sauntered around the stage, lit up by neon red light.

A whistle sounded next to him.

"I will give you bloodsuckers credit where it's due. Least you have style," Malcolm noted.

"What is your plan, Malcolm?" Cassius scoured the room for Ava, panic surging through him when he could not find her. There were many vampires scattered about on the lounges, some with vixens in their grasp, openly feeding while others entertained other forms of attention. Though he'd never been one for voyeurism or multiplicity, he could not deny the arousal such a sight brought him.

He shifted his stance farther from Mal, feeling quite on the spot. If the other man noticed, he didn't say anything, and for that Cassius was grateful. It was awkward enough being down here with the scent of blood and sex permeating the air, although his hunger for blood had been abated thanks to his trip to the morgue. He only had to ride out the toxin, but that was manageable—or so he told himself it was prior to setting foot in the main den.

The doors encased within the walls all bore red-lit occupied signs, and his stomach turned as the thought of Ava in one of those rooms pushed forth.

Mal slid his phone out, the light illuminating his face.

"It's showtime," he said with a smile.

The sound of a laugh cut through the air, and Cassius followed it like a beacon. There she stood, legs wrapped around the Incubus, giggling as his lips traversed the skin over her neck. But he was too late.

For as quickly as his feet picked up pace, the damage had been done, and all Cassius could do was watch as he sank his fangs into Ava Crowley, and then kissed her before whisking her away into the darkness of a locked room.

CHAPTER THIRTY-TWO

SOMETHING HAPPENED THE moment Sam's fangs pushed forth. It was as if she'd been replaced by someone else, forgetfulness now taking over. She forgot who she was, where she was. What she was supposed to be doing. In that space, instead, she had given in to her darkest desire, and let it bring her to salvation.

The thought of Sam's fangs in her neck was no longer a fantasy.

But it didn't *feel* right.

Something in the way he touched her and in the sound of his voice, she knew. Her blood rallied against the intruder, furious as her mind fought to make sense of it all.

The temperature dropped, a chill running all along her skin. She fought the fog that threatened to settle, holding on to the memories she often conjured when fighting a vampire's thrall.

But this was different.

Because it wasn't thrall she was fighting, it was her own demons.

"Your lust tastes so sweet..." Sam groaned as he

pushed her up against the locked door. Her mind protested, but her body sang a different song as her hands made steady work of unbuttoning his pants, driven by lust and lust alone.

When she gazed up at him and his luscious, divine lips, his eyes flashed bright red, flickering in and out with an emerald-green glow as the demon tried to take the form of the thing she wanted most.

"I can take it away, if you let me," he whispered darkly, kissing her much more roughly than he had previously. All the other times he'd kissed her, he tasted sweet, took his time.

But now...

Now, it was as if he couldn't move fast enough, his lips falling back to her neck, sucking the blood that rushed to the surface.

And for a moment, Ava wanted to give in. Because what he promised was too difficult to say no to.

Freedom.

To end the mark.

To be free of Cassius.

To be free of the hold he had over her.

It was him who had brought her here. She'd been foolish, fallen into his net. For as much as she tried to fight it and tried to hide it, in this moment she understood what frightened her the most was that in spite of it all... he was her weakness.

Damn Cassius...

Damn this fucking bond!

"Yes," she moaned in response, sliding Sam's boxers to the floor as his hands roughly slid up her legs, her thighs, his fingers hooking into the sides of her panties, grasping at them as if they were a lifeline.

"Make it go away," she breathed as his lips pressed over her collarbone. When he pulled away, her pulse throbbed, and she felt a burning pain.

Her gaze fell on him, and she watched as his eyes shifted to a glowing solid red, as his fangs tore into his own wrist, crimson blood rushing to the surface.

And though her insides ached, her body awakening with need once more to feel him, be possessed by him...

The sight of his fangs in his own flesh ignited something within her, and lust was replaced by anger and disgust.

She needed to save this man, to exorcize the demon within him. Sam Kingsley deserved to be free, too.

She fumbled with her skull clutch, her fingers shakily grasping onto the clear quartz pillar she'd managed to fit inside.

She wasted no time as she held it to his chest, chanting the words Tito and Dallas had coached her to say.

Sam's lips turned up in the corners into a wicked smile, and his features... flickered. They shifted into someone else, something else. Where dark, inviting chocolate eyes once laid, there were pools of crimson fire; where golden skin once stood, he was now ashen gray like a stone. And he was somehow much larger, towering over her like a gargoyle instead of a man.

His fingers covered hers and he pulled the stone away with a smirk.

"Perhaps, you should stick to slaying, *meum delicium*." he hissed, his pink forked tongue sliding out of his lips. The sight made Ava want to throw up.

She'd let this *monster* into her heart?

Her body?

She shook with anger, with fear.

Oh, hell no.

"And perhaps, you should go back to Hell where you belong."

His hand nearly crushed hers as he forced her arm down, while his free hand slid up her neck, fingers tightening around her throat as the warm, sticky blood of his wrist seeped down her neck. With his tightening grip, she could feel it spreading, feel his claws in her open bite, and it hurt like hell.

"And here I thought we were on the same page." He pressed himself against her, her back aching as it meshed with the hard wall, and she could feel him and his putrid member against her thighs, wet with arousal.

She fought his hold, feeling stronger than she ever had. The toxins and adrenaline melding to give her a boost she hadn't expected. Ava brought her knee up, connecting it with his groin, and he stumbled back.

"Sorry about this, Sam... but you'll thank me later."

Screams echoed in the distance, but Ava did not flinch. She made a beeline for her crystal, spouting the chants louder, just as the door crashed in.

Dallas stood there, blade in hand, and upon hearing her chants, was at her side immediately. Combined, the Incubus started to singe, smoke billowing from his eyes and orifices.

"What the fuck took you so long?" she growled.

"There's a lot of rooms down here, Kitten. You could've texted me."

"Oh, for the love, when would I have had time—"

Dallas hefted his body on top of the Incubus, the door swinging behind him.

"We can do this later, Ava." He straddled the Incubus by the legs, and Ava didn't miss the Incubus's flailing erection.

God I'm never going to be able to erase that from my brain.

Ava repeated the words, Dallas echoing them in

tandem as she came up beside him and slammed the crystal down on his chest.

She watched as the demon before her flickered between gray skin and red eyes, back to kind brown eyes and golden skin. Watched as the gray smoke turned black, smelled the burning flesh as the crystal lit with a crimson glow.

"It's working!" Ava exclaimed, her fingers tightening around the crystal.

But just as the crystal started to fill, Ava felt a stabbing pain.

"Fuck!" She squinted her eyes, tears coming to them faster than a flood.

"Ava what's wrong..."

"It hurts..." she gasped, her neck throbbing. She shakily brought one hand up to her neck. The scent of fire and ash filled the air, and it was horrid. She felt as if she were going to be sick. Her stomach twisted, her loins aching fiercely, as if someone had taken a knife to her from the inside.

"Dallas... something's wrong... Ahhhhhh!" She clamped her legs together, curling into a ball, her fists shaking.

"Stay with it, Ava! We're almost there..."

"It burns!" she cried in agony, her vision blurring from tears and pain. She could see the steady stream of black smoke surrounding Sam Kingsley's lifeless body, and then it was over.

The smoke dissipated, filtering in a steady stream toward the crystal, and a burst of red smoke settled in its wake, like a sonic boom, edging out like a ripple on the surface of a lake, covering everything in its wake.

Ava let go of the crystal as the force blew her back into the wall.

Her entire body felt as if it were on fire, as if she was

burning from the inside out.

CHAPTER THIRTY-THREE

CASSIUS FELT A pain deep within him as the scent of smoke and fire filled the air.

It all happened so quickly.

When the Incubus had shifted, he knew.

They all knew.

The Succubi couldn't deny the call of their maker, any of which were in the proximity of him, that is. The ever-present stench of demons filled the air, and if that hadn't been enough, there was the struggle, the screams of chaos.

It was a free for all of demons, vampires, and Malcolm somewhere, likely staking those who got in his way as he collected the employees and evacuated them in the middle of the madness.

The scent of death and decay was prevalent, the putrid scent of smoke, demon expulsion, and burning flesh made his eyes water.

But none of that mattered as he felt the sting, the racing pulse in his veins.

And then he saw her.

The smoke filled the room—he could see it all

spiraled into one clear crystal—just as it glowed red and as the energy stabilized, trapping the exorcized demon in the stone, it sent a shockwave out, hitting everyone in its wake, including him.

Cassius fell back from the blast, sprawled against the floor. His chest ached from the impact, his muscles tensing immediately. The crash of toxin ebbed as he sat up, his vision blurring as he clutched his chest. The ringing in his ears subsided as he shook his head, blinking furiously.

He could withstand the pain; it was surely not the first time he'd been knocked around or fallen flat on his ass. He crawled on the floor through the red haze, below the smoke, with only one goal and one line of sight.

The sound of coughing and Ava's pain would be etched into his brain forever, and he hated the sound. His vision cleared enough for him to see Ava against the wall, writhing in agony, screams of terror escaping her throat. "Ava?" he called in as thick smog filled his lungs, making it hard to breathe.

"Cas?" she cried, a mixture of shock and pain. The sound was like breaking glass.

He waved his hand through the smoke.

"What the fuck are you doing—" Her words dissipated in the air as another scream erupted from her.

"Make it stop!" she cried.

He hated to see her like this.

It was torture.

The Ava he knew did not cry or scream.

She fought.

To see her this way set every nerve in his body on edge. He was next to her in an instant, kneeling beside her.

Her eyes fluttered, her chest heaving with heavy breath.

"I'm here..." the words fell out of his mouth without warning as he scoured his gaze over her, trying to assess what could be causing her so much pain.

"What happened, Ava, talk to me..." He licked his lips as the sweet, divine smell of blood invaded his passageways. His fangs ached as the scent made its way throughout his senses, his cock twitching. Frustratedly, he growled at the response.

This is not the time...

Ava's head rolled to the side, her hair falling over her shoulder, and then he saw it.

Her pale neck smeared with crimson, wet, sticky blood.

His throat suddenly felt constricted, his thrall pushing forward, trying to find its way out. It was instinct, he knew that, and it was as if the world stopped. As if there was no fire, no fight.

Only him, her, and the *blood.*

Instinctively he reached out, his shaky fingers brushing along her skin, along the blood that smelled sweeter than any dessert. But there was also the scent of a demon, and he swallowed hard, trying to fight his nature.

His insides lurched with another wave of ache; panic, fear coursing through him.

He'd never known an Incubus to challenge a vampire's claim. And by the looks of things, he knew the Incubus had managed to start the ritual somehow. Given Ava was still clothed, he knew it was blood.

It would be so easy...

Venom pushed through his fangs, and his entire body felt the drive, the desire to sink his fangs into the woman he'd previously claimed. To save her, draw out the poison. To finish what he'd started two years ago, the night he'd saved her life.

Not only had the Incubus bitten her, challenged his claim, he'd spread his toxin, his blood, before he'd been exorcized from the mortal vessel's body.

No...

Not like this...

Cassius closed his eyes, pushing back against his thrall.

The world was giving him a second chance. In that moment, the one he went over in his mind time and time again, she'd said yes.

She hadn't known what that meant.

The sight of her as she cried out in pain, as she twisted on the ground, fists balled together, he knew if she were in her right mind, she'd say no and that was his last thought.

A deep coughing sound rattled in the air, pulling Cassius from his realization, and his gaze settled on another body; it was enough. Enough of a distraction that for one split second he could breathe. But it would not last long, as a force pushed him back, away from Ava, up against the wall with a knife to his throat.

"Don't touch her, you fucking tick," the man growled, his blue eyes full of rage.

Ava's coughs echoed in the background.

"Dallas... Sam..."

"He'll be fine, Kitten. But we need to get you out of here."

Another sharp pain shot through him from head to toe, but he pushed it aside, his fingers wrapping around the man's thick wrists.

"Ava..."

"Wait a minute, you're the vamp from the church—"

Ava coughed violently, and Cassius struggled

against Dallas's hold.

"You are wasting time, she—" The way this man held him, Cassius wasn't sure he had much of a chance, but his only thought, his only worry was for the woman he loved who was struggling from the separation, the death of the Incubus who had poisoned her and started a mating ritual.

"Cassius!" Familiar voices rang out, male and female, and Cassius fought to look to where they came from.

Cora lunged for Dallas, bearing her fangs, and he swiftly changed course, swinging at Cora instead. Leon wrapped his arms around Cassius from behind, pulling him against his chest.

"Cassius, we must go..."

Cassius coughed, trying to find his breath.

"Leon, I'm sorry I—"

"It's all right, we can worry about the details later, right now we need to get out before this place goes up and takes us with it," Leon said sternly.

In the distance, he could hear Cora hissing, could hear *Dallas* slamming her up against the wall; it was white noise. All of it was white noise, because as the toxins crashed, as his mouth watered, he could feel her racing pulse in his veins.

That was what he held onto.

Malcolm stood in the doorway, covered in blood, his voice panicked.

"What did you do to her..."

"I did nothing, the Incubus, he—"

Malcolm charged Cassius, knocking Leon off of him, and within seconds his stake was against his chest.

"Malcolm, listen to me..."

"Why should I listen to a word you fucking say?" Malcolm's lips pulled back in a snarl.

"Give me one good reason why I shouldn't dust you right here and set you on fire."

Cassius hissed, rage fueling him once more. He glanced from Malcolm and his stake pressed against his chest, to *her*.

"Ava..." Cassius's gaze fell on Ava as she stared up at him.

"She's been bitten by an Incubus," he breathed heavily, his eyes staring into her with all that he truly was.

"She needs anti-venom."

His words hit Malcolm instantly, and he watched as his expression shifted, considering his words.

"Why should I believe you?"

"If you love your sister, you can't afford not to," Cassius growled.

"Cassius, there is no time, I am sorry—"

"She bears my mark, Leon. I'm not leaving without her."

"You're the one responsible—" Dallas shifted once more, angling himself between Leon and himself, and the sound of labored breathing and coughing; of beams breaking sounded all around them.

Dallas's fist connected with Cassius's face, once, twice, splitting his lip in the process.

The man who lay lifeless only moments ago struggled to sit up, looking dazed and confused.

"What the hell..." he coughed.

"Dallas, stop..." Ava cried as she pushed his leg, knocking him off balance. She scowled up at him as clutched at her abdomen.

"He's mine." She coughed, but her eyes were still full of fire, menacing.

"Grab her, Dallas, I have the anti-venom. If what they say is true..."

His punches stopped and Cassius broke away, seizing his chance to get away from the violence as he knelt beside Ava once more, the man—*Dallas*—arguing with Leon behind him.

"We need to get you all somewhere safe," Leon commanded.

"I'm not going anywhere with the likes of you—" Dallas growled.

"And what is your plan? To stay here and die?" Cassius asked, turning his head, angling his furious gaze at the lumbering man just as a flaming beam fell from the ceiling.

Cassius pulled Ava by the arm, just out of the way of the raining debris. She did not fight his touch, or his pull. Instead, he felt her hand on his bicep, fingers grasping on as if she was trying to ground herself, trying to push herself up...*fighting.*

Fighting to hold on, to live once more.

"The hotel will be crawling with cops. And I doubt the local emergency services will know how to treat her or..."

"Lead the way," Malcolm said, sheathing his stake.

"The fuck are you doing, Malcolm?" Dallas roared.

"Saving my sister," Malcolm yelled back as another rumble from the rafters echoed in the chamber.

"Ava, I need you to get up." Cassius focused on keeping his voice calm.

Tears streamed down her face, her eyes of fire, glassy and red rimmed. She looked back at him and nodded.

"It hurts, Cas...it hurts so fucking bad..."

"I know, Ava, but not for much longer..."

"We must hurry." Leon nodded to Cassius.

Cassius reached out to help her stand, but Dallas pushed him aside with one large arm.

"Touch her again and you die."

Cassius knew better than to argue as the fire started to spread, the alarms ringing loudly, sprinklers spewing water like rain. He wanted to protest, wanted to tell this lumbering bag of muscle where he could shove his attitude, but he knew that would not get him anywhere.

Instead, he watched as Dallas wrapped his arms around Ava and picked her up. Her arms wrapped around his neck, her face buried in his ripped shirt. Dallas turned away from the man sitting up in the center of it all, the mortal fastening the buttons of his pants, running his hand through his hair.

As Leon led Mal, Dallas, and Ava out of the room and toward safety, Cassius had a split second to make the decision.

I could leave him here.

Leave him to disappear with this god-forsaken place...

But that was not who he was.

Cassius looked death in the eye and he said, "not today."

So, instead of turning his back and letting the flames consume the man who'd wronged his sweet Avarice, he approached the man. Cassius's gaze settled on the dark ones of the mortal man. He was delirious, confused, and scared, and Cassius did not feel anger.

Instead, he felt *compassion.*

Understanding.

After all, he's been possessed by a demon for lord knows how long...

Cassius grabbed Ava's skull purse from the floor as he made his way to the man, shoving the crystal inside, zipping it shut before reaching a hand out to the Incubus's second victim.

Though Cassius wanted to hate this man for what he'd done to Ava, he knew the man in front of him was not responsible, and so he helped him up. During this time, he let the man lean on him for support, and did not waste another second as he carried the weight of the human against him, with adrenaline fueling him.

He fled, with as much haste as he could, out of the burning Dark Hearts Club and into the shadows of the night.

Sirens bathed the street in shades of red and blue as Cassius helped the man to the nearest ambulance, and when the medic turned from him to tend to the man's wounds, Cassius disappeared into the night.

***

When Cassius walked through the doors of Leon's home, everything was different.

Cora sat on the chaise in the foyer, her hands placed delicately in her lap, looking sorrowful.

"I'm sorry, Cassius." Her voice was soft.

"You are sorry?" he scoffed as he stood just barely in the foyer. The distance between them was overwhelming.

"I did not think..."

"No, you didn't. You didn't think about anyone but yourself."

"I know that!" She sniffled, her voice shaking.

"Were there any human casualties?" The sound of his footsteps echoed in the large room.

Cora shook her head.

"Human casualties, no."

When her eyes did not meet his, he let out a deep sigh.

"And the man who'd been possessed?"

"Sam Kingsley seems to be all right. Reports say he's

a bit disoriented, but he's stable."

Cassius stopped next to her, the silence between them deafening until she spoke.

"I never meant to hurt anyone," she whispered.

"That doesn't excuse what you did."

"I know."

When Cassius entered Leon's library, he was not surprised to see him milling about with a stack of books, chewing on the arm of his glasses.

"I expected you much sooner," Leon said nonchalantly, not looking up from his book as he swayed back and forth.

Cassius's shoulders relaxed and it was as if all the world came crashing down all at once, and he held his face in his hands, a deep sigh leaving him. In the distance, he could hear the closing of the book, and within moments he felt arms around him. Warm, familiar arms, and he could not hold in the pain or emotion any longer.

"It's all right, let it out."

"No, it's not. It's a fucking disaster," he said through the first onset of tears.

Leon's hands smoothed over his arms, and the touch stirred long forgotten feelings of guilt and pain.

Even his own father had never hugged him like this.

"Your club, the murders, Ava..." His voice hung on her name, and Leon let out his own sigh.

"Why didn't you tell me, Cassius? Hmm? Why didn't you tell me you'd claimed a mate?"

"Because I thought I could handle it."

Leon let out a soft laugh, shaking his head.

"She was dying, and I... I just couldn't leave her there. I know the repercussions of what I did. It was on Boracelli territory."

Leon held him at a distance, and Cassius wiped his

eyes.

"And you thought what? You'd just fight a supernatural bond to avoid being discovered?" Leon said as he turned away, heading back to his desk.

Cassius blew out a frustrated breath.

"Something like that."

"And how's that going for you?" Leon snickered.

"Terribly." Cassius let out a shaky laugh.

"Is she...is she going to be okay?"

Leon nodded.

"Yes. I administered some anti-venom, thanks to her brother, which may take a few hours to take hold, but should do the trick. Thankfully, your mark is strong. Had it not been there, the toxins likely would have spread much quicker and we may not have made it in time."

"So, you're saying my bite..."

"Saved her life again."

Cassius blinked in shock, unsure how to process such information.

"Her fever will pitch and delirium will set in, a side effect of the anti-venom fighting off the toxin. She may say things or do things that don't make sense. Things she won't remember, but that is par for the course. Once the anti-venom is in full effect, the loopiness will taper off, and she may not remember everything fully or clearly."

Cassius processed Leon's words, unsure how to feel about them.

"And Dallas?"

"Dallas is still here, yes. He refuses to leave. Malcolm, too... You've come a long way from High Covens, haven't you, Cassius?" Leon sighed.

Cassius could not find it in him to answer and just nodded.

"Cora tried to drug me with Succubi toxin."

"She told me," Leon said as he folded his hands in front of him on his desk.

Cassius stood to the side, feeling quite tired.

"She also told me you vehemently denied her advances, even under the influence of the toxin." His tone had shifted to a much more serious one.

"Do you plan on turning the girl? Ava?"

"It is not up to me."

"You do not wish to spend immortality with her?" Leon cocked his head in surprise.

"She does not want this, and I will not force her hand."

"But if she did want this... If she came to you and asked to be bitten, would you do it?"

"In a heartbeat."

Leon crossed his legs, spinning in his chair.

"And if she never asks? How long do you think you can keep up this ruse? Vampiric Law states that you have seven years to fulfill your claim or the Boracellis can challenge you."

"I will deal with the Boracellis when the time is right. I cannot hide from them forever, I know this."

"Your father came to me one night, much like this one. Stormy. Rainy. He came to my library in Rome and told me he'd made a mistake. In the heat of passion during his stag night, he'd bitten your mother."

"He didn't turn her for seven years, though."

"He struggled with the decision to do so as well, you know."

Cassius's eyes widened in surprise.

"Come again?"

"It was an accident. He hadn't meant to bite her, claim her. Though, he'd become quite smitten with her, and he struggled whether or not to make her his for eternity. And then he found out about you."

Cassius pursed his lips.

"If he was so smitten with her, why did he wait seven years to turn her? Why did he leave us? Why did he seek out the bed of other women if he was so *smitten* with her?" he scoffed.

"You are like him in so many ways. Smart, loyal. Stubborn."

Cassius glared at Leon, as he continued.

"Sooner or later, Cassius, you will need to make a decision."

"I know."

Leon stared at Cassius, a deafening silence falling between them.

"A word of advice?" He raised an eyebrow at Cassius, who nodded.

"Of course."

"Stay as far away from her as you can."

"Leon..."

"No, Cassius. Listen to me on this. If you do not wish to turn her or feed off of her... do not put yourself through the agony. A claiming bond is not meant to be drawn out. It is meant to be an eternal *bond*. It is meant to happen, naturally, in the blink of an eye. A bite for a bite. Your father sought out other women, sought out binges of blood to quiet the madness he felt around your mother because he thought he could deny his nature. And he couldn't. He did not win the fight. He surrendered."

Cassius looked away.

"I will never be like him, and if for one moment I think I am anything at all like him... I will have Ava put a stake through my heart."

Cassius pushed off the desk, slowly walking away.

"To deny our nature is madness. To give in is

salvation." Leon's voice echoed in the cavernous room.

Cassius stopped at the doors, responding without turning around.

"My salvation is not worth the price of her choice," he said as he walked through the doors, closing them once and for all.

Cassius softly padded over to the guest room, the very one he'd been staying in before he left to stay at the Silver Starling.

Dallas lay with his back against the wall, his eyes shut. His chest rose and fell, the sound of snoring like a buzzing frequency.

Cassius quietly shifted past him, carefully pressing on the door, opening it ever so quietly. The room was dark, lit up only by moonlight pouring in through the windows.

Malcolm lay crumpled in an armchair, snoring away just as Dallas was outside. Even in the dark, he could make out the outline of her body on the bed. Slowly, he approached her side, his gaze roving over her sleeping form.

She always looked so peaceful, so beautiful when she slept. Long, full dark lashes fluttering ever so slightly in deep sleep against her porcelain skin, the way her mouth opened just the slightest, how she gripped her pillow, her hand behind it—usually holding a stake.

Curious, he lightly pushed her pillow up with his pointer finger, a soft smirk forming on his face when he saw the familiar stake curled in her fist.

It's nice to know some things never change.

As he drew his fingers back her eyes fluttered.

She was awake.

"Cas?" she whispered groggily.

"Yes, my sweet Avarice?" he breathed. It was as if

her words gave him life, not her blood.

The way she said his name was a spell he wanted to hear over and over.

"Where the hell am I?" she whispered, her eyes looking up at him with panic and fear.

His fingers trailed down her pillow, brushing the edge of her knuckles. Her skin was soft, but slightly clammy.

The fever.

"You are safe. Malcolm is just over there in the corner, and your lumberjack lapdog is just outside the door." He smirked.

Ava's lips turned up in the corners.

"Dallas didnt hurt you, did he?" she drawled, her eyelids fluttering once again.

"Thanks to your command, no. He did not."

"Mmm, good. I wouldn't want to see anyone wreck that annoyingly pretty face of yours." She hummed, and his heart skipped a beat.

"Besides, I have a claim on you," she whispered.

"Yes, you do," he whispered back.

"You're mine to slay," she whispered, looking up at him with fire and delight in her eyes.

His voice caught in his throat, and the words tumbled out of his mouth without warning.

"Yes. I am yours. Forevermore."

"I would kill for a donut, right now, and a drink," she grumbled, and he couldn't help but smile.

"What kind?"

"Red velvet supreme," she whispered as she closed her eyes.

His fingers traced lines over her knuckles, his thumb brushing the scar on the underside of her wrist, and he could feel her pulse quicken at the touch both beneath his fingertips and in his veins.

"I thought you preferred jelly filled. Cherry, raspberry."

"Cas likes red velvet. And Bordeaux." Her fingers unfurled from their hold on her stake, splaying out beneath him.

He let his own intertwine with hers, squeezing just the slightest.

"Go to sleep, my sweet Avarice."

"When I was little, my mom used to sing to me when I was sick. I miss her."

Cassius could feel the heat from her hand rising against his palm.

"I can only imagine." He sat next to her, the bed creaking only minimally.

Malcolm shifted in his chair at the sound, but he did not wake.

There was only the sound of her breath in the silence between them, and he thought for a moment she had fallen asleep.

"Seasons don't fear the reaper," her hazy voice whispered softly.

Cassius reached out softly, brushing her wet, sweat-slicked hair from her face.

"Nor do the wind, the sun, or the rain." His voice was strong and so full of hope, of love. If anyone would have heard it, they'd have handed him the stake themselves. But no one would hear this, no one would know, and there was the chance Ava herself would not remember this, but he would.

Ava curled closer to him, and Cassius didn't see anything else. He'd never see anything else and would never forget this stolen moment as long as he lived. Even if she woke up, thinking it was all a dream, for him, it would be enough.

It would be enough to get him through however long

his sentence was.

"We can be like they are," she whispered, her breath warm on his skin, glassy eyes staring deeply into his, eyelashes fluttering before they closed once more.

"Don't fear the reaper." He didn't miss a beat, the words a prayer on his lips.

Ava's whispers turned inaudible, a string of incoherent mumbles as she faded back into slumber.

Though, he knew the words quite well.

"Baby, I'm your man," he whispered to the darkness, a silent promise before he let go and disappeared into the shadows once more.

EPILOGUE

1 month later

AVA WATCHED THE television in the corner of the Third Eye, flipping through the channels. It was a slow day, and she had already stocked the shelves, rearranged the bookshelves. There was no excitement in Chester, not like there used to be. She stopped on a news station as reporters hounded a hooded figure that looked oddly familiar.

She read the caption below, "Sam Kingsley pulls long-awaited documentary and announces his last season of *Hell on Earth*. Fans are outraged."

"Well, that sucks, I was really looking forward to that," she grumbled. Her best friend, Ember, looked up from her tarot card spread, raising an eyebrow.

"Isn't that the guy you met at TerrorCon?" she asked.

"Yeah. We had a drink at the bar together. He was actually kind of nice."

"Did you two... you know..."

"Oh yeah." She nodded, waggling her eyebrows in

response.

"You're pulling my leg…" Ember said with a blush.

"I'm not. It just kinda happened. Right before everyone came down with that awful food poisoning."

"I still can't believe that. What a time for food borne illness. All those people were sick for days, good lord. That really sucks when you have to spend the rest of your vacation sick, you know."

"Yeah, it definitely bites," Ava said as she set down the remote.

"Wanna read my cards?" she asked nonchalantly.

Ember nodded.

"Yeah, sure. I'm trying to learn some new spreads, so if you're up for experiments…" She shuffled her cards and Ava pushed off from the counter and headed toward the folding table Ember had taken residence at.

"All right, Miss Cleo, deal me."

Ember dealt the cards as Ava continued to watch the television. The news of the club responsible for the food poisoning, it looked like, had closed, the owner vanishing overnight, after a mysterious fire left the place burned to a crisp.

The camera panned over the landscape, showing the beautiful Silver Starling set against a stormy gray sky as they discussed what the media called "Con Crud."

Ember counted her cards, and the camera panned to an unsuspecting building with a large open window, yellow tables with hardly anyone inside sitting at them, behind the woman being interviewed, and Ava's stomach growled.

"Did you eat breakfast?" Ember asked as she placed her cards in a spread Ava didn't recognize.

"Not unless you count the venti caramel macchiato I woofed down in ten seconds on the way here."

"Want to get some lunch after this?" Ember asked as she placed the last card down.

Ava's phone vibrated in her pocket, drawing her attention away from her wandering thoughts.

"Actually, I could really go for a donut."

Ember smiled. "Cherry filled?"

Ava blinked, feeling the strangest sense of déjà vu, but she shrugged it off.

"No, red velvet supreme," she said as the news prattled on about the upcoming Chester Witch's Festival.

"Since when do you like red velvet anything? I thought you hated chocolate."

"People change, I guess."

Ember flipped over the first card.

"This is your situation, or what is going on with you right now," she stated matter of factly.

Ava glanced down at the card, recognizing the imagery immediately.

The three of swords.

She knew the suit of swords well.

"Oh wait, I actually know this one," she said excitedly.

Ember leaned back and motioned to her friend.

"Heartbreak, grief. Oversensitivity. Usually indicates turmoil in one's love life." Ava smiled smugly.

"Or a breakup." Ember smirked.

"Ah, Em, that's the trick. Can't have a breakup if you don't commit to anyone." She winked, letting out a small laugh.

Ember rolled her eyes.

"It could also just mean a separation. Maybe someone in your life is pulling back."

"Maybe." She nodded to Ember to pull the next card.

"What's the obstacle?"

"Are you doing this reading, or am I?" She teased.

"You." Ava batted her eyelashes sweetly at her friend.

"Then let me read." Ember continued to flip the card.

"The two of cups is your obstacle, and I'm reading that as upright," she stated positively.

Ava raised an eyebrow. She knew the cups was the suit of love. Coupled with a tragic card such as the three of swords, she couldn't help but feel annoyed.

Love was not something she had time for, something she sought. It wasn't as if she had the best track record. Every relationship she'd had seemed to fall into disaster.

Ross, dead by vampires.

Sam, romantic involvement thwarted by demon possession.

Dallas...

Ava shot the thought down immediately. There was nothing between her and Dallas. He'd proved that when he'd stayed silent for two years.

And then, there was Cassius.

The only man who remained a constant visual in her life wasn't a man at all.

He was a creature of the night.

A creature of blood and lust, incapable of such human emotions as *love*.

Nothing would ever matter more to him than blood, and it was best she remembered that.

She'd only seen him once since returning from Oklahoma. He'd stopped by the Third Eye a week after her return with a cup of coffee. A coffee she needed desperately, since sleep was not her friend, lately.

The nightmares, it seemed, had only gotten worse since her trip to TerrorCon. She still relived the death of Ross, the sight of her parents. It seemed the memories of a painful bite, the glowing red glare of demonic eyes, waited for her in the dark and left her in a cold sweat with a racing heart.

And when she'd awakened to the cold chill of the air with her stake in her hand, ready for the monsters, she found herself alone. And just as the terror of loneliness set in, the wind would blow and her skin would prickle with the slightest of goosebumps.

She'd wrap her arms around her legs and close her eyes and she'd whisper to the night, the words her mother would always sing to soothe her to sleep.

Seasons don't fear the reaper.

And on some nights, when exhaustion was too much to fight, she could swear the wind answered, "Nor do the wind, the sun, or the rain."

Turn the page for Blood & Ash, Book 3 in the Ava Crowley, Vampire Slayer series!

BLOOD & ASH

AVA CROWLEY

VAMPIRE SLAYER

BOOK THREE

ARIEL DAWN

NAUGHTY NIGHTS PRESS LLC • CANADA

BLOOD & ASH

Blood will be spilled & bonds will be tested...

Ava's not afraid to get a little bloody... unless it comes to matters of the heart, that is.

When things get too close for comfort with Jake Dallas, Ava finds herself packing her bags to rescue a friend from the pitfalls of internet dating... with the vampire who bit her. What could go wrong?

Cassius knows the clock is ticking and he will have to make a choice—turn Ava into a monster like him, or feed on her blood until there's nothing left.

When Cassius discovers his corpse blood supplier has gone missing, he and Ava embark on a rescue mission that will test Cassius's loyalty in more ways than one.

Can Ava and Cassius work together to slay the monsters that lurk in the shadows as well as the ones in their hearts?

Blood & Ash is book three in the Ava Crowley, Vampire Slayer series, filled with snarky heroines, sexy-as-sin monster hunters, and other seductive supernatural beasts.

Blood & Ash

Ava Crowley, Vampire Slayer

Book Three

Copyright ©2023 Ariel Dawn

ISBN: 978-1-77357-511-7

978-1-77357-509-4

978-1-77357-510-0

Naughty Nights Press LLC

Cover Design by Willsin Rowe

These sudden joys have endings. They burn up in victory like
fire and gunpowder.

— William Shakespeare

What fire does not destroy, it hardens.

— Oscar Wilde

CHAPTER ONE

"HARDER," AVA BREATHED as her back was slammed up against the wall. A sheen of sweat had already started to form on her skin, and her muscles were starting to ache, but she didn't care. Dallas grunted in response, his hand around her throat.

"Is that all you've got?" she said with a smirk. His fingers rested there, just above her jugular, and a part of her wanted to feel the force, the tight grip she knew he was capable of. Because in those moments, the ones that were far more frequent these days than they'd been before, she was free.

Free from the nightmares that plagued her, free from the ghosts that haunted her.

Well, the vampire who haunted her, really. Though with the way Cassius appeared and disappeared at will like the wind, he was quite ghostlike at times. Always there, watching.

Waiting.

Ava brought her lips to Dallas's, forcing the thoughts away. She could taste the saltiness of the sweat on his lip, the metallic taste of blood that hadn't quite dried yet from their last go-around in the ring, or more accurately, the mattress of Motel 6 that was acting as a boxing ring in place of the Bat Cave's comfortable gym.

"You drive me up a fucking wall, you know that?" Dallas bit back as he moved his lips from hers to her neck. Ava started to feel lightheaded from all of it—the sparring, the secrecy, the memories, the feel of Dallas and all his hardened edges encompassing her.

Now was her chance. She wrapped her legs around his waist, dragging her nails up his arm, fingers finding their way into his hair, twisting softly before tightening her grip.

She forcibly yanked his head to the side.

"Oh I know, Dallas, that's the fun of it," she said between breaths.

Dallas smiled devilishly back at her before breaking her tight hold, his eyes full of heat and desire.

Desire that echoed beneath her skin.

Her muscles ached, her head was splitting, and she was certain she'd be sore tomorrow, but she didn't care.

It was getting harder and harder to care, and a part of her almost *wished* the others would knock on the door, would find them tangled up together so that she could breathe again. She hated lying to her brother, hated having to pretend everything was fine and nothing had changed, when in fact, *everything* had changed.

Dallas slid his hands underneath her thighs, turning her around before slamming her back onto the mattress of messy sheets once more, his weight heavy on top of her.

Ava wriggled and writhed beneath him as his large hand held her wrists together, his grip firm. She moved around, twisting and turning, her breasts brushing against his sweat-soaked chest. In the amber light of the motel room, he looked like every dream, every fantasy, every bad decision a girl could ever dream of.

"Fight me, Ava," he growled, grinding his rigid length against her thigh.

She grunted and huffed in annoyance, her muscles tightening, her leg starting to go numb from the weight.

It wasn't all that different from the first time they'd done this, four years ago. She could still remember how it felt when he wrapped his arms around her, held her close. How badly she'd wanted to submit and give into the temptation of Jake Dallas, even then.

But now...

"Jake," she whined, a strange feeling working its way up her body, through her blood, into her heart, her mind.

"I can't, I—" Her breath started to come in faster, and panic started to set in.

She was trapped, and there was no way out.

"Fight me, Kitten. I know you can," he said, his voice strained, but yet full of something she'd never heard before.

"I don't want to fight!" she bit back, tears starting to form behind her eyes.

Dallas loosened his grip but he did not let go. Instead, he entwined his fingers with hers in a soft gesture that felt foreign to her. Jake Dallas wasn't *soft* in any sense of the word. No, Dallas was a force of nature, a hurricane that would undoubtedly wreck her and destroy her into a million pieces.

But still, she wanted the wrath of his storm. She wanted to be caught up in the eye of all that he was, because death was not an option. As long as she wore Cassius's mark, death would one day come for her and she would not submit to it. Not over her dead body.

"Ava," Dallas's voice turned softer, his free hand pushing her sweaty, wet strands of hair behind her ear. When she looked up into his eyes, she could see her own fear reflected in them, and she hated it. She hated herself for not being strong enough.

"Ava, I—" He brushed his thumb over her bottom lip.

Her heart racing, the world around her started to fade back into reality, and she swallowed harshly.

"I can't do this right now," she said as she fought the tears.

Dallas was quiet for a moment, his gaze settling on her. He let go of her wrists, easing his weight off of her. She expected him to just leave her alone. That was what he normally did when she'd been pushed too far; given her space to ground herself again. Training with Dallas was always like that; it always pushed her past her limits, because the intent was to be stronger than her fears. To be strong enough to survive vampire Jedi-mind tricks as well as to combat their strength. It was the difference between life and death, and it was familiar.

But the tears weren't.

"I don't know what happened, I just—"

Dallas wrapped his arms around her and pulled her into his lap, brushing his fingers along her arm in the gentlest of touches. He tilted her head up, and looked in her eyes in a way that was quite different than the other times. The heat, the lust had diminished and in its place was something far more dangerous.

Sympathy.

The touch felt... intimate.

Loving almost.

"Don't look at me like that," she said as she pushed

him in the chest, though not hard enough to move him, though she could have. If she wanted.

"Like what?" he asked, his brows furrowing in concern.

Ava didn't like it.

"Like I'm some fucking damsel in distress. I don't need your pity, I just... need a fucking break." She shoved him, and he fell back against the mattress, running his hand over his face.

"From this—" He motioned to the hotel room, which looked to be in disarray from their steamy 'sparring' session. "—or..."

The words hit Ava like a brick as she considered them. She moved off the bed, snatching up her clothes from the floor that had come off at some point after the second round, when sweat and heat made them both uncomfortable.

Ava froze.

Before she could even speak, both of their phones started going off, rattling against the end table. Dallas sighed, getting up from the bed as she pulled on her Blue Oyster Cult shirt.

"It's Mal," Dallas said, turning to her.

"Yeah, and?" She slid her jeans on slowly.

"Get your stake. We have a nest to infiltrate." He said the words plainly, as if they were the most normal thing in the world. As if the strange moment they'd just shared, the one where he *held* her hadn't happened at all.

Maybe it's better if I just try and forget about it. Forget about today, forget about whatever this is that's happening between us.

Ava nodded as she buttoned her jeans.

"Riding separately?" she asked, her nerves starting to settle.

Dallas stood there, the light of his phone illuminating him and his double star tattoos, the shadows falling on the planes of his chiseled jaw, his dark features.

He nodded. "Of course."

"All right. See you there," she said as she grabbed her phone, silencing it and sliding it into her pocket before throwing on her leather jacket. She reached for the door, pausing for a moment.

It was just a moment, a split second of waiting as she realized Jake Dallas did nothing to stop her. He did not protest or beg her to stay. Instead, he let her walk out the door and into the crimson sunset without a sound.

Ava settled into her Impala, turning the keys in the ignition.

The familiar guitar strings of *Heart's Magic Man* filled the car, and Ava sighed as she backed out of the Motel 6 parking lot, speeding off for the highway, off to hunt something she could catch.

CHAPTER TWO

CASSIUS WATCHED THE rain fall outside the window. The days were getting shorter now, and fall, it seemed, had started to settle into Chester once more. The moon hung in the sky, lighting up the property he called home. The dark, black waters of the pool reflected the moonlight like a mirror, and the sight was almost soothing. Almost enough to get lost in.

The house was far too quiet for his liking, with Jasmine and Tajiri gone until daybreak. The silence never used to bother him as much as it seemed to these days. In fact, he'd enjoyed it once. His pulse thumped away beneath his skin faintly, his insides warming instinctively.

She is near.

He knew without a doubt, the stolen pulse in his veins belonged to the one and only Ava Crowley, the very reason for all his restlessness.

The desire to be near her, even in this moment, was damn near too much to bear as thunder roared in the distance.

Four years.

It had been *four years* since he'd tasted her blood on his tongue, since he'd marked her as his... mate.

Cassius watched the rain as it fell against the glass, long drops seeding into other drops until they connected and dispersed, the moonlight illuminating them like fractured diamonds.

When he could not stand the shadows of his own loneliness anymore, he grabbed his leather coat—a proper coat that came down well past his hips and near to his ankles—and slipped on his boots. Perhaps a walk through a November rain would be just the thing to clear his head.

He slid his cell phone in his coat pocket, if only out of habit. It wasn't as if he made many calls on the thing, but Ava did have a tendency to text him once in a while.

When she needs my help on a case...

Cassius shut the door as he stepped outside into the woods, the scent of rain most invigorating to his senses. A rainstorm in Chester during the fall was nothing quite like a rainstorm at the beach in Italy, or a rainstorm in Paris, but it was not without its grandeur and romance. There was something about the stillness of the forest when it stormed that soothed Cassius's spirit.

His stomach growled, and he fought to ignore it. It was Saturday, after all, and Brian would not be working the weekend shift, which meant he would have to wait a few days for his routine serving of corpse blood.

Before he knew it, he'd made his way out of the forest and into town, a deep sigh escaping him as his pulse ebbed with intensity. He stood on the side of the street, underneath a bright streetlamp, scanning his surroundings. She was close, so very close he could almost taste her. The memory of her blood in his mouth on that fateful night, the night both of their lives had been forever changed, would always be burned in his brain. He'd only bitten her to start the healing process, to save her from death's doorstep.

His venom had sealed her wounds, but it appeared it had opened some new ones as well.

For ever since that night, Ava Crowley had made it more than clear where he stood with her; yet time and time again, it seemed the opportunities to end his life had passed them by without their noticing. It was hard for him to believe she truly wished him dead, but he was not certain she had accepted his presence for it what it truly was, either.

A mate bond.

A bond that meant he'd claimed her blood.

Claiming a mate was something he'd never intended, and he didn't wish to commit Ava to a life of immortality, no matter how bad he wanted her for the rest of his cursed existence. As an Aurelia—a pure bloodline among his kind—he possessed the ability to sire a mate, a feat that had become much more rare nowadays. Though, being born into a high coven bloodline, Cassius knew what it was like to not have a choice in such things, and he vowed not to take such a choice from the spitfire that was Ava Crowley.

Cassius leaned against the streetlight post as the rain fell, a symphony around him. Puddles rippled with fresh raindrops, and water ran down the sides of the cracks of the road, diverging into sewers. He watched as the neon purple lights in the window of The Third Eye dimmed, as the bell atop the door jingled in tandem. But it was not Ava who exited the shop, and for a moment his heart sunk.

Had he dreamt it?

Fantasized such things?

The pulse beneath his skin was still hot, still aching...

"Looking for someone?" The venomous tone was music to his ears, and a smirk formed on his face at the sound. He did not turn around. There was no need. He'd know that bite anywhere.

"Not anyone in particular," he teased.

"You're a terrible liar, Cas, you know that, right?" Ava huffed, and he could practically hear her eyes rolling in the back of her head, and he finally turned around to look at her.

She was dressed in an oversized maroon hoodie and ripped jeans, her hands in the frayed front pouch. The hood covered her short, brown hair, but he could still see several strands peeking out the sides. She took a step closer, and he pretended not to notice.

"I have never lied to you, Ava. Nor do I have the need or desire to do so."

Ava rolled her eyes as he pushed off the streetlamp post, taking a step closer to her.

She crossed her arms.

"Then tell me the truth. Why are you standing like a fucking stalker outside my place of work?" she said as she chewed her lip.

Cassius let out a soft chuckle.

"Would you believe me if I said I wanted to clear my head?"

"Well, I didn't think you had any brains underneath all those golden locks, so no. I do not believe you," she said as she narrowed her eyes at him.

"You are a terrible liar, my sweet Avarice," he said with a grin.

Somehow gravity had pulled them closer, close enough he could reach his hand out and push back her hood, run his fingers through her chocolate brown hair, kiss her perfectly pink lips, and watch the blood he'd claimed flush into her cheeks.

But all he could do was stand there like a stone, captivated by the sight of the woman who made him feel less like a monster and more like a man.

"I have no reason to lie to you, *Cassius*." She hissed as she said his full name, something she did not do very often, if at all.

The sound of his name on her tongue made his slow, dying heart spring to life.

CHAPTER THREE

AVA'S HEART THUDDED in her chest as she realized she was close enough to kill Cassius without a second thought. It would be easy. She could slide her hand beneath her shirt—beneath Dallas's hoodie—and swiftly pull out her stake she kept tucked in the band of her bra.

With the way Cassius was looking at her, his gorgeous green eyes full of sparking embers, she could not look away. Surely he was doing *something* to her to make her stand so still. She knew without a doubt what a vampire's thrall felt like, and at this moment, she did not feel that. Perhaps it was some type of vampire juju that was special to this pain in the ass vampire who filled her thoughts more than she wished to admit.

Ava could feel her blood heat, rushing through her veins. In the presence of Cassius, it was like her blood *knew* it was his, and she hated that.

She forced herself to turn away from his beautiful face, keeping her hands in the front pouch of Dallas's hoodie.

She had planned on going home immediately after she'd arrived back in Virginia, but it seemed fate had other plans for her. Once she'd parked the Impala in the driveway, staring up at the dark, empty plantation house that now belonged to her, she could not bring herself to enter. She hated coming home from a case. Back to reality. So instead of walking up her steps, she'd walked down the driveway, with no destination in sight. Her feet led her to walking the streets of Chester in the rain, trying to avoid what was now her home. It didn't feel like home, though Ava was not sure what home really was anymore. Home was once Salem, Massachusetts, when life was perfect, happy.

Until vampires took everything from her.

Malcolm, her brother had divulged as much only after he'd realized she'd been bitten, and she couldn't help but fall into a spiral of painful thoughts every time she thought of them. Home was a dorm she'd left behind, and motels and hotels she'd crashed in on the road whilst helping her brother and his Goon Squad hunt vampires and other creatures of the night.

Now that her guardian, Becky Lee Michaels, had passed, leaving the magnificent property to Ava, she felt truly alone. Her brother had made being a hunter his top priority, forever searching for the vampires who had killed their parents and a way to clear Ava of the mark.

Cassius's mark.

Malcolm had made it more than clear that while her backup was helpful at times, he was adamant that she keep 'the fort down' in his absence, which was he nonchalant way of sitting her at the kids table. Even though they were no longer children. After all, she was twenty-three years old, she could more than take care of herself, and she'd proved that on numerous occasions.

Now going home to her inherited plantation home, complete with a pseudo-parent housekeeper, just made her feel small, insignificant. It was a stark reminder that Ava was alone. She hadn't had a real relationship since her college boyfriend, Ross, who'd unceremoniously ended up dead by vamps. She would have met the same fate, had it not been for Cassius... which she did not want to think about.

Ava had not known at the time when the angelic faced vampire asked her permission, what he truly meant. She only knew in that moment as she lay bleeding out on the floor that she would have agreed to anything if it meant she would live. She had not known the cost for such things. Aside from the demonologist, Sam Kingsley—who had turned out to be possessed by an incubus, and an alcohol infused makeout with Sawyer Thorne, the closest thing she had to a relationship was... whatever she had with Dallas, her brother's partner, and even that was sparse. After all, Dallas was just as much a nomad as her brother. When they'd discussed their arrangement only two years ago, she'd been more than fine with such things.

No attachment meant no pain.

She'd told herself it was better to be alone, a sentiment her brother echoed. Even Dallas himself had said the very same—*If you had no one, no one could hurt you.* But Ava was a Crowley, and she was restless, always searching for something. A way to break a bond. Strong arms to know when to hold her and when to let her go.

So why was standing in front of a vampire she longed to kill—who she could not bring herself to do so—the only place she could be still?

"Are you working a case?" Cassius said as he slowly ambled forward, nodding for her to follow him. To walk with him.

Ava knew trusting Cassius was dangerous. He was suave and attractive, and his proximity lit her blood on fire while giving her goosebumps at the same time.

But he was a monster.

A blood-eating, undead creature who would kill her himself if she was not careful.

She knew she should walk away. Go home as she had planned, but her bed was cold without Dallas to make her forget about the things that haunted her.

Jake Dallas had a way of exorcising her demons that she was certain no one else would ever match. His brand of love was not love at all, but a perpetual war. A macabre dance over hellfire, and she was never certain which of them would escape alive when she was with him, a sentiment she'd relished at the beginning of their *arrangement*, but now had started to feel trapped by.

So, Ava followed Cassius as he led her down the street, like a moth to a flame.

"I just finished a case. Guess it's time to go back to my boring ass life," she said in disdain. She stole a glance at the vampire next to her, noticing he was dressed in a long, leather trenchcoat and boots. She had to admit the outfit was a departure from his normal grey shirt, black leather pants, and low-top converse tennis shoes, and it wasn't a bad look on him. Amidst the grey fog and the rain, he looked every bit an evil vampire come to drag her to hell.

Why is that sexy?

Because it's the fucking bond.

It makes him appeal to you because that's what he needs to fucking end you.

You to be smitten with him.

Was she smitten with him?

She wasn't sure, and the way her heart lifted at the possibility forced her to push down the thought.

That would be insane, after all.

"I would hardly call your life boring," he said with a smirk.

"You're right. Your life is probably a lot more boring than mine. Surprised you haven't thrown yourself off a fucking cliff yet out of insanity."

"Of course not. I'd hate to rob you of the chance to slay me," he said as a small laugh escaped his throat. The sound was... kind of sexy, if she was being honest. Her insides fluttered and she looked away. They had come to the library. It was only four years ago, they stood here and he had divulged he was a vampire.

She hadn't believed his words, but her blood knew the truth.

I should have killed him then.

She'd vowed to slay him if he didn't stay away from her, and she hadn't even come into her slayer training yet. She'd only known with every fiber of her being that he would be the death of her, vampire or not, and such a thing was just as frightening a concept as the reality that monsters existed.

"You make it sound like you're looking forward to your inevitable demise," she said as the rain suddenly stopped. The light from the lamppost out front, and the low ceiling lights of the library, cast amber ribbons of reflections in the puddles between them. Cassius shifted his weight, his golden hair falling in his eyes. The light fell on him, making the raindrops in his golden hair shimmer, his bright emerald eyes imploring her gaze.

"Do not tell me you are not? You only threaten my very existence every time you see me."

"That's because you don't how to fucking leave me

alone. Because you are a stalker." She was very flustered at his words and her cheeks felt warm.

"Perhaps I like your company."

"Wow. Does that kind of thing really work for you, Cas?" she bit.

"I beg your pardon?" he asked.

"Nevermind. I should probably be going..." She sighed and turned toward the direction of home.

"Ava..." he called out to her, his voice full of something she'd certainly never heard before.

"Go home, Cas." She waved at him as she walked away, though she had to admit a part of her wished he'd reject her plea and run beside her, insisting on seeing her home safely. That he'd walk her up her steps, as he had many other times, leaving her at her door.

Or that he'd show up in her room, climbing in through her window just as she'd awaken from a bad dream.

But Cassius did not chase after her, and that made her feel a mixture of sadness and relief.

When Ava had reached her large plantation home, she breathed a sigh of relief as she opened the door. She locked it immediately, flicking on the light, and the silence was deafening, and her heart heavy.

Fucking hell.

She pulled her hood down, and headed straight for the fridge. She'd been gone a week, and had told Connie, her aunt's housekeeper—now her housekeeper—not to worry about cleaning, or stocking the fridge. When she opened it, she could see the Chinese woman had not regarded her request. The refrigerator was stocked with all her favorite things, including a bottle of Bordeaux.

Ava did not truly care for red wine, she much

preferred a solid, hearty scotch or whiskey, but Cassius did. He'd mentioned it once, and she'd gone to purchase a bottle to see how awful it was, and she had to admit there was something about the bitterness that soothed her soul. And when she would undoubtedly awaken in a cold sweat from the memories that haunted her in her nightmares to a golden-haired, green eyed angel of death, she longed for its bitterness.

Ava poured a glass of wine, pausing for a moment as she closed her eyes, wrapping her fingers around the glass. Her cell phone vibrated against her ass, and she let out a breath she did not realize she had been holding.

She slid the phone out of her pocket, opening her eyes. The artificial light of her phone lit up the small space as she read the notification from the man she referred to as *Asshole* in her phone.

Jake Dallas.

You up, kitten?

She licked her lips as she took a sip of the bitter wine.

You know I am. Otherwise you wouldn't be texting me.

She took another sip of her drink as she waited for his response.

I miss you.

Three small words.

How was it that three small words felt so heavy on her heart?

Should I say it back?

She did miss him, in a way. She missed the warmth of his body curled around her in the middle of the night, and she missed going head to head with him in a ring or a motel room. Hell, she even missed pushing his buttons and pissing him off.

She did not miss his voice, or his bipolar personality. One moment he was fine with their arrangement, and the next he was ignoring her, or running his hands through her hair, holding her in his lap and being... caring. It was exhausting keeping up with his fluctuating moods.

She'd been clear two years ago that she was not looking for a man to settle down with, or a boyfriend to bring to game night every week at the Third Eye. She had vowed not to get attached to anyone, and Dallas had been upfront with her, too. He wasn't looking for anything serious, either. He could not afford attachments with the lifestyle he'd become accustomed to. Hunting came first, and it always would. They'd agreed to keep it casual, after all, it was just sex.

Really, really good sex at that.

She let her thoughts drift. It didn't mean anything, and that was how she preferred it. It didn't change anything about their friendship, or their hunter partnership. Feelings were off the table.

But lately, these rare moments with Dallas were becoming more frequent, and Ava was not sure how to respond, or where things had changed.

Did they change?

She texted him back.

Good to know.

Ava took a long drink and refilled her glass before he had responded.

Are you pissed at me?

Ava rolled her eyes, letting out a frustrated laugh. For a thirty-five year old man, he was often quite dense.

Not everything is about you, you know.

It seemed an eternity until he'd responded.

Are you trying to start an argument with me? I just wanted to let you know I was thinking about you.

Just as soon as he'd sent the first text, another came.

Don't you miss me?

Ava pursed her lips, feeling a mixture of annoyance and anger. How dare he make her feel like the asshole. Clinger was not a good look on him.

I can't miss you if you don't fucking go away, Ava texted harshly.

She wasn't sure where the anger was coming from, but she didn't shy away from it. In fact, she embraced it. Anger was familiar, cathartic even.

Is that what you want, Ava? For me to go away?

Ava felt her stomach turn.

Is that what she wanted?

For him to leave her alone?

She wasn't sure. She only knew this conversation made her feel rather anxious. It felt too much like an argument with a boyfriend, and Dallas was certainly *not* her boyfriend.

For starters, no one knew about their relationship. Well, no one but her best friend, Ember, and she was not Dallas's biggest fan, either. They'd kept everything hush for the last two years, since they'd first crossed that line when she was only twenty, while on a case in the tiny mountain town of Mahoning, but if she was being truthful, whatever existed between her and Dallas had been going on much longer than that. It had all started when Cassius bit her four years ago, when Dallas became her mentor, her trainer, and the unattainable, emotionally unavailable, wishy-washy asshole she could never quite pin or quit instigating.

And the last two years had been a blur of sex and fighting, moments stolen in shitty motel rooms, bars, and even cars, and once on Dallas's motorcycle, when they weren't driving stakes into vamps like toothpicks in cheese.

Not once had Dallas shown up to her doorstep outside of a hunt, not even on Thanksgiving when Mal had come home, when he had done so before...

Before we fucked.

Ava drained the last of her drink before sending a final text.

I want to go to bed. I think you should, too.

She placed her glass in the sink before heading to her bedroom.

Okay. Good night, Ava.

Ava tossed her phone on the end table as she crawled into bed, curling atop her burgundy covers, feeling colder than ever, and she knew it wasn't because the window was open. The wind whistled outside, and she felt overwhelmed with sadness.

Why am I like this?

She closed her eyes tightly.

Why do I push people away?

The scar on her wrist heated, her skin prickling with goosebumps, and she couldn't help but feel a tightness in her chest. Though, when she looked up, Cassius was nowhere to be found, and the feeling had disappeared, and that hurt her heart most of all.

CHAPTER FOUR

CASSIUS STROLLED THROUGH the parking lot of the Willow Creek Morgue, feeling rather famished. It was now Tuesday, and the last two nights had been practically torturous.

Jasmine and Taijiri had decided to stay a bit longer wherever they were, since Cassius did not press for details when Taijiri had texted him. His friend had only said he wished to spend some 'quality time' with his companion and Cassius could not fault him for such things, though a part of him was jealous that Taijiri had a companion to spend time with in the first place.

It had been ages since Cassius had been with another. His life of solitude had been more than deliberate. After Eden had exposed her true colors, after she'd admitted her hand in his father's death, among so many others of those he held dear, it was the final straw. They'd been strained for years, trying to keep up their rouse, their engagement. And he had *tried* so very hard to be the man Eden needed, but alas, she had no room in her heart for him. He could not compete with the ghost of the only man she truly loved,

Marcellus. And despite his pure bloodline and his genetic ability to reproduce with mortals and vampires alike, they had not managed to do what their union was intended for.

Once he'd discovered the truth about her miscarriage, about how she'd *used* him as nothing more than a pawn to cover up the truth, he knew there was nothing left in his heart for the vicious Eden Boracelli. With her admission, she'd taken the last remains of any feelings he'd harbored for her.

Cassius had spent the last few decades in hiding, knowing that Eden would not take no for an answer. She'd tried to thrall him from leaving all those years ago, after all, realizing she was far too late. Even now, Cassius hated to think about everything—no, *everyone*—he had left behind.

At the time, Eden had moved up in rank, and was one of the Boracelli Queen's closest allies. He'd agreed with Francesca's proposal, to be betrothed and united with Eden because of the sins of his father, and the need to protect his mother.

The Boracellis demanded an Aurelian stud.

After his father had left the high covens altogether, running away with his mother so they could live their life in exiled happiness, they were left to make arrangements with covens who did not possess such pure bloodlines. And with his father dead, without his protection, his mother was exposed and fair game. He'd agreed to the arrangement for her.

His mother had offered him and his seed up in exchange for protection from Lucious Aurelia's enemies. And though it had angered him, made him feel as if he was nothing more than a prize pony on the auction block, he could not throw his mother to the wolves. He would always protect her, the woman who gave up everything to have him. When he'd left without word to anyone but Leon, his closest friend, he'd left her, too.

It was better she did not know what I planned...

He still felt remorse. Cassius did not miss much of his life prior to his arrival in Chester, but he did miss his mother, and often he wondered if she was still alive, kept in the halls of the Boracelli castle still to this day, and if she was happy, if she was all right.

Cassius pushed through the door, smoothing his hair back as he came to the front desk. His stomach felt so hollow, and the pain was maddening. His throat was parched. Just the sight of the woman at the desk made his mouth water, knowing her blood would be fresh and warm, but Cassius had mastered a level of control over the years that would drive Eden to drink. The woman who claimed to be in control all the time was a slave to impulsivity, and she had the body count to show for it.

"Can I help you?" she asked with a bored sigh.

"I'm here to see Bryan. We are... meeting for lunch," Cassius said with a well practiced smile that hid just enough of his fangs that he could pass for a human.

This song and dance wasn't one he practiced often anymore, he'd grown rather accustomed to his routine corpse blood delivery, and therefore, crashing a morgue was a thing of the past for Cassius. He hadn't done so in two years, not since he'd been in Oklahoma to help Leon clear his name after he"d come under investigation for murders that he had no part in.

Murders committed by an incubus, no less.

Though the experience had been refreshing, the blood he'd consumed had not been. It had been laced with incubus toxin, and had thrown him into a lust-filled haze. It had been a miracle he'd had enough control not to throw Ava up against the vending machine in the Silver Starling hotel and ravish her until she begged to be bitten.

Cassius pushed the memory away.

No, that is not who you are.

"Oh, I guess he must not have called you, either," the woman, a short, petite teal haired woman spoke.

"I beg your pardon?" Cassius asked, his voice going flat. He did not like the sound of this.

"Bryan didn't show up today. No call or anything. I hope he's okay. Boss said if he doesn't hear from him by tomorrow, they might have to do a welfare check or something."

Cassius's blood chilled, his thoughts immediately turning dire. Bryan was, if anything, a stickler for routine. Since his first brush with death—where Cassius had saved him from a vampire in the woods— he'd become highly reclusive. His job in the coroner's office provided him the means to supply Cassius with a steady supply of corpse blood as a return favor, but it was usually quite an isolated job. The man had become something of an occultist, a mad scientist since his brush with death—and aside from his return favors, Bryan kept his distance from Cassius.

Most humans with a sense of self preservation are smart to stay away from monsters.

His melancholy would have to wait, though, because suspicion was driving the boat right now, and Cassius knew he needed more information. His guilt and despair would always be there, swimming just beneath the surface of his cold, pale skin.

"I am sure it must have slipped his mind, you know how hyper-focused he can be sometimes," Cassius said, using his smile, and only an ounce of his thrall to flood the woman, preventing her from asking too many questions.

Her eyes glazed a bit as she looked at him, her demeanor shifting to more flirtatious and wanting.

"But I'm not doing anything for lunch, if you need some company," she said with a giggle.

"I'm afraid that won't be necessary. But thank you for the offer," he said as she nodded, sighing. Cassius pulled back on his thrall as he waved her goodbye, and walked out into the fog-laden afternoon toward the woods.

As he came to the clearing, he heard a rustle in the bushes. Pausing for a moment, he was hit with a wave of hunger that made his stomach tighten. It seemed using his thrall on the woman, even if it was only for a short moment, had only exacerbated his thirst. A cold sweat formed on his brow as images flooded him. Of fangs in neck, of the memory of blood on his tongue. But not just any blood.

Her blood.

Ava's.

Cassius let out a groan of defeat, feeling his cock twitch from the memory. He hated that even now, the memory itself could awaken such desire in him. Ava was so much more than his perfect feast. She was feisty, sarcastic, and rough around the edges, but he'd had the privilege of catching the woman beneath the armor when she thought he wasn't looking, or when she'd let her guard down.

The woman who tried to fight him for his donut when she had a dozen of her own, or who offered him her umbrella, while her pulse raced, insinuating it was just 'polite'. The woman who listened to music too loud so no one would know she was singing along. The woman who suffered from nightmares and tried to stifle them with wine, whiskey, and men like Jake Dallas, who would never understand the gift she truly was.

Cassius adjusted himself, trying to shake off the thoughts. As he did so, a deer appeared in the clearing. Cassius watched its ears twitch as it looked at him, and he did not think.

For, he couldn't.

He could only act on impulse, starved as he was, and closed the distance. Cassius moved with lightning speed, chasing the doe into the woods, cornering her until he was certain he was out of sight. He could never be too careful. He'd gotten this far keeping his nose clean and under the radar, he did not wish to risk it now. Not when he was so very hungry. The hunter inside of him—no, the *monster* inside of him—reared to the surface as Cassius caught the doe in his hands. She looked up at him with pleading eyes, scared out of her wits, and he hated himself.

He hated that his need for blood prevailed over everything else, and that after only two days of no corpse blood, he was here in this forest, with a frightened animal between his hands.

"I'm so sorry about this," he whispered, feeling the shame and guilt mix with his hunger, his need. His predatory instinct. Cassius did not waste a moment as he brought his fangs down on the deer's neck, holding its body still as it tried to fight him, tried to kick out of his grasp.

But he was stronger than an average human, and as Leon had once disclosed, stronger than the average vampire.

Warm blood hit his tongue, and it was sour and bitter. Cassius felt his gag reflex kick in, and he was disgusted with himself and the taste.

It wasn't like *real* blood. It wasn't even like corpse blood, which he had grown accustomed to.

He drank with a shudder, letting the gamey, slick blood slide down his throat, and he felt better. Better enough that his stomach had settled, though he knew it wouldn't be for long.

It'd been nearly fifty years since he'd had fresh blood, save for that night four years ago whence he'd tasted Ava's once he bit her.

He'd subsisted on corpse blood solely, breaking into morgues and crematoriums like a criminal until he'd met Bryan. The urge to feast on animal blood had not been a prevalent one, as Cassius had discovered in his earlier years, it made him ill.

Cassius let go of the body of the deer, and it slumped to the ground, lifeless. He backed away as reality hit him, and found himself up against a tree. He closed his eyes and let the shame, the guilt, rise to the surface.

His thoughts wandered to Ava and her sweet blood, her bite, and her thriving pulse that was alive in his veins. Even if she did not care for him, even if she found him appalling and a thorn in her side, Cassius could not deny that being in her presence soothed the demons inside of him that would not let him be.

He opened his eyes, wiping the back of his hand over his mouth, as the first wave of nausea hit him.

So much for a satisfying meal.

Only a monster was capable of such things, and how could anyone love a monster?

CHAPTER FIVE

THE DOOR BELL jingled, alerting Ava that a customer had finally decided to show up. She groaned as she shut her book, *East Anglian Witches & Wizards*, readying to have to put on her customer face and be chipper, friendly.

When she saw the customer in question sauntering in with a fresh coffee and a bag of something that smelled like a cherry danish from The Mean Bean, though, she wasn't sure if she was relieved or annoyed. Perhaps a bit of both.

"Well, look what the cat dragged in this afternoon," she drawled as she leaned against the back counter, following Cas's graceful stride to her counter. He gingerly set the bag of pastry deliciousness down, pushing it to her like some offering to a caged, vicious animal.

"I need your help," he said as he set the coffee down next to it. On the other side of the counter, he stood perfectly still, looking at his offerings, then at her.

Waiting.

Ava narrowed her eyes and her stomach growled.

She was not much of a morning person, and therefore, nine times out of ten, she rarely ate breakfast at home. Ava's idea of breakfast was coffee on the run. She could never wake herself early enough to leave the house in time to make it to the Mean Bean to eat something substantial, and she hated cooking first thing in the morning when she was barely awake. If she'd had any time, it was for a bowl of cereal, and this morning she'd had difficulty waking.

For the third night in a row, the nightmares had persisted. Ava had tossed and turned, never quite finding a modicum of comfort as her mind raced against her, not wanting to fall back into the darkness and the awful memories that awaited her.

Ross's scream of terror.

Her parents bloodied bodies on the floor.

Sam Kingsley being exorcised.

A large, heavy werewolf with its jaws at her throat.

Being wrapped up in a vampire's thrall.

She leaned forward, only enough to pull the brown paper bag off the counter, rifling it open only to catch a divine whiff of cherries, cream, and flaky sugar pastry.

Cherry danish, my favorite.

She regarded Cas as she broke off a small piece of the confectionary delight and chewed on it, wondering if this was some sort of trick. Cassius was many things, but he was not one to ask favors, especially from her.

Was it some sort of trap?

Was this how he got her?

Lured in with breakfast and glowing green emerald eyes?

Was she that easy?

"What the hell do you need my help with?" she said through a mouthful of danish. The tart cherry filling on her tongue was still warm, and it was rather delicious.

"It's Bryan."

Ava stilled for a moment. There weren't many things she and Cassius had in common; in fact she doubted they had much in common other than their mutual contact, Bryan.

She'd been working a case, one of her own, when she'd come across Bryan's services. The beautiful bloodsucker had urged her to visit the man, who was something of a laboratorial genius when it came to antidotes, potions, and preventative measures. If one needed dead man's blood, or a crystal to force a demon into, or protection oils, Bryan was capable of whipping up the best.

He was also a bit eccentric, but Ava knew beggars could not be choosers. It was not as if Chester had a white pages for hunter-adjacent occultists who you could rely on in a pinch.

"What about him?" Ava pressed.

Cassius leaned his arms on the counter.

"I think he may be in trouble. He is missing," Cassius stated sternly.

Ava shrugged. "Maybe he finally went off the deep end."

"He did not show up for work today. My gut tells me something is amiss."

Ava set the bag of half-eaten pastry down. Something about Cassius's tone felt off. He sounded legitimately worried.

But why would he be worried about Bryan?

It wasn't like they were friends or anything. Ava pushed the thought down, feeling the strange impulse to soothe the vampire's worry.

"Maybe he's just not feeling well."

"I went by his residence as well. He is not there."

"You went inside?" Ava asked, surprised. "I mean,

maybe he's just you know... indisposed with the flu or something. Wrapped up in a blanket burrito."

"No. I did not, but I knocked. No answer. From what I was able to discern, he was not there. I could see through the door window. The house looked... unkempt."

"You didn't just like... break in..." Ava suggested as she reached for the coffee.

"I am a lot of things, my sweet Avarice, but a locksmith I am not."

Ava rolled her eyes. "I mean, it's not that hard. Just a wiggle here and a pinch there..."

Cassius's eyes lit up as she licked her fingers clean of the sticky danish icing. She did not miss the way his gaze fell to her lips, how he fixated on her slender fingers as she licked them. He let out a breath as he licked his own lips before meeting her gaze. Something about the way he looked at her made her blood boil beneath the surface.

"Perhaps you could..."

"Are you asking me to break into a man's home?" Ava said with a smirk. Cassius pursed his lips.

"I suppose I am," he said plainly.

Ava sighed as she looked at the clock.

"Guess I'm going to lunch early," she said, taking a sip of her coffee. The perfect mix of cream and espresso made her insides flush, and her heart flutter with excitement as she grabbed the rest of the bag of danish, tucking it beneath her arm as she grabbed her cross-body purse, reaching for the store keys.

Cassius stood back while she readied herself, and she could keenly feel his gaze on her. She turned away just as she felt a blush creeping into her cheeks.

What the hell is wrong with me?

She stormed past Cassius, and he followed without

question. He squeezed through the door after her, the narrow passageway causing him to brush against her, and the touch, as innocent as it was, made Ava stop dead in her tracks, key in the lock.

It wasn't the first time she'd ever *felt* him, though it had been quite a long time since she had. She could still remember the night he saved her life, how he'd taken her wrist in his hand, how his fingers brushed over her skin. Though the memory brought forth a myriad of other touches, other sensations she wanted to forget.

His fangs piercing her skin, his tongue on her flesh.
The pure bliss of being in his thrall.

Ava swallowed harshly, forcing the haunting memories away. She hated how they had a mind of their own, and filled her psyche so often. Especially, when she was alone, with no one to make her forget, and no one to satisfy her burning desires, the ones she tried to lock deep within.

Cas's body against hers sparked a fire in her blood, in her nerves. The feeling of his chest against her back, his stomach against her waist, caused her stomach to flip and a warmth to blossom between her thighs.

Ava angled herself away from his sight, feeling her cheeks flush once more.

Jesus Christ!
This should not be happening!

She chastised herself, locking the door and scurrying away to the curb where her car was parked.

Cassius stood on the side of the street, looking like some Calvin Klein model in his signature grey shirt and leather pants, all glowing green emerald eyes and golden hair blowing in the chilly Chester wind.

Ava folded herself into the driver seat, unlocking the passenger door from the inside. She swallowed as she stared at him from inside the car, feeling as if this crossed some sort of invisible line.

But the prospect of a case was much more enticing.

"Well, don't just stand there, get in," she grumbled as Cassius stared back at her.

He shook his head, obviously shoving away his own random thoughts or daydreams. If he thought this was how he would take her, feast on her blood and kill her, he had another thing coming. Ava's Impala was more secure than Fort Knox. Not only was she equipped with at least two stakes on her person, she kept a multitude of elixirs and weapons stashed all throughout the car. Her brother and Dallas had taught her well.

Cassius opened the door, angling himself in slowly, and Ava's blood heated as she watched him do so. The motion drew attention to his long, slender, leather covered legs.

She turned around, not wanting to stare at the beautiful monster any longer.

Ava started the car, and sped off quickly, in search of danger once more.

CHAPTER SIX

CASSIUS WAS NO stranger to getting in cars with beautiful women, and it certainly wasn't the first time he'd been in Ava's Impala. It was, however, the first time he'd been invited inside without a second thought, and that notion made him feel some sort of mix of confusion and hope.

Do not be silly, it has everything to do with Bryan and nothing to do with you.

For a moment, Cassius could have sworn as he got in the car that Ava was blushing, though she'd turned away too quickly for him to be sure. But it did not matter. The racing pulse beneath his skin was more than evidentiary, and he could not help the twitch of a smile on his face.

Ava could deny many things, but she could not deny her blood, her racing pulse.

Ava turned up the radio, focusing her sight on the road intently. The crooning sounds of a man singing about looking for something he could not seem to find—or rather someone who evaded him every time he tried to find her—filled the space as Ava grumbled, changing the station.

"I liked that song," Cassius said, if only to try and lighten the mood in the car. He could not shake the feeling that something was amiss with his lost friend. He had a bad feeling in his gut, but he was not one to jump to conclusions. Perhaps they would arrive at Bryan's humble abode just as he was pulling in. Perhaps his friend had a reasonable explanation for not showing up today. Perhaps Cassius had overreacted, let his imagination get the best of him.

"You don't even know who Nick Jonas is," Ava bit.

"Does that matter? I thought the sound was... soothing."

Ava rolled her eyes as she turned down the street.

"I mean, yeah, sure, if breathy heartthrobs with purity rings in need of a fucking haircut is your thing..." She turned down another street, entering the patch of forest that would soon take them to Bryan's house, every second like an eternity between them.

"Unless you're really a teenage girl in disguise," she said with a laugh.

Cassius could not help but rise to her bait.

"I can assure you I am neither a teenager or a girl."

"Could have fooled me with your ballerina leather tights and your floppy california bob." She giggled.

The sound was beautiful and rare. It was almost as if in that moment, she was... comfortable.

But before Cassius could grasp it, the moment slipped through his fingers like grains of sand in the hourglass when Ava pulled up to Bryan's... home.

The shipping container-style residence was sleek and sophisticated and rather isolated. Against the foggy onset of mid-afternoon, it looked almost heinous. Threatening even.

How could anyone truly live here?

Ava exited the car without warning.

Cassius shook his head, dispelling the stolen moment for good as he walked slowly behind Ava who was now digging around in her trunk, opening boxes, and bags, and...

"Aha! There you are! Damn little fucker thought it could escape, but no way! Not today Satan..." Ava tucked a leather pouch underneath her arm, the sound of leather upon leather filling the silence.

Cassius moved to shut the trunk, and Ava nearly jumped five feet off the ground.

"What the fuck are you doing?" she said, her guard up once more.

Cassius fought a frown, remembering only mere moments ago when she hadn't been so brash.

"I just thought..."

She focused her eyes as she slammed the trunk, causing Cassius to jump back, if only to avoid getting shut in the trunk with the rest of her slaying paraphernalia.

"You thought wrong," she bit, leaving him in her dust as she headed for Bryan's front door. She looked around the front of the yard—if the dried grass and unkempt pile of weeds could be called a yard to begin with—before sliding the leather pouch out from under her arm.

"The coast is clear, Ava. I do not think we will be disturbed."

Ava scoffed at him as she pulled out what looked like a long, slender metal toothpick with a curve at the end. The metal tool reminded Cassius of an instrument he'd seen long ago, and one that had nor provided relief to anyone it touched. He shuddered at the memory.

"Yeah, well, don't take it personal, Cas. I only trust my own fucking judgment, okay?" she said through her breath as she kneeled in front of Bryan's door, angling the pick inside. She let it rest in the lock as she turned her attention to the remaining tools in the pad.

Cassius watched as she concentrated, laying them out on the pavement, selecting them like a surgeon selects his scalpel.

"Of course. I understand." He nodded as she selected her tool and started working. The motion of her tweaking the tools together looked almost like crocheting, and Cassius had to fight a laugh as an image of Ava knitting black lace doilies with curse words came to mind.

"All right, and... I think I'm in," she said as a small click sounded.

Cassius watched her stand, noting the motion drew attention to her rather long, sinful legs. Even in jeans they looked to stretch for miles, and he did not miss the opportunity to trace over her lithe form.

She gently pushed open the door, and for a moment time stood still. There they were on the edge of Bryan's doorstep. At this proximity, he could smell the lingering scent of jasmine and bergamot, feel the heat radiating from her body like a bonfire.

The desire to reach out and touch her, to set his hand at the small of her back and run his nose up her neck and through her hair, to breath in her floral, seductive scent was too much to bear, and so Cassius reached his finger tips out, but they would not make contact with their target.

They would only grasp at the nothing, at the faint breeze left behind as Ava wasted no time, heading into the shadows of Bryan's home, into the unknown once more.

CHAPTER SEVEN

AVA HAD BEEN to Bryan's modular home a handful of times over the last two years.

After TerrorCon, she'd come across the squirrely man while working a local case in which she'd thought vamps were responsible, but it only turned out to be a group of bored teenagers messing with spirits. Though it was out of her wheelhouse of fanged creatures, Ava had always been interested in all the facets of the occult and did not waste the chance to learn upfront about spirit possession, and how to prevent such things.

Cassius had been there that night, with a steaming cup of coffee by her car after she'd learned vamps were not to blame. It was almost as if he knew somehow exactly where she'd be, which both irritated her and, if she was being honest, made her feel a sense of relief. It made her feel less alone, even if she would not say it out loud.

He offered her a cup of coffee and a contact when she'd admitted her search turned up no vampires to slay, but rather stupid teenagers who'd bitten off more than they could handle.

Cassius led her to Bryan that evening, an eccentric man living in a shipping container passing as a modular house, who looked exactly like the kind of man who would live on the outskirts of society with the brain to match such isolated things. Ava was not certain why a vampire would have such a contact as Bryan, though, someone who was well versed in occult elixirs and preventatives. It wasn't like Cassius needed elixirs or preventatives for anything.

He was a vampire, what use would he have for a possession potion?

Vampires couldn't be possessed.

Only the living could be possessed.

In the times Ava had visited Bryan, he hadn't been the cleanest human, but there was an order to his chaos and she appreciated his eccentricities. But now, as she stood in his living room, the overhead lights turning on of their own accord, buzzing with ominous flickering to accompany the ambiance and the severity of the situation, Ava felt her heart sink.

The place was a wreck, more so than normal.

"Holy fuck," Ava grumbled as she made her way across the floor, through a small smattering of strewn papers. Cassius's footsteps sounded behind her, soft and slow. As if he was trying to keep his distance.

Good.

He should stay the hell away.

She thought the thoughts instinctively, but her heart lurched at the bitterness of them.

Did she want him to stay away?

She was not entirely certain the answer was yes, given the fact she'd damn near lept at the chance to investigate Bryan's disappearance with the gorgeous monster. But Ava could not lose herself in the labyrinth of thoughts Cassius usually brought upon her with his presence, and she pushed them aside. She would deal with them later.

"It does look a little chaotic in here," he agreed as he turned away from Ava, heading toward the kitchen area, which doubled not just as a kitchen, but Bryan's alchemical lab.

"It looks like a bomb went off," she said as she stopped in front of his desk, staring at his computer. She gingerly pushed around papers on the surface, not quite sure what she was looking for, but knowing that whatever it was she would know it when she saw it.

"Be careful what you touch, you don't want your fingerprints on anything," Cassius called as he opened and shut cabinets.

"What's the matter, Cas? Worried they'll whisk me away into a cage where you can't get me?" She smirked, turning around to look at the vampire, whose face had gone cold. His green eyes were blank, as if he was remembering some unpleasant memory, and he looked away.

"There is nowhere you could go that I would not find you," he murmured and Ava's skin prickled with goosebumps, her blood boiling just beneath the surface at the darkness of his tone.

"God, you are a grade A creeper, you know that?" She shook her head, pulling her hand into her leather jacket sleeve before touching the ON button to Bryan's computer.

"What are you doing?" Cassius asked, slightly panicked.

"Um, if CSI has taught me anything with its reruns, it's that there's always a cyber trail."

"I told you not to touch anything," he huffed.

"I didn't touch it! I used my jacket! But if you're so

fucking worried, then maybe you should get over here and start fingerprinting up everything. I doubt you're in the system, being the ancient pain in the ass you are. Unless, of course, you've been moonlighting as a serial killer or something," she said as she narrowed her eyes at him.

Cassius scoffed, closing a cabinet rather harshly and Ava cracked a small smile.

So I can piss him off.

Noted.

Cassius sauntered over to her, the flickering lights casting shadows on his features and making him look far more threatening than normal. With his hands in his leather pants pocket, golden hair falling in front of those glowing green eyes, he looked like the villain from one of those 1920s film noir flicks her Aunt Becky used to be so gung-ho over.

Ava took in the sight of him like this, and she did not miss the way it made her blood boil, made her stomach flip. Memories of the first time he'd emerged from the shadows played on repeat in her brain, and she had to swallow the compulsion to *sigh.* To fall into the aura, the thrall of the vampire who'd saved her life, and could not for the undead life of himself, seem to stay away from her.

She turned around, facing the computer which had started up, knocking some papers off the desk.

Cassius caught them with ease, with perfect timing.

He's so fucking extra.

One glance at the paper, and Ava did a double take.

"What the hell is this?" she said as she grabbed the paper off of him.

"Ava..."

The crinkled paper touted an upcoming event in Albright, Ohio, a town she'd certainly never heard of.

The flyer boasted a rather haunting looking house in black and white, with text that read *Marquis Masquerade & Fun House: Where your darkest desires and your worst nightmares come to play.*

"What is it?" Cass asked as he leaned his head over her shoulder. The proximity made her skin flush, her blood race. This close, she could smell his natural, spicy scent. It wasn't something she often thought about, except in the dead of a lonely night where the thoughts had become too much to bear. When there was only one way to quiet them, where she could let the memory of his warm, wet tongue on her skin mix with the memory of his scent, his touch, and the sharpness of his fangs piercing her skin until she'd brought herself to release, before the guilt and shame took over.

"A hunch," she said as she looked at the computer. "Check his history."

"I beg your pardon?" he asked, his voice much breathier than usual in her ear.

Ava had to step away, for the sound caused a wetness to bloom between her thighs that was quite unwanted at this moment.

"I mean, you do know how to use a computer, right?" she taunted him, finding solace in the sarcasm.

This was easy, this was normal.

Cas breathing sexily in her ear was *not* normal, and her liking it was also not normal. So, she refused to acknowledge such things, shoving them down into the dungeon inside where she cast all thoughts of Cas to, the dark prison where she'd lock up such things and never let them out again.

"Of course I know how to use a computer. I frequented the university, too. I sat in on many lectures and classes."

"Aww, how cute. The old man learns basic computers 101. Did they teach you how to browse a user's history or did they just stop at email because the rest was too difficult?" she said with a laugh.

Cassius pursed his lips as he nudged her aside, moving his fingertips on the touchpad.

Ava watched as he brought up the browser successfully and accessed the history. She had to admit she was kind of... impressed.

Maybe he can be useful after all.

"You were saying, my sweet Avarice?" He smirked.

Ava leaned closer to the screen, scanning Bryan's somewhat questionable search history. It seemed Bryan favored the darkweb and two singles sites. AltGothGirls.Com and GothBabes4ME. She pointed to the screen on one of the GothBabes4ME links.

"Bring that up, please," she ordered, and Cassius did as she asked without hesitation. Ava shook her head as a small smile crossed her face.

"Bryan, you little fucking pervert," she said with a laugh. The website displayed a rather drunken looking picture of Bryan and his GothBabes4ME profile. Under the listings of his preferences, Ava couldn't help but giggle, or the comments left on his page.

"Scroll down," she said through a giggle.

"What is so funny?" Cassius asked, but he did so all the same.

"Just... I mean... I guess I didn't think Bryan was like... looking for someone... I guess."

"Is not everyone looking for someone?" Cassius's voice was smooth, even. Like warm chocolate cake straight from the oven.

Ava felt her heart catch in her throat as she stole a glance at him.

What the fuck is wrong with me?

"Some people like to be alone. I thought Bryan was one of them."

Cassius's voice softened. "No one *wants* to be alone."

Ava's stomach twisted at his admission. She almost felt a sting of sympathy for the monster.

Monster.

Ava had to remember that was what he was. A monster who feasted on the living, a wolf in sheep's clothing. And he would do the same to her if she was not careful.

"Stop!" she exclaimed as she saw a comment from a "Enchantress" on his page. The woman was breathtaking. Long, black hair and blue eyes and a silver nose ring stared at them. The woman had commented with an invitation to the Marquis Masquerade & Fun House, some sort of Labyrinth event. She had stated Bryan could message her with details on meeting up beforehand to discuss... *opportunities.*

"Check his DMs," Ava ordered.

Cassius swallowed harshly, looking lost in thought, but he did so.

What is his deal?

He's acting weird today.

The notion that Ava had come to expect a certain way of behavior from the bloodsucker was startling and she did not want to think about the implications of such things. Instead, she watched as Cassius brought up Bryan's messages, and sure enough, she had her culprit.

Enchantress had messaged him with a location, a date, and a time.

"Motherfucking bingo," Ava said proudly.

"Care to clue me in on your epiphany, Mrs.

Sherlock?" Cassius teased her.

"I mean, it's kind of obvious, isn't it? Baby Tim Burton over here fucked up and didn't follow the rules of internet meet ups. He probably went to go meet Enchantress, didn't tell anyone... I mean, like, who is he going to tell? You? Pfttt." She waved her hand in the air.

Cassius raised an eyebrow at her as she continued her crime-drama worthy monologue.

"Then, he probably got up there and got fucking catfished and is sitting in Enchantress's—whoever they really are—in their basement somewhere tied up and gagged."

"You have deduced all of this from a flyer and some DMs?" Cassius asked, stroking his chin. The slow, rhythmic motion of his fingers made Ava's blood rush.

"I mean, it's a theory."

"It is a good theory. What do you suggest we do next?"

"What is it with you and this *we* crap? I told you, Cassius. There is no we."

"So, I suppose I should just embark to Ohio myself, and leave you to your devices and your riveting life as it were. I understand," he said as he gingerly pulled the flyer from her hands.

Ava stared at it, feeling as if she was once again crossing an invisible line, pushing past the pit of snakes in Indiana Jones' Temple of Doom. There would surely be another booby trap waiting for her on the other side of the pit, but what was one more in the grand scheme of treasure?

A man's life may very well be at stake, and what if Cassius took more lives on said trip?

No, she needed to go to see this through, to rescue Bryan and to make sure Cassius didn't sink his fangs anywhere they did not belong.

"Fuck you. I'll have you know I'm off until Monday from my *riveting job,*" she bit.

Cassius smiled, showing just a hint of his fang, and Ava's insides turned to molten lava. She clenched her jaw, knowing the only way out was through.

"Then I take it *we* are going to Ohio to find our... Baby Tim Burton, as you called him?"

"I am going to Ohio. You can tag along, since, you know, you and Bryan are such fucking besties. I wouldn't want you to get your panties in a bunch and blow up my fucking phone while I try to save the day."

"You may need back up when you go in and save the day," Cassius smoothly said as Ava folded the flyer up and stuck it in her pocket.

"The day I ask you for back up will be a cold day in Hell, Cas," she grumbled as she headed for the door, wondering if she'd just signed her death certificate.

"When do we depart?" he called out, his voice oddly chipper.

Ava stopped in the doorway, turning around to look at him once more.

"I get off from work at eight, so eight thirty?" She said the words, but they felt heavy.

Ominous even.

"I shall meet you at your home at eight thirty, then," he said triumphantly.

She turned around, not bothering to look at him any longer. She needed to get the hell out of Bryan's apartment. Away from the prospect of a case, away from the sinfully delicious vampire who made her blood rush and her heart skip a beat.

CHAPTER EIGHT

CASSIUS SMOOTHED HIS hair back as he neared the gate of Ava's residence.

Though he hadn't migrated to Chester until 1985, he'd certainly seen his fair share of plantation homes in the south when he and Eden had traveled along the eastern coast in the twenties, and he'd been in plenty of castles, mansions, and estates in his rather long life. But he'd never felt as nervous, as on the spot as he did at that moment as he walked through the gates to Ava's newly inherited digs.

It wasn't as if it was his first time seeing the place. He frequented it often, in fact; though most of the time he was sequestered to either the front porch or Ava's bedroom in the middle of the night when he did visit. On nights he couldn't sleep, he'd stroll by the estate until he was certain she was all right and then, he would retire to his favorite piano lounge until the place closed, drowning his sorrow, his memories, and his pesky desire to *hope* perhaps Ava would come around to their predicament.

Predicament.

That is what he was to her, some thing that happened to her that she did not agree to. Although, to be fair, she had agreed, but as Ava had reminded him on countless occasions, she hadn't truly known what she was agreeing to. The fine print had been evaded, because there was no time to waste. She was dying, and he had a way to save her, so he did.

And Cassius speculated bond or no bond, he would do the same if anything, or anyone threatened to put Ava Crowley into an early grave.

He took a breath as he made his way up her steps, standing in front of the door feeling as if he was crossing over into another dimension. One where upon the door opening, a beautiful, snarky slayer would look at him with bright eyes and a wicked grin, spout some sarcastic nonsense and invite him in—into her home, her heart, and her bed for all eternity.

He pushed the thoughts away, knowing they were dangerous, blaming such things on his recent corpse feeding. Blood always incited lust, it was just vampire biology. Nothing more.

Cassius had rationed breaking into the morgue was risky, even if there was no one currently working there at the time. Though it wasn't something he could keep doing, for regularly scheduled break ins would draw attention, and Cassius could not afford such things. He'd laid low, kept his nose clean, if only in an attempt to live outside the grasp of Eden, the high covens, and everything he'd left behind.

He hated skulking around like some criminal or some junkie in need of a fix, but the truth was rather simple. If Cassius did not fill his stomach and feed the monster inside of him before embarking on a trip—no matter how short—he would be a danger to Ava. And as far as Cassius was concerned, that just could not happen. He would never put her in harm's way. Not now, not ever. They were bound by blood, for better or for worse.

The corpse blood was cold, as he'd had to pull it directly from the fridge, and it was not the best as far as taste. Later, he'd have to explain to Bryan about the missing logs, but it would be a small price to pay once they'd rescued the squirrely man and everyone made it through unscathed. At least, that was what he held onto, it was the outcome he hoped for. He wasn't sure he could face a much harsher reality.

Bryan had been gone for at least a day, if not longer, which was suspicious enough, but if Ava was right, and he was truly locked in someone's basement, then time was of the essence.

Cassius breathed a slow, deep breath as he balled his fist, and knocked on the door. His heart slowly thudded in his chest as it seemed like forever until the door was opened. But it was not Ava who greeted him, no. It was a tiny Chinese woman.

"Can I help you?" she asked sweetly, eyeing him up and down.

Cassius cleared his throat.

"Is Mrs. Crowley home?" he asked, feeling unsure of himself for a moment. Ava hadn't mentioned living with anyone, and he'd never seen any evidence otherwise, but then again, he hadn't spent much time anywhere but her bedroom in the middle of the night.

"And who may I ask is calling on *Mrs. Crowley,*" the woman said with a smirk. The potent smell of cinnamon and sugar wafted toward him, and his stomach twisted with recognition.

Cookies.

Cassius straightened his stance, looking the woman in the eyes poignantly. "My name is Cassius." He did not bother to give a last name, feeling on the spot. Such things held no value to him anymore. He'd been taught to keep his Aurelian heritage a secret, until he'd met Eden. He'd adopted her late husband's surname, Wright for a time, and she did not seem to mind his taking it then. Though the rouse of Cassius Wright had dissolved rather quickly whence he was spotted at a coronation for the Meidici's, another lineage of damn near vampire royalty. It wasn't long after that, the Boracellis had discovered his true bloodline, and Cassius Wright was put to rest until he'd joined forces with Eden again, when they'd been betrothed.

After fleeing Eden and the Boracellis, last names served no purpose. It would only make him easier to find, documented or not, and Cassius wished to be lost.

"Cassius, hmmm." The woman's eyes smiled, giving Cassius the impression she would not let him go if he stepped inside. "Well, Cassius, I am Constance Chen." She waved him in the door, and Cassius felt as if he was surely walking toward his inevitable death.

But if death included cookies and Ava Crowley, he would die a thousand times.

"Ava should be home soon..." She tutted as Cassius crossed the threshold into the Michaels estate.

Becky Lee Michaels, Ava's aunt, had been somewhat well known to the town. She had her hands in nearly every committee, every event. A single woman with no children, and no family left, Ava's aunt had amassed a wealth of her own in addition to the inheritance bestowed upon her.

Cassius knew Ava did not talk about her parents much, or her croming to Chester. In fact, their conversations mostly consisted of her reminding him she would kill him, or in some instances, details about the cases she'd taken on, or supernatural knowledge.

But Cassius wondered as he stood in the grand foyer of the estate, what had truly transpired to bring Ava and her brother to this haunting town, and why Ava had never mentioned a Constance Chen before.

"Feel free to have a seat," Constance gestured to the white sofa, and Cassius nodded, escaping his thoughts.

"Thank you, Mrs. Chen," he said graciously as he took his seat, setting his hands in his lap.

Why am I so nervous?

"Would you like a cookie?" she asked, her demeanor shifting from suspicious and deadly to sweet and caring in the blink of an eye.

"I would love that, actually." He politely nodded, smiling; careful to hide his fangs behind his lips. It was a feat he'd long mastered, and truly the only time he let them show was around Ava, and he only did so because he enjoyed knowing the effect it had on her, even if she did not admit it. Her pulse would *race* beneath his skin.

Constance Chen scuttled off to the kitchen and Cassius watched her do so. He took in the sight of the estate, all pale colors, white, and grey, and it reminded him of the Medici's estate in France.

That was a lifetime ago, Cassius.

You need to forget such things...

Constance set a small appetizer plate down before him on the glass coffee table, just as the front door opened.

"What the fuck?" Ava bit as she set her eyes on Cassius. He felt strangely warm under her viscous gaze.

"Ah, Ava, you are home..." Constance tuttled.

"I said eight thirty," she growled, glancing from him to Constance.

"A gentleman is always early." Cassius smiled.

Ava rolled her eyes.

"I swear one of these days I'm going to need a fucking restraining order," she said as she stormed up to them.

"You didn't have to invite him in, Connie." She huffed.

"Ava..." Constance sighed. Ava looked at the plate of cookies in front of him,

"God, and you're feeding him, too?" Her cheeks flushed, and he could tell she was most perturbed.

Cassius offered her the plate.

"Perhaps some sugar will soothe your frayed nerves," he said with a smirk.

Ava grabbed the cookies, clutching the plate to her chest as she regarded him with a solid, heavy gaze.

"Don't fucking move. I will be out in five minutes. And don't harass my housekeeper."

Housekeeper?

"As you wish."

Ava rolled her eyes again, mumbling to herself as she stormed off, plate and all, toward her bedroom, leaving Cassius alone once more.

CHAPTER NINE

AVA SHOVED A cookie in her mouth as she packed a bag. It was still warm, and the gooey chocolate relaxed her, if only a fraction.

She did not plan on being out of town long, but she knew the drive to Ohio would take at least five or six hours if they were making good time. Running on little sleep as it was, she was certain she'd have to find lodging accommodations somewhere at some point, even if it was only a few hours to sleep.

Bryan would have probably needed somewhere to rest as well, and the reality of just how little Ava knew the man made her feel slightly overwhelmed, but it was easier to focus on than anything else.

The thought of lodging with a vampire made her feel quite on edge, despite the fact Cassius regularly visited her bedroom.

In the middle of the night.

When she'd had nightmares.

She did not feel right throwing him out in the cold, or asking him to stay in the car, but at least if he was *near* her, she could account for him.

And this is why you sleep with a stake under your pillow.

Ava threw a pair of jeans and some clean shirts in her bag. She knew it was rude of her to react the way she had earlier, not just to Cassius, but also to Connie. Connie did not know the danger she had put herself in, and therefore, she could not entirely blame the woman.

No, that blame had fallen on Ava.

Neither Mal or Ava had wanted to bring Connie into the fold, both vowing to keep the truth of what it was they got up to, hidden. But she certainly would not have lost her cool if Cassius had just listened to her instead of showing up ten minutes before she'd told him to be there.

Though to be fair, she would have been home sooner, had she closed the shop on time, which she would have had the pesky yoga-enthusiasts not shown up five minutes before close just to peruse the store and not actually buy anything.

Ava headed toward her armoire, opening it and taking stock of her weapons. She wasn't entirely sure what she would need, and it wasn't like the car wasn't stocked itself. A part of her knew she was just procrastinating and prolonging the inevitable. Bryan's disappearance likely had nothing to do with vampires or monsters, but she rationed one couldn't be too careful, or too prepared. She settled on grabbing an extra stake, some holy water reserve, and one of the decorated blades she'd bought earlier in the year from a guy on Craigslist who claimed it could kill anything undead. Perhaps she'd find out if it were true on this rescue mission.

She zipped up the bag hastily, throwing it over her shoulder. She grabbed another cookie, shoving it in her mouth, making quick work of eating.

They really did need to get moving.

When she'd come back out, she saw Cassius standing in front of the fireplace. His back was to her, and for a moment, Ava could imagine him somewhere regal, somewhere else than their present time. A mansion, a castle, or perhaps even a historical bed and breakfast, like some ghostly attractive inn keeper. Tall and slender, his silhouette stood out, his dark grey shirt, his pale skin and of course, those annoyingly sexy leather pants. Even his golden blond hair shimmered with sophistication.

Ava cleared her throat, gripping the strap to her duffel tighter as her blood rushed beneath the surface. They needed to leave.

Now.

Cassius turned as she cleared her throat. His green eyes glittered with excitement.

"Okay, so this train leaves right now," she barked as she headed toward the kitchen, to Connie, tapping her on the shoulder. Connie turned with a wicked smile.

"Cassius seems very nice, Ava."

Ava pursed her lips. "Yeah, well don't get any ideas. That's not going to happen, like ever. He's just a—"

What could she say?

A vampire?

A pain in my ass?

"A friend," she said the words, and they felt strange on her tongue. They felt... right.

Though she didn't really believe she and Cassius were friends. Friends meant you *liked* the person, and Ava did not *like* Cassius.

She was grateful he'd saved her life, but they had already settled the score, hadn't they?

"Well, it is nice to see you making friends, then," Connie said as she returned to her dishes.

"Connie, I... I'm going out of town for the weekend. I'll be back on Monday, okay? Don't worry about coming in or—"

Connie waved a sudsy hand at her. "Have a good time with your *friend.*"

Ava nodded, if only because she wanted to end the conversation. She was starting to feel on the spot.

"Okay. Bye." She stood tall, turning around once more and exiting the kitchen toward the gorgeous vampire waiting at the door. As she approached, he smiled, showing just a hint of fang, and her stomach flipped.

He opened the door for her.

"After you, friend."

Ava rolled her eyes as she brushed past him.

"We are not friends, Cas. We are... co-workers, at best."

"Still, you did not call me your co-worker. You called me your *friend.*"

Ava huffed as she unlocked the door of the impala.

"Eavesdropping was once a punishable crime, you know," she bit.

He only had the audacity to look just as enticing as ever as he smirked at her. He was gloating.

"There is no need to eavesdrop when I have impeccable hearing, but I could not have avoided your sweet voice if I tried. The architecture was built to be loud. The walls echo."

Fucking pain in my ass.

"Then hear this," she countered, her voice clear as a bell. "You will be *dead* in a minute if you don't shut the fuck up," she nipped as she opened her door and threw her bag in the back seat.

Cassius opened the passenger door and climbed in, grinning devilishly, twisting his fingers along his lips to show he'd zipped it.

If Bryan isn't fucking dead, I'm going to kill him for this.

CHAPTER TEN

"LET ME DRIVE," Cassius pleaded.

"I'm fine, I just need to find a motel or... something... When is the next goddamned exit?" Ava moaned.

"There is no need. Pull over and let me drive. You can rest, and when you wake we will be at our destination."

Ava shot him a scathing glance.

"Was this your plan all along? Tag along until I get tired and then bam! Vamp chow? I don't think so."

Cassis furrowed his eyebrows.

Is that what she thinks of me?

That I'm just waiting for her to let her guard down and I'll finish the claim?

Her words hurt him, because he could not understand why she would think such things. It had been four years since he'd bitten her, and he'd done everything in his power to prove to her he would not force her hand, despite the fact it would be easier.

Everything would be so much easier if he could complete his claim. If he could make her like he was.

But Cassius would not take such a choice from Ava. He knew all too well how it felt to be born into a life of blood and ash without any say. His words to Leon echoed in his brain.

My salvation is not worth the price of her choice.

What more could he do to make her understand that he could never harm her?

"Your words wound me. But it does not change the truth. You *are* tired, and you need rest. My only *plan* is to see to it that we arrive on time, and that you are well rested enough to... how did you say it? Save the day?"

Ava yawned, her jaws stretching like that of a cat in an irrefutable sign that she did indeed need rest.

"Trust me, Ava," Cassius pressed.

Ava sighed, glancing at Cassius for a moment, and he could see she was more than just tired of driving.

She was tired of hiding, too. Hiding behind vicious words and walls erected around her that prevented anyone from seeing the truth. Cassius understood such things. It wasn't as if he hadn't erected walls around himself or his residence. He'd purposefully refrained from telling *anyone* other than Leon that he was leaving the glittering world of the high covens, leaving Eden for good.

He'd hidden in the forest, skirting by on corpse blood for nearly fifty years, passing his endless nights with somber piano music, dry wine, and guilt until he'd followed Taijiri to that frat house.

Until he'd laid eyes on a struggling, dying human with fire in her eyes and a will so very strong it made Cassius drop to his knees that very night and take her hand.

He knew then that nothing else would matter. Nothing else mattered in that moment except her delicate wrist in his hand, the blood in her veins that begged to hold on to dear, dear life.

It was clear to him then, before he even knew her, that she was more than a beautiful college student who had ended up in the wrong place at the wrong time.

Ava was, and continued to be, a fighter, and if the last four years had taught him anything, it was that. And as Cassius looked at Ava's tired eyes, he knew he needed a fighter.

He needed *her,* and she would be the death of him.

"Fine. But if you try anything, and I mean anything..." she nipped as she pulled the car over to the side of the road.

Cassius watched as she threw the car in park, as her hands gripped the steering wheel. She looked on ahead for a moment before letting her shoulders relax and then, she turned her eyes of fire on him.

Would it ever cease?

The feeling of warmth spreading through his veins, lighting him up and making him feel alive?

He hoped it never would.

"If you try anything I will fucking stake you in this car and I won't be sorry about it. Got it?" Her words were full of bite, but Cassius knew it was an empty threat. After all, she threatened him constantly, and yet here they were, pulled off to the side of the road in the middle of nowhere in the dead of night.

Together.

That has to count for something right?

"I promise." Cassius nodded.

Ava sighed as she opened her car door and he did the same. As he rounded the front of the car, meeting her in the middle, she stopped. She looked up at him in the midst of the headlights for a moment. He could feel her pulse racing, the blood rushing beneath his skin like a river. His stomach twisted into knots, and he knew it wasn't due to hunger.

He longed in that moment to reach out to her, run his fingers along her soft, supple skin and tilt her head up until his lips could claim hers, and perhaps then she would understand.

That they were *bonded.*

Not just by blood, but by circumstance.

By fate.

But Cassius did not reach out and touch her. He did not invade her space or attempt to annihilate the fortress that protected her from the outside world, from him.

Instead, he walked past her, rounding to the driver side without a word, the only sound the purr of the Impala's engine, and Ava's tired sigh.

He'd never driven Ava's car before. In fact, he had not driven a car since the 80's.

There was no need for Cassius to own anything. Paperwork meant there was an evidentiary trail, even if he used one of his aliases, and it was not as if he could not walk, or find other transportation, not to mention Taijiri would not object to him borrowing his Camaro, as long as he was home.

He familiarized himself with her controls, appreciating the simplicity and the mechanics of the 1969 car that Ava called hers. He was not entirely sure how she'd come to own such a beautiful machine, but it suited her nonetheless.

Ava curled up in the passenger seat, tucking her legs to her chest. She wrapped her arms around them, and he noticed she poignantly posed her fists in front of him, one hand gripping a stake, as a display of dominance.

Though it was not needed, he knew it made her feel better and so he did not say anything. Instead, he only pulled the car out on the road.

"Sweet Dreams, Ava."

"Fuck you," she grumbled sleepily, and he had to contain his laugh. Her prickly attitude was both charming and endearing to him, for she was not the first woman in his life who'd had a sharp tongue.

Though the immediate thought pushed images of Eden forth, Cassius combatted them with one look at the pretty slayer in the seat next to him.

She is nothing like Eden.

She has a heart.

The darkness that blanketed them on all sides was thick, and Cassius hoped they would arrive at their destination soon.

Cassius grabbed her phone on the dashboard, checking the map when a notification came through.

A text.

From an *Asshole.*

Cassius wondered for a moment who Ava would deem so terrible they would not have a name in her contacts.

You up, Kitten?

Cassius felt his blood slow. Not only was it an invasion of privacy, but the tone suggested this was someone she knew well. Well enough this *Asshole* had given her a pet name.

Curiosity got the better of him as he looked to his side, noting that Ava was sound asleep. Her fist still curled tightly around the stake, but her mouth had gone slack, and her head lolled to the side. She was, as he would say, out like a light.

Cassius swallowed lightly as he scrolled up her text log, and it did not take him long to realize who *Asshole* was.

Cassius set her phone on the dash once more, as an

air of shame and guilt befell him.

His suspicions were in fact, confirmed. Ava and Dallas, it seemed, *did* have a relationship. One they were not public about. His heart ached at this knowledge, and he looked at her once more. He was not angry, nor jealous. He was only numb.

What did Jake Dallas possess that he did not?

Was it because he was... human?

Cassius had his suspicions about Malcolm's partner, ever since TerrorCon. He'd seen the way Jake Dallas looked at Ava in the Dark Hearts Club, felt his anger, the rage from his fist when he'd seen her bleeding on the floor, in his arms of all places.

Together.

Albeit, Cassius had been fighting the overwhelming desire to sink his teeth into Ava at the time—her blood was on display from her bout with the Incubus who'd bitten her, and Cassius had only acted on instinct with concern for Ava—Dallas's reaction was more than telling. Dallas had feelings for the slayer, too.

Perhaps even *loved* her.

How did Ava feel about him?

Did she love him as well?

Cassius abandoned the thoughts, for they were a dangerous road to take. He'd been down it before, with Eden.

No, he did not need to know such things. Not if he wanted to remain focused on the task at hand, and that was finding their friend.

Ava twitched, drawing his attention. A soft whimper left her throat, and she gripped her stake tighter. Of course, the nightmares that haunted her would not rest just because she was far from home.

Instinctively and without warning, Cassius reached his right hand out, tracing his fingers over her fist—the very one curled around her precious stake. He ran them smoothly over her knuckles, before letting his palm kiss the back of her warm hand, and in that moment Cassius knew.

It would never matter what she did or did not do. It would never matter who she loved or didn't love.

For it would never change the reality of their bond, and it certainly would never change how he felt about her.

And such a realization was more brutal a death than any at the hand of her stake.

Cassius let go of her hand as he turned the radio up a fraction, letting the soft sounds of Taylor Swift and a man crooning about living forever fill the space. It pulled him back to the here and now, the real reason he'd come on this trip.

To save his friend.

And as Ava's breathing settled to a steady hum and her pulse stilled, that was exactly what Cassius vowed to do.

CHAPTER ELEVEN

AVA STOOD IN the darkness, the smell of blood and death pungent in the air. Though everywhere she looked was nothing but shadows, and there was no way out that she could see.

"You will never escape," a voice echoed in the darkness.

Ava held her arms close, a chill overtaking her. Her feet were cold, covered in thick, wet liquid.

Blood.

She was standing in a puddle of blood.

Ava looked up to the black, starless sky, and she knew the voice was right. Perhaps this was where it ended. Perhaps this was where it was always supposed to end.

Ava turned in the darkness, and a trail of slick, wet, shimmering blood stood out to her. So she followed it, like a moth to a flame. One bare foot in front of the other, letting the crimson liquid run over her skin. She did not slip or trip, her gait steady.

A figure stood at the edge of the path, illuminated by light. One sole light in the darkness. It called to her, filled her with a warmth and a peace that settled all the demons inside of her.

But who was the man silhouetted by the light?

An angel?

Before she could find out, she was startled.

"Ava," another voice called to her from the darkness, and she turned around abruptly. She could see nothing in the vast blackness, but she could feel a presence.

"Hello?" she called out, her stomach churning. But no one responded.

When she turned around, the light had dimmed, and she had gotten further away.

It was so dark, so cold.

Ava huffed indignantly as she set forth for the light once more, this time with steadfast feet. She skipped through the pools of blood, picking up into a run.

Ava ran and ran as fast as she could, needing to find the light again. Needing its warmth, its awe and wonder.

But every step she took, every moment her feet hit the ground beneath her, the light only receded.

"No, come back!" she called out, but it was no use.

Ava stopped to catch her breath as reality blanketed her like a thick fog.

The blood covered her legs and feet, and when she brought her hands up she could see they were stained too.

"Come back!" she called out in agony, but all there was, was the scent of fire and ash, of death and blood.

There was no response. No voice to call out to her, no light to comfort her. She was well and truly alone, in the darkness. Her mind replayed the death of her parents, of Ross, and the monsters she'd slain like a highlight reel.

Blood, fire.

Ash.

Ava closed her eyes, forcing back tears. She would always be alone, because those closest to her were nothing but cannon fodder. She would always be alone, because she was a monster.

A soft, featherlight touch stroked her skin, and her blood warmed on contact. The warmth she sought blossomed throughout her being and she opened her eyes. The light was blinding, and she could not make out a figure.

She could only lean into the light, praying that it would dispel the darkness.

Ava felt a soft touch nudging her. Sleep disintegrated from her as she opened her eyes. Her muscles were cramped and sore, and for a moment she wasn't certain where she was, but it certainly didn't feel like home.

When her vision sharpened as she laid her eyes on the culprit who had awakened her from her slumber, her blood chilled. Cassius sat in the driver seat of her Imapala, looking like a damned oasis in a desert.

"I thought you may be hungry," he said as he nodded to the Stop-N-Go in front of them. Artificial light filled Ava's car, and she glanced at the clock radio. It was near four in the morning.

"Guess I slept a little longer than I wanted..." she grumbled as she wiped her eyes.

Cassius's voice was soft when he spoke as if he was sad. Upset. Which was strange to Ava.

What the fuck does he have to be upset about?

As she thought the bitter thought, she remembered the events of yesterday, the very ones that led her to this car, with him.

Bryan, of course.

Way to be insensitive, Ava.

"Sleep okay?" he asked.

Ava focused on his glowing green emerald eyes, and opened her mouth to respond, but it was as if she was at a loss for words. Something about the way in which Cassius spoke made her feel as if he was asking something else, some question she was not sure how to answer. She shook her head, dispelling the strange thought.

I am just out of sorts because of that stupid nightmare.

"Like a baby," she said with a smile as she opened the door.

Cassius remained in the car, and he did not move.

Ava stretched in the crisp, cool air, her Blue Oyster Cult shirt rising up above her navel as she reached above her head for the moon hanging in the sky. She wasted no time heading into the Stop-N-Go, her stomach growling ferociously.

Good call, Cas.

Though she would never admit out loud that perhaps stopping for food was a good idea, she was thankful he'd decided to do so.

Ava perused the ready made counter, noting there were at least three other individuals in the store aside from the burly cashier. A side glance told her they were all men, and judging by the sound of their heavy boots and slurred speech, they were on their way home from the bar.

Ava quietly opened the Krispy Kreme Donut case, selecting a jelly filled donut for herself. She closed the donut case and headed over to the self-serve coffee machines, at the same time one of the men seemed to stumble up.

"Why hello there," he said mid-burp.

Ava rolled her eyes, ignoring him.

The man looked to be about six foot at least, stocky but not as muscular as Dallas. Though the scruffy five o clock shadow and the light wrinkle at the corner of his eyes reminded her of him.

"Sweetheart, I'm talking to you," he drawled, and Ava pursed her lips.

It wasn't that she felt threatened or worried at all in this man's presence, but more or less that she'd just woken up, and was not ready to deal with the normal breed of asshole she often found herself dealing with quite yet. She hadn't even had herself a coffee yet.

"Let's get something straight here, dickwad. I aint your sweetheart, and I don't give a fuck if you're talking to me."

One of the other men joined tall, big and stupid, this one a much skinnier version, but dressed in the same grungy digs with the same heavy boots and look of inebriation.

"Woohoo, Earl, seems like you found yourself a biter," he taunted.

Earl?

Really?

Could they be more stereotypical?

Ava finished filling up her cup, and moved to grab another one, if only to show the presence of two cups, which meant she was not alone.

Not that she *needed* Cas's help or anything.

Besides, it was his idea to stop.

As she started to fill the cup with liquid, the third bristly bear joined the party. Ava hurriedly capped off the second coffee, trying to get around them, but it seemed as if they'd boxed her in.

"Excuse me, *Earl,*" she nipped, but he blocked her from moving.

"Not until you apologize to Daddy, little brat."

Ava felt her stomach turn. It wasn't as if this piece of work knew anything about her, but the words left her feeling disgusted.

There was truly only one man who could call her a brat and get away with it.

"Look, asshole. It's early, and I'm really not in the fucking mood. Move. The. Fuck. Out of my way."

"Or what, sweetheart?" he asked with a lascivious grin. His cohorts chuckled behind him, and Ava heard the bell on the door jingle.

"Okay, so I guess you're big, and stupid, too. Cool. Wanna play fuck around and find out? Be my guest."

She swung her leg out, applying pressure to just behind Earl's knee. In his drunken state, he went down just as she suspected, like a sack of potatoes, falling on his ass.

Ava stepped around him, just as the cashier was filling up the donut case with more donuts, completely unphased. Although, Ava had to wonder if that meant this was a normal sort of occurrence in these parts or if the cashier was so over their job, they just didn't care.

She scanned the new additions, noting one of them was red velvet supreme. She'd never much cared for the flavor before TerrorCon, but after she'd returned home she'd had a strange craving for it. So, she grabbed a fresh one, tucking it into the bag with her jelly filled donut, the groaning sounds of Earl behind her like music to her ears.

"I'll just take these, when you're ready," she said to the cashier, noting her two coffees and donuts.

Earl's friends helped him up, scoffing.

"Fucking stupid man. Really thought going to that bitch bar would have gotten me laid, but fuck no..."

Ava's blood stilled.

Bitch bar?

What were they talking about?

Tall, skinny and stupid helped his friend up, answering her thoughts.

"All the bitches up in the Drowned Clam's aint good 'nuff for ya anyway. Maybe we'll have better luck at the Marquis."

Before Ava could process the idiot's words, the cashier rung her up. Ava fished around in her jeans pocket, pulling out a small wad of cash. She never left home without at least forty dollars in cash in her pocket, just in case. After she'd left her wallet in Sam Kingsley's room at TerrorCon, she'd vowed to always keep it on her.

The events of TerrorCon were still blurry to her. She remembered parts of it so vividly, and others she worried were lost forever.

She remembered Sam Kingsley sharing a drink with her, remembered being wrapped up in his arms, how he felt as he filled her. But she also remembered his fangs sinking into her skin, his erection flailing about as she and Dallas exercised the demonic incubus possessing him.

But after that, much was a blur and neither Malcolm nor Dallas seemed to want to talk about it. Bits and pieces surfaced every now and then, of things that didn't make sense, and all Malcolm had offered her was "the anti-venom took awhile to combat the toxin, which can cause hallucinations."

But Hallucinations didn't touch you, or sing to you, and Ava could have sworn she heard someone singing to her, "Don't fear the reaper."

Ava tossed her money on the counter. "So, you, uh... wouldn't know how far the Marquis is from here, would you?" she asked nonchalantly.

The young woman behind the counter sighed.

"That place is nothing but trouble. You don't want any parts of it."

Ava stood straighter.

"Oh really? Why's that?"

"That place is cursed."

"What do you mean cursed?" Ava tucked the donuts underneath her arm.

"Before it was the Marquis, it belonged to a wealthy couple. Lots of murders happened in those walls. Place should be torn down."

Ava grabbed the cups.

"Let's just say... I like a little danger. How far away is it?"

The cashier looked at her cautiously. "About thirty minutes south of here. But it'll be closed until Friday. The new owners have been working on a 'Masquerade' bar or something, sposed' to open up then."

Ava nodded. "I thought it was the Marqius Masquerade and Funhouse?" she asked.

The cashier nodded absentmindedly.

"Place changed owners not that long ago. Some high-brow chic bought it about a year ago. Amara something or other. Guess they wanted to add some luxury to the place."

"Of course. What's more luxurious than a cursed bar?" she teased.

"Don't say I didn't warn you."

And with that, the bell jingled and another couple of patrons walked in.

"Keep the change," Ava said as she exited the store, only to find Cassius leaning against the hood of the Impala.

Watching her.

Amidst the hazy dusk light, he looked stunning. Like a model on the cover of a rock album or something. His expression was unreadable, as always, though.

Ava leaned on the hood next to him and offered him a coffee.

"Spur of the moment. I don't even know if you drink coffee, since you never show up with one yourself but..."

Cassius looked at the cup like it was made of lava and he would expire if he touched it. She almost pulled it away, but he stopped her. He slid his hand over hers, taking the cup gingerly.

Ava noted the feel of his skin on hers was light, like a feather.

Soft.

Her skin prickled with goosebumps and her blood boiled beneath the surface. Her entire being felt warm. Surely it was not because of his touch. Surely it was due to the warmth emanating from the outside of the flimsy cardboard cup.

"Thank you," he said.

She held out the donut bag.

"I do know you like these, though," she said quietly in response as she held the red velvet donut out to him.

Cassius smiled, showing just a hint of fang.

"Are you sure you do not want it? You nearly mauled me for it last time."

Ava rolled her eyes.

"Just take the fucking donut. Pain in my ass."

CHAPTER TWELVE

CASSIUS'S HEART LIFTED at the kind gesture. While rare, these moments fueled his desire more than he cared to admit. He shifted closer to Ava against the hood of the Impala. She pretended not to notice.

When she shifted her weight only a fraction, moving an inch closer to him, he pretended not to notice.

"So, the cashier said the Marquis is about thirty minutes down the road, but she says it doesn't open until Friday. Something about them adding a Masquerade Bar onto the property." Ava shrugged as she finished her donut, the red jelly staining her lips bright red. The sight flared the beginnings of bloodlust in Cassius's stomach, causing his throat to go dry. He looked away, taking a sip of his coffee, which was much more bitter than he cared for, but it was a welcome distraction. He puckered his lips from the overbearing burnt taste.

"You do drink coffee... right?" she asked, her voice carrying a hint of concern.

"Yes, I do. It is just very... bitter."

"So, you're not one of those 'I drink my coffee as

black as my soul' assholes, then."

Cassius let out a small chuckle. "I assure you, I am not," he said as he popped the last bit of donut in his mouth. "But I have had worse."

"Cashier says the place is haunted, too." Ava's lips pulled up into a wicked grin.

"Thinking of doing a bit of recon are you, Detective?"

"I mean, if it's closed, then there won't be anyone else poking around there, will there?" Her eyes sparkled with anticipation.

Cassius picked up his coffee, crumpling the remains of paper from their breakfast. Ava did the same, heading for the driver seat.

The sun would soon be up, and another day laid to rest. Cassius could not help the dread that continued to build in his stomach, worrying that Bryan had already succumbed to an ill fate, and they would be too late. He also worried that maybe they were way off base, and would come up with nothing once they found the Marquis, and that all of it would be some wild goose chase. If only there was a way to know for sure instead of taking a shot in the dark.

But despite knowing the odds may be against them, Cassius stole a glance at the slayer beside him, taking in the sight of her slightly disheveled hair, her fixed gaze of determination, and her jelly-stained lips, and he knew there was no one else he'd rather be in the dark with. A faint stirring in his blood told him perhaps she felt the same, even if she did not say so.

"Stop looking at me like that." Ava sighed, never taking her eyes off the road.

"Like what?" he said smoothly.

"Like you want to eat me."

Cassius couldn't help but shake his head, turning his gaze to the window.

"I do not wish to *eat* you."

"You lie like a fucking rug. Just remember the deal. Keep your fangs to yourself or I will fucking stake you."

Cassius quietly stared out the window at the passing forests as the sun started to peek through the silhouetted treetops, all amber and ochre, like the light when it caught in Ava's eyes.

"So you say," he murmured as they rounded a long, winding road, in chase of ghosts once more.

CHAPTER THIRTEEN

AVA TURNED THE car off, but she did not vacate right away. Her heart would not stop racing and she felt as if it would burst right out of her chest. Surely Cassius could hear it thumping away like a drum this closely.

Cassius did not move either, and Ava noted he looked lost in thought as he stared out the window at the Marquis Masquerade and Fun House. The sign itself was ornate, gilded with unlit bulbs, and reminded her of the Las Vegas sign she'd seen in all those travel channel shows she'd binged in college.

She felt a sting of guilt, wondering if she'd been too rude or brash with Cassius, but she knew there was no other choice. She could not afford to get too comfortable with the vampire beside her, no matter how smooth his voice sounded, or how good he smelled, or how enticing he appeared. Falling victim to Cassius was truly a death wish.

But maybe I like a little danger, she had told him once.

Was it still true?

She thought it was, but she was certain there were

some alleys she did not want to venture down, lest she be met with harsh realities and truths.

The sun was starting to bathe the world in the beginnings of dawn when she decided to turn the idling car off.

Cassius was in no danger of turning to dust.

She had learned some vampires could walk in the daylight without harm, him being one of them. History and lore did not seem to have an answer as to why some had this ability and others did not, but Ava suspected it had to do with age, or perhaps when the vampire was sired or turned. She had no idea how old Cassius was, and though she'd wondered on occasion, she could not bring herself to ask. Fleeting were the moments she wondered about the creature beside her, and when the thoughts came, she quickly diminished them. They would not make a difference in the grand scheme of things. Come hell or high water, one day, she would undoubtedly put a stake through his heart. Though he hadn't made a move to do so yet, she knew the day would come when Cassius would have to give into what he was. He could not fight this bond between them forever, she was sure of it. All the lines converged into one point, all the lore said the very same thing. No bond was meant to be contested, to be ignored.

It was kill or be killed.

He may have saved her life that fated night, but by doing so he also condemned it.

The only choice he had was to either drain her like a juicebox or make her a monster like him, and neither of those options appealed to her. She'd wondered in the depths of her own despair on lonely nights if she would have still clung to the sliver of life he promised her by claiming her blood, had she known then what she knew now, and the fact she could not answer herself caused her a great deal of turmoil regarding the matter.

Cassius moved to open the door, and Ava followed suit, banishing all stray sugar-induced thoughts and daydreams of the golden haired vampire from her mind. She had bigger things to worry about.

Set against a rather scenic landscape, the Marquis was not as opulent as its name or signage would suggest. While one would expect ivory pillars and Grecian grandeur, the Marquis itself looked more like a weathered plantation, left alone on the edge of the forest to fade into the shadows with time.

"Well, it's definitely got the 'someone was murdered here' vibe," Ava said as she bent over slightly, sliding out the stake she kept between her jeans and the inside of her boot.

Cassius's gaze dipped to the sliver of wood that could end him at any moment.

Ava stole a glance, noting that doing so made her blood heat like molten lava. One day she would not feel such things, and she had to remember that. She had to remember what she was fighting for.

A chance to live.

"It is hard to believe this is where your darkest desires are brought to life," he drawled, his tone laced with judgmental apprehension.

"What's the matter, Cas? Does the haunted mansion scare you?" she teased him as she quickened her pace, strolling to the front doors.

Cassius shook his head. "The only thing that scares me, my sweet Avarice, is that we may be too late."

His words sobered her. He was right to worry. There was a sliver of a chance they'd be too late. Find Bryan chopped to bits or left for dead in this very building, but she refused to fall into such awful thoughts. She had also been left for dead once, and here she stood.

No, she had to have *hope.*

Hope that Bryan was somehow here, alive and waiting for them.

Ava walked up the steps, the stairs creaking and groaning in her wake.

The windows were fogged, strewn with fresh cobwebs in the corners, and she could barely make out anything inside.

"I'll take the right, you take the left," she commanded, not giving Cassius much time to answer as she headed back down the steps, rounding about to the right.

"Of course," he agreed, and Ava noted his voice sounded off. As if he was not entirely focused on the matter at hand; as if he was distracted.

Ava held her stake close to her chest as she crept quietly around the wrap-around porch. The parking lot had been stark empty upon arrival as she expected, but she could not shake the feeling like she was being preyed upon.

Stalked, watched.

By something *other* than an annoying vampire who looked good in leather pants.

She slid her back up against the faded paneling, catching her breath as a rat skittered across the floorboards, nearly making her jump. Clearly, whoever had purchased the place did not care to upgrade the outside as much as the inside.

"Fucking rat," she huffed out breathlessly, feeling both on edge and embarrassed.

She continued slowly creeping around the porch. No windows existed on the side of the house, and she found that quite odd. While the house looked ancient enough, she was fairly certain even old colonials had windows on the main floor, but the only ones she'd seen were those in the front of the house, flanking both sides of the door.

And just as she quickly turned the corner, a heavy force slammed her back against the wall and she nearly dropped her stake, being caught off guard,

"What the hell? Ava? What are you doing here?" the familiar dark, deep voice caused Ava's heart to race and her blood to heat, although it had nothing to do with vampirism.

Ava held her stake against a solid, defined chest, pressing the sharp tip in just enough she truly could draw blood if she desired.

But that was the thing about being trapped in Dallas's large, solid arms, backed against a wall.

She didn't *want* to escape, and she hated how his dominant nature brought out the parts of her she hated the most. The weak, needy, submissive part of her that longed to be held, to be worshipped, and to be *loved.*

But Ava did not love Jake Dallas. No. What they had was far from love.

"Put me the fuck down, asshole." She twisted in his grip, driving the tip of her stake into his chest only a bit to prove she wasn't in the mood to play games right now.

What the hell is he doing here?

Dallas grabbed the edge of her stake and with one pull, he had it out of her hands, despite her tight grip. Ava whimpered in defeat, scowling in protest.

"Not until you tell me what the hell you're doing in this hellhole."

Dallas pressed his chest against hers, which wasn't a hard feat, considering he was built like a brick house. The man had more muscles than was probably necessary, but that was due to an extensive work out regimen that Ava had assumed had more to do with working out stress than staying in shape, though she couldn't be sure. It wasn't like she and Dallas talked much when they were together, especially outside of hunting. When they were alone, there was hardly any time *to* talk, being as most of their interests were centered around training and...

"Hey, D, look what the fucking cat dragged in. Ava's gonna have a conniption when..."

Malcolm shoved Cassius forward, and Ava's eyes widened in surprise. She looked between Cassius—who didn't look too offended by the gesture, only annoyed—back to Dallas who still had her pressed against the wall. She noted the flicker of something in Cassius's gorgeous green eyes; something she couldn't quite place. But it looked like pain. Disappointment, even.

"I can explain," she said, looking back at Mal and Cassius.

Cassius crossed his arms, drawing back his lips to reveal pointed fangs, visibly *hissing* at Dallas.

"Put her down, you big brute. She is not the enemy. *We* are not your enemy."

Mal snapped. "You don't fucking call the shots here, tick." He pointed his own stake at Cassius, inches from his chest.

Dallas growled, but he moved back enough to give Ava some space.

Suddenly, her cheeks felt flushed and her thighs became slick and wet.

Now is not the time!

"Just calm your fucking tits, Mal. I said I can explain," she said as she pushed Dallas in the chest. He faltered only a bit, a murderous look in his eyes she'd never quite seen out of the boxing ring or the bedroom.

"Then start talking," Mal bit.

"We don't have time for this," Cassius growled as he laced his fingers around Mal's stake. He pulled it away, and the sound of cracked wood was most prevalent in the air.

Ava's stomach twisted as she realized he'd *snapped* the wooden stake in half. With his hand.

All the more reason to remember your end game.

"We have a... mutual contact," Ava started.

Cassius's gaze focused on Ava, his lips tightening.

"A friend. He... he needs our help. I think he was kidnapped."

"Isn't that a job for the police?" Dallas asked, crossing his arms. He took a step closer to Ava, still giving her space but letting her know he was not done with her, by far.

"He was on one of those singles sites, and this chick messaged him about meeting up and coming here." Ava motioned to the empty building.

"And you didn't tell the police?" Mal said as he regarded Cassius.

"No. Because I firmly believe that whoever is responsible for taking my friend, isn't your run of the mill hot goth babe."

"What makes you say that?" Mal asked skeptically.

Ava growled as she stomped her foot in annoyance. "Call it a fucking hunch! I just know, okay!"

"What are you psychic now, too?" Dallas quipped.

Ava glared at him. "You never questioned my judgment, before."

"That was before I found you sneaking around a Djinn nest with a fucking vampire."

"Djinn?" Ava asked, feeling her temperature rise. How dare Dallas insinuate such things.

Who the hell does he think he is?

"Yeah. We got reports about some locals who claimed to have escaped, thought it might be vamps, came down from Michigan to check it out. Turns out..."

"Vamps aren't the only invasive species in town," Dallas growled.

"Just you two? Where's the rest of the Scooby Gang?" Ava asked, crossing her arms.

Hunter and Tito are following up with Vinny on a lead about..." Mal's gaze quickly flashed to Cassius, and Ava understood.

The lack of words told her all she needed to know. She'd never been forthcoming with the vampire in her presence about her endeavors to try and lift his blood claim, and she didn't have any intention of doing so right at this very pivotal moment in time.

"Djinn are usually more isolated," Cassius said smoothly, pulling her attention once more.

"Got something you want to share with the class, Cas?" she bit out at the same time Dallas spoke, effectively canceling out her speech.

"You think we're fucking lying?" Dallas's shoulders tensed as he took a step toward Cassius.

"I said no such thing. Just making an observation." Cassius's voice was like velvet, tinged with a venomous bite Ava had never heard before, but she could not deny the sound stirred something within her.

Something she did not wish to acknowledge even in the dead of night, alone.

"There's also been reports of a vampire coven in the area for some time, but they didn't seem to settle until recently. That's the problem with hunting, too many ticks, not enough of us to go around and put them in their place," Mal said as he slid the pad of his fingertip over the sharp, broken point of his stake. His eyes met Cassius's, both of them staring at one another like a

Mexican standoff.

"Two birds one stone. I understand," Cassius said, his voice falling back to normal.

"To answer your question, Ava. Yes, I know of the Djinn. Their kind have been around since the dawn of vampires, but we are not... allies. The Djinn operate similar to that of the demons, the Incubi. Like us, they need human blood—" His words hung in the air for a moment, leaving Ava feeling rather nervous. His eyes met hers for a moment and it seemed as if he regretted saying such things. Which would be insane.

"They need human blood, but not for the same reason we do. It does not fulfill them. What they seek is the essence, the desire. The *hope.* Djinn pray on wishes."

"Or your darkest desires," Ava mumbled, remembering Enchantress's message to Bryan.

Where your darkest desires come to life.

"Maybe we should work together," Mal said cautiously.

"Are you fucking crazy?" Dallas growled at the same time Ava chimed in with "Absolutely not"."

Mal looked everyone over before settling his gaze on his sister, raising an eyebrow.

"If your friend *is* in custody of the Djinn or the vampires, you'll probably need backup anyway. Unless, of course, you've killed a Djinn before," Mal snarked as he pulled out his cell phone. He looked at the glowing device, tapping out a text, though Ava wasn't certain to who.

Cassius looked as if he wanted to speak, but he thought better of it.

Ava's gaze flickered from one man to the next, all standing before her as her brother's words sunk in. He was right. She hadn't thought there would be any other threat, outside of vampires. She'd never faced down a Djinn before, and though it seemed Cassius *knew* what they were, she wasn't entirely sure she could trust him, though she wanted to.

A part of her buried deep beneath the surface *begged* her to trust him. He hadn't hurt her yet. In fact, he'd come in handy and aided her on more than one occasion.

But was it enough?

Faced with a monster she knew nothing about, could she put her life in the hands of another monster?

A monster who saved your life once before...

"Fine," Ava answered, not missing Dallas's cursing behind her.

"Wise choice, Simba," Mal said as he looked at Cassius with a smirk.

"In that case," Mal cleared his throat as he slid his phone back into his back pocket. "Cas, you come with me. Dallas, take Ava back to base and get her up to speed, and give Vinny a call. If anyone can find some blueprints on this place, it'll be him."

"Where the hell do you think you're going?" Ava nipped.

Cassius sank his hands into his pockets, sending her a reassuring look.

"Hunting of course," Mal smiled wickedly.

A hurricane of concern fluttered in her stomach, though she could not discern who she was more concerned about—her brother, or the monster accompanying him.

CHAPTER FOURTEEN

CASSIUS FOLLOWED MALCOLM around the back of the building toward the woods. In any other scenario, he would have been more cautious of the man, but with Ava near, he knew he was safe. For the moment, anyway.

"I have to give you credit, Cas. You have more balls than I thought you did."

"Excuse me?" Cassius responded, taken off guard.

Malcolm stepped down from the porch, looking up at Cassius, who stood still as a stone.

"It's been what, four years since you marked my sister?" Mal pulled out a package of cigarettes from his back pocket and Cassius pursed his lips.

"I can assure you, it is not what it looks like."

"What was your plan?" Mal lit his cigarette, and Cassius wrinkled his nose at the smell of smoke. He'd never cared for it.

"Make up some little story about a rescue, sequester my sister on a road trip to the middle of nowhere, and BAM!" Mal clapped his hands, loud enough it stirred the birds in the nearby trees.

"Believe me or not, I have never lied to you once, Malcolm. Our friend is in danger, and we are wasting time."

"How do I know you didn't pluck the poor bastard off yourself? All part of your devious little plan to get Ava to trust you."

"You are implying she trusts me at all," Cassius bit as Mal blew smoke in the air.

Malcolm turned with a nod as he headed for the woods.

"Well, I don't. Trust you, that is. Not as far as I can fucking throw you."

"So why ask for my help?" Cassius kept his distance if only to avoid the putrid smoke.

"Keep your friends close, but your enemies closer."

"I am not your enemy, Malcolm. I never have been." Cassius sighed as he followed him into the woods. Just a hair into the woods, he could see two motorcycles parked just behind a large bush next to an old cellar door in the ground. Of course, that was why they hadn't seen them. Cassius stood still as Malcolm threw his leg over the seat.

"I take it you were not able to break the lock?" Cassius nodded to the doors.

"It's old, rusted. Probably locked from the inside. Dallas and I were looking for a way in, scouting the area until..."

"And now what? You've abandoned your search on account of me? I'm flattered, Malcolm, really but—"

Malcolm nodded to the larger cycle, which boasted painted flames. It was a large bike, bigger than anything Cassius had seen in a good while.

"You know how to drive one of these things?" Mal said, taking another drag of his cigarette.

Cassius shrugged. "I have never cared for

motorcycles."

"So that's a no, then." Mal cracked his neck.

Cassius felt rather agitated. "I only said I did not care for them. Not that I don't have experience." He stared at the beautiful chrome, the shimmering paint, and his stomach growled with hunger. He closed his eyes as he realized with a wave of nausea that it had been longer than twenty four hours since he'd fed on the stolen blood from the Willowcrest Morgue. As if perfectly on cue, his throat constricted, feeling dry and desperate. His senses kicked into gear, and he was all too aware of the pain in the ass hunter snickering behind him, egging him on like some town bully.

If only he'd possessed a shred of Eden's heartlessness, he could eliminate Malcolm Crowley and all his interference. It would make things so much simpler, but alas, Cassius could not find it within himself to be so callous toward humans, no matter how annoying one of them may be.

"Then quit pussyfooting around, and let's go," Mal bit as he tossed Cassius the keys and started up his motorcycle.

Cassius caught them in midair, his reflexes much more heightened than the average human's due to his vampirism. He ran his free hand along Dallas's bike, finding himself wondering if Ava had ever been on it. Thoughts of her legs hugging the side of Dallas's hips shot a fire through him, and he knew he should dispel such thoughts, push them down deep into the caverns of his soul.

Cassius threw his leg over the seat, and he had to admit, sitting behind the bars of such a sleek, well kept machine made him feel a sense of power he thought he'd lost long ago. And when the engine roared to life, for a moment, Cassius felt alive in a way he'd never felt in all his years.

***

"It is a bar," Cassius drawled. "And it is ten o'clock in the morning."

"I have it on pretty good authority that it is five o clock somewhere. This is where the Djinn have been spotted. It's also rumored this is where the coven operates out of."

"A hotspot, then," Cassius murmured.

"A literal den of fucking monsters," Malcolm retorted.

Cassius stared at the Drowned Clam, which looked just as run down as the Marquis, and every other building in the town of Albright, Ohio.

"You pulled me from a rescue mission to drag me to a bar—a hotspot—you *think* is full of immortals."

"Are you slow? Have all the years of daywalking rotted your feeble tick brain?" Mal snickered.

"I do not see the point in your actions," Cassius said, dismounting the motorcycle. It was nearing a quarter after ten, and Cassius was starting to feel rather antsy. For such an early hour, the bar itself looked to be quite busy. A pair of women giggled as they walked past him, one of them stealing a glance at him that he could only describe as tempting. He had to admit with her long, dark hair and excited eyes, she was rather attractive.

The blood that flushed her cheeks as she took in the sight of him stirred his hunger, the stolen pulse beneath his skin next to non-existent. His pulse was faint, and he longed for what was out of his grasp. Even the sight of a beautiful woman as it were, was not enough to make his heart race or his black blood rush beneath the surface, and he was certain no one else

596

would ever again. Not now that he'd claimed the sweetest blood for himself.

Wherever Dallas had taken Ava, it was far from his reach, and he was equal parts grateful and angry, but also very hungry.

He forced himself to look away.

"What's the matter, Cas? Feeling a little under the weather?" Malcolm said with mock concern.

"Let us get whatever it is you intend to do, over with. A man's life depends on it."

Malcolm dismounted his bike, heading for the doors with Cassius right behind him.

The inside of the Drowned Clam lived up to its name. The walls were a dark, aged mahogany that reminded Cassius of another place, in another life. It reminded him of Penny's tavern in Portofino.

It reminded him of home.

Cassius had called many places home since those years. Paris, Rome, Ansley. Chester. But nothing had ever truly felt like home, not in the way Portofino did. Even now he missed its salty breezes and the warmth of the tavern when the air turned to a chill.

The man tending the bar was a burly man, with a pointed beard that hung just above where Cassius would assume his navel to be, given the portly shape of the man.

Malcolm pulled up a spot at the bar, not bothering to wait for Cassius. "Two whiskeys, please," he said arrogantly.

Cassius raised an eyebrow at him. "I do not drink whiskey."

Mal chuckled as the bartender set to pouring. "Bold of you to assume it was for you."

Cassius huffed indignantly as the bartender shoved the glass toward Malcolm.

"And for you, Sunshine?" he grumbled.

Cassius's lips twitched, the scent of sweat and liquor clinging to the man was making his stomach flip. His throat was dry, and he knew nothing in the Drowned Clam would clench his thirst.

And then he saw *her.*

Long, silken black hair sprawled down her back, and her vibrant blue eyes sparkled in the light amidst her porcelain skin.

Enchantress.

Cassius shook his head, feeling a strange sense of deja vu. She reminded him of someone else. Someone he longed to forget.

It seemed the ghost of Eden Boracelli would haunt him wherever he went.

"Excuse me, Malcolm," he said as he strode over to the other side of the bar, not giving a care to the annoying Crowley behind him sputtering some nonsense.

Cassius sauntered toward the woman who'd messaged Bryan, his blood running colder than usual due to his lack of sustenance. She sat in a corner booth with two other women who looked like carbon copies of her, albeit with varying facial features. But they were all dressed in black, with the same onyx hair and fair skin. How hadn't he seen it before, he wondered. Though one could argue that photographs on the internet did not do the siren Djinn justice, and perhaps it had been too long since he'd seen one in person. Centuries, even.

The same pair of women who'd passed him on the way in sat at a booth not far away, and he could feel their gaze on him as he walked on by. The air was thick with the perfume of the Djinn, a mix between woodsy citrus and spice. He had to admit it smelled *divine* and stirred a wishful sort of lust in him that was hard to ignore, but that was par for the course for the beautiful creatures. They fed on blood and desire, after all, albeit their desire was less sexual and more to do with hopes and dreams. Cassius had to remember to stay focused. If he wasn't careful, one could fall into the fantasy far too easily and end up deceased, even a monster such as him.

"Can I help you?" The raven-haired kidnapper said as she appraised Cassius with judgmental blue irises.

Cassius hated how easy it was for him to flip his switch. He mourned the time he was naive, trusting, ignorant to the wills and charms that were pure instinct for a vampire, once they'd learned how to use them.

"You look oddly familiar to me," he said, dropping his voice low enough that bystanders could not hear him. A low hiss echoed near him as Enchantress licked her lips.

She did not betray much. She only smiled softly with a shrug as she roved her gaze over him.

"I've been told I have a... familiar face." Her voice was smooth, but it carried the hint of an accent. Coupled with her deep tone, it was almost hypnotizing.

The two girls in the booth next to them appraised him as well as he stood there, and Cassius noted they looked... *hungry.*

Had Malcolm not said there were reports of deaths?

He wondered how many innocent lives these venomous snakes had caught in their coils, and how long it had been since their last meal. He made a mental note to ask Malcolm about the reports later. After all, if they were to work together, it would certainly be helpful to know the full story.

"Well, perhaps I shall jog your memory." He shifted

his stance, loosening his shoulders as he leaned his head to the side. The woman known as Enchantress twisted her lips in thought before responding.

"A face like yours would be hard to forget, but it has been a long week."

Cassius stepped forward, his thrall testing the waters and begging to be free. He hated to use such things, but as Eden had once taught him, power was only as strong as the man who wields it. Though he did not favor using his vampire abilities on other creatures as it often required more strength and energy, and unless one was full and sated, it could be quite draining.

He reached out, feeling the edges of Enchantress's natural aura.

She smiled wickedly as she took a step closer.

"Well this is a surprise. I don't often snag vampires in my nets, but for you I may make an exception." Her eyes glistened as her aura glowed, pulling him in by his thrall, practically

Before Cassius could answer, another voice stopped him dead in his tracks.

"Tous les pécheurs seraient misérables au ciel." The saccharine voice was ghostly, stirring up memories he thought he had long buried. He spun around, taking in the sight of a petite woman, dressed in a pale pink sweater that was rather tight on her small frame. White heart buttons pulled from the overabundance of fair, bountiful cleavage, accented by long, pale blonde curls falling over her shoulders, framing her breasts. Her bright, blood-red lips and dark makeup made her look young—perhaps early twenties—but Cassius knew she was much, much older than that.

"Elle brûlait trop fort pour ce monde." Cassius spoke the words as if he'd gone back in time, and perhaps in

a way he had.

"Cassius, what a lovely surprise," she said as she slowly approached him, reaching out to hug him in a polite gesture. Enchantress scoffed, her demeanor shifting from the surprise appearance of the queen in her presence. Though when Amora Medici embraced Cassius, planting a kiss on his cheek, he could not deny the memories as they came flooding back to him.

"This is madness, Amora, I can not..." Cassius's heart raced as he tried to catch his breath. She smelled like blood and strawberries mixed with fresh-pressed linen. The scent of blood and sex was prominent, and he was starving.

Amora traced her long, pale fingernails along his jaw, tugging his face toward her.

"Why not? Do not tell me this is because of... Eden." The way in which she spoke of his betrothed was bitter, spiteful. Though Cassius knew Amora had more than one reason to harbor such hatred for Eden.

"I am betrothed to her, Amora. And you are tied to Marcellus." Cassius softly plucked her hand from his face, holding her delicate wrist in his hand, his thumb brushing the underside of her wrist.

"Marcellus is my consort, not my mate. We are not as bound as you think."

"He is my friend, and I—"

"Do you think I don't know what he does? I am a queen, Cassius, there is not much that goes on under my nose that I am not aware of."

Cassius turned away, dropping her wrist.

"Marcellus loves you, even if he does not show it," Cassius said in defense. Though he knew better than anyone that love was complicated. Marcellus was not unlike his father; raised in blood, wanting for nothing. The world lay at their feet and they were encouraged to

partake in all its riches, for that was the mark of a powerful man.

"Love does not factor into the equation, Cassius. Our marriage is not so different from yours, you know. The only difference is I have given this coven an heir. I have fulfilled my duty," she bit.

"How can you say love is not part of the equation? How can you stand there and preach such things to me, when you are begging for my love?" Cassius exclaimed, feeling hot remorse and guilt mingling with his desire.

A part of him longed for love, and he thought perhaps one day Eden would grow into their arrangement, perhaps one day their lovemaking would not feel so empty or one-sided. Perhaps one day, he would be enough. Children or no children, as long as they were together his family could be safe.

"You deserve more, dear. You deserve a queen."

The party could be heard still, the sound of strings and laughter echoing in the halls of the Medici estate.

"That may be so, but I am a man of honor, Amora. I would not put you, or him... or Eden in such predicaments."

"What would it take, Cassius? Name your price."

Cassius closed his eyes and breathed deep. The scent of fresh blood was so tempting. His cock strained in his pants, knowing the satisfaction the crimson nectar would bring inevitably.

But he was stronger than this.

Wasn't he?

"My heart is not for sale, Amora," he said sternly. "And neither is my bed."

"She will never love you, Cassius. Mark my words. Eden is not capable of love for anyone or anything other than her own selfish needs."

Cassius shook his head as he headed for the door.

"Friend of yours, Ami?" Enchantress's tone had shifted to pure intrigue, and Cassius felt a sting of panic. He'd been hiding for so long... the only person who truly knew of his presence, of his whereabouts was Leon.

Would Amora expose him?

Though their affair was brief, he hadn't said goodbye...

Amora pulled back, flashing her bright eyes to Enchantress before speaking.

Ami?

Is that what she goes by now...

"Ah yes, a friend who I have missed," Amora said sweetly as she tucked her hand underneath Cassius's arm, pulling him away.

CHAPTER FIFTEEN

"SO, THIS IS why you were avoiding my calls," Dallas grumbled as Ava walked with determination toward the Impala.

"I'm not doing this with you," she bit, feeling a flurry of emotion. She hadn't expected to run into her brother or Dallas. She knew they were on a case, in Ohio, but they could have been good and gone for all she knew. It wasn't like either of them kept her apprised of their plans on a day to day basis.

They were grown men with agendas of their own to service, just as she was a grown woman with her own ghosts to chase.

She didn't owe either of them, especially Dallas, any explanation for... well, anything.

Besides, it wasn't like they were a couple, but the way Dallas was lumbering after her, seething with anger, it felt like maybe...

"Oh no? But you'll creep around with fucking monsters, won't you?"

Ava stopped, dragging her keys out as she came to the car. She reached for the door, but a large, solid hand smacked the side of the door, making her jump. She looked up at Dallas, who was practically fuming.

"And so what if I am? What's it to you? I'm not some Susie fucking homemaker waiting for you to grace me with your calls, Jake. I'm capable of chasing leads and putting said fucking monsters in the ground myself, and I don't need permission form you to do any of it," she bit.

"I never said—" Dallas huffed in frustration.

"Get. Out of my way, Dallas." Ava could feel her temperature flaring. A part of her wanted to take the bait, rise to the fight. She loved to fight, especially if it would undoubtedly end in Dallas putting her in her place—consensually of course—but there was also a part of her that knew at the moment such things would likely be trouble... more trouble than it was worth. Trouble was practically her middle name, after all, she was a Crowley. A death wish was genetic.

Dallas only pursed his lips, nostrils flaring as he looked at her, his eyes alight with something she had seen only a few times before.

Jealousy.

Was he jealous of Cassius?

The thought was absurd to her.

Why would he be jealous of a vampire?

"I don't think so, Kitten. I'm driving," he said as he shoved her back against the side of the car, the door handle just out of reach. He loomed over her like a much hotter version of The Hulk, the little vein in his neck standing out. Fury looked good on him, but it also stirred feelings within Ava that she despised.

Fear, anxiety, powerlessness.

She'd been training with Dallas for years to break through such barriers, but here she stood, frozen as he pressed his solid frame against her, staring her down with wordless command like the hurricane he was.

At that moment, something in her awakened, rising like a phoenix from the ashes.

Ava's eyebrows furrowed.

"The hell you are, this is my car!" she said as she pushed him aside.

"Why do you insist of being so defiant of everything I say and do?" he growled in response.

Ava opened the door, slamming it into his midsection if only to convey she was not in the mood for his bullshit. He had the audacity to grab his groin and hip, hissing in pain as if her outburst should make her feel any sense of remorse. But it didn't. In fact, Ava wished she had hit him a little harder, turned the tables of punishment on him for a change.

"I don't have time for this. Get in or stay here, I don't give a shit."

She closed the door, but Dallas was in the passenger seat faster than she could start the car and drive off.

"You don't even know where base *is*."

"Then by all means, do something useful and tell me instead of being a jealous dick." The words escaped her mouth, and she almost regretted them.

Almost.

"I'm not jealous of a fucking tick. I'm concerned. About *you*."

"Thanks, but I'm a big girl, Dallas. Or have you forgotten that?" she nipped as she pulled out on the road.

Dallas looked as if he wanted to respond, but thought better of it.

"This conversation isn't over, but right now we have bigger things to worry about. Take route 30 north."

***

Ava pulled into the driveway of what looked to be the most perfect house she'd ever seen. The residential area looked like something out of a movie. Idyllic, even. Dogwood trees flanked the sides of the road along sidewalks, their blooms starting to peak. The sun shone down on the blue house with white trim, and Ava had to do a double take.

This is base?

She'd known her brother and the rest of the Goon Squad to take up in motels most of the time when they were on the road, but she also knew they had other secret hideouts like the Bat Cave where they could train, or keep a stash of weapons. Just in case.

Though the idea of anyone training in a house with a white swing on the porch and pale blue shutters made her slightly uncomfortable.

It reminded her of home, as a stray memory pushed forth.

Ava ran up the steps, nearly missing her mother sitting on the porch swing.

"It's eleven thirty." Her mother's voice sounded in her ears. Ava turned on her heel, the leather of her cheerleading shoe squeaking against the wood.

"I lost track of time," she lied.

Lenora puffed on her cigarette, blowing smoke into the air.

"Nice try, baby, but I wasn't born last night."

"Mom…"

"I'm not mad, Ava. Just disappointed." Somehow the words made Ava feel worse than if her mother would have been angry. If she would have grounded her on the spot.

"You just don't like Jeremy." She crossed her arms.

"Jeremy is an idiot," her mother said, like it was

common knowledge. "And he doesn't respect you. A boy worth your time will respect you."

"Why are you trying to ruin my life?" she grumbled.

Her mother raised an eyebrow. "Oh, Ava. Baby. This isn't ruin. Far from it." She took another drag of her cigarette, pushing herself on the swing. The rusty metal springs squeaked from the movement.

"Whatever. I'm going to bed."

Ava pushed the memory away, feeling the threat of tears. She didn't think of her mother often. She thought she'd buried all the hurt and pain of her death deep down inside of her, but every once in a while, it would creep back up and grab her by the throat.

"What the fuck is this place?" Ava asked as she turned the car off.

Dallas opened the door, his inflection full of venom.

"Base."

"It looks like a fucking bed and breakfast. You sure you and my brother aren't on a honeymoon or some shit?" she asked as she opened the door, watching Dallas circle around to the front. The sunlight shone on his tan skin, his tousled dark hair, which he'd neglected to cut, against his skin, his almost six-o-clock shadow. He looked rather out of place in such a cozy neighborhood.

He didn't answer her. He only hurried up the white wooden steps and she followed, reluctantly.

Whatever it was they had to do, she wished it to be over as soon as possible so she could get back to the task at hand.

Finding Bryan.

Her thoughts wandered for a moment, to her brother and Cassius.

Where were they and why did Mal need him all of a sudden?

What did he have planned?

Dallas lifted up the mat in front of the door, pulling out a key.

Ava crossed her arms, listening to the sound of the birds chirping. The white swing swung from the light breeze, but the metal didn't squeak.

Dallas opened the door, glaring at her.

"Ladies first."

Ava brushed past him with a huff and into the house. It didn't look as she had expected, in fact it looked quite bare, minimalistic. She slowly walked into the foyer, and Dallas came up behind her after shutting the door. He set the key in a ceramic bowl on the end table in the center, making her jump.

"Welcome to my house," he growled as he stomped toward the kitchen.

The words hit Ava in the chest like a brick.

His house?

Dallas never mentioned having a house of his own. As far as she knew, his home was the open road, like her brother, or the rest of the hunters. Then again, there wasn't much about Dallas's past that was open for discussion, if she wanted to discuss it at all. She'd known the man since she was fifteen, well before they'd ever formed a mutual friendship over monster hunting. Dallas did not dwell on the past. He only focused on the present, but she had always been curious.

Every one of them, including her brother, had come to the dark side to hunt vampires and other creatures of the night because, like her, they'd been exposed to the world in the shadows. But even after several years with the Goon Squad, no one seemed keen on bringing up such ghosts. Instead, they chose to avenge them with every stab and every match.

Ava stood stone cold for a moment as she watched

Dallas head for the kitchen, opening the refrigerator. She tried to match up the cottage aesthetic with the motorcycle riding, tattooed man in front of her but she could not see it. Surely, he was joking, or he'd hired one hell of an interior designer.

Nonetheless, she made her way to the kitchen.

Dallas poured himself a drink. A whiskey it looked like. He took a long pull before grabbing her a glass as well.

"This is what's going to happen, Ava. You're going to tell me the truth. And then, I'm going to fill you in on our investigation, and if you listen to me, you can stay and help us."

"How very noble of you to offer me such a deal," she bit, grabbing her drink and nearly downing it. "Maybe you've gotten knocked around a bit too much or that senility is finally kicking in, but last I remember, you don't tell me what the fuck to do."

Dallas glared at her with fire in his eyes.

"I called you. Texted you. You didn't respond, and I thought maybe you were in trouble."

Ava scoffed as she took another drink. "Typical fucking man."

"I'm serious, Ava. You've been avoiding me, ever since..." His voice disappeared into the air, but she knew what he meant. What he wasn't saying.

The last time they'd seen each other things had gotten... blurry.

They were both so very frustrated, stealing moments away on the case they were working together with the rest of the crew.

Training with Dallas had always been a surefire way to blow off steam, to re-circuit herself back to neutral.

But that night... something changed. When Dallas held her down, as he had so many times before, begging her to fight him, Ava's demons rose to the surface.

She'd always attributed the painful memories of powerlessness as part of her process when facing down vamps. Remembering that night she'd almost died, her legs dead weight as they bled out on the concrete floor. The feeling of thrall she'd experienced time and time again from her exposure as vampire bait was hard to combat, but her brother had taught her that the most difficult, painful memories could be a powerful weapon.

But pinned underneath Dallas at that moment, she wanted to give up.

She didn't want to fight Jake Dallas anymore. She wanted to submit, but that was not who she was.

Was Dallas changing her?

When did that happen?

And when he had *held* her in his arms after her momentary lapse of self, she felt a sting of guilt.

Panic.

"Not everything is about you, Dallas," she said, her voice carrying in the small space. "I don't need you to take care of me. I can take care of myself," she bit. "I was trying to save a man from the pitfalls of online dating!"

"With the fucking vampire who bit you!" he roared.

It's not like that! God, you are such a..." she yelled back.

Dallas balled his fist, slamming it against the other side of the refrigerator as he pulled out the bottle of whiskey, pouring another round.

"An asshole? For giving a shit about your safety? Well, excuse me for wanting to protect you."

"Really, Jake? You want to 'protect' me all of a sudden? When the last two years you've done nothing but teach me how to protect myself against vicious monsters? I'm not some fucking damsel and you know that! I don't *need* you or your 'protection'. And besides, if Cas is with me... he isn't killing anyone, and that's a win in my book."

"I'm going to give you to the count of three, Kitten. To. Tell. Me. The. Truth." Dallas's eyes were full of fury, his voice solid and unwavering.

Coupled with his hunched shoulders, and the grip he had on his glass, Ava could not deny he looked quite menacing. When he slowly stalked his way over to her, she found it hard to move. Ava looked up at his bright blue eyes, feeling emboldened as ever, as if she was staring down a scary monster come to drag her to hell. And in a way, that was what Dallas was to her. A monster of her own making. Something she needed to conquer in order to move on with her life. He certainly wasn't anything... more. But even as she tried to convince herself, she knew it was a lie.

When had things gotten so complicated?

"Are you in love with him?" Dallas asked seriously.

Ava's eyes widened in surprise as his words hit her. Surprise gave way to anger, to panic. Her blood ran cold.

"Absolutely not! Are you fucking insane?" she yelled, feeling defensive.

How could he insinuate such a thing?

Didn't he know she loathed the leather-clad vampire for what he had done to her?

Did he not know her at all?

Dallas looked down at her with fire behind his eyes and reached his hand out, grabbing her by the neck. His thumb slid over her jaw, and his grip was stern, fierce.

"Are you in love with me?" His voice was barely a whisper.

Ava could not tear her gaze away from him. Her heart pounded in her chest, and the air felt as if it had been sucked out of the room.

Instinctively, she reached out to push him away, to tell him to fuck right off with his emotional, manipulative words. But instead, her arms slid around his neck, her fingers teasing the edges of his hair. This was familiar, the pain, the force. His hand around her throat.

But what wasn't familiar was the fact she could not bring herself to say 'no.'

So Ava said nothing.

Instead, she leaned up and kissed Jake Dallas with anger, with fury, and guilt.

And when he kissed her back, sliding his tongue into her mouth, she could not resist.

She pulled him closer, seeking the feeling of numbness Dallas always brought her.

Lines blurred when he grabbed her by the hips and lifted her up onto the counter. Glasses skittered across the surface as lust overtook them both.

Ava tugged at Dallas's shirt, sliding it over his head. Bright, golden light shone through the window, lighting up his tan skin and making his double star tattoos stand out even more.

Dallas grabbed her waist, sliding his heated palms up the expanse of her skin under her shirt. His touch was rough, hurried.

Possessive.

Ava shimmied out of her leather coat, feeling the heat of the moment.

Dallas sucked at the flesh of her neck.

The motion caused Ava's eyes to close in ecstasy, but in the dark confines of her mind, she imagined someone else. Memories of Cassius's lips on her wrist, his tongue against her flesh, assaulted her, mixed with the sensation of Dallas's lips on her skin.

Her thighs clenched in response, wetness blossoming between them as the memory of fangs piercing her skin danced with the desire to feel such perfect bliss again. She moaned in response, feeling a mixture of guilt and need. She didn't want to think about Cassius.

Not now, not ever.

But it seemed the sinfully delicious vampire who remembered how she liked her coffee had a hold on her that would never cease.

Not until she could remove his mark.

Ava opened her eyes, noticing the faint sparkle on her skin from where he had bitten her. Dallas worked at the buttons of her jeans, and she did not stop him.

"That's what I thought, Kitten. You know who you belong to," Dallas growled in her ear.

"Jake…" she groaned, feeling her heart catch in her throat.

"Tell me you're mine."

She could feel the tears starting to pool in her eyes.

The guilt, the pain… he was supposed to make it go away.

He always made it go away, so why was this time different?

Dallas slid her jeans off, throwing them across the room. The cold air of the kitchen kissed her skin, shocking her like ice.

He grabbed her neck, imploring her eyes with his.

"Who do you belong to?" he asked again, his voice heavy with command, with need. The words were no different than what she'd heard over the last two years. After all, Dallas delighted in dominating her and up until this very moment, she'd been more than happy to receive his rewards and punishments in the privacy of their stolen moments.

But something in the way his words sounded now, how his voice trembled in the slightest, it was as if he was asking her for more than just sexual consent.

When he fingers slid his beneath her panties, caressing her slick folds before diving in, she cried out in ecstasy. The slow drag as he slid them in and out of her was mind-boggling and she could feel her orgasm starting to culminate, making her feel foggy, unfocused. She longed for release, to be set free once more.

Her words came easily, but they felt empty.

"You, Jake. I belong to you."

"That's right, Kitten," he growled as he slid her panties down her legs over her ankles and boots. The cool stone of the countertop was soothing to the heat radiating throughout her.

"And I'm going to make sure you don't forget it, do you understand?" His voice was dark and called to the demons inside of Ava she thought she'd buried. The sound of his belt and pants hitting the tile floor echoed around her like a church bell, loud and ominous.

Ava closed her eyes, nodding in response. "Yes. I understand."

At that moment, she did not understand what Dallas was truly saying. She only focused on the familiarity of the action itself. After all, it wasn't the first time they'd gone about this song and dance.

She'd given herself to Dallas plenty of times. He needed to know he was in control, that she was at his mercy. And for two years, she'd found solace in their arrangement because for the sliver of however long it lasted, with Dallas she could be free.

Free of the ghosts that haunted her, the burdens that had become so heavy for her to carry.

Memories surfaced. Hazy, blurry memories of burning buildings, blood, and deep, satisfying pleasure. In the space of her consciousness, all she could see was bright green eyes, and sharp, pointed fangs.

And when Jake Dallas entered her in a swift, sharp motion, Ava cried out as she held onto the memory of Cassius's bite like a life raft. Nothing would ever feel as blissful, and she hated that.

Dallas slid his hand underneath her thigh, hooking her legs around his hips as he thrust into her with steady force. Ava held onto to Dallas's large shoulders, her fingernails digging into his warm skin as he picked up his pace. She could feel his control slipping, and her own fading into darkness. She was so very close to the edge she felt as if she might fall. Into the darkness, into *him,* so far that she would lose herself.

Dallas took her face in his hands, bringing his lips to hers as he stilled, spilling himself inside of her.

When he pulled away, leaving Ava dripping wet and unsatisfied, alone on his kitchen counter without another word, Ava could feel herself shatter like the glass of whiskey on the floor into a million pieces.

CHAPTER SIXTEEN

CASSIUS LOOKED OVER his shoulder, expecting to see Malcolm, but the older Crowley was nowhere in sight.

The bar was not packed, but it was busy for a mid-morning shift with various tables filled with women sharing appetizers and mimosas. It dawned on him that save for Malcolm, himself and the bartender, he hadn't seen any males in the establishment, only cementing the older Crowley's suspicious actions and claims of a nest.

He did not trust Malcolm entirely, not in the way he trusted Ava. For better or for worse, he and Ava were bound in a sense, and he had a feeling he'd trust her, mark or no mark. But her brother was another story.

Though Cassius had done all he could to prove to both Ava and her brother he was not a threat, the man did not take any liberties with his feelings on the matter.

He'd been far too amicable when they'd discovered one another, looking almost nonplussed that Ava and he had shown up on *their case*. He knew Malcolm was using him, but to what end he was not certain.

Amora tugged on Cassius's arm as she led him through the bar, through the kitchen to a small office where once in, she closed the door. The room was small, only big enough to fit a small loveseat among a desk with scattered papers and used mugs of what smelled like stale coffee and blood.

"I thought you were dead, Cassius," she said softly as she locked the door.

In the small space, Cassius felt only slightly claustrophobic.

"In a way, I was. Dead, that is," he said as he traced his fingers along the messy desk nonchalantly, looking for what he was not sure. He only knew that whatever it was, it would stand out when he saw it. A name, a printout, perhaps a sticky note with a *Bryan is here!*

Amora slowly made her way over to him, forcing him to look at her. Bountiful blonde curls spilled over her cleavage and she looked up at him with deep, forest green eyes. The way she was looking at him was familiar. Too familiar, and Cassius felt a tinge of panic.

Had he traded a fox's den for a lion's instead?

"So much has happened since..." Her voice was sweet, carrying the hint of ner native French accent.

Cassius pursed his lips, but he did not break her gaze. He felt as if he was on a cliff, and the wrong word, the wrong movement would surely throw him over the edge. Give Amora the wrong idea.

But a part of him still felt sentimental toward the Medici queen. After all, they'd once been friends, and he considered her an ally. And for a brief time... they were perhaps a bit more. But Cassius did not want to think about such things. He wanted to let sleeping dogs lie.

"How are your children?" he said, changing the

subject.

Amora shrugged. "Donatello is fine. Stirring up a ruckus in Paris like his father at his age. Lilibet is in Spain with her father, Thomasse, wanting nothing to do with me, but isn't that the will of daughters anyway?" She rolled her eyes. "Henry met an untimely death. Hunters."

"You... took other consorts?" Cassius could hear the weight of that word, heavy in the air.

Consort.

He'd almost been one himself. Amora had unofficially propositioned him all those years ago, when he and Eden were... together. Yet, if Eden had succeeded in rising to such stature as a queen herself, if she hadn't told him the truth...

Is that where he would be now?

Would he be the consort to the Boracellis his father couldn't be?

By Eden's side living in the luxury of the high covens, father to a small brood of powerful little vampires?

The thought made Cassius pale, made his blood run ice cold. For remembering those moments with Eden was far too painful. The life he'd been sentenced to was full of desire, hunger, pain, and lies. So many lies he'd been naive to believe.

"I had to. Luckily, I'd given birth to Donatello when Marcellus was alive, so that bought me my spot on the Medici throne in his absence, but..." Amora looked away, and he could see the strain in her jaw. "Had I not had our son, I would have been easily replaced, and they would have had to institute a new, fresher model as those archaic rules state." Amora tossed her hair behind her shoulder, looking away for a moment as if she too were remembering a painful past.

Cassius's heart broke for a moment, thinking of all the things she must have had to endure while he hid in the shadows. He'd never gotten the chance to truly tell her how sorry he was about what had transpired with her consort, Marcellus.

The only man Eden ever truly loved.

He felt a sting of guilt that while he'd been on the run, finding a suitable place to disappear, Amora not only had to mourn her consort, but fight tooth and nail to keep the spot on the throne she deserved.

"A queen is only as good and powerful as the heirs she provides." Her voice cracked at the words, and Cassius wanted to reach out. Pull her into his arms and hug her.

He understood all too well what it was to be beholden to ancient laws and forced bloodlines. Though immortal, they were but slaves to their own blood as well as the life source humans provided. Only the strongest of bloodlines prevailed, the high covens practically untouchable. All the other bloodlines were diluted and would never be as strong as the pure Medicis, Aurelias, and of course, the Boracellis. Though there were others, even they paled in comparison of wealth and standing.

His Aurelian bloodline was highly coveted for its purity and the ability to sire—an ability that was much rarer these days—and produce viable, blood born heirs was both a blessing and a curse to Cassius. It was the reason he'd grown up a secret, the reason Eden had been betrothed to him, and it was one of the main reasons he left the life of the glittering high covens.

He wanted more than the life of a consort, bound to another in a loveless arrangement that the only use was to provide strong, powerful heirs. When Eden had come clean, it had been a blessing. The way out was more than clear, but it came with its costs.

"Unless you are the Boracelli queen." Amora's words were thick with bitterness, pulling him from his melancholy thoughts.

"She is... still..."

"Queen? Yes. Childless? Yes. No consorts either, just blood slaves."

The words made Cassius nauseous. He'd heard about Eden's rise to the throne when it happened, and his heart was conflicted. It was what she always wanted, but knowing she fought Francesca, eliminating her... it did not sit well with Cassius.

How many innocent lives had she taken?

How many people had she stabbed in the back, bought their alliance in order to slay a sitting queen?

Amora took a step closer, reaching her hand out to caress Cassius's cheek.

"Your mother is well. I can... get word to her if you would like?" she whispered.

Cassius could not fight the undeniable stirring in his stomach.

"She is still in Eden's possession?" Cassius felt his voice shake, but he needed to know.

Amora nodded, tracing her fingers over his jaw, and he could not help but settle his hand over hers as she did so. He looked at her with pain, guilt, and concern as he waited her answer.

"She is. But I have allies, Cassius. My reach is far."

The chill of her skin against his palm was somewhat soothing and he knew better. This is who Amora was.

Calculating.

Manipulative.

Alluring.

It was a wonder she herself was not a siren Djinn, for she was just as tempting.

Cassius shook his head. If his mother was safe, that was all he needed to know. Despite Amora's promise, he knew allies could be bought, and Eden was not a forgiving woman. If one breath of his name reached her ear...

"I can not risk that, but I appreciate the gesture," he said as he dropped his hand to his side, feeling the guilt over his decision all over again.

"Oh Cassius..." Amora's eyes sparkled with intensity.

"After all these years, you are still so stubborn aren't you?" She let out a laugh as she pulled away, heading to the chair behind the desk.

"Old habits die hard, *Ami.*"

Amora giggled. "Oh, that is just a nickname my... employees gave me."

"Employees?" Cassius was confused.

Amora sat back in her chair, crossing her legs as she focused her gaze on him.

"Well, a single mother of two needs a hobby, darling. It was either this or a casino and I rather detest all those blinking lights and buzzing machines."

Cassius shook his head.

Still the same old Amora.

Restless and full of ambition.

"And what kind of *hobby* do you have in which you have employed sirens like Enchantress?"

"How do you know Caroline?" Amora's voice was no longer sweet and flirtatious. It was full of seriousness.

Cassius slid his hands in his pockets as he walked closer to her, leaning against her desk.

Down to business, finally.

"Enchantress?" he asked.

Amora nodded. "Yes, Enchantress is her handle, but I prefer to address my employees by their given names.

It feels more... personal."

"I've seen her on AltGothGirls.com."

Amora laughed, the sound saccharine. She grabbed a coffee cup, taking a long pull before answering him. When her tongue licked crimson liquid from her lips, Cassius's throat constricted, his stomach turning with hunger.

"Oh dear Cassius, have you fallen that far?" she teased as she rose from her chair, closing the space between them.

"I have not fallen at all, Amora. That is the point." The words fell out of his mouth without warning. The lines of past and present were starting to blur.

"You always did have a type, I suppose." She offered him the cup.

Cassius stared at it, the smell of fresh blood like sweet honey.

His cock twitched in his leather pants and his stomach turned. He needed to eat, soon.

"And what type is that?" Cassius looked at the beautiful woman in front of him, offering him exactly what he needed at the moment, and he fought the compulsion to take her offer.

"Tall, dark, and bitter. Like black coffee. Incapable of giving you everything you deserve."

Her free hand slid around his waist, playing with the loops of his pants.

He'd always found Amora attractive, found her warm and comforting even in some of his darkest days.

But she was as much a predator as Eden. They only wore different crowns.

Cassius steadied his gaze as he pushed the cup of blood away.

"I'm on a diet. I do not feed on the living, anymore."

Amora shrugged as she drained the last of the

blood, and Cassius stifled a groan. She set it down on the ledge of the desk.

"Always so noble," she purred. "Here we are centuries later, free of our bindings, and still you deny your instincts. You haven't changed at all."

She settled her hand over the small of his back, and he did not move. He couldn't.

It was as if he was paralyzed, but he knew no vampire other than Eden possessed such an ability.

"We are never free, petite étoile."

Amora slid her hand up his back as she pulled him closer. In her eyes, he could see yesterday, visible and bright.

The glittering chandeliers.

The fountains of blood.

Amora's reflection in the mirrors as they danced across the floor like ghosts in a haunted ballroom.

His reflection in the mirrors of her bedchambers as they lay entangled together in her sheets.

"Freedom is an illusion, Cassius. The rabbit thinks it is free of the fox, but as fast as it is, it will never outrun its predator."

Every bone in Cassius's body told him to run. Run far away from Amora and her pretty, pink claws. But he also knew in the depths of his soul that Amora was the fastest way to uncover what he'd come to Ohio to do. Find his friend. If her reach truly was as far as she advertised, then she'd know exactly where his friend would be, given Enchantress was her *employee*. Unless of course, Enchantress—Caroline—had gone off script, which could be a possibility.

"Is that so?" he purred, pushing away his instincts and his own qualms. He knew the way to Amora's heart was rather like picking up a motorcycle after nearly thirty-some years, and he also knew he could catch more flies with honey than with vinegar. This game of cat and mouse was familiar. Eden detested games, but Amora... Amora loved the *chase.*

Amora smiled wickedly at him as she nodded, leaning up on her tiptoes to meet Cassius's lips. It was a strange feeling, like time had somewhere gotten away from him while at the same time he'd fallen back to yesterday, to Paris in the 1800's. Her body pressed against his did nothing to quell the bloodlust that had formed in his being, his hunger recognizing a means to an end despite his best efforts. Amora tasted of sour blood and cherries.

Like a cherry danish.

Images pushed forth Cassius could not fight, nor did he want to. He knew the answer lay on the other side of Amora's sweet kiss, but he wished in that moment, that she was someone else. That the lips that parted for him, inviting his tongue into her mouth, belonged to a wicked slayer, a woman whose kiss he was certain would taste like heaven itself, and not of sour blood and mistakes.

Amora let out a soft moan against his lips, and he knew he had her.

"You are hungry," she whispered, biting her bottom lip.

Cassius sighed, regrettably acknowledging the truth.

"Starving, actually," he whispered.

Amora's eyes glowed with excitement.

"Perhaps I have just the thing to sate your hunger, *Mon étoile,*" she cooed as she slid her hand into his.

CHAPTER SEVENTEEN

AVA COULD NOT fathom how much time had passed. Her mind spiraled, trying to figure out where she'd gone wrong, where things had changed, and she could not pinpoint it. Though Dallas had left her feeling guilty on plenty occasions, he'd never left her feeling so empty, so unfulfilled before.

Ava buttoned her jeans, catching her disheveled reflection in the sleek silver of Dallas's refrigerator door, and she had to turn to look away.

The woman staring back at her was not one she recognized.

She kicked the broken glass on the floor aside with the heel of her boot as she stuffed down the pain, the shame, and the guilt, locking it all in a coffin at the bottom of her soul with the rest of her demons.

Dallas sat on his couch, shirtless. He leaned his large, muscular arms over his knees, tapping away on his phone. Dressed in a pair of fresh jeans, she could see his hair was wet from a recent shower. The room was soft, boasting the same white and gray color scheme, accentuated by dark indigos, bright ochres and pale blue accents. It looked like something out of a magazine.

"You going to tell me what exactly you and my brother are up to, or am I wasting my fucking time?" she bit as she leaned against the wall, keeping her distance.

A part of her ached for him. To throw herself around him and apologize. To placate this man who held her to such a higher standard, who tried irrefutably to break her defiance.

But the larger part of her wanted to walk away from it all. From him, from the graves she needlessly dug to keep her secrets buried. She was plain and simply, tired.

Dallas ran his hand over his face, shaking his head before turning to look at her and setting the phone down on the coffee table.

In his bright blue eyes, all she could see was pain.

But Ava would not run into the arms of a hurricane so soon after destruction.

She knew better.

"Your brother seems to think the Djinn and the vamps are working together." He sighed, wringing his hands together. In the light of the living room, sitting on the pale gray couch, he looked every bit his age. But he did not look like he belonged anywhere but on the back of a motorcycle, chasing sunsets and sunrises.

"It's never a simple thing, is it?" she asked.

Dallas spoke softly. "No, I guess not."

Ava fixed her gaze on the attractive, freshly-showered Dallas, the scent of his Old Spice bodywash thick in the air. "And you haven't taken them out yet? You two must be loosing your magic."

Dallas shifted his stance, looking at her with sad eyes.

"You can sit down, you know." He spoke evenly.

"I'm good where I'm at, thanks," she sternly replied.

Dallas pursed his lips as he nodded.

"Ava, I'm..."

Just as he opened his mouth to speak, the front door opened to reveal a grinning Malcolm, who strolled in and plopped himself down on the couch across from Dallas, kicking his feet up on the coffee table.

"What the fuck has you so happy?" Ava bit as she turned to look for someone else.

"Where's Cassius?" she asked, feeling strangely panicked.

Malcolm looked happy as a clam as he clasped his hands in his lap. "Catching us some big fish." Malcolm smiled. "You know, Dad always taught me you catch bigger fish with bigger bait."

Ava felt her blood chill.

If he laid one finger on him, I will kill him myself.

That monster is mine to slay.

"So you went to the Clam?" Dallas spoke.

Ava watched as his demeanor shifted, like nothing had happened.

Nothing had happened. Nothing out of the ordinary anyway. It wouldn't be the first time they'd gotten into a heated argument that ended up in sex.

So why did his dismissal, his change of character make her feel so small, so insignificant?

They'd been quiet about their affair for the last two years, but in all honesty, they'd been keeping secrets since he and Malcolm had discovered she'd been bitten. Everything was the same as it always was, except... it wasn't. Something had changed. Between them, in herself.

"I got a good look at the place, and it's crawling with

Djinn."

"No vamps?" Ava asked, shifting her focus to her brother.

Mal nodded. "Well, there was one vamp." He snickered.

"Real pretty thing, too." He whistled before continuing. "My money says she's the ring leader. I have to say, your little vampire puppy seems to have some game. She ate him like he was fucking filet mignon."

Ava's lips strained into a straight line.

Why did her brother's words make her feel so cold?

"And you just left him there?" Dallas asked, his voice rising.

Malcolm smiled. "Of course. Your bike's equipped with a tracker."

Dallas's eyebrows furrowed and Ava looked between them, sensing the next hurricane was coming.

"You let the fucking bloodsucker touch my baby?" he grit out through his teeth.

"Honestly, I was surprised he knew how to drive the thing. Thought I was going to have to get all up close and personal."

"Wait... so... Cassius knows how to drive a motorcycle?" Ava asked, dumbfounded.

"That's your takeaway?" Dallas bit at her.

Ava shrugged. "What can I say? I have a thing for leather pants and bikes," she nipped back at him, if only to wound him. The desire, the instinct to rub salt in Dallas's wounds was prevalent and she was feeling quite on edge. She hadn't had enough coffee for all this bullshit.

Malcolm rolled his eyes, knowing she wasn't serious.

At least, as far as he knew she wasn't serious.

Though she had to admit, she did like riding on the

back of Dallas's motorcycle and she could not deny Cassius looked good in leather pants, despite being an annoying bloodsucking pain in her ass.

A startling thought pushed through her shock. "Wait... if we didn't show up... if you didn't have Cas... who would have been the bait?" she asked, looking between them.

Dallas's jaw tightened and she could tell he was grinding his teeth.

"D, of course." Mal shrugged. "He's always the bait when it comes to the pretty monsters."

Something about her brother's words made Ava hot all over. She never pretended to be unaware of the normal day to day operations the Goon Squad partook in, and she and Dallas had never discussed jobs outside of the ones they worked together.

But the reality of what went on while he was away... from her... both pissed her off and made her feel even worse.

Knowing Dallas was out there sidling up to vampires, trapping them with his roguish good looks, his dark, commanding voice, and his sex appeal.

It wasn't any different than what she did, so why did the realization of such things make her want to drive a stake through every vampire he'd cornered, when she knew damn well he'd ended their life himself?

Ava felt flush, and she knew she needed to get out of the claustrophobic cottage. She needed air, for she felt like she couldn't breathe.

"Where are you going?" Dallas asked as she turned heel and headed for the door.

"Out," was all she said as she ran down the front steps of the porch, racing to the car. She turned on the ignition, peeling out of Dallas's driveway with lightning speed, in search of sanity once more.

She pulled her phone from the dashboard where it lay, glowing with notifications.

Meet me at The Sweet Shoppe. We need to talk.

Ava stared at the text from *Cas*. She found herself wondering what he'd gotten up to left to his own devices, with the *pretty blonde* Malcolm had described.

She also knew, it could be a trap. If he'd fed recently...

But as she thought such things, a part of her heart ached.

Surely, he wouldn't do such a thing... would he?

Guilt befell her at the thought of a casualty that one of them could have prevented had they kept him closer. Malcolm had given him too much of a leash.

She decided it was best to see for herself, and besides, they were supposed to be working together, right?

At least, that was how she rationalized things.

Curiosity bested her and she did not desire to turn around and head back to *base* any time soon.

She needed to be as far away from Jake Dallas and his wildfire heart as possible.

CHAPTER EIGHTEEN

CASSIUS LEANED AGAINST Dallas's motorcycle, the wind blowing his soft, golden hair into his eyes. He felt guilty for what he'd done, leading Amora on as he had, taking advantage of their history.

Was she right?

Was he just too stubborn?

Perhaps.

Amora had lost Marcellus, just as Eden had, and though she'd paid her dues to the high covens, taken other consorts... fate had severed those bonds as well.

Like himself, she was alone.

Her words rattled around in his brain. He'd made so many mistakes in his long, immortal life. Trusting Eden, covering for Marcellus. Covering for Eden when he'd discovered the truth about her affair with Marcellus.

He'd used Amora to get back at her, knowing full well the Medici queen favored him.

And he'd used her again, only this time a man's life was at stake.

The memory of earlier that morning, as Amora clung

to his back on his borrowed transportation, he knew what he was doing. He'd rationalized it was for the good of everyone, driving off to the Marquis with Amora for an early lunch. As it would appear, her *business* was the Marquis, but of course he should have known that. The ornate signage boasted a sort of Moulin Rouge aesthetic, a callback to their younger days in Paris.

Amora tugged his hand through the Marquis, the masquerade bar.

"When we open, I plan to have the doorway like one of those sensory deprivation tunnels. Imagine walking through the darkness, into a room full of illusion, only to find such grandeur on the other side," she said wistfully as they entered a room full of mirrors.

"The door is—"

"A mirror. Yes. Of course, those invited to the opening will know how to reach the ballroom, but I suspect it could be rather fun for the mortals in question. Apparently escape rooms are all the rage these days." She giggled, opening the door.

She was right. It was positively wondrous, with its vaulted ceilings and cavernous appearance. Incandescent amber lighting illuminated the room by baroque-esque sconces adorned on the mahogany walls. In the low light of the place, it looked like something from another time. The sleek mahogany bar and its black marble finishings, the crystal chandeliers dripping with golden finishings. The tufted red leather booths and chairs. When they came to the center, Cassius laid his eyes on the large terrarium.

"What is this?" he asked as he took in the sight of the oversized tank. He could see through it; it looked like a living terrarium, with hedges set up like a labyrinth.

"That is my main attraction. The labyrinth."

"What is it for?" Cassius asked, his throat dry.

"My patrons can buy a spot in the labyrinth. Their spots—mortals, of course—will be placed in the labyrinth, and my employees as well as very generous benefactors with... generous donations... will have the chance to exert their long-lost instincts. To hunt."

Cassius's blood chilled.

"And how much does a spot cost?" he asked.

"For you, I would make an exception. That is, if you had a mortal to place."

She cooed as she pulled him through the room, toward another door, unlocking it.

"Where are you taking me?" he asked, starting to feel as if he'd walked into a trap. She'd promised him blood, after all.

"My stock room. I don't keep my reserves in the Clam. Too risky."

"Reserves?" he asked.

"This isn't my first rodeo, Cassius. It is only my current one," she said as he followed her down the dark hallway. The basement smelled of death.

Bloody, rotting death.

His eyes befell the doors set in the walls, similar to cells or stables. They all held small slivers of windows.

"What are the pens for?" he murmured, strolling up to one. Though he had a feeling he knew the answer.

"For the spots, of course. Livestock needs to be kept and primed before the big event, after all."

"Primed how?" His voice dropped as he set his hand on one of the doors, peeking in through the window.

What he saw chilled his blood, made his slow, dying heart still.

Bryan was huddled in the corner. Though the room didn't look entirely in disarray, it looked just as ominous, boasting a bed and a small latrine. It reminded him of the prisons in the Bastille, only with better furnishings.

And just as Amora spoke, his eyes opened, and he stared at Cassius in shock. Cassius quietly, as indiscriminately as possible, held his finger to his lips. How he wished he could implore the man with his loyalty, tell him he would indeed find a way to bust him out. Though he could not risk doing so with Amora watching, that he knew. He would simply have to convene with the Crowleys and Dallas, and they would have to make a plan.

Perhaps he could even use one of them as a spot...

"The Djinn of course. Give them a taste of heaven and then set them loose in the labyrinth. All men need something to chase too, you know."

The sound of a purring Impala startled him from his thoughts. The blood bag Amora had given him was cold, much like that of the one he'd stolen from the Willowcrest Morgue. While Amora preferred live kills, she'd always been one to keep reserves, in times of scarcity. It appeared she hadn't changed, either.

He straightened his stance, the stolen pulse in his veins awakening with life once more. He felt a mixture of guilt and satisfaction. His thirst would be abated, for now.

Ava opened the car door, looking as breathtaking as ever in her band tee, her dark wash jeans, and jacket, and he felt as if he could finally breathe.

No matter what ghosts chased him, they all disappeared when he looked at her.

The woman he loved, who he'd lain claim to.

The woman who wanted to kill him six out of seven days of the week.

You have a type. Amora had said. Perhaps she was right on that account as well. After all, she wouldn't be the first woman he'd fallen for with a penchant for blood.

Ava sauntered over to him, scowling. She stood in front of him, but kept her distance. He did not miss that she did not look at him immediately, but instead her gaze fixated on the motorcycle he was leaning against.

Dallas's motorcycle.

"My brother said so, but I gotta say I had a hard time picturing it." She spoke plainly.

Cassius smiled. "And how did you picture it?"

"I mean, you're not exactly, like, the biker type. You're missing the muscles, not to mention the vest with some stupid ass graphic stitched on the back." She crossed her arms.

"I have many talents, my sweet Avarice, I can assure you."

"Mhmm. Better to lure your victims with. If they're into that sort of thing, I guess."

Cassius noted the annoyance in her voice.

"Are you hungry?" he asked. He knew if she did not have nearly a thousand calories of sugar or coffee before noon, she could get quite an attitude, though she would deny such things if he said them out loud.

Before she could even speak, her stomach answered him with a rumble.

"I'm fine," she bit. "You wanted to talk."

"Will coffee suffice, then?" He slid his arm out, his hand bracing against the painted seat.

Ava shifted her stance, bouncing her leg.

"Why don't you just tell me what you want, Cas?" she bit.

Cassius furrowed his eyebrows. Ava was always sarcastic and there was always a sort of venom in her voice when she talked to him, but something about her tone, about her body language, the way she was looking at Dallas's motorcycle...

Panic flooded him, mingling with a sort of possessiveness Cassius had never felt before. It made him hot, worried, and it stirred his bloodlust in an entirely new way.

The desire to reach out across the canyon between them and pull her into his arms was overwhelming. All he wanted was to comfort her, but he couldn't.

She would surely push him away, threaten to stake him, or worse... maybe she would follow through on her threat in the obvious state of upset she was in.

Ava was temperamental on most days, let alone bad ones.

He wanted to persist, wanted to push further and ask her what had happened.

If Dallas hurt her somehow... The thought caused his bloodlust to fill him with a deep, burning desire to *kill.* The thought of sinking his fangs into Dallas's neck, snapping it until he heard the definitive crack, caused his cock to harden and his mouth to go dry. Mixed with his recent meal, the need to protect what was *his* was a primal desire he'd never felt before.

But Ava was not his.

Not really.

Her blood belonged to him, but he knew it was only a matter of time before the hourglass would run out. She could never be his as he wanted her to be. His time with her was limited, and so he pushed the dangerous thoughts away, conceding to her demands once more.

He would always give her exactly what she wanted, whatever that may be, until the last grain of sand dropped from the hourglass.

"Bryan is alive," he said solidly. He pushed away from the motorcycle, taking one stop closer to her. "We do not have to stand out here in the cold. Come, let us go inside," he tried again, his voice gentle, as if he was talking to a frightened animal.

Ava glanced up at him, her amber eyes full of questions. Her stomach rumbled again.

"Fine. Pain in my ass." She rolled her eyes as she turned away from him, heading for the door.

Cassius smiled, but she could not see it.

"But you're buying this round!" she shouted as she opened the door.

Cassius slid his hands in his pockets.

"As you wish, my sweet Avarice."

***

Ava picked at her cherry danish, and Cassius felt a sting of guilt. The memory of Amora's lips on his, the thoughts that filled his brain, made him feel like a monster.

Ava tore a piece of flaky dough off, sighing in defeat.

"Where is he?" she asked quietly.

"He is in the Marquis. You were right," Cassius answered her softly.

"And you just left him there? Some friend you are."

"He is under lock and key. I was not able to seize him myself at the moment. I was... indisposed."

Ava smirked, raising an eyebrow.

"With Vampire Barbie?" she bit, her tongue laced with familiar venom.

"I do not know what Malcolm told you but..."

"I don't care. All I care about is getting Bryan out safely." She took a long drink of her coffee.

Cassius watched her, feeling his stomach turn with hunger. The blood bag he'd swiped from the blood bank on the way to the Sweet Shoppe it seemed was not enough.

"Her name is Amora. She is... an old... friend." He

was careful with his words.

"I don't suppose this *friend* of yours would be amenable to just like, letting Bryan go?" she asked, twisting her lips.

Cassius shook his head. "I am afraid not. She has plans to use him as..."

What could he say?

Bait?

Vamp chow?

Entertainment?

"She owns the Marquis. There is a labyrinth inside which mortals will be... donated... as entertainment. Creatures like myself, will be able to pay a hefty price to chase them, to hunt... and the event will be visible to all the patrons of the masquerade as a show of sorts."

He watched as she sank her teeth into the red, cherry filled pit of her danish, some of it smearing along her fair skin.

Images of blood running down her chin pushed through his psyche, causing his cock to twitch. He crossed his legs, tightening them as he cleared his throat.

How was it something so simple caused him such detriment?

It was just a pastry for god's sake.

Though Cassius felt somewhat perverse that he often took enjoyment in watching Ava eat such things, if only because he knew inevitably she would end up with red jelly all over her perfect, luscious lips.

Her lips look beautiful stained so red.

Ava looked up at him as she swallowed the confectionary delicacy. Her gaze was full of fire.

"So what you're telling me is he's alive until he hits that labyrinth. How the hell do we get him out? Crash the place or..."

"That is the part I will need your help with. Well, I will need Malcolm and Dallas's help, too."

Cassius watched as Ava stiffened completely.

"We don't need them," she said too quickly.

Cassius did not miss her words. They hit him like a silver bullet.

"I thought you said there was no *we*, Ava," he said, his voice softened.

"Well, I can do this myself. I just thought *maybe* you'd want to..."

"Amora said she would make an exception for me. I could easily be a part of the games. It would be an inside job. Malcolm or Dallas could be the red herring, and we could work together, to rescue Bryan and escape the labyrinth. Though someone will need to be responsible for causing a distraction upstairs, I—" He stilled, realizing he was rambling too much, and he needed to tread lightly. Especially given the fact he'd already starting planning and arranging the rescue mission.

Ava huffed in annoyance.

"What is it Ava?" He cocked his head to the side, watching her expression fall.

"You know what, it doesn't matter. I don't need them, and I certainly don't need you," she said as she rose, grabbing her coffee.

"Ava..." His heart fell, seeing her in such turmoil. Something was wrong. He knew it in his bones. It wasn't as if they worked a lot of cases together, but enough that he knew she should have leapt at the chance to tell him all the faults with his plan and fabricate one herself. The way her mind worked always seemed to fascinate him.

"The Masquerade is a monster's ball. The patrons will be vampires likely of high stature. The Djinn will also be there, preying on the mortals. Enchantress isn't the only Djinn cultivating a population for this event," he said, just as she turned her back on him.

She stopped in her tracks, turning to face him once more. Ava looked back and forth, but she did not return to her seat.

Cassius rose, grabbing their napkins and garbage. He threw away the trash before moving over to her side. Of course, he left space between them, as he always had.

But every fiber of his being wanted to close that space, sidle up next to her and wrap his arm around her waist. To hold her, soothe her. Quell her fears and worries.

His throat felt dry as he looked at her, and he sucked in a deep breath.

Knowing what he was going to say next, he was not sure how she would react. She may be tempted to stake him as it was, and so he kept them both in public, in eyesight of the Sweet Shoppe cashier.

Ava's face paled.

"And *creatures* such as yourself get to hunt down victims like Bryan? Like a safari? How do I know I can trust you won't fuck us all over and devour the spots yourself?"

He did not miss the bite in her tone as she settled on the word trust.

"Because, Ava, I am not your enemy. Bryan is my friend, and I do not have many of those. I am a man of my word, and I promise you I will do everything in my power to protect all of you." He paused, gazing at her upon that one word, *you*. It carried so much weight, as he wished he could make her understand. He would never hurt her, or anyone she cared about. It was not within his nature, bond or no bond. She would always be safe with him. But his next words would likely sound suspicious, and so he sighed, knowing what he was about to say would potentially land him a stake in his chest, or worse, a punch to the gut.

"I bought a spot. To ensure us a way into the event."

"You what?" Her voice escalated, enough to garner the attention from a nearby janitor.

"We will have an easier chance this way."

Cassius motioned for her to follow him outside and she did, waiting for him to continue.

"Who are you planning on putting in the big monster royale, Cas?" she asked, pinching the bridge of her nose, squinting her eyes.

"I would prefer your brother. I have full confidence he would be able to hold his own against a room full of monsters and likewise victims."

Ava scoffed as she turned around, angrily opening the door.

Cassius followed her into the light of day like a moth to a flame.

"I bet I could take them," she bit.

Cassius smirked behind her. Of course she would feel emboldened by his denouncement.

She hurried down the steps toward her car, toward his current ride. He threw his leg over the seat, not missing her gaze as it flashed to his legs as he did so. The metal between his legs was a most welcome distraction from his strained cock.

Ava scoffed, crossing her arms as he started the motorcycle.

"Then who would distract them?" he purred.

Ava pursed her lips. "Is that all I'm good for? Vamp bait? Distractions? Just another pretty thing to turn heads?" Her tone was highly agitated.

"There are darknesses in life and there are lights,

my sweet Avarice, and you... you are one of the lights. The light of all lights," he said, his heart in his throat. "Besides, I thought you would relish in getting a chance to dress up. It is a masquerade, after all."

"Did you seriously just fucking quote Dracula to me?"

Cassius smiled slyly. "Smart as a whip, too."

Ava rolled her eyes. "Whatever. Where the hell am I supposed to get a costume this last minute, *Dracula*?"

Cassius smirked. "You are resourceful. You'll figure something out."

"Mhmm."

Cassius kicked the stand up.

"Where are you off to now?" she asked, her gaze roving over his arms, his fingers, as he gripped the handlebars. The stolen pulse in his veins *throbbed* with excitement.

Cassius's lips pulled back just enough to show a hint of fang, and her pulse raced within him. Ava could deny many things, but she could not deny her body's natural reaction to him. She could not deny the bond.

"Preparations must be made," he said smoothly.

Ava scoffed.

"I will keep you informed. In the meantime, speak with your brother and tell the lumbering oaf I will return his motorcycle in one piece. I know he must be beside himself without it."

"You trying to tell me what to do, Cas?" She smirked at him, her eyes lighting up with interest.

There is the light I know.

"I would not dare do such a thing," he purred.

Ava waved him off.

"Thanks for the poison," she said as she opened her car door, but she did not get in immediately.

Cas nodded to her before taking off toward the

setting sun.

CHAPTER NINETEEN

AVA SLAMMED DOWN her whiskey, pushing it toward the portly bartender.

"Hit me."

The Drowned Clam was thick with patrons. Cassius's information, as helpful as it was, both angered her and made her more than appreciative. Whether she wanted to admit it or not, a part of her trusted him, and she knew that was dangerous.

As it turned out, the Djinn-filled bar actually served decent drinks, but they were not on a social call. Vinny had been more than helpful in providing them with the blueprints to the Marquis, despite being on a case himself. Malcolm sipped his own whiskey, raising an eyebrow.

"You okay, Simba? You seem a little... on edge."

"I live on the edge, Mal."

Mal shook his head as the sounds of some pop artist droned on about wanting attention and not anyone's heart.

Her gaze flickered across the room to Dallas, who was currently talking to a woman. A Djinn. She was tall, with the same dark features as Enchantress. Despite her handy vampire radar Cassius had cursed her with, she'd learned vampires were easy to identify if one knew what to look for. Their skin carried a pale glow, their features practically model-esque, and a chill breeze often accompanied them. But in the presence of the Djinn, she felt nothing, which concerned her. The leggy Djinn with its arms around Dallas's neck looked young, and Ava wondered how old she truly was.

Dallas leaned in, whispering something in her ear, and she knew exactly what he was doing, what he was planning to do.

Amora had taken Cassius to the Marquis.

Enchantress had taken Bryan.

The idea that Dallas would be taken, sequestered alone with the creature made her blood boil.

He'd never lay with a monster.

But a part of her thought she'd never do so either, and at this point in her life, she'd been with at least one. The thoughts of a possessed Sam Kingsley threatened to push forth and Ava drank some more.

She'd done the same thing on countless occasions.

If you can get close to them, you can kill them.

The fact Dallas hadn't protested to being a honeypot, or even blinked an eye at the suggestion, left Ava more than bothered. It was as if he truly did not care who his mark was, as long as the outcome ended favorably.

Ava needed to stake something, and at this point she did not care if it was a creature of the night or a thirty-five year old mortal who knew how to get underneath her skin.

"I swear it's like shooting fish in a barrel sometimes." Mal shook his head as he nodded at Dallas.

"You think creatures that old would have better taste," Ava bit.

"You two have been at each other's throats all evening. What happened? Dallas piss in your cornflakes?" he teased her.

"Nope," she said as the bartender gave her another drink.

Mal sighed as he looked around the room.

Ava's wrist suddenly flared with heat, goosebumps rising on her skin. She looked up to see Cassius, on the arm of a rather tall blonde who was dressed in a tight, pale pink bodycon.

She looked like a Playboy Bunny, or some erotic version of Elle Woods.

"He always gets shitty around her anniversary." Mal shrugged. "Don't take it personal if he's being a dick. It's normal for him this time of year."

"Anniversary?" Ava asked, never tearing her gaze off the leggy blonde sliding her hand in Cassius's. His smile was soft as he looked down at her, and she felt a twist in her stomach.

Her fingers ached to stake something.

To strike a match and watch a bitch burn.

It'd been too long since she'd felt the rush of death, since she'd watched a monster turn to ash.

She watched as Dallas slid his arm around his mark, pulling her aside with no remorse. He didn't even steal a glance at her, despite Ava's fiery gaze burning a hole into his back.

"Yeah. The anniversary of his wife's death. Always messes him up."

Ava's glass slid out of her hand and onto the floor, her heated blood going cold.

"What?"

"I thought you knew. You two have always been

close, and I assumed when you were bitten he told you what happened."

"Nope. Guess we're not that close," she said, recovering quickly. The bartender grumbled as Ava slid some bills on the counter. She stepped over the glass, feeling only a little hazy. It wasn't enough, but she needed more than alcohol to settle her demons.

Jake Dallas was married.

Suddenly, the little blue cottage with the charming swing and magazine-worthy interiors made sense. Her heart caught in her throat as the memory rose from its ashes of their argument, of their heated moment, threatening to make her lose the whiskey she'd drank.

"You take the left. I'll take the right," Mal said as he slid his own bills on the counter.

Ava nodded, but his words didn't stick. She made her way through the crowd.

"Ava?" Cassius's voice stopped her dead in her tracks.

She turned, her vision jarring for a moment. The light above him cast an angelic glow on his the planes of his face, taking her back to the night he'd saved her.

The night he bit her.

He'd come from the shadows, all glowing eyes and sex appeal, and she thought he'd been an angel then.

How very wrong she was.

"Cas..."

"I did not expect to see you here... are you... alone?" he asked as he guided her toward a corner booth, away from Dallas and his target. She huffed in annoyance, wanting nothing more than to run away from Cassius, toward the shadows where she knew salvation lay in the form of her stake.

She knew this playbook by heart.

Lure the monster, get close.

Stake, burn.

Though according to Hunter and his extensive research, Djinn needed a silver blade and not a stake. Thankfully, she kept a set of etched silver knives in her trunk, not to mention her brother and Dallas kept a steady supply in the Chevelle as well.

It wasn't like Dallas needed her help, but if she didn't quiet the need to kill something soon, she was sure she'd explode.

"No. I'm not," She bit.

Cassius leaned closer, looking at her with concern.

"Perhaps we should convene elsewhere, discuss our... plans... for tomorrow. Together."

Ava huffed in annoyance as Dallas rounded the corner with Malcolm behind him, sans Djinn.

Damn it!

Something in the way he spoke, the way he looked at her, made her blood rush, made the hair on the back of her neck stand. He looked at her the way she looked at whiskey.

As if just one hit could cure all of life's problems.

Ava turned to see Dallas's bright blue eyes staring at her from across the room. She watched the two hunters make their way through the crowd of humans, vampires, and Djinn.

"Barbie going to let you off your leash?" She could hear the fury, the frustration in her voice.

"You are not the only one with allies, Ava."

She did not miss the way his gaze flashed to her lips, or the way his tongue licked his lips, inciting deep desires Ava did not wish to acknowledge.

Not here, not now.

The crowd roared as some country song came over the airways, the singer droning on about saving a woman if she falls made Ava feel even more keyed up.

"I do not have, nor do I need, *allies.* All I need is my fucking stake and nothing else. Ever," she said.

Cassius crossed his arms, regarding her with concern once more.

"Blood will not satisfy you forever, Ava."

"Forgive me if I don't take the word of a fucking vampire when it comes to blood and death."

Dallas and Malcolm met them in the center of the floor.

"We need to talk," Cassius said, his glowing green emeralds fixated on her.

On *only* her.

Dallas grumbled, "Not here."

Cassius nodded in the opposite direction. "I have just the place."

***

The scent of grease and sugar was nauseating to Ava. Perhaps the whiskey she'd consumed was not helping either.

At this hour, the Waffle House was empty. Save for a drunk man in the corner snoring away and a couple of teenagers high off their asses giggling like children.

"The Marquis Masquerade's grand opening will start at nine. Bryan and the other spots will likely be loaded into the labyrinth around ten. Amora plans on getting everyone loosened up first, give their instincts a chance to come out."

Malcolm nodded. "So how does this work? We just show up together or..."

"I will need to present you to Amora myself. Preferably, *before* the event so you may be... primed."

"Like fucking cattle," Dallas bit as he leaned back in the booth, glaring at him.

"The spots will be primed by the Djinn. From what I

have gathered, that means that they will likely be looking into your head for what you desire most. They need a carrot to dangle so you will run, chasing a wish while we chase blood."

Ava crossed her legs underneath the table, her foot bouncing with anxiety.

"Fan-fucking-tastic," Mal bit.

Ava didn't like any of this, but she knew it was a means to save her friend. Still, it felt as if Cassius was leading them all into a trap.

He'd told her to trust him, but could she?

Could they?

Being in the same space with the hunters and the vampire who bit her was starting to make her feel more than queasy.

It was as if her worlds were colliding and she'd only just realized they were separated.

Her heart raced as she shifted away from Cassius. She was practically on the edge of the booth as was.

"Would you prefer to be the bait, Dallas? You looked quite comfortable earlier, or is that just with women you want to sleep with?"

Ava felt her blood turn to ice. She never wanted to vacate a Waffle House so bad in all her life.

She fought to control her facial expression. Cassius had no clue about her and Dallas, nor did her brother.

He was only making an observation. He must've seen Dallas and the Djinn earlier at the Clam, and put two and two together.

If looks could kill, Dallas would have murdered Cassius on the spot.

"I don't fuck monsters. I have morals."

"So you say, but I have seen no evidence of such things," Cassius said smoothly.

"I need you to get Bryan out and that's all that

matters," Ava said, cutting through the thick tension that had somehow formed.

"Of course, Ava," Mal softly reassured her. "We'll get him out. And take out some fucking ticks and Djinn while we're at it," he said, his tone cocky as hell. Where her brother got his confidence, she was not sure, but at the moment she wished she had some.

"And what about Mal? How can I trust you'll get *him* out?" Dallas bit, grinding his teeth. Ava could see the tension in his jaw, how his fist shook.

Cassius sat straight, folding his hands on the table. He glanced at Ava before speaking.

"Because I am a man of my word. I do not make promises I can not keep. I know you do not trust me. I know you very well may try to kill me yourself, though you will find I am not as easy a target as the women you lure, but I digress. I will do everything in my power to protect you." Cassius looked at Ava for a moment before fixing his sight on Malcolm and Dallas.

"Because I am not your enemy. I am your ally, and I always have been."

Ava could stand no more as she got up, heading for the door.

"Ava..." Cas's voice was smooth like silk and she hated how it nearly stopped her in her tracks.

After this job, she vowed to put as much space as possible between her and the vampire who was starting to affect her more than she wanted to admit.

Her heart was in her throat as his words ricocheted through her.

How was it his words carved such a deep cut?

Memories of blood and fire surfaced, begging to pull her under.

Burning pain in her neck radiated throughout her blood, and she felt powerless as the Incubus toxin overtook her.

Dallas had been right there, fighting the monster who'd hurt her. Trying to protect her. But he'd failed.

And in that moment, it dawned on her. She hadn't called for him.

She'd called for someone else.

Her memory was hazy, and she was told it was because of the fever from the toxin, mingling with antidote. She'd never remembered it clearly, but suddenly it all made sense.

Panic surged through her, and all she wanted to do was run. Run back to the Clam, find a vampire or Djinn to slay and quiet the uncertainty, the fear in her heart.

Cassius pushed a stray strand of hair behind her ear, his touch cold, yet gentle.

"Ava!" Dallas hollered as she burst through the door into the empty parking lot, feeling as if her lungs were going to explode. She welcomed the cool air, closing her eyes.

"Leave me the fuck alone, Jake!" she hollered back.

"Ava, look at me," he commanded.

Tears formed at the edges of her eyes and she could not stop them.

"No! You don't get to do this!" she said as she turned around, looking at him with anger.

So much anger.

Dallas strode toward her, closing the space between them. He grabbed her by the neck, pulling her closer.

"Dallas, stop... they'll see," she whispered.

"I don't fucking care, Ava. I don't. I'm done hiding. I... I love you, Ava I'm sorry."

She shook him off.

"Love me? You're not supposed to love me!" she yelled. Her blood raced, and the tears fell freely. "That was the deal, remember? No feelings."

"I didn't fucking want this either!" he growled.

Ava ran her hands over her face in frustration. She hated crying. Crying meant she was weak.

And Ava was not weak. She killed monsters for goodness sake. But yet, in the overbearing presence of this man she was broken.

"You say you have my back. That you want to protect me. But throwing yourself into a locked box with a bunch of fucking monsters is not protecting me."

"And you'd throw your brother in there?" Dallas bit. "Put your own flesh and blood at risk? Why don't you volunteer, huh? Or would your pussywhipped little vampire have a fucking problem with that?" he snapped.

"Leave Cas out of this. He has nothing to do with it."

"Are you really that fucking stupid? He has everything to do with it, Ava. You should have killed him a long time ago."

Ava felt a part of her snap, the last stitch coming undone as she got in Dallas's face, pointing her finger at him.

"It's no different than when you fucking dangle yourself in front of monsters, Dallas. Besides, I can trust my brother. I can't say the same about you anymore, can I?"

His eyes darkened at her words.

"Since when do you not trust me?" He gritted his teeth.

The cold wind was like ice on her skin.

"Were you ever going to tell me you were fucking married?" She felt herself falling apart at the seams.

Would he stitch her back together or cut the threads?

The moment she said the words, she wished she

hadn't.

Dallas looked as if he could barely breathe.

He looked... hurt.

"Ava... I..."

The memories broke into a million pieces as they spiraled to the ground.

Dallas yanking her by her long ponytail into his arms, his brutal kiss like a match to gasoline.

His anger when he'd found out she'd slept with Sam, the Incubus.

His jealousy when he'd cornered her in Howlers the night they'd crossed the line. After Sawyer hit on her.

The grip of his fingers entangled in her hair, his dick down her throat.

The pain in his eyes when he saw her scars, the deep cuts where she'd been attacked by vicious vampires, scars that healed because of Cassius's venom.

How Dallas turned her away in that moment, because she was damaged.

Broken.

The tears streamed down her face, one fractured memory at a time.

The sweat from their sparring matches covering her like armor.

The way he felt buried inside her, ravaging her with his lips, the rough sensation of his facial hair brushing her thighs.

The look in his eyes as she stared up at him, telling him she was his.

The way he made her forget everything, everyone. The way he smelled, like tobacco and whiskey and un kept promises.

And for the first time Ava understood.

She'd fallen for Dallas, too, and she was more

frightened of that than anything else. She could not afford to fall for anyone. Love was not in the cards for Ava Crowley. Love only meant death.

So she did the only thing she knew how to do.

She fought back.

"What? You wanted to what? To fuck me until you forgot about her? About your pretty little white picket fence house and your former life?"

"Don't fucking talk to me like that," he roared. "Don't fucking talk about *my wife* like that!" He was enraged.

"What are you going to do about it? Fuck me into being your little good girl? Hmm? You going to dominate me until I fucking give in to your stupid Big Daddy Dallas bullshit? I got news for you Jake, I don't belong to you. I never have. So save me the drama. You want to fuck around and find out with the monsters, as far as I'm concerned that's where you belong because that's what you fucking are. A monster."

"Ava Marie Crowley, don't you fucking walk away from me."

Ava did not think twice as she turned heel, walking toward the woods in search of the only thing that would truly quiet her pain.

Blood and ash.

CHAPTER TWENTY

AVA'S HANDS SHOOK as she removed the stake from the nameless vampire she'd lured at the Drowned Clam. Blood ran down her stake, the scent pungent in the air. She shook, as the tears begged to come forth again.

Why did it still hurt?

She dropped her stake as she took out the matches from her jacket pocket. The smell of sulfur was welcome amidst the scent of decay, and she watched the flame settle, wavering in the darkness of night.

Ava paused for only a moment before she threw the match on the dark-haired vampire who'd been far too easy to catch. All it took was a little eye batting, a show of Cassius's bite mark, and they flocked to her like flies to honey.

It should have bothered her, how easy it was for her to kill.

But it didn't.

She'd been fighting forever. Fighting for peace within her mind, her heart. Her soul. No, Ava Crowley knew there were only two options, kill or be killed.

And she did not relish the idea of submitting to death so easily.

She watched as the flames engulfed bones, watched as the skin decayed before her very eyes in the middle of the forest.

He'd thralled her, the vamp with no name, and for a moment she wanted nothing more than succumb to it. The heat in her body, the lust in her belly. The desire to be had, to be worshipped for her blood, and to be free of the pain that would not relent.

But it wasn't the nameless vampire she wanted to be thralled by.

His thrall didn't feel... blissful.

His thrall didn't quiet the noise, and she suspected no vampire's thrall would ever feel as perfect as Cassius's.

She'd only felt it once, that very night, but it was enough to poison her thoughts forevermore.

When the last of the vampire's ashes blew away in the wind, she headed back through the woods to the Drowned Clam. Her hunger was not abated, though she wished it was.

Perhaps a drink will help.

Her phone vibrated in her pocket. She removed it, glancing at the screen.

She had four missed calls, one of them her brother.

The other three belonged to Dallas.

She swiped up on Malcolm's number, stopping just outside the door. Her brother picked up instantly.

"What the fuck? Where are you? Dallas said you blew up and left."

She pursed her lips.

"I'm fine Mal. I just needed a drink."

"You're not with that fucking tick, are you?"

Ava bristled at his words and their insinuation.

"No. When I left, Cassius was with you..."

"I don't know what you're running from, Ava, but whatever it is, you won't find the answer at the bottom of a glass. I know that better than anyone," his voice softened.

"That's the pot calling the fucking kettle black. You're the last one who should be giving me a lecture on running, considering you never come home."

Mal sighed.

"The boys called. After you ran off and Cassius left..."

Ava's blood chilled.

"They may have found something. Something we haven't tried..."

Ava braced herself the wall, her heartbeat stilling.

After all these years of searching for a way to break the mark... could it be they finally found something that would work?

"What is it?" she asked, feeling anxious but needing to hear the answer all the same.

"You are never going to believe this, but... blood of a Djinn."

Ava glanced at the door of the Drowned Clam, feeling as if freedom was finally tangible and the answer was on the other side of the door, in a room full of vampires.

But how did one catch a Djinn?

Would it be as easy as luring a vampire?

"That's it? What do I have to do, drink it?"

"Cut open the bite mark and spread it. The Djinn are known for granting wishes, and that power comes from their blood."

"So if I open myself to their blood and wish really hard, it'll sever the bond?"

"Tito says it's a little more of a process than that,

but yeah. That's the gist of it. Djinn's blood is highly powerful. Even among other supernatural beings." He paused.

"Come back to base, Ava."

"Thanks for calling, Mal. I'll talk to you in the morning."

"Ava don't hang up on me... Ava!"

Ava clicked the phone as a soft voice pulled her from her thoughts, heading into the Drowned Clam once more.

***

The world was starting to look rather hazy after her third drink. She could still feel the blood on her hands, smell the scent of burning ash even though her hands were clean.

The Drowned Clam was much more vibrant at this hour, and she'd had no shortage of men willing to keep her cup full, and she was starting to feel numb. But numb was what she wanted.

She wanted to forget.

To be lost.

But she wasn't certain who was a mortal and who was a Djinn.

Smooth arms wrapped around her, pulling her close. She rolled her head back against the shoulder of a man whose name she could not remember. He felt... different. She knew it was dangerous. But danger was all she knew. There was no rest for the wicked, after all. She couldn't quite place it, but she would have bet he was a Djinn.

"Come with me," he purred in her ear.

Ava smiled wickedly as the alcohol hit its peak. He smelled good, felt good. She could feel her walls crumbling as his hand slid into hers, as his fingers brushed over her scar. She despised small talk, anyway.

"I thought you'd never ask," she said as she closed her eyes.

***

When Ava opened her eyes, she was in a dark room. Panic flooded her instantly as memories resurfaced of a nameless man, a sense of danger.

Of sharp teeth and rough hands, and regret.

Ava sat up in a bed, and she could see she was not alone. She was half-dressed, missing her pants. The scratchy sheets fell to her waist and panic set through her. Bodies littered throughout the room were in various states of slumber, and her wrist heated with fire where fangs had laid claim on her blood four years ago.

One look around told her she was in a basement, and wherever she was, it was not well kept. She moved slowly, planting her feet on the floor. She was still wearing her panties, and for that she was thankful.

The air smelled of blood and sulfur. She turned to take it all in, her gaze falling on the body beside where she had been laying. Blood stained the sheets, and the memories assaulted her.

The loud hiss, the bright blue glow of the eyes of Djinn.

Ava looked at herself in the broken mirror across from where she stood. She was covered in blood.

Dark, black, crimson blood.

Vampire blood.

Djinn blood.

She couldn't tell the difference.

She shakily held up her wrist. It did not look any different, save for the dried black blood stains on her skin.

Had she found the cure?

A sound pulled her from her thoughts, her concerns. A loud bang.

Ava quietly tiptoed over the bodies on the floor, most of them breathing. Her skin prickled like ice, her blood hot like liquid magma.

She opened the door to see a long, dark hallway, and the stone walls looked faded and old in the light. Voices sounded in the corridor and Ava hid against the wall.

It wasn't the first nest she'd been in, but it was the first time she'd woken up in a room full of monsters. The realization made Ava's stomach turn. She covered her hand with her mouth to keep from throwing up.

"The rest of the spots should be arriving soon," a man's voice said.

"We'll have to make sure the Djinn butter them up real good for the chase."

Ava stood still as a stone as realization overcame her.

Hadn't Cas mentioned the spots were to be delivered to the Marquis?

Was she...

The two creatures passed her and she held her breath. When she was certain they had disappeared, Ava set out down the corridor, looking for a way out. Door after door, it seemed the exit was nowhere to be found, and Ava wondered if perhaps she had been too careless. If she could not get out... Ava stamped her foot, cursing under her breath as she pinched the bridge of her nose.

Think, Ava.

Think!

She looked up toward the ceiling, praying for a sign,

an answer. Instead, she only saw a clear ceiling, or rather... a floor. Above her, all she could see was glass, a giant terrarium. Plants and walls lined the space and Ava'a breath caught in her throat.

The labyrinth.

That's where Mal and Cas will be...

A creak sounded and she stopped dead in her tracks. Her head was pounding, her heart racing.

"Wake up the others. We're going to need the room."

Ava could see the sliver of light from above, and she knew it was her ticket out. She nearly tripped over a broken piece of brick, the sound echoing in the space.

"You hear that, Romulus?" the voice called, sniffing the air.

"I smell a human."

Ava held her breath, picking up the brick and throwing it down the opposite end of the hall.

When the vampires took off in the other direction, Ava sprinted toward the light, hoping to reach her brother in time.

CHAPTER TWENTY-ONE

CASSIUS PADDED DOWN the steps of Amora's condominium toward the kitchen. Sunlight filtered through the windows. He ran his hand through his golden hair, feeling tired. He did not need sleep, but sometimes he wished he could truly rest.

He texted Malcolm. Today was the day. Everything needed to be in place and he would have to present Malcolm to Amora this afternoon, so that there would be enough time to get Malcolm in the building. Thanks to one of the other hunters, Mal had disclosed he had blueprints to the place, which would help in their escape.

All that was left after that was making sure Ava and Dallas were on the same page.

The plan was rather simple.

When the Marquis opened, Ava and Cas would cause a distraction and slip downstairs. Amora had agreed to let him in to the labyrinth, excited at the prospect of watching Cassius channel his instincts, and he knew a way in was not an issue. Rather, it would be making it through the labyrinth untouched and with his collective that would be challenging, but Cassius was not all that unfamiliar with the odds stacked against him. Fate as it seemed, always underestimated him.

Dallas would be on the bottom level, ready to receive them and guard their transports and Ava would be safe, with him, away from the labyrinth. Though he hadn't disclosed that Ava would be on the receiving end to her as of yet, knowing she would only fight him if he gave her too much time to process. She worked best under pressure, when she let her instincts shine.

Cassius started the coffee pot as Amora strode down the stairs in a fluffy pink robe.

"You're up early," she cooed.

He did not turn to look at her.

"I have always been an early riser."

She slid her hands around his waist and he felt the weight of the world. He could not deny that the touch was nice, but it didn't feel *right.*

The hands he wanted to touch him belonged to someone else.

So he moved away, out of Amora's grasp.

"Oh, Cassius, why do you fight this?" she asked as she leaned against the counter.

Cassius opened the cabinets, looking until he'd found a mug.

"Amora..."

"Tell me why, Cassius. Why do you deny the things you were made for?" She motioned around the sparkling kitchen. It was pristine, crisp and reminded him of the Medici estate.

"And what is it do you think I am made for *petite étoile?*" He poured himself a cup of coffee, opening her refrigerator. It was empty.

Amora tutted at him as she opened a cabinet,

pulling out a container of sugar and powdered creamer. She set the items before him with grace.

"You were made to be a king, Cassius. To live your days in immortal opulence, wanting for nothing. Not to live in the shadows."

"And is that what you have here, Amora? A Kingdom with no King?"

He took the creamer, sniffing it first, and it smelled chemical. He pushed it away, settling on sugar alone.

"What I have is protection. I am a queen, Cassius. I have armies. Fortresses. I can protect you, if that is what you are worried about..."

Cassius took a sip of his coffee.

"Like you protected Marcellus." The moment the words left his mouth, he regretted them. It was a deep cut, even for him.

Amora crossed her arms, the motion driving her breasts together to produce a rather tempting vision. She stood in the light of the kitchen look like someone from another time.

"I know what you are doing. It will not work. You will not wound me with your words so easily. I have fought for this life fang and nail, and my kingdom is of my own making. Marcellus may have given it to me, but it is I who made the Medici name one to be feared, Cassius."

"Not everyone wants a life in the spotlight, on a pedestal. I may have left because of..."

Eden's voice stopped him from breathing.

He'd never discussed what had happened with anyone other than Leon, for fear she would make good on her threat and find him.

Amora closed the space between them, her forest green eyes full of hunger.

"Stay with me, Cassius. You can feast all you want

on fresh, dried, semi-warm blood, whatever you wish, in the comforts you deserve. I would be good to you, Cassius. I could give you what you desire most."

Cassius stared down at her, searching her eyes for an answer he knew he'd never find.

Because the thing he wanted most was not blood, or sex, or beautiful lies.

She slid her delicate fingers along his shirt, her pink nails catching on the fabric as his phone lit up with a notification.

Saved by a Crowley.

He removed her hand gingerly. "I must go."

"Cassius..." she whined as he left his bitter coffee on the counter, heading for the door.

When he reached the elevators, he was met by a woman with sparkling eyes and jet black hair, and for a moment his blood chilled. Though when Enchantress flashed him a smile, he settled only a fraction.

Eden was not here.

She was only in his head, in his memories.

"Rough night?" Enchantress smirked as she pressed the elevator button.

Cassius slid his hands in his pockets.

"I must admit tonight's festivities have me a bit... anxious," he politely answered. He looked over the woman who'd kidnapped his friend. The hallway was empty except for them.

"You vampires are far too dramatic for my taste. Always brooding over everything like some middle grade emo."

Cassius shirked her words. "Excuse me?"

"What do you have to be nervous about? Think you're going to loose?"

"No. I do not. I only mean that I have not been... social... in many years. Crowds tend to make me nervous.”

He knew from his own research, his own intuition Enchantress—Caroline, as Amora had called her—favored loners.

The elevator dinged and he motioned for her to step in. Just because she was a monster did not negate the manners he’d been raised with.

“That’s the beauty of the labyrinth. You’ll be so focused on the game, you’ll hardly realize the people in the room. At least, that’s the intention.

“Have you seen the guest list? Know something I don’t, my lovely Enchantress?”

Her blue eyes shimmered with mischief. She shrugged.

“Let’s just say… this isn’t my first labyrinth… what was your name again? Cassius?”

Cassius stilled at the mention of his name on her tongue.

“You have done this before?” he asked as she hit the button for the first floor.

“It’s been awhile, but yes. It is a time honored tradition for my kind.”

“The Djinn?”

Enchantress’s eyes glowed bright aqua for a moment. “Yes. Many a times we have given man… and creature everything they desire. They only need to prove themselves worthy, and say the magic words, of course.”

Enchantress smiled wickedly as the bells sounded on the sixteenth floor.

Cassius’s gaze settled on her, the weight of her words hanging in the air between them.

“And what reasons would a Djinn have to be working underneath a vampire like *Ami?*”

Caroline leaned closer to him as the tenth floor

dinged, the doors opening and closing of their own accord.

"The same reason the rest of us are drawn to Ami. To take back what is ours."

Cassius swallowed nervously. Something about the way her words sounded, their sharp sting made him feel on edge.

"And what is that?"

"Power, darling. What else?"

"Amora promises you power?"

"Ami promises us the chance to have our cake and finally eat, Cassius. We are hungry, too, but we do not have the means to eat whenever we wish. We can only feed every so many years, and we must make the meal worthwhile."

He watched as the elevator neared the fifth floor.

"I supposed I will see you there, Cassius, was it?"

Cassius nodded his head in approval. "Of course."

CHAPTER TWENTY-TWO

THE GRAND OPENING of the Marquis Masquerade and Fun House was apparently a larger event than Ava had realized. It seemed as though everywhere she went, the only thing the folks of Albright wanted to talk about was the masquerade bar. The costumer where she'd purchased her dress at the last minute raved about the amount of costumes she'd sold in preparation for the event alone, with a smile, as if it was some sort of accomplishment. Though Ava could hardly see the accomplishment knowing that the individuals arriving at the bar this evening would only be dressed for death. She hoped that perhaps they could stake or kill at least a few of the ticks and Djinn. Perhaps she could try to ritual again, smear some dead Djinn juice on her mark. Clearly, she'd missed a step in her alcohol induced haze the prior night.

Ava sighed as she scrubbed at her scalp, letting the shampoo run in sudsy streams down her back. The hot water was soothing, calming even. After one last Scooby Gang meeting in which her brother and Dallas had discussed in great detail the plan, she did not wait to jump into the shower. It'd been nearly forty eight hours at this point, and while she was certain no one else could notice, she could.

She'd just turned off the faucets, wrapping herself in a pale blue, fluffy towel when Dallas called her name from the doorway.

"Ava." His voice was soft, pulling her from her thoughts as she turned around in the bathroom. Dallas stood against the door, shirtless, his large arms crossed in front of his chest.

"What do you want?" she grumbled as she tightened the towel around her front.

"There's a lot of things I want, Ava, but right now? I just want you to look at me."

Ava fought the desire to meet his eyes, losing miserably.

"Jake..." She sighed tirelessly.

"Just listen to me, Ava. I need to say this. I didn't ask for any of this to happen. You, me. Us. I tried to fight it, I really did, but..."

Ava suddenly felt cold, despite the steam in the room.

"But what?" Her voice was barely a whisper. "There was never supposed to be an us. It was just supposed to be sex, no strings attached... We have a job to do, Dallas." Even as she said the words aloud, she could feel the sting, the pain of them. She'd never said it out loud before.

"I know. But somewhere along the way Ava, in the middle of all the blood and the bullshit... I... I fell in love with you."

He took a step closer, and she did not stop him. He reached out, brushing her wet hair back behind her shoulder, his thumb tracing over her jaw. Ava felt as if she couldn't speak.

"I can't be what you want me to be, you know that right? I'll never be this—" She waved around the pale, seashell blue bathroom, with its beige towels and perfectly set tile.

"I'll never be this person. I'm defective. I don't run right, I..." Thoughts of waking in a room filled with monsters threatened to pull her under, the words on the edge of her tongue.

Dallas slid his hand around her waist, shifting the towel just above her thighs.

"This is who I was Ava, not who I am. You know me better than anyone."

"Loving me is a death wish, Jake. Nothing good can come from it..." she whispered.

"I'm not your parents, or Ross," he said, running his fingers down her heated skin. He closed his eyes, leaning his forehead against hers.

"Those fucking ticks took everything from me. Until I found your brother, until I found you..."

Ava slid her hands up around his neck, feeling the edges of his short hair.

"I forgot what it felt like to have something to fight for." The rumble of his deep voice echoed through her entire being as his lips brushed hers. Her tears melted against his skin as he kissed her softly.

It was... new. He'd never kissed her with such sweetness before.

"What it felt like to have *someone* worth fighting for."

"Oh, Jake..." Ava cried out as she kissed him with trembling lips.

He broke away, leaving her feeing more exposed than she'd ever been before. His fingers brushed the underside of her wrist, dancing along the raised skin where fangs had once claimed her blood.

"And I'll fight to the death for you, if that's what it

takes. I promise."

His words were a promise she was certain he couldn't keep, but in that moment, Ava believed him, because no one had ever made such a declaration to her before.

"I'm sorry for the things I said," she choked out.

"I know, Kitten. Me too."

When his lips met hers again, Ava pulled him close. Dallas backed her against the sink, lifting her with ease. Her towel fell to the ground with a soft thump as he carried her across the hall, the cool air of the house causing her nipples to stiffen, shockwaves of lust ebbing through her body as she brushed them against his heated chest.

Dallas laid her down on cool, upturned sheets, and she did not waste a moment. The sheets welcomed her into their soft prison as desire flooded her from head to toe. She was frustrated, she was angry, she was scared.

Of all the things they were, and all the things she knew they could be.

She removed his shirt, her fingers deftly working at his jeans, sliding them down as her insides started to twist, readying herself for what she knew was to come.

Dallas's cock sprang free as he settled himself on top of her, dragging his thickness along her wet seam.

"I don't want to fight anymore, Jake," she whispered, gazing into his bright blue eyes with a burgeoning desire she'd never felt before.

Hope.

Her thighs clenched as she bucked her hips off the bed, seeking the friction, wanting nothing more than to be fulfilled by the promise of Dallas's cursed words.

She knew they were doomed. From the moment she kissed him in a boxing ring all those years ago.

But death at the hand of Jake Dallas was as close to

bliss as she was going to get.

***

Dallas parked the car up the road from the parking lot, which was already starting to look full.

Thanks to Vinny's blueprints, they discovered a cellar storm door in the woods off the property, which Ava had exited from previously. Lights were lit up on the porch of the Masquerade, and the sounds of electronic symphony music abounded in the chilly air.

Ava bunched up her skirt as Dallas opened the door. Like her, he'd opted for a costume if only to blend in among the crowd when the doors opened. She hadn't asked where he'd gotten his Phantom-esque costume, and she suspected by the frayed edges of his collar it was older than the costume she'd been saddled with.

Ava was still unsure of just *what* she was going to do to distract a room full of vampires and Djinn, and she hoped whatever it was would buy them all enough time for Malcolm and Cassius to find Bryan and escape.

The unmistakable sound of Dallas's motorcycle broke the silence, and Ava let her iridescent, eighties-style ball gown down to the ground.

Of all the ensembles in the costume shop, did the only one in her size *have* to be white?

She longed for pants.

The headlight on the motorcycle shined on her like a laser beam, catching the fabric and making the sequins pop to life.

Dallas stood behind her in his costume, which she had to admit didn't look half bad on him, especially with his phantom mask. The way the fabric clung to his muscles—particularly the pants—she couldn't deny he was a sight for sore eyes.

But as Cassius pulled up on Dallas's motorcycle, Ava felt the air leave her lungs.

He still wore his signature leather pants, but he'd traded his normal heathered shirts in for a ruffled blouse, the kind that exposed a sliver of his pale chest just enough. Combined with his golden hair and glowing green eyes, he looked like something out of a fantastical dream, like a Goblin King come to whisk her away to a world of floating stairs.

"You clean up nice," she teased him. "A little on the nose, though, if you ask me."

"Says the woman who looks like a frosted cupcake," he said smoothly.

"Where's your mask?" she asked, feeling strangely on the spot.

Cassius pulled out the black venetian mask, sliding it over his head.

"And yours?" he breathed, his voice full of darkness.

Ava took in the sight of him, standing before her and she could not deny the way her blood responded. Her body heated at the sight, but she was certain it had to do with the prospect of slaying and nothing else.

"I've never been one to follow the rules." She smirked.

Dallas shook his head.

"I am certain you don't need one, what with your blinding frock and all," he teased her. "Are you ready to save the day, Ava?" Cassius offered her his arm. She contemplated taking it. Setting her hand on his forearm, letting him lead her into a den full of monsters hungry for blood.

Her scar burned in his presence, as if it knew her blood truly belonged to him.

So instead of giving in to the instinct, she pushed past Cassius and headed for the Marquis.

ARIEL DAWN

CHAPTER TWENTY-THREE

CASSIUS LOOKED JAKE Dallas in the eye as he sauntered past him, after Ava.

"I trust you will find that I have taken good care of her," he said smoothly, his lips curling back to expose just a hint of fang.

Dallas's eyes narrowed, his breathing steady.

"Well, I would hope so. After all, she wasn't yours to begin with," he said gruffly.

"I even polished the chrome." Cassius slid his hands in his pockets.

Dallas grunted as he set toward his motorcycle, swinging his leg over it.

"You fuck this up for us and I will kill you. And I won't be sorry about it."

Cassius picked up his pace as Dallas started up the shimmering, silver bike, taking off toward the Marquis.

They'd been over the plans enough. While Malcolm was inside, biding his time until the labyrinth would start, Dallas was to stake out their exit, ready to receive them all once he and Malcolm had obtained their target and completed the rescue.

He knew from Amora's admission that the conspiracy-theorizing coroner was being kept in the suit closest to the labyrinth's underground entrance, if only for convenience.

Cassius hoped at the very least Bryan had been treated well in captivity. When it came to servitude, Amora did have a history of being quite... demanding. But she could also be quite amenable and manipulative.

Eden preferred to kill to have her way, whereas Amora preferred a much slower, painful sort of torment to get what she wanted out of her subjects.

He'd seen such things firsthand. Given the fact the Djinn had been feeding the spots their deepest desires, he wondered how strong Bryan would be.

Would he falter?

Or would he persist to escape?

Ava tromped through the grass on the side of the road, and he could see that underneath her poofy, shimmering skirt and tulle, she was wearing her signature black studded boots. The sight made him smile. Underneath it all, there was no hiding the real Ava Crowley. Though he had to admit, she was quite stunning in her shimmering ball gown. The sweetheart neckline showed off her ample cleavage, the sash that fell off her shoulders exposing her slender, pale neck.

Cassius's throat constricted, the sight a most favorable one to him. He could feel her pulse in his veins, steady like a river. He hoped the blood bags he'd stolen from the hospital morgue on his way would suffice enough to get him through the masquerade. Dallas was not the only one worried that things would go awry.

Cassius hated large events such as this, for many reasons. But for his friends he'd always proven loyal to a fault.

Penny, Marguerite, Marcellus.

Leon.

Eden.

Her words reverberated in his head, the sting of them still fresh even though the'd been uttered ages ago.

"Do what you do best, Cassius."

"What is that?" he asked.

"Be the hero," Eden whispered.

Though as Cassius looked at the fresh-faced slayer, her stark profile and her ruby red lips, staring at the Marquis with determination, he knew he was far from a hero.

At least where Ava Crowley was concerned.

"How many stakes are you hiding in there?" he teased her.

Ava huffed as they came to the parking lot.

"Bold of you to assume all I am hiding is stakes. A girl likes to accessorize, you know."

"And what sort of accessories do you favor, my sweet Avarice?"

"Sharp, pointy, sparkly things, of course. And matches, naturally."

"Plan on starting a fire this evening?"

"We all have our vices, Cas," she said as they approached the front of the Marquis.

Up close it reminded him of another place, a long time ago.

The Duquensian manor where he'd first danced with Eden. He hadn't known much of the world he'd been born into at the time, and he was so fresh, so new. He'd only just completed his transition, and the thirst was maddening. When a beautiful, raven-haired woman found him in the shadows, feasting on blood with guilt and remorse, he hadn't known what she was truly offering. He'd been far too trusting then, far too naive to the evils of the world around him.

Cassius shoved the thoughts of his past down, back into their coffin where they belonged as he stared up at the lights, feeling strangely anxious.

Ava shifted her stance, the movement bringing her closer to him. It was just an innocent motion, something she probably didn't even notice. Still, he felt a sort of peace in her proximity every time she closed the space between them, every time she absentmindedly fell into the gravitational pull that existed between them, and every time he pretended not to notice.

"If we pull this off... you owe me a donut," she said seriously.

"My sweet Avarice, do not sell yourself short. *When* we pull this off, I will buy you a dozen donuts. And coffee with French vanilla cream, and two sugars."

Ava lifted her skirts as she walked forward, taking the lead.

Cassius was more than happy to let her lead him.

CHAPTER TWENTY-FOUR

AVA WAS NOT sure what to expect from a funhouse slash masquerade, but she was certain the shadowed, dark, winding hallway was not anywhere in her imagination.

"Amora has always had a thing for theatrics," Cassius mused, and Ava twisted her lips.

"I thought you said this was a party. You know like... full of people?"

"I believe it is the light at the end of this literal tunnel," he said as he motioned to the hallway. Like many haunted houses, it looked as if inflated black bags stemmed from the walls to create a claustrophobic tunnel in which sensory deprivation was the terror experienced.

No light, only darkness.

"The only way out is through," she mused aloud as she lifted her skirts, moving to take one step in front, but Cassius did not let her.

"For a fan of horror movies, are you not missing the most obvious trope? The beautiful woman *never* goes headfirst in the darkness lest she has a death wish," he teased her.

Ava felt the heat in her blood start to boil. She wasn't scared, knowing what lay at the other end of the stupid hallway.

Monsters.

A labyrinth.

A friend needing to be rescued.

A Djinn who could possibly break the Goblin King beside her's claim on her.

"With this contraption—"She gestured to her dress. " I'm fairly certain I've got enough of a buffer."

Cassius stepped in front of her, sliding his arm in between the crevice, extending his opposite arm toward her. Offering her his hand, yet again.

Ava looked at it, feeling strangely warm. But she knew time was of the essence, and so she took his hand.

His long, pale fingers curled around hers. His touch was cool, gentle, as his fingers brushed the scar on her wrist with care as if it were fresh.

Her palm heated like a fire, her body temperature rising.

Surely it is from the overabundance of tulle.

Cassius tugged her hand with a force that was somehow both strong and soft, as if he was terrified to let her go but frightened all the same.

She watched as the darkness swallowed him, and followed him down the rabbit hole.

In the darkness there was only the two of them, molded together by fire and ice.

And as soon as it was there, it was gone. For the light appeared, but it was not golden or incandescent. It was ultraviolet and neon, and it was reflective.

They'd come to a room of mirrors, bathed in hazy blue and violet, their reflections infinite.

He was everywhere.

All around her, encompassing her like air.

The sound of music echoed around them, and by the sound of it, they were close to the party.

"I guess this will have to make up for the haunted houses I missed this year," she said sarcastically. Though she had no reason to do so, she could not help but tighten her grip on the annoying vampire in front of her. Every bone in her body told her this was a trap. She'd been had. She'd finally lost her mind, and this was it. This was how he would take her, in a fun house, surrounded by mirrors and a thumping base.

Cassius let go of her hand, turning to look at her with deep, glowing green eyes that made her feel a sting of guilt.

Her hand fell to her side and the heat subsided.

When they'd arrived on the other side of the room, the path became much easier.

As they entered the grand ballroom, Ava had to admit it looked like something out of a movie. The room was large, cavernous, and it was difficult to believe it existed within the size of the building she'd laid eyes on.

In the center of the room was what looked like a large enclosure or fish tank, able to be viewed from all sides. Her wrist flared with heat, burning beneath her skin like lava as her skin prickled with goosebumps.

She glanced around, uncertain of who was a vampire and who was not. There were plenty of individuals wearing masks, which only added to the mystery. She knew the Djinn were hiding somewhere in the crowd...

In the years she'd been tracking vamps, she'd rarely come across other monsters. Save for the time she'd spent in Mahoning, in the mountains hunting werewolves, or that time she'd been bitten by an Incubus...

But in all those situations, she'd been able to pick them out with a defining factor. In the presence of an Incubus, her mark felt like ice, and in the presence of the werewolves, she could tell by their glowing gold eyes and physique, not to mention they all looked... similar in appearance.

"What's wrong?" Cassius's voice was soft in her ear. He was right behind her, yet he kept his distance.

"I cannot tell the difference," she whispered. "Between vampire and Djinn."

Cassius let out a breath, his voice low enough only she could hear.

"I don't feel anything in their presence, but they all share a similar... aesthetic."

Ava turned to look at him. "You do realize everyone's wearing masks, right?"

"They all have the same aquamarine eyes, the same complexion and dark hair. Their aura is inviting. It is not dissimilar from a vampire's thrall. It is meant to lure, so it will smell heavenly, make you feel relaxed. But their scent is spicy, citrus-like. Woods like. They smell like the lands they originated from."

"Great. So I'm looking for blue-eyed goths who smell like Morrocan oil. That helps a ton," she spewed.

Ava could feel eyes on her, and she wanted to grab her stake. Instead, she put one foot in front of the other and approached the glass, if only to get a better view.

Cassius followed her, keeping close. He left a modicum of space between them, enough that only she could hear his whispering plea.

"Stay close."

When they'd arrived at the glass, she set her sweaty palm against it. Looking down into the glass, she could see the hedges and walls set up, and she could see the spots waiting at various corners.

"My money's on that one," a man said as he came next to her. His olive skin was sickly in the artificial light that emanated from the labyrinth.

"The skinny one?" she asked.

The man with grey eyes pointed to a spot on the other side of where he stood.

"Yeah, that one. Ami got a last minute spot. Heard he took out a guard on the way into the labyrinth when they was loading 'em up. Scrappy one, he is."

"Where is *Ami?*" Cassius asked smoothly.

"Probably downstairs fussing over the details. Woman and their parties," the man scoffed.

Ava's heart stopped as she ventured around the man, looking through the glass to see he was pointing at a man dressed in ripped jeans and a Led Zeppelin shirt.

Her brother. Of course he'd stick out like a sore thumb.

You're supposed to blend in, Mal.

"And who are you placing your bets on?" the man asked curiously, but Ava was certain he was not talking to her.

"Wise choice, my friend. That spot belongs to me."

The words on Cassius's tongue angered Ava. It sounded wrong coming out Cassius's mouth, but yet...

He was a monster just like the rest of him, and she had to remember that.

She had to remember who he was, and who she was.

For once she got her hands on the blood of a Djinn—perhaps she could find Enchantress—she would be free of his bond, forever.

"Does this lovely delicate flower belong to you as

well?" the man asked smoothly.

Ava's stomach felt nauseous. She belonged to no one, but how could a monster understand such things.

"She is free to answer you herself. She has a voice."

Cassius looked to her for only a second, exposing a hint of fang. He regarded her with a sly look.

Ava's fingers ached to drive a stake through *something,* and this man's words caused her fire to spark. She could not very well walk into a rich vault and not leave with a small fortune. Perhaps she'd found the distraction they all needed.

"I belong to no one," she said boldly.

"What a pity," he said as he offered her his hand. "But perhaps in that case, I can persuade you for a dance?" The man smiled.

"I'd love to," she mused sweetly, if only to seem appreciative. Ava could feel the beginnings of a thrall reaching out to latch on to her with desperation.

Of course, Cassius had said Djinn were capable of similar things...

She tried to get a good look at the man's eyes, but it was hard to discern amidst his brown leather bird mask.

But Ava would not so easily give in. She'd been here a hundred times. In the arms of a vampire, fighting their jedi mind tricks. Djinn or not, she had faith she could take this monster either way.

And so, she pretended to fall into the arms of the unknown man, channeling her inner Christine. Ava let him pull her to the center of the ballroom floor, and she could feel Cassius's gaze on her like a sun burning down on the sidewalk in July.

She stared up at the man, his facial features strangely familiar to her, though she couldn't place them. His eyes were the shade of oceans.

"Do I... know you?" she asked.

He slid his hands around her waist, turning her around so her ass was smack against his groin. A deep rumble left his chest, and she could feel the faint stirrings of lust in her belly as his thrall-aura-whatever jedi mind tricks he was using, seeped out toward her like an invisible Kraken ready to sink a ship.

Ava called on the memories like they were weapons themselves. And in a away, they were.

The moan of pleasure before Ross's scream.

Her parents cold, dead eyes staring back at her across a bloodstained carpet.

Sam Kingsley floundering around on the floor of a burning building as she exorcised him.

Watching Dallas disappear with Midnight at the Drowned Clam.

"I am hurt, my dear. I would have thought you'd remembered our time together, however brief it was." His left hand pulled along her waist, sliding down her thigh. His right grasped her wrist.

Ava stilled as he dragged his fangs along her neck torturously and it all came rushing back.

The drinks, the dancing. His hands around her waist, pulling her closer. His eyes as he took in the sight of her before him, his teeth along the scars of her thigh, his blood smeared in her open wound, his hand wrapped around his cock as he stroked himself until he'd brought himself to release with a groan, while Ava felt *free.*

Hopeful.

Wishing for release of her own.

The nameless man from the bar. Her insides twisted with nausea once more, but her face did not betray her sudden remembrance.

"How could I forget... silly me." She shoved down the

panic, the disgust and the regret, bending over to grind her ass against him as she bunched her skirts just enough she could grasp her knife. As she had told Cassius, she'd opted to bring silver with her in case of Djinn. And if she was correct, the silver would turn this man, this creature, to putty, causing him to die a slow and agonizing death. Just enough to buy them some time...

When she whirled around faster than a hurricane, her knife striking his chest, he growled ferociously.

"You little bitch!" He grunted as she pulled the knife out. She watched the blood pool against his white shirt. "She's a slayer!" he yelled, and suddenly Ava felt more in danger than ever before.

As she drove the blade in the nameless man's gut, she could feel the stare of those around her, and hungry growls sounded.

Vampires stared at her with hunger, and at the Djinn who was now kneeling on the floor, the blood seeping through the spots she'd stabbed him. She'd heard not all supernaturals were as picky when it came to their prey. Though there was the legend or two of vampires who relished in supernatural blood, such as the ones they'd run into in Mahoning, but they'd killed those vampires...

"Ava, run!" Cassius hollered, just as the man roared an animalistic, angry sound. The sound was answered, echoing in the dark space like a war cry. The scent of blood was pungent in the air.

His blood smelled rotten and awful and she wanted to throw up. She did not have time to strike a match as the crowd closed around her. She did not have time to process or steal the blood as she wished, to see if it would fix her cursed mark.

If it would cure her.

Ava looked Cassius in the eye, seeing the fear shine in his gorgeous irises, spreading like wildfire. He was scared, too. His gaze darted to the puddle of blood forming beneath the man.

She did not think twice about running.

This was it, this was the moment they'd been waiting for. She ran toward the other end of the room, remembering Vinny's blueprints in her head. She hoped the gamble she'd taken was worth it.

Vampires hissed, Djinn snarling behind her as they fought one another for the body on the ground.

Cassius grabbed her hand as she ran to him. His grip was firm, strong.

"I said a distraction, Ava, not a free for all," he said as he pulled her toward the other end of the room. A creature with dark hair and fangs lunged for them, but Cassius easily dodged her.

Ava could barely keep up with his pace, but she didn't care. The scent of woodsy citrus perfumed the air as she started to feel hazy. She focused on the looming exit sign and the door beneath it that led to the basement below, and she followed it like a guiding star.

CHAPTER TWENTY-FIVE

"WHERE DO YOU think you're going?" A deep voice sounded as Cassius and Ava came to the door.

He held Ava's wrist tightly, squeezing, if only to tell her without words to follow his lead. He prayed she would not open her mouth, or try anything.

"Taking this one down to the cells where she belongs, of course. Thought she could get one up on us."

The guard appraised them both, and Cassius did not miss the way he looked over Ava.

"All that caused by this little thing?" The guard set his hand on his hip, and Cassius could feel thrall in the air.

Instinctively, he pushed back against it, causing the man to look at him with curiosity.

"I can take her from here."

"That won't be necessary," Cassius said solidly.

Ava faltered in his grasp, and he could see her eyelashes fluttering.

Cassius moved toward the guard, bearing his fangs. He forced Ava behind him.

"Get downstairs to the labyrinth, Ava."

'Cas…" She sounded as if she wanted to protest, but thought better of it.

"When I say now…" he spoke evenly as the guard bared his own fangs, drawing his own weapon.

A gun.

Cassius did not think twice as he lunged for the guard, dropping Ava's hand.

"Now!" he hollered, as hands and bodies collided.

Out of the corner of his eye he could see her glittering sequins, glinting like pixies in the sunlight, and within seconds the slam of the door told him she was gone.

Well on her way to the labyrinth.

The guard pushed back against him, and they danced a waltz of hissing, of bared fangs. The guard grabbed him, pulling him against his chest, the barrel pointed to his jugular.

"Give me one good reason I shouldn't blow your fucking brains out," he hissed.

"Amal, that is enough!" A sweet, saccharine voice called, and the guard stilled. His hand shook, but he did not remove his gun.

Out of the shadows, Amora emerged.

"Oh, Cassius, you haven't changed at all, have you?"

Cassius laid his eyes on her, and she looked positively regal, dressed in a long, blush colored silk dress. The high slit at the thigh made her naturally petite frame look longer, taller even. Her pale golden hair cascaded down her shoulders, her blood red lips pressed into a thin line.

And she was not alone.

The well dressed Djinn woman behind her smirked devilishly as her icy eyes appraised him.

"What is her name this time? Helen? Rose?

Jennifer?" Amora shook her head.

Cassius bit his tongue as he looked away.

"It is not what it looks like," he said.

Enchantress took one step closer to him.

"He is no different than the rest of them, Ami. He lies to you."

Amora pouted before sighing. "Amal, lower your weapon."

The guard broke out into a sweat, shakily obeying.

"I wish I could say I was surprised, Cassius. I really do. But it seems you have crossed me for the last time. Fool me once, shame on you. Fool me twice, well..."

Enchantress stepped forth and the air burst with woody, citrusy perfume, and Cassius started to feel hazy, relaxed. As if heaven was so close, but somehow so far away...

"Amora... petite étoile," he called.

Amora sighed. "Do what you wish, Caroline. I have no need for traitors," Amora said as she turned on her heel.

At that very moment, Amal fell to the ground, his gun skittering to the floor.

"Please, don't hurt me, I'm sorry, I—"

Cassius watched in shock and awe as the guard looked to be seeing something that wasn't there. A hallucination of sorts, but whatever it was he was seeing, it was obviously distressing.

"Oh, I'm going to enjoy this," she said as she reached out, grasping a hold of Cassius.

He felt immobile, as if he was not in control. He fought to try and move, but it was useless. Panic coursed through him as he worried perhaps it was not Enchantress or Amora who controlled him.

Perhaps his worst nightmare had made itself known again... after all these years...

Enchantress grabbed him by the throat.

"Any last requests?" she purred just as she sunk her claws into his skin, her fangs into his neck.

Cassius could feel his blood rushing to the surface, but he felt strangely at peace.

"Such desperation, such pain. You are ripe with hope, aren't you?"

Cassius struggled to move his arms, to fight the Djinn off.

Her eyes glowed bright like bioluminescent algae on the surface of a lake.

The world around him started to fade, disappearing into something else. His blood slowed, his heart rate stilling.

The world was so... beautiful he had to close his eyes.

When he opened them, he was right back where he'd started. In the ballroom, holding Ava's hand as she ignored the man talking about the spots.

"Perhaps I could ask for a dance?" he spoke softly as he tugged her closer. Ava looked up at him with curiosity, a blush creeping onto her cheeks.

"You can always ask," she teased him.

"But will you ever say yes?" He pulled her closer, settling his right hand around her waist.

Ava smirked, shaking her head as she set her hand in his open left palm.

"Yes," she spoke the words softly. The swooning melancholic melodies of a song he'd heard long ago echoed in the room, the words filling him with faith in every step.

The music ebbed and flowed as the people around them waltzed and wallowed, hiding behind their grotesque and stunning masks. The scent of blood in the air was thick.

Ava leaned her head to the side, showcasing the expanse of her slender, pale neck.

"Is this what you want, Cassius?" she asked.

His thirst was insatiable.

"Yes," he whispered. The world was spinning and his heart felt as if it could leap right out of his chest.

Ava slid her arms around his neck, pulling him to her. Her fingers grasped the edges of his hair at the nape of his neck. Chest to chest, he could feel her heartbeat, her stolen pulse in his veins.

"Is this what you wish for?" she asked.

Cassius felt the overwhelming need to say yes, but something stopped him. It sounded like someone was calling his name.

Her voice...

"Cassius! Run!" Ava hollered.

Ava...

But she is right here...

A wet, crunching sound followed by a hiss filtered through his thoughts, and he blinked. The world started to dissipate again, the wondrous moments gone with the wind.

Enchantress fought against Ava, baring her fangs, her face contorted in the grotesque true form of the Djinn.

Ava kicked at her, knocking her on her back as she drove her knife through Enchantress's pale, exposed chest.

The Djinn writhed beneath her, underneath the torn and shredded edges of Ava's white ball gown, which was covered in debris and blood. Burgundy stains spattered along the iridescent fabric, along her pale arms. Blood oozed from her wrists, where he'd lain claim to her blood.

His neck throbbed, and he brought his hand to the

spot. When he pulled away he could see blood. Thick, black blood covered his hands. He'd been bitten.

Ava rose from the Djinn who lay lifeless on the floor, waving her hand in front of his face." He blinked once more, focusing on her.

"Get Bryan out of here," she commanded. He blinked once again, realizing he was on the floor beneath the exit. The way out was not too far, but he was aware of the fighting going on still, and the sounds of sirens outside.

How long had he been out?

When his gaze landed on his friend, it all came crawling back. Bryan's tired, heavy eyes and sullen appearance was both disheartening and full of relief.

He was alive.

He was alive, and now he was safe, as long as they could get out of this hellhole in one piece.

"Go, get out of here! Get Bryan back to the car and—"

"I am not leaving without you," Cassius said as he got up. Bryan stood beside him, covered in sweat and blood, and Cassius hoped it wasn't his. The scent caused his stomach to turn, his throat to dry and he had to fight it.

A wretched scream tore through the air, and Ava's eyes widened in fear.

"Just go! Fucking listen to me!"

She shoved at them, and Cassius felt between a rock and a hard place. He wrapped his arm around Bryan, trusting his gut.

"We will wait for you," he said, hoping she understood.

Ava nodded as another scream echoed in the air, and she wasted no time disappearing into the darkness below, leaving Cassius and Bryan to fend for themselves.

CHAPTER TWENTY-SIX

THE SOUND OF Dallas's scream made Ava's blood curl. She raced down the stairs, practically leaping all the way down.

When she finally got down to where she'd left her brother and Dallas, her heart stopped.

They were fighting off a handful of monsters.

Ava's wrist flared with heat and prickled with goosebumps, and she wasted no time defending her brother and Dallas. The world moved in slow motion, as she, Dallas, and Malcolm moved in perfect symmetry, a symphony of knives and stakes.

When she was certain they'd cleared out the herd, she let her hand fall, her gaze falling on a bloodied Malcolm, whose shirt was in shreds.

"We did it," she said as she caught her breath.

Malcolm pulled her into his arms.

"We fucking did it," he said with a laugh.

Ava had never felt so accomplished.

And then she smelled the scent of burning wood and citrus.

"Ava, look out!" Dallas's voice cut through as he

shoved her and Malcolm aside.

The sound of fangs sinking in through flesh and muscle echoed in the air as Ava turned around, expecting to see Dallas strong-arming whatever monster had decided to show up late to the party.

But that was not the sight that greeted Ava.

"Dallas!" she hollered as the Djinn clutched a writing Dallas to its chest. Blood seeped out of his neck and he cried out in pain.

Ava and her brother lunged for him, fighting to pull the Djinn off. Malcolm sunk his blade in its back, the creature hissing in pain.

It let go, Dallas falling limp to the ground, and Ava scrambled to him. His eyes looked scared as he looked around. Her hand settled over his neck, trying to stop the bleeding. But it just kept coming.

"Come on, Jake, you gotta get up. We gotta get out of here," she exclaimed, her voice shaking.

"I'm sorry, Kitten, but that's not happening."

"Jake..." Malcolm rushed to his side, flanking Ava.

"You guys need to get out of here." His voice sounded garbled, like he couldn't breathe.

Ava felt sticky, warm blood seeping all through her dress, and as she moved away a hair, she saw he was bleeding from the chest. A long, gaping gash in his side oozed blood. She could see the faint coloring of bone.

"Rule number one," Ava said as tears came to her eyes. "No one gets left behind," she sobbed.

Dallas reached out, brushing away a strand of her hair.

His touch was cold.

Because he was dying.

She knew it in her heart, but she couldn't process it. For this was Jake Dallas. He was a lot of things, but he was not so easily bested.

She'd seen him take down much stronger monsters, and she'd heard the stories. The man practically had nine lives from all the hunter tales she'd heard.

Malcolm's arms wrapped around her.

"You have a job to do." He coughed.

"*We* have a job to do," she pleaded.

Dallas shook his head, looking up at Malcolm.

"I can see her," he said wistfully.

Malcolm's sobs echoed with her own as he spoke.

"She's waiting for you. They both are." Malcolm pulled Dallas to him, and then that was it. The sound of his knife driving deep into his blood soaked body was the last thing Ava heard.

She let out a bloodcurdling scream as she felt Dallas's cold hand fall from hers. The world was blurry as Malcolm wrapped her in his embrace, as he pulled her by the hand through the dark cavernous hallways, through the basement of the Marquis.

***

When they'd made it to the clearing, she could see Cassius leaning against the hood of her Impala, could see Bryan's defeated eyes gazing out at them through her windows.

"You are all right, you..." His voice faded. "Where is Dallas?" he asked, his voice a whisper.

Malcolm only shook his head. Ava could not speak, the words stuck in her throat, making it hard to breathe.

Dead.

Dallas was dead.

CHAPTER TWENTY-SEVEN

THE DRIVE HOME was much quicker in time, but it felt like an eternity.

The news of the murders at the Marquis Masquerade had made the radio stations and the papers by morning. According to the news outlets, they'd come across six bodies, and Cassius could not help but feel a sense of guilt. Ava could have been one of them, but she wasn't.

Was it wrong to feel a sense of relief that the slayer had survived when her lover did not?

Cassius felt conflicted on the matter. He was glad they'd accomplished their mission, they'd rescued their friend, who was sleeping soundly, snoring like a grizzly bear in his own bed. Cassius shut the door, vowing to stop by in the morning to make sure his friend was alright after all he'd been through.

Ava leaned against the drivers side door, standing as still as a statue.

At least she's moved since we left Ohio...

Cassius came to her side, his heart aching. Her stolen pulse throbbed in his veins, slow and steady.

The light in her eyes had darkened.

"Ava—"

"Don't." She spoke concisely, curtly. "Don't you fucking—" Her voice shook, as she pinched the bridge of her nose. "Just... listen to me for once and leave me the fuck alone," she cried.

Cassius reached his thumb out, resting it on her cheek.

She grabbed him by the wrist, her nails digging into his skin.

CHAPTER TWENTY-EIGHT

A SINGLE TEAR melted into her skin as he brushed it away. Ava threw his hand down.

"Get the fuck away from me," she growled.

A part of her wanted to fight. To lay a stake in his chest and blame him for what had happened. Had they not embarked on this journey to find Bryan, perhaps Dallas would still be alive, texting her in the middle of the night, and she would ignore him out of annoyance while secretly dreaming of the next hunt, the next time they'd see one another.

The next fight, the next kiss.

The next case.

But there would be no next anything's.

Not anymore.

The other part of her longed to fall into the vampire in front of her and disappear.

Cassius let out a sigh as he took a step back, his gorgeous green eyes imploring hers as he spoke breathlessly, in defeat.

"As you wish, my sweet Avarice."

And with that he was gone, faded into the shadows

of night and Ava was alone once more.

She double checked Bryan's doors were locked, walked the perimeter of his humble abode merely four times before she felt as if she could leave. She wiped her tears away as she started the car, turning the radio up.

The familiar sounds of *Don't Fear The Reaper* played through her speakers, but even that could not soothe her broken heart or her fractured soul.

EPILOGUE

Four Days Later

"JAKE DALLAS WAS my best friend. My partner. He was a hell of a lead singer, a pain in my ass, and a fucking gem," Mal said as he stared into the fire.

To the rest of the world, Dallas had simply died in the brawl at the Marquis. Malcolm had stayed behind to make arrangements, retrieving his body, burning it. Scattering the ashes as Dallas would have wanted.

Malcolm had told them all his wishes were granted, his ashes scattered over the graves of his wife and their unborn child.

Laura and Kelly Dallas.

The hits just kept coming, Ava thought.

Would they ever stop?

Would the pain ever subside?

Malcolm set his beer down, and Ava could see he was making his way over to her. He'd asked several times if she wanted to talk, but clearly he did not understand. No amount of talking would fix how she felt, it would not bring him back.

She simply had to cauterize the wound left by Jake Dallas if she wanted to have a semblance of a normal life again.

Whatever normal was for a cursed Crowley.

"How you holding up?" Mal asked, swishing the liquid around in his beer bottle.

"I'm alive, so I guess that counts for something," she said with a scowl. She clutched the maroon hoodie around her waist. The only piece of Jake Dallas she had left.

"You know, this... this is what I was trying to protect you from. This life... it's not for the faint of heart. It's lonely, full of losses. Gruesome, fucked up shit. I wanted to spare you, but... D... he saw something in you, just like he saw something in me."

The bonfire crackled behind them. Though the courtyard slash backyard of the estate was rather large, Ava couldn't help but feel claustrophobic.

"I don't know if I can do this anymore," she said, her voice filled with defeat.

"It's not us we do this for. It's them," Malcolm said as he nodded to Vinny, Tito, and Hunter all sitting around the fire, beers in hand, telling stories of their friend, their fallen comrade.

"For the ones we've lost. We keep fighting for *them*." Mal let out a shaky breath. "You aren't the only one who loved him, you know. He was my brother, and I can promise you, I will keep fighting for him because I know it's what he would have wanted. And I know he'd want you to do the same."

Ava could not listen to her brother, or to the stories of Dallas being passed around. Not when she could not speak of her own stories, not when she couldn't speak his name out loud without breaking into tears. Though she wished she could share her memories, be a part of the camaraderie.

To tell of how they'd shared a bucket of wings that first night after Ross's funeral, playing darts, or when he'd gotten all pissed off at her at TerrorCon and kissed her.

The way he hogged the covers in the morning, or the way he held her when she'd been pushed too far.

Perhaps Jake Dallas was not the only one who'd failed miserably.

And now he was gone.

The monsters had taken him, too, just as they had taken Ross, her parents, his wife and child, and once again Ava was alone. Left to bear her heartbreak in silence, her pain, on her own.

"I think I need some air," she said as she rose from her seat, taking her leave. She walked through the house, her footsteps echoing in the space. Malcolm had politely asked Connie to take the day off, if only so they could talk freely about their hunter lives, not having to worry about anyone misunderstanding or asking too many questions.

She settled down on the bench on her porch. The wind kicked up dead leaves, and she sat there for what felt like eternity until a pair of black and white converses peeking out from beneath leather pants came into view.

Ava looked up to see Cassius standing there, looking as gorgeous as ever, holding out a steaming cup of coffee and a box of donuts.

"What the fuck are you doing here?" she bit.

"I came to express my deepest sympathies," he said softly.

"For a hunter?" she said defensively.

"For a man," he said as he nudged the coffee cup in her direction. "A man who was important to many.

Including you."

"Is there whiskey in that?" she asked coldly.

Cassius set the box of donuts down on the patio table, popping the lid open. Ava could see a full box of a dozen donuts, and her stomach lurched for the sugary goodness. She hadn't eaten much in the past few days.

"Only one way to find out," Cassis said with a soft smile.

Ava pulled the coffee cup from his hands, her fingertips brushing his. The touch sent tiny shockwaves through her system that made her feel almost a spark of peace and she pretended not to notice.

"Do you want to talk about what happened?" he asked quietly.

"No."

"May I?" He gestured to the open space beside her.

Ava shrugged. "I don't fucking care."

Cassius sat next to her, leaving nearly a canyon between them.

"Then we will not talk," he said simply.

Ava glanced at the long expanse of his legs in his signature leather pants before sipping the coffee he'd proffered to her.

The unmistakable burn of whiskey in her throat made her eyebrows raise.

"There *is* whiskey in this!"

Cassius shot her a smirk. "A smart woman once told me that coffee fixes most things, and for the rest of life's ills, there is always whiskey."

Ava breathed in the sweet, coffee and cream scent, with a hint of cinnamon, stifling a hint of a smile as he threw her own words back at her.

"I'm too tired to kill you today," she said as she wrapped her fingers around the cup, letting it warm her skin and body. She was tired, near exhausted, and it did help but she would not divulge such things to the vampire beside her.

Cassius crossed his ankles, leaning back against the bench, leaving a modicum of space between them.

"Perhaps tomorrow then."

Ava took another pull of her strong, alcoholic coffee.

"Tomorrow," she agreed.

They both sat there in silence as the leaves bristled about like tumbleweeds until Ava's insides felt warm, and she'd found enough courage to face the hunters once more. When they'd gone, it was just her and Malcolm.

"I'm leaving tomorrow," he said plainly.

"I'm not surprised. Didn't think you'd stay in one place long."

"I'll be back soon, I just... I have some leads to follow up on. I'll be in touch and I promise I'll be home for Christmas," he said as he pulled some keys out of his pocket. He held them in his hand for a moment before handing them to her.

"What's this?"

"I think he'd want you to have it. The bike."

Ava's chest tightened.

"I can't take that," she said softly.

"Then leave it in the garage with Dad's." Malcolm's voice was quiet.

"I miss him. Dad. He always knew the right thing to say, didn't he?" she said as she wrapped her fingers around the keys tightly.

"Yeah, he did." Mal sighed.

"We're going to avenge them, you know. Mom, Dad, Dallas..." Malcolm pulled her into his arms, and she couldn't help but hug him back.

"I know," she whispered.

"After all, we're fucking Crowley's. It's in our blood," he said as he broke apart from her.

Ava nodded in response.

"What was that saying Dad always used to say? About fires and rising?"

Mal smiled.

"Ah. I believe it was Carl Sagan's quote, 'stars are phoenixes rising from their own ashes.'"

Ava nodded. "Yup, that's the one."

"Tonight we burn, Ava. But tomorrow, we rise. I promise." He leaned in and kissed her on the cheek.

"Call me when you get in," she said, suddenly feeling exhausted.

"Of course, Simba," Mal said as he headed for the door.

Ava watched from the porch as he drove off, chasing leads, and doing what he did best.

Hunting.

And as she watched him leave, she made a promise to herself to do what she'd been training for for years.

Like a phoenix, she would rise from the ashes of her own destruction and she would fight.

Ava & Cas will fight another day.
In The Blood is AVAILABLE NOW!
http://books2read.com/Forevermore2

Turn the page for a preview of Blood of the Lost…

PREVIEW

THE AIR WAS thick with broken promises, tainted memories, and the scent of blood. The sound of Ava's screams would haunt Dallas for the rest of his undead life.

Because as Dallas lay motionless on the blood-soaked ground of the Marquis, suspended in motion between life and death, he could feel his insides hardening, changing.

Like a moth inside a cocoon, all he could do was wait. For the transition to take hold.

"Get up," the sound of a woman's voice called to him, but he did not recognize it.

Dallas tried to move his fingers, his toes, but everything felt heavy.

He grunted in response as his eyelashes fluttered. The room he was in was dark, the only light the bright flash from a phone screen.

"Fucking shut that off," he growled, stretching his fingers. He moved his hand to shield his eyes. The light was so bright, blinding almost.

"Oh, this one's got spunk," another woman's voice

carried excitedly.

"Who do you think is responsible for making him?"

Dallas attempted to move his legs, the effort nearly exhausting.

His entire body felt as if he'd been hit by a freight train. He held his hand in front of his eyes, noting the mess of blood all over his skin.

Memories filtered back into his brain.

The Djinn heading for Ava and Mal.

How he'd pushed them out of the way, without a second thought.

There had been so much blood...

Dallas ran his hands over his chest, feeling for the gaping wound he knew should be there.

But he felt no such thing, just cold, congealed blood, and soft, sore skin among the shredded remains of his costume.

"Can you get up?"

Dallas's gaze settled on one of the women, the one with the excited voice.

She kneeled before him, long raven waves falling over her shoulders. Her pale skin and glowing aquamarine eyes were indicative of her breed of monster.

Djinn.

She looked strangely familiar...

Dallas leaned in close to the Djinn, letting her scent fill his airways. She smelled of woods and citrus and he could feel her natural siren aura trying to capture him.

"You got a name, sweetheart, or should I just call you mine?" he asked, the words empty, soulless. It wasn't anything he hadn't done before, but this time... it felt different.

Because there was only one woman he wanted to call his, and he'd left her with the vampire who'd claimed her blood...

The Djinn giggled.

Fucking giggled like an innocent child.

"You can call me—"

"Midnight?" Her name came to him without warning as the memories flooded him.

"Oh! You're the guy from the bar... the...hunter..." she said as her eyes widened in surprise.

"He's a hunter?" the other woman shrieked, and Dallas's gaze was pulled away. The other Djinn resembled Midnight, though she was taller with short chin length black hair that boasted bright blue streaks.

"Ami will have a field day with him..."

Midnight pursed her lips as she set her hand on his shoulder, imploring him with her gaze.

"Perhaps he could be of use to us... to Ami," Midnight said as she tugged Dallas's sleeve.

"Can you get up?" she asked again, her voice soft.

Dallas wiggled his toes in his boots, bending his legs and knees slowly. They still ached, but feeling had come back. He motioned forward, getting up too fast as he started to feel dizzy.

"I'm fine..." he bit, shaking off the touch of the sweet-voiced Djinn.

He could hear the sounds of sirens in the distance, and he knew they were right. He did need to move.

He needed to find Malcolm, Ava...

The thought of the Crowleys caused an ache in his heart as his stomach twisted in nauseous knots.

He was starving. He grabbed his stomach, a painful growl escaping his throat.

"What the fuck..."

"He needs to eat," Midnight protested.

"The damn police will be here any minute, Midnight!" the other one bit out.

Dallas jumped as Midnight slid her hand in his, tugging him toward her.

"Whoever made him doesn't look like they're coming back. He's one of us now. I won't leave him to the fucking wolves."

Dallas tried to make sense of her words, but he couldn't. His head was pounding, his body aching, and he was *starving.* His gaze fell on the short vixen in front of him, his mouth going dry.

I wish...

The sound of doors opening, of rushed footsteps, told them all they needed to know.

And so, Jake Dallas followed the Djinn into the shadows, escaping into the night.

Watch for Blood of the Lost at your favorite retailer!

OTHER BOOKS BY ARIEL DAWN

The Hunter Games
Blood Of My Enemy
Blood Of The Lost
Thorne Of Blood

Speed Dating with the Denizens of the Underworld Series
Hecate
Hades
Orion
Athena
Spike

The Forevermore Series
In The Cards
In The Blood
In The Shadows
In The Deep
In The Garden
In The Night-coming soon!

Shifters Of Starfall Creek Series
Hollow's Sunrise
Hollow's Sunset
Hollow's Legacy
Shifters of Starfall Creek Collection: Books 1-3

CONNECT WITH ARIEL DAWN

Website
http://www.ariel-dawn.com/

Goodreads:
http://www.goodreads.com/authorarieldawn

Bookbub:
http://www.bookbub.com/authors/ariel-dawn

Facebook:
http://www.facebook.com/authorarieldawn

Twitter:
https://twitter.com/ArielDawn10

Join Dusk Chasers—Ariel Dawn's Official Readers
Group for access to exclusive content!

Get a special treat when you sign up for Ariel Dawn's
newsletter!
https://mailchi.mp/e5f326e433bf/dawn-breaks-official-
newsletter

ABOUT ARIEL DAWN

USA TODAY BESTSELLING AUTHOR Ariel Dawn grew up as an avid reader and is a creative soul.

What started out as writing reviews for indie romance authors led to featuring quirky, stereotypical, and weird covers on her Instagram Wrong Turn Romance, which gave her the courage to finally decide to live her dream and become an author.

Ariel writes plot driven paranormal romance and hopes to venture into fantasy and rom-com in the future. When she isn't writing, she can be found cosplaying, attending conventions, creating all sorts of artwork in her studio, or editing photos for her photography business.

A self-professed geek and foodie, she loves hanging out with family and friends and playing video games and board games with her retro gamer husband.